Praise for
Bond Girl

"I'm crazy about *Bond Girl*. Erin Duffy is a fresh, funny, and fabulous new voice in literature. Her heroine, 'Bond Girl' Alex Garrett, has moxie and drive, her veins are pumped with Red Bull while her heart is full of hope. At long last, thanks to Ms. Duffy, I grasp the world of high finance, and the hearts and minds that drive it. Great story. Delicious debut." —Adriana Trigiani, author of *Lucia, Lucia* and *Brava, Valentine*

"*Bond Girl* is . . . witty and very racy. . . . Trust me, you won't be bored with this Wall Street story." —*Washington Post*

"Despite financial details that may make your head spin and a workplace that will make your stomach churn, Duffy's fresh take on the single-in-the-city tale does a terrific job of reviving chick lit (not every girl works in publishing or PR, after all)." —*Library Journal* (starred review)

"Writing with an addictively acerbic sense of humor, Duffy gives readers a sassy new heroine and an unforgettable tour of financial trading." —*Chicago Tribune*

"A compelling, fun read." —*Kirkus Reviews*

"Duffy's first novel is a sharp, witty look at the intricacies of the trading floor and the people who populate it. The writing is clever and articulate, and Alex's story of personal growth makes her a sympathetic, likable heroine. Filled with too-good-to-be-true anecdotes and enough of a biting, cynical bent to offset the chick-lit romance angle, *Bond Girl* is a fun read—alike to the canons of Weisberger, Kinsella, and Green. Duffy's acknowledgment of the recent financial collapse and ensuing recession makes *Bond Girl* an entertaining and timely read." —*Booklist*

"Told in first person in Alex's voice—and what an appealing voice it is, one that makes Alex likable from the first page—*Bond Girl* is a smartly written comic novel that's great fun to read."

—Richmond Times-Dispatch

"If you're looking for a great weekend retreat or a great book for the beach, look for this one. For any woman who's ever had a love-hate-detest relationship with a job *Bond Girl* is truly perfect."

—Wisconsin Rapids Tribune

"*Bond Girl* is a sparkling debut, smart and snappy but never weighed down by financial terminology. Who knew Wall Street could be this much fun? A-"

—Entertainment Weekly

BOND *girl*

ERIN DUFFY

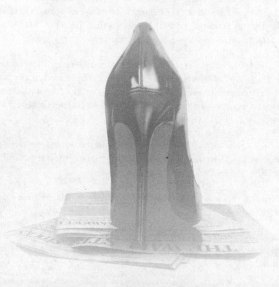

WILLIAM MORROW
An Imprint of HarperCollins*Publishers*

7
3/23

BOND GIRL. Copyright © 2012 by Erin Duffy. All rights reserved. Printed in the United
States of America. No part of this book may be used or reproduced in any manner whatsoever without written permission except in the case of brief quotations embodied in
critical articles and reviews. For information address HarperCollins Publishers, 10
East 53rd Street, New York, NY 10022.

HarperCollins books may be purchased for educational, business, or sales promotional
use. For information please write: Special Markets Department, HarperCollins Publishers, 10 East 53rd Street, New York, NY 10022

A hardcover edition of this book was published in 2012 by William Morrow, an imprint of
HarperCollins Publishers.

FIRST WILLIAM MORROW PAPERBACK EDITION PUBLISHED 2012.

Designed by Lisa Stokes

Library of Congress Cataloging-in-Publication Data has been applied for.

ISBN 978-0-06-206590-2

12 13 14 15 16   OV/RRD   10 9 8 7 6 5 4 3 2 1

For my family.

For my brothers: Scott, James, and Christopher. Thank you for always making me laugh, hard.

But especially for my parents. For my father, my idol, who always encouraged me to go to the Street, a life I still don't think I deserve but am so proud to have. And for my mother, my mentor, who quietly supports even the worst of decisions (and believe me, there are many) and who always thought I should write.

I guess you both had a point.

How I love you all.

BOND GIRL

The Giant Adult Sandbox from Hell

I AM TOO old for this.

Click.

At 6:00 A.M., my clock radio turns on, and music blares from the speakers, shattering the blissful morning quiet, the latest Beyoncé song reminding me that the weekend is over. Waking up on Mondays is bad enough, but waking up on Monday when you have a really bad hangover, the kind of hangover that makes your toenails hurt, is damn near impossible. Half in a coma, I dig around under the mass of pillows crammed against the dark green wood of my headboard, searching for the radio's remote control to snooze for another blessed ten (maybe twenty) minutes. Mercifully, my hand makes contact with the remote somewhere in the upper right-hand corner of my bed, and I wave it in the direction of the nightstand, silently begging for the room to fall silent. That is to say, as silent as a third-floor apartment in Manhattan can ever really be.

A lot of people dream about waking up in New York City. Hell,

Sinatra wrote an entire song about it. Unless of course you are *trying to* sleep, in which case New York is where very tired, cranky, hungover people go to die. If you're like me and decided to drown your Sunday-night anxiety in a bottle and a half of pinot noir and a pack of Parliaments while watching *Law and Order* reruns until 1:00 A.M., New York City, at six in the morning, is undeniably, irrefutably hell on earth. I probably should have realized when I rented my shoebox-sized apartment in the West Village for $4,000 a month that having a third-floor window overlooking Greenwich Avenue with a direct line of sight to a firehouse did not bode well for REM sleep. Since I moved here the concept of sleeping late—of sleeping in general—is pretty much one I have long since forgotten.

I begin to doze off again, when the damn radio clicks back on. Now the annoyingly perky DJ announces time, traffic, and weather. "Better get going people. It's another hazy, hot, and humid day in the Big Apple." Clearly, the DJ didn't handle his Sunday-night blues the same way I did. Or maybe he just liked his job and didn't find excessive Sunday-night boozing necessary. I hear that some people have it that lucky.

I give myself "the pep talk," the same speech I give myself every morning before heading to work at Cromwell Pierce, one of Wall Street's biggest powerhouses. *You can do it, Alex. You can handle it. You will not let him break you.* Talking to myself has become a habit since I started working on Wall Street. If this pace keeps up, by the time I hit thirty I'll be certifiably insane.

Much to my horror, I realize the industrial-size bottle of Advil I've been working my way through over the last six months is in the bathroom and, since I'm pretty sure my head is about to explode, I have no choice but to get up. I swing my legs out of bed, my feet hitting the cool wood floor. In minutes, I'll be shoving my battered toes into any number of pairs of four-inch heels that make my twenty-four-year-old knees feel like they belong to a sixty-year-old woman. I shuffle to the bathroom, flick the switch on the wall, and experience a full assault on my eyeballs courtesy of the fluorescent lightbulbs lining the top of the medicine cabinet. I groan as I try to shield my contracting pupils from the blinding light, blinking until the blue dots disappear and I can actually focus on my reflection in the mirror. Blindness would be a welcome reprieve. Surveying the damage after a night of heavy drinking was never this bad in college, and for some reason, only two years after graduation, I look much more haggard than I did after a similar night back at the University of Virginia. I decide to blame the lightbulbs.

Gazing into the mirror, I discover I must have slept facedown in the same position all night long, because the sheets have left creases on one side of my face that I fear may need to be surgically removed. My long, dark hair is tangled and it will take me an hour to comb the knots out if I'm lucky. My usually rosy complexion looks sallow and dry, and there are dark, puffy circles under my green eyes. I neglected to brush my teeth before face-planting; this morning they're blue and my lips are crusted with a deep ruby stain, which, to tell the truth, would make a really nice lipstick shade. I wonder if the people at Sephora could come up with a way to turn your lips this color that didn't involve alcohol poisoning.

"Just five more minutes," I mutter to myself as I lean against the shower wall, allowing the scalding hot water to blast my half-asleep body. I begin to wonder if humans could sleep standing up, you know, like cows. It occurs to me that if we can't, falling asleep in the shower could very well lead to my being found dead and alone two days from now, after the water in my flooded bathroom seeped through the floor into the apartment below. Juan, the super, would force open my door to discover two empty wine bottles, an overflowing ashtray, a carton of chicken lo mein on the coffee table, and my naked, pruned body in the bathtub.

Oh no. No, no, no, no. I will *not* be written up in the *New York Post* as the girl who drowned from a hangover in her own tub. I limp out of the shower and get dressed in khaki pants and a white button-down shirt. I tie a bright scarf around my once narrow waist, figuring that if I'm well accessorized maybe no one in the office will notice I'm still drunk. The constant drinking has made my clothes a bit too snug for comfort, one of many unwanted side effects of working on the Street. Joy. I search for the usual necessities: iPhone, wallet, and keys.

One of the worst things about not remembering going to bed the night before is trying to locate all the pieces of your life the following morning. I finally find my iPhone behind a sofa cushion, and for reasons that I can't fathom, my wallet is in my fridge next to yet another bottle of wine. Yet for the life of me, I can't find my keys. Anywhere. And my apartment, as I previously mentioned, is not large. I glance at the filthy, overflowing ashtray on my coffee table. I know I didn't have cigarettes in my apartment when I came home yesterday, because I quit smoking last Thursday. Which means I went down to the twenty-four-hour bodega at some point last night . . . which means I had to have my keys to get back in. (At least the alcohol hasn't done any permanent damage to my powers of deductive reasoning.) It doesn't take me long to figure out where I had left them, and when I throw open my front door my suspicions are confirmed. This is why I insisted on living in a building with a full-time doorman. Without one, I probably would have been killed in my own bed last night, and my face would've been splattered across the front page of the *Post* anyway. There are no small victories in life.

I scoop my gym bag and my newspapers off the floor with one hand, scurry out of my apartment, and hail a cab. I scan the front page of the *Wall Street Journal*. The headlines chronicle yet another massive investment bank going under, the stock market declining the most in a single session since the 1920s, and more layoffs being announced throughout the financial sector. This isn't helping my headache. Working on a fixed-income trading floor, the government bond desk specifically, has been torturous lately. Treasury bonds are the safest place in the world to put your money (except for under your mattress), so we've been mind-numbingly busy as everyone's been selling stocks and other securities in exchange for bonds guaranteed by the government. The last few months have been incredibly stressful. I promise, if you polled a random sample of Wall Street employees, the majority would admit to getting drunk more frequently these days. (Though I don't know how many of them would admit to finding their wallets in the refrigerator the next morning. But they lie.) I vaguely remember the way things were just a few months ago, before everything got really bad, before we all needed to drink ourselves to sleep. It didn't use to be like this. I check my phone quickly and notice that I have missed calls from my two best friends, Annie and Liv. I don't bother listening to their voice mails, because I already know what they say. They're well aware my mental state isn't good. They also know the liquor store delivers.

Twenty minutes later I hop out of the cab and race through a set of massive gold doors, the name Cromwell Pierce proudly engraved in the marble lintel. I try to walk lightly across the floor so that the *click clack click* of my heels won't reverberate throughout the cavernous lobby as I make my way to the escalator. I repeat my new morning mantra as I walk:

Click, clack, click. A few hours, you can handle anything for a few hours. Easy.

Click, clack, click. Maybe he won't be in today.

Click, clack, click. Of course he's in today. He's always in. You're fucked, Alex. You're royally fucked.

I bow my head and stare at the metal slats on the escalator as I ride it to the second floor. As I step off, I'm immediately confronted by security guards and place my bags on the conveyor belt running through the x-ray machine. I hate the x-ray machines with a passion. One morning I had a thong in my bag (for reasons that I'd rather not recount at the moment), and that was the one day the security guard made me empty the entire contents of my tote in front of everyone, so he could ensure that I wasn't carrying some sort of concealed weapon. Security on Wall Street is second only to the White House. I'm not complaining. All I'm saying is that sometimes you don't want your purse x-rayed. That's all.

The elevator is packed, and I find myself standing next to two middle-aged men in perfectly pressed pants and pastel polo shirts. I don't know who cast the movie *Wall Street,* but whoever it was never took a lap around Cromwell Pierce. If any of my colleagues even remotely resembled Charlie Sheen or Michael Douglas, coming to work would be a whole lot more enjoyable. As I stare blankly at the *Journal,* I listen to their conversation. Casually, the man in the blue polo says to the guy in the yellow polo, "You out east this weekend?"

"Yeah, Southampton. Played Shinnecock on Saturday."

"Ah, beautiful course. How'd you play?"

"Had some trouble off the tee, but pretty well, thanks. What about you?"

"Westhampton. Spent some time with the family before my son heads off to school this weekend."

"Oh, that's nice. Where?"

"Brown. He's going to play lacrosse."

"Fantastic. What position does he play? My son's a sophomore at Harvard."

"Harvard, huh? That's terrific. He's a defenseman. Yours?"

"Middie."

"We'll have to go to a game together sometime, cheer the kids on, you know?"

"Definitely. Can't wait for the season to start. The Bears versus the Crimson will be a great game."

Both men nod in agreement. Of course, that is only the surface conversation. Underneath the polite banter, which you can decode if you've spent enough time in the Business, the real conversation went something like this:

"I belong to a more expensive golf club than you do, which means I make more money than you do."

"Screw you and your exclusive, world-famous club. My kid's going to play lacrosse in the Ivy League."

"Oh, you think that makes you special? My kid *already* plays in the Ivy League."

"That's great. If your kid is a middie, that means he's smaller and weaker than mine. Hopefully, they can match up against each other and my son can level yours out on the field."

"We will never, ever, talk to each other at games. I will pretend I have never seen you before in my life."

"Harvard's for fags."

"Brown's for pussies."

News flash: I work in the giant adult sandbox from hell.

I haven't always felt this way. Just last year I would have found that conversation amusing. I would have cared what was going on in the markets. I would have been excited to come to work. But 2008 has sucked on every level imaginable.

one

Leatherface and Starfish Ted

IT'S NO SURPRISE that I ended up working in an industry ruled by
men. I always loved playing with the boys. I loved to get dirty, skin
my knees, and catch frogs. I would rather have tossed a baseball with
the three Callahan boys down the street than played hopscotch with my
little sister, Cat, in the driveway. My parents laughed when I came home
covered in mud, an interesting counterpoint to my quiet sister, who
wanted nothing to do with any physical activity that didn't involve a jump
rope or thick colored chalk. At first, the Callahans didn't mind having
me around, and why would they? I was an easy opponent, someone who
helped reinforce their developing, fragile male egos; until the day that
I hit a home run, a soaring, fast, uncatchable hit to right field (otherwise known as the hedges that lined the Callahans' front lawn). I ran
the bases fast, my knobby knees knocking each other. When I hit home
plate, marked by a kitchen towel, I jumped up and down savoring my
victory, loving that I had managed to score against boys who were older,
bigger, faster, and stronger. Benny Callahan, at ten, two years older than

me and the strongest of the group, didn't like it. In fact, like most boys (and later men), he hated that a girl had challenged him—and won.

"I don't want to play with a stupid girl. Why don't you go home and play with your dolls?"

"Don't be such a sore loser!" I cried. It was my first lesson that success, small or large, comes with consequences.

"Go home! Your parents probably don't even want you. That's why you have a boy's name. My mom told me your parents wish you were a boy."

"That's not true! Alex is a girl's name!"

"Alexandra is a girl's name. Alex is a boy's name. Your parents don't like you and neither do we!"

I had never thought about the fact that my name was just plain Alex, not Alexandra. Ouch.

"I hate you!" I yelled, the joy of my victory vanquished in a flash. I sprinted off as the last of the evening sun disappeared over the horizon, arriving just as my dad returned home from work.

"What's wrong?" my mother asked, as she hugged me. "Did you get hurt playing baseball?"

"No," I sobbed, pulling out of her grasp. "Benny said that I have a boy's name, and that you didn't name me Alexandra because you wished I was a boy!" I wailed loudly, the way an eight-year-old does when faced with the reality that her parents don't love her.

My father kneeled on the floor, as if somehow matching my size would better enable him to console me. "That's not true," he reassured me. "Your name is Alex because it's unique, just like you. There will be a million Alexandras running around, but there's only one Alex."

"I don't believe you!" I sobbed hysterically and ran out of the room. How was I going to live in this house until I graduated from high school with parents who didn't want me? My parents found me in the living room, curled up in a ball on the couch.

"Hey, would you like to come to work with me tomorrow?" my dad asked.

"I can't," I said. "I have school."

"Well, how about tomorrow you don't go to school? Come to work with me instead, and we'll spend the day together. Would you like that?"

I looked at Mom for confirmation that I could miss school and spend the day in New York City with my dad. She smiled and nodded.

"Really?" I asked my dad. Until then, all I knew of my father's job was what I saw when I went with my mom to pick him up at the train station. I would sit in the backseat of the car and wait for the train to pull in. When it did, I'd watch dozens of men wearing suits, ties, and trench coats briskly exit the train and descend the stairs into the parking lot. A few women got off the train, too, wearing skirts and matching jackets. They carried soft leather briefcases and wore socks and sneakers with their skirts. They all looked so *important.* I couldn't wait until the day I was able to ride the train with the grown-ups and carry a briefcase of my very own. Of course, I could do without the sneakers and the socks. I wiped my eyes with my sleeve. "Can we take the train into the city? The one you take every day?"

"You bet. We can ride the train in the morning and you can come see where I work. Then we can go to lunch and to FAO Schwarz. How does that sound?"

Sounded good to me. Who needs the Callahan boys when you have new toys?

It became a ritual. My dad would take me to his office a few times a year, even before there was an official "Take Our Daughters to Work" Day. On days when the markets closed early and he wasn't busy, he'd allow me to come see his office and watch grown-ups at work. We'd take the train from Connecticut to Grand Central Station, and then ride the subway downtown to Wall Street where he was a banker at Sterling Price. I'd sit at his desk in his office and play with all his computers. He had two different keyboards, more phone lines than I had friends to call, and I had access to unlimited candy and cookies from the cafeteria downstairs. From the first time I witnessed the glamour of the Wall Street machine, I was hooked. Downtown buzzed like no place I had

ever been; it was and is the economic epicenter of the universe. Everyone walked with purpose: you never saw people casually strolling or
window-shopping along the twisted streets south of Canal. Down there
people were busy. Time was money, and money was all anyone thought
about: how to make it, how to keep it, how to make sure someone else
didn't have more of it than you did. It was electrifying.

"Hurry up, Alex. You'll get run over down here if you don't pay attention!" My dad would wave for me to follow him, weaving in and out of the
surging crowds as I tried to keep my eyes on his navy suit jacket. Men
in the Financial District wore their pinstripes with pride and a swag-
ger—they were the Yankees of Lower Manhattan. Everything and everyone I saw downtown looked expensive: men wearing fine Italian suits,
silk Hermès ties, shiny leather shoes. The first time I saw the New York
Stock Exchange in person it was like seeing the Parthenon. The American flag hung proudly from one of the many Ionic columns, the building
stretching the length of an entire city block. I was only eight years old,
but I already felt like I was part of something special. I felt sorry for the
people who would never get close enough to know what they were missing, and so amazingly lucky that I wasn't one of them. I decided to make
sure that that never changed.

My father had no idea those days would alter the course of my life.

"The Business" was what my father and all the other Wall Street
guys called the finance industry, as if there was no other profession
on the face of the earth. And, to them, there wasn't. The very first time
I went to his office, I knew this was what I wanted to do. My parents
always joked that I had a lot of energy, sometimes too much. My teachers
commented that I talked too much in class, that I ran in the hallways,
that I had to learn the difference between my "inside" and my "outside"
voice. I always found it all difficult to do, no matter how hard I tried. I
could never seem to harness my energy, and I worried that it was something that would end up being a problem for me when I grew up. But
everyone ran in the hallways at Sterling Price. Furthermore, from what
I could tell, there was no such thing as an inside voice, and all anyone

seemed to do all day was talk on the phone or to each other. It was like a giant adult playground, where people could do everything I was always told not to do. It was fantastic! I felt like I had walked into a world where every quality that made me a difficult child was actually valued. I felt like it was where I belonged. From then on, working on "the Street" was the only dream I ever had—I never wanted to be a ballerina, an astronaut, or a teacher. I became the eight-year-old who wanted to work in finance—the quirky, precocious, "interesting" child. My teachers found me amusing. My mother figured I'd grow out of it. But there was no way that was going to happen. I didn't know where I wanted to go to college, or even what kind of Trapper Keeper I wanted for fourth grade, but I knew what I wanted to do with my life. And once I set my mind on something, there was nothing anyone could do to change it.

I DEDICATED THE NEXT TWELVE years to getting a job on the Street. Originally, it was because I thought it seemed like a really fun job, but in college, it became about something else, too. As I grew up I realized that I was privileged. My father made a good living as a banker, and money was never something we worried about. When I arrived at UVA, I realized how many students had taken out loans to pay for their education. I hadn't. Some kids couldn't get home for Thanksgiving or Easter because flights were too expensive. I didn't even check the fares before I made my reservations. Some kids had to work for spending money. I had my parents' credit card. My father's career afforded me luxuries I didn't even know I had until I left the cocoon of suburban Connecticut and entered the real world. (And college wasn't even the "real world," really.) It was eye-opening and scary. I didn't want to live my adult life without the luxuries I grew up with. I didn't want to worry about paying bills once I graduated, or end up a grown woman completely dependent on a man. I wanted to give my kids the same blissful upbringing I had no matter what my marital fate. I wanted it more than anything. The Street could make that happen. Besides, no one went to work in the Business because they really liked stocks or bonds, right? They liked financial security. And so did I. So, come senior year of college, I dropped my résumé off in the campus business center and researched various companies to determine where I wanted to work.

As soon as I started educating myself on the differences among the top ten brokerage firms, I realized that Cromwell Pierce was where I wanted to be. My father worked at Sterling Price, Cromwell's fiercest competitor. Sterling is a more uptight, old-school firm. Cromwell had a reputation for being younger, hipper, and a more fun place to work. The headquarters were located downtown, away from the tourist mecca that was Midtown Manhattan (where some of the banks had migrated over the years), and was close to the waterfront. I decided I wanted to apply to the sales and trading program and not the investment banking division. One thing I didn't like about my father's profession was that he worked obscenely long hours most of the time, and he told me that starting out I would be expected to work sixteen-hour days and weekends. Not something I had any interest in doing. Salespeople and traders worked much more humane hours, and weekends were rarely required. It was an easy enough decision to make. My mother sent me a black skirt suit that made me look like Working Girl Barbie, but was a necessary evil if I wanted to impress the people conducting the interview. More than one hundred students were interviewing for just three spots, and while we all sat in the campus business center waiting for our names to be called, the tension was palpable. I had done my due diligence: read the *Wall Street Journal* every day for two weeks, watched CNBC during the day to bone up on industry lingo and jargon, some of which I already knew from my dad, and learned as much about Cromwell as I could. I felt prepared; at least, I thought I was.

When my name was called and I was escorted to a small windowless room, my knees were weak with fear and anticipation. At a large mahogany desk sat two middle-aged men, waiting for me. I took my seat facing them and exhaled one last deep breath before flashing a smile and folding my hands demurely in my lap.

The man on the right, a broad-shouldered blond guy named Ted something or other, wearing a pink tie with yellow starfish on it, spoke first.

"So, Alex, it says here that you're a finance major. Do you think that makes you adequately prepared for a job on the Street?"

"Well, no, the short answer is, I don't. I think a solid understanding of the fundamentals will help, but from what I've been told, there isn't a course in the world that can prepare you for a career on Wall Street. You have no idea what it's really about until you actually do it."

They both nodded slightly. Ted's sidekick, a slightly older man who was graying at the temples and had leathery skin that suggested a lot of time spent outdoors, was next to ask a question.

"What's the square root of two?"

The square root of two? Does two even have a square root? The square root of a number is the number that you squared to get the first number. So the square root of sixteen was four and the square root of four was two. What the hell was the square root of two? It couldn't be one, because one times one is still one. So it had to be some number greater than one but less than two. Fractions. Shit. Leatherface smirked. Then it hit me.

"The square root of two is the number that you multiply times itself to get two. I don't know what the exact number is but the square root times itself will equal two."

Leatherface leaned back in his chair and smiled approvingly, while Ted straightened his starfish tie.

"Interesting answer. You have a unique way of thinking, Ms. Garrett. We like that in the Business. Thinking outside the box is an important ability, and it can't be taught. You either have it or you don't."

"Thank you." I breathed a sigh of relief, crossed my legs, and noticed a slight tear in my nylons by my left anklebone. Swell.

Starfish Ted looked at me intently. "Do you squeeze the toothpaste tube from the bottom or the top?"

I shifted uncomfortably in my chair. *What the hell did that have to do with anything?*

"Do I what?" I asked him, confused.

"Do you squeeze the toothpaste tube from the top or the bottom?"

Okay, seriously what kind of screwed-up interview was this? I fig-ured the best way to answer the question was honestly, because trying to figure out what these guys were up to seemed futile. "I umm, I don't. I use one of those toothpaste pumps."

Leatherface laughed. "You're the first person that didn't try to fig-ure out what we wanted you to say."

"Is there a correct answer?"

"Yes," Starfish answered. "It's moot now though, Pump Girl."

Pump Girl? I didn't think I liked being called that.

The rest of the interview was easy. We discussed my résumé and my family background. I think having an investment banker for a father scored me a few points. When I left the business center, I felt pretty good about my meeting with Leatherface and Starfish Ted. Two weeks later, I received a letter in the mail, offering me a position in the 2006 analyst program. I was assigned to the government bond desk in the fixed-income division, starting in July. My lifelong dream had been realized. *Watch out Wall Street,* I thought. *Here I come.*

S INCE MY NEW JOB STARTED in July, and there was no way in hell I was going to get up at 5:00 A.M. every morning to catch the train into the city from Connecticut, I quickly set about the brutal task of find-ing an apartment in the city. Thankfully, my best friend, Liv, was look-ing to move right away also, so the two of us ran around Manhattan for two weeks after graduation, looking for a non-rat-infested building we could afford. We finally found a place suitable for two people and moved in June 15. We divided our tiny one-bedroom Murray Hill apartment into two bedrooms by erecting a fake wall in the living room. I had the real bedroom, and Liv had the fake one, no larger than a prison cell, but with better flooring. The living room could barely accommodate one sofa, a tiny coffee table, and four people comfortably. Our combined income was more than $100,000—a lot by normal standards—and yet neither of us could afford her own place. Of all the things that are great about New York, rent isn't one of them. Liv had a job at another investment bank, but in Human Resources, and so we both needed a Manhattan address to spare us the horror of commuting.

We lugged all our belongings, which wasn't much, into the service elevator and up to the twelfth floor with the help of my friend Annie. Annie and I had become friends the first week of freshman year at UVA. We lived on the same floor in the same dorm. One night, when our resident adviser was locked in her room with her boyfriend, we stole the sofa from the lounge and moved it into Annie's room at the end of the hall. When she was caught a week later, she was forced to sort mail at the university post office for a month as punishment. But she never told the RA that the great couch caper of 2002 was orchestrated by yours truly. For that, I will love her forever.

Annie had decided to prolong school as long as possible by attending NYU to get a master's in psychology. After discovering how early Liv and I had to get up now that we were part of the working world, she was pretty sure she didn't want to enter it.

"How on earth are you going to get up at 5:30 and not be a zombie by 3:00?" Annie asked. "That's just unholy." She looked at me the same way I look at people over forty who aren't married: with unabashed pity. She sat on the living room floor and pushed her curly blond hair behind her ears. Annie had done gymnastics as a kid and possessed a flexible, toned physique I wouldn't have even if I lived on carrot sticks. I know this for a fact. I tried for most of freshman year.

"I'm sure I'll get used to it," I said as I jammed sweaters in my closet.

"I'd rather die," she added.

"Are you excited?" Liv asked as she broke down boxes with a razor and laid them flat against the wall next to a bookshelf. She picked dust bunnies off her black spandex shorts with a perfectly manicured nail and ran her sleeve across her forehead. "I don't start until next week, and I'm kind of dreading it."

"I'm excited. I guess a little nervous, too. It's like the first day of school all over again. New people, new places. I hope I don't screw up anything too badly."

"You'll be fine," Annie assured me as she stood to leave for her own apartment on the Upper West Side. And by "her own apartment" I mean the one her parents kept in the city for the two times a year they came to Manhattan to see a show. She gave me a quick hug and waved good-bye to Liv as she headed for the elevators. "Call me tomorrow and let me know how it goes," she yelled over her shoulder.

I helped Liv lug boxes to the refuse room down the hall, and we spent the next few hours unpacking, cleaning, hanging, ironing, scrubbing, organizing, and discussing how excited we both were to have our very own apartment in Manhattan. I went to bed at 9:30, still leaving a lot of boxes untouched, and prayed that my first week of work would be merciful. *I'm sure it won't be too bad,* I assured myself. *It's just a job. How bad could it possibly be?*

two

She's Cute. Would I Do Her?

O N THE FIRST day I was so excited I could barely breathe. I couldn't believe that I had managed to achieve the goal my eight-year-old self had set all those years ago. But I had. And I was ready to do whatever it is people actually did inside this building. I sat with the rest of the incoming class of new analysts, twenty-five of us in all, in a conference room on the main floor of the building. I looked around at the other new kids, knowing that they were all there for the same reason—cash (and maybe some stock options)—and worried that my more romantic motivations of fond childhood memories and a desire to follow in my father's footsteps would result in my not being able to compete. I convinced myself that the rest of the group probably had memorized the Fibonacci sequence by the time they were twelve. My excitement quickly turned to fear, and the longer I sat in that conference room, the faster my fear turned to all-consuming terror. We sat quietly and listened to an over-weight woman with dark curly hair and bright lipstick lecture us from a podium.

"Welcome to Cromwell," she said enthusiastically. "My name's Stacey, and I'm the firm's head of Human Resources." The fuchsia lips flashed a brief, not entirely convincing smile. "Please make sure your name tags are visible at all times for the first week or so. It will help you get to know one another, and it will help your new colleagues learn your names as well. Please open your orientation packets." We dutifully opened navy blue folders on the table in front of us and began to flip through the contents. "Inside, you'll find a copy of the employee handbook, which addresses all of Cromwell's rules and regulations. It goes over everything you should and should not do, common ethical dilemmas that, as new analysts, you may come up against and how to handle them and, more important, what we consider to be fireable offenses. Pay close attention to the section on electronic communication. You should not write anything in an e-mail or instant message that you wouldn't want published on the front page of the *Wall Street Journal*. If you think it could embarrass the firm or yourself, don't write it. If you receive incoming e-mail that contains inappropriate pictures or material, delete it. If you respond, you will be held accountable for disseminating material that is inconsistent with the firm's principles and your employment can be terminated. Make sure you read the handbook because from this moment on, you're responsible for knowing everything contained therein, and if you violate any one of the rules, you cannot use the excuse that you didn't know. Does everyone understand?"

We sat silently. A few of the eager analysts in the front row nodded, but apparently Stacey didn't like the halfhearted response. She leaned forward on her elbows and asked us all again, louder this time, "Do you understand?" This time, there was no smile as she enunciated each syllable. We responded "yes" in unison. *What is this—nursery school?* I wondered. *We get it Stacey, you own us.* It wasn't that hard to understand.

"If you have any other questions, your orientation packet contains the names and numbers of the desk managers and the appropriate contacts in HR. You all should know what floor you are heading to. There will be someone from each group waiting to greet you at the elevators and escort you to your desks. Other than that, have a *great* day, and again, welcome to Cromwell Pierce. You are now part of one of the most respected firms in the industry."

We stood, and I moved with the crowd out to the elevator banks. I counted seven girls. The Ivy Leaguers walked together in front of the rest of us, acting like a pack of alpha girls I knew in junior high. I had gone to the University of Virginia, an intellectually inferior school as far as they were concerned. I felt, warranted or not, like an outcast. Not exactly how I wanted to start my first day.

The hierarchy in most Wall Street firms is clearly delineated. You spend your first few years as an analyst, responsible for learning as much as you can, and making sure the rest of "the team" gets their lunch orders picked up from the lobby in a timely fashion. From there, you move up the ranks to associate, then to vice president, then director, then managing director and, from there, I was pretty sure you jumped to the executive committee or something. For my purposes it didn't really matter. All I needed to know was that I was as junior as junior could get, and I therefore worked for *everyone*. I figured as long as I kept that in mind, I would be okay. At least I hoped so, because from what I had heard, forgetting your rung on the corporate ladder was a very bad idea.

I was one of ten analysts who stepped off the elevator when the doors opened on the eleventh floor, all of us assigned to various "desks" in the fixed-income division. There were people waiting in the hallway for us as we exited the elevator, everyone somehow knowing which clueless analyst he was supposed to claim ownership of. As I stepped onto the marble floor I was immediately intercepted by a stocky man with shocking green eyes and short brown hair. He was imposing and suave, attractive in a rugged way, the kind of guy who instantly commands your attention. I figured he was in his midforties, due to slight graying at his temples, but it was hard to tell. Men are annoying like that. He seemed to excrete charisma from his pores as easily as a normal person sweats. His khaki pants and blue-and-white-checkered shirt were pressed within an inch of their life, and his brown tweed blazer fit him perfectly. He looked like a brunette Ken doll, live and in the flesh. When he extended his hand to greet me, I noticed that his fingers were thick and squat, but that his skin was smooth and his nails were perfectly manicured. Here was an interesting dichotomy: a guy who oozed machismo but who also valued immaculately buffed nails. This was my first introduction to a legitimate Cromwell salesman and, more important, my first introduction to Ed Ciccone, otherwise known as Chick. My boss.

Chick was a trading floor veteran. I'd come to learn that he'd spent twenty years in the Business, fifteen of them on this very trading floor. He was smart, ferociously competitive, and could sell just about anything. He was well known on the Street for his hard partying, his lavish entertainment spending, and his ability to function on little to no sleep. He was wildly successful, extremely popular, and hugely intimidating. He didn't waste time with formalities; after a perfunctory shake of my hand, he turned and walked toward the trading floor, a vast room that encompassed nearly the entire floor of the building, except for the foyer by the elevator bank, a coffee stand in the hallway right outside the elevator vestibule that was swarming with people who probably didn't need more caffeine, and a few offices lining the perimeter. I could hear screams on the trading floor from the elevator vestibule and felt my hands begin to sweat. It seemed like total chaos. People—nine out of ten of them men—raced through the hall, their loafers crushing the once-plush carpet fibers flat and thin, talking, laughing, cursing. Some wore ties and jackets. Most wore khakis and their moods tattooed on their foreheads. We wove in and out of people as we approached the small staircase that led down to the floor, and for the first time I could see huge banners hanging from the ceiling marking the accolades the division had earned over the years, the way the championship banners hung in Madison Square Garden. The room was enormous. A girl could get lost in there and need the dog teams from the New York City Police Department to be found. I felt my legs begin to tremble.

Chick spoke insanely fast, like his lungs didn't need oxygen at the same rate as a normal person's. His smile was friendly and his demeanor was welcoming, but at the same time I had the sense that if I screwed up he would make sure I spent the rest of my Cromwell career stuffing FedEx envelopes in the mailroom. We made a left before we hit the small staircase that led to the floor and walked down a hallway lined with glass-enclosed offices. Small plaques mounted next to the doors displayed the occupants' name, a small sign of stature that differentiated the office-endowed from their peers. Only very senior managers received offices, because they were a scarce commodity on the floor. The majority of employees only had a seat on "the desk" on the trading floor; no hope of privacy, no direct-dial phone numbers, no chance of having two minutes of solitude during the day unless they locked themselves in the bathroom. Chick wasn't one of the majority.

We walked past his secretary, who Chick quickly introduced as Nancy, and pushed open a heavy glass door into his office. I found myself staring through floor-to-ceiling windows on the opposite wall that afforded an uninterrupted view of the Statue of Liberty and Ellis Island. Photographers could have used Chick's office to shoot postcards to sell in Times Square—I wasn't entirely convinced they didn't. If I had this view, I'd sit in here all day, but it didn't seem like Chick spent much time in his office at all. His shiny lacquered desk and aerodynamic chair were squarely in the middle of the room, and there were two leather-backed chairs facing his desk. The walls that abutted the adjacent offices were completely bare, although with the view I guess he figured artwork was unnecessary. I scanned his desk, which held a monitor with two keyboards, and a phone, and was covered with disorganized stacks of papers and books. A mini basketball hoop was attached to the rim of an empty wastebasket on the wall on the right, next to a large fish tank containing three tropical fish. That was about it.

He sat down behind his desk, with his back to the view of the water. I found it kind of funny that the people who occupied these offices sat with their backs to one of the most iconic New York landmarks, but I guess

Cromwell figured the view was meant to impress guests, not employees. "Take a seat," Chick commanded from his chair as he motioned to the empty chairs facing him.

I did as I was told and placed my hands on my knees to keep them from shaking. This guy terrified me.

"Okay, Alex," he said as he put his hands behind his head and his feet up on his desk, so that I was staring at the soles of his brown Gucci loafers. He leaned back in his chair and talked to me while he stared straight up at the ceiling. It was very disconcerting having a conversation with someone when the only way you knew for sure he was actually talking to you was because you were the only other person in the room. "I run my group pretty openly. There aren't a lot of rules you need to know, but I'll go over the basics. You're smart, I know, because if you weren't, you wouldn't be here. I promise you, though, that you aren't the smartest person in this building. What that means is that I expect you to work hard; I expect you to be the first person here in the morning and the last person to leave at night. Unless, of course, you think that you know more than some of the guys who have been busting their asses for twenty years. Do you think that, Alex?"

I wasn't really sure if the question was rhetorical. It was difficult to tell when he still hadn't taken his eyes off the ceiling.

"No, Mr. Ciccone. I don't think that." There was a piece of pink gum stuck in the tread of his left shoe.

"Good. I'm here by 6:30 every morning, so you do the math and get in before me. That's rule number one. Rule number two is don't call me Mr. Ciccone. I'm not your high school math teacher and we're all adults here. Call me Chick like everyone else. You will not ask for anything. The way I see it, you don't deserve anything. No one knows you, you haven't done one productive thing to help this group make money, and until you do, you should just thank God every day that you're able to clear the turnstiles in the lobby. Your job, until I tell you otherwise, is to learn as much as you can by observing the rest of the team and asking questions without annoying them to the point where they punch you in the face. Help out when they ask you to. If that means you pick up some-one's laundry and drop it off at his apartment, or buy a birthday present for his wife, then you do it and you do it with a smile. It might not be in the job description, but you can take comfort in knowing that you will at least be the highest-paid delivery girl on the planet. I personally interviewed more than eighty applicants for the one spot in this depart-ment this year, so I know for a fact that there are hundreds of kids out there who want this job. If you have a problem with any of this, turn in your name tag downstairs and walk right out the front door. I'll have you replaced by lunchtime with someone who will wipe my ass for me if I ask him to."

Lovely visual.

He continued very matter-of-factly, "You will get coffee, pick up lunch, mail packages, and enter numbers into spreadsheets until you go blind if that's what we ask you to do. I don't have time for tears. There aren't a lot of women on the floor. There are two or three on most of the desks"—my quick math put that number somewhere around thirty— "and before you ask, no, it's not because we have a problem with women at the firm. We always try to hire smart females, but most of them real-ize they're not cut out for the Business and quit, or they get married and quit. I have milk in my fridge that has lasted longer than some of the girls we have hired over the years. I'd put the aggregate number in fixed income around forty or fifty, not including the administrative assis-tants who mostly keep to themselves. You're one of two women in my group, and if that dynamic is a problem for you, then take the train to Midtown and see if the broads at Condé Nast have a job for you, because I won't. You're not to answer phones. Under no circumstances are you allowed to execute trades of any kind, and you are prohibited from talking to clients unless someone introduces you directly. You're also required to pass the Series 7, 63, and 3 exams by October fifteenth at the absolute latest." Christ. I had less than three months.

He pushed three huge binders toward me. I felt my stomach churn in fear. A passing grade on the exams he'd named was required by the

Securities and Exchange Commission if your job necessitated speaking to clients. The tests covered industry rules, regulations, ethics, fraud, and market basics. They were notoriously hard, and a lot of people failed because there was so much material to memorize and so many different ways to make mistakes. From what I'd heard, if you failed them, it basically advertised to everyone you worked with that you were an idiot, and the humiliation alone was enough of a reason to quit. I flipped open the binder for the Series 3 exam, which covered futures and options, and read one of the practice questions: "What would a farmer in Iowa do to hedge himself if he was worried about the effect rising grain prices would have on pork belly futures?"

Pork belly futures? I thought I was working on the Treasury bond desk. What do pigs have to do with anything?

"I don't know what's going on lately with some firms allowing their analysts to fail the tests and still keep their jobs while they study for a second try, but that's not how we do things here. You pass all of them on the first try in October or you're fired."

Great.

"As you know, we are business casual here. I trust that you'll dress appropriately. If you wear a tight skirt and someone smacks your ass, don't come running to me or to HR about it. This is a place of business. Not a nightclub. The team is fantastic, one of the best in the Business. They work hard, play hard, and are some of the funniest human beings you will ever meet in your life. Personally, I think being a little crazy is what makes us so good at what we do, so prepare yourself for just about anything. It may seem like a tough group to crack, but once you earn their respect and are accepted, there's no better group of people to work with."

Yeah, especially if they smack me on the ass.

"Other than that, keep your head down, work hard, and stay out of the way. Use your brain, and you'll be fine. Are we clear?" He finally took his feet off the desk and turned his gaze on me.

"Yes, Chick. We're clear."

"One more thing. I'm not your father, and I really don't give a fuck what you do with your personal life, but I don't encourage interoffice relationships. You're a good-looking girl, and it won't surprise me if half the floor hits on you, but I expect you to be smart. I do *not* expect you to date anyone on this floor, certainly not anyone on *my* desk. The last thing I need is a weepy employee fucking up right and left because she's upset that someone here didn't return a phone call. Capiche? Let's go."

Chick stood without giving me a chance to answer. I had never in my life met anyone who seemed so nice and so completely insane at the same time.

We walked out onto the floor, a giant room shaped like a horse-shoe with enormous hermetically sealed windows and ceilings high enough to accommodate a circus tent. I wasn't expecting the floor to look the way it did. Every time I'd gone to work with my father, I had never stepped foot on a trading floor. Bankers were kept separate from everyone else. They had inside information on mergers, stock offerings, and acquisitions and had to be segregated from the traders to ensure that inside information stayed classified. Banking floors were clean and tidy—all polished wood, plush carpets, and private offices. They even used a different elevator bank. The stories my dad had told me about my new work environment didn't begin to do it justice. The difference between the Cromwell Pierce trading floor and the Sterling Price banking floor was staggering. This place looked like it was stuck in the '70s. The walls had probably been white once upon a time, but they were now a dingy shade of cream. The Formica desks were chipped and stained, broken corners revealing the brown cork underneath. The fact that these desks were basically Generation One Cromwell was something I tried not to focus on; because if I thought about how many people had sneezed, coughed, eaten, and God knows what else all over them for the last forty years, I would have to come to work in a plastic jumpsuit wearing latex gloves.

I kept my eyes on the floor as I navigated the obstacle course of rows to our "desk" in the back corner of the room. I could feel the stares from the men as I walked by. The guys surveyed the length of my skirt and the fit of my sweater, just in case I had missed a button or, God forbid, had visible panty lines. It was something I'd have to get used to.

The energy in the room was palpable. People bellowed out numbers, screamed instructions to pick up phones, yelled just for the sake of yelling. The shouting made my ears buzz, and I didn't know how anyone was able to understand anything above the chaos. There were at least four hundred people on the Cromwell Pierce fixed-income trading floor. Most of them were loud. Most of them were aggressive. Most of them relished the opportunity to mess with the new kids.

Most of them were male.

Chick suddenly threw his hand up in front of my head and intercepted a football that had missed its intended target. Unless of course, the target was me.

"Watch it, Smitty! Hitting the new girl in the face with a football on her first day will get you called to the principal's office."

I tried to find something to say to break the awkward silence, and the best I could come up with was, "You guys play football?"

"Sometimes *we* do. *You* don't. You'll be too busy learning to have time to play. Capiche?"

"Sure. I'm really excited to be here and I'm ready to work hard."

"That's good, Alex, because we don't want you here any other way."

A slight, pale man with red hair and an absurdly thin blond girl approached us. They stopped, and the guy nodded in my direction. His skin was translucent and his eyes so light they were almost clear. I was immediately reminded of the weakling on the high school football team who had to carry the equipment because he wasn't big enough to actually play in the games. I had always assumed those scrawny kids bulked up later in life. I was wrong.

"Who's this?" he asked, his voice almost robotic.

"Alex. My new kid," Chick answered curtly.

"Hi," I said.

"Hi!" The blond stick figure gushed, as she threw herself on me.

"Oh, this is great! I'll have a friend now! There aren't a lot of girls to talk to in this place!" she said as she hugged me.

The redheaded leprechaun surveyed me and said, "Chick, yours is cute, but mine is better." He snorted as he walked away, the girl trotting off quickly behind him. I wondered if he took the train to work, or if he just slid down a rainbow into the lobby.

I held my breath. Chick started walking again and said, "That was Keith Georgalis, more commonly known on the floor as Darth Vader. He's a prick. He runs the high-yield desk. His sidekick is his analyst, Hannah. She's a freaking moron, but she's a treat to look at so we keep her. She doesn't work for me, so what do I care? If you make even half the mistakes that idiot has made, I'll bounce you out on your ass so fast your head will spin."

Before I could say a word Chick stopped in front of a group of people and waved his arm in a sweeping motion as he proudly announced, "This is the desk."

A "desk" was the Wall Street term for the team of people who worked in a specific product area. My desk, the government bond sales desk, was composed of forty people sitting in three long rows like diner counters—covered with papers, phones, and flat screen monitors. Each person sat in an aerodynamic chair, his specific workspace segregated from the person sitting next to him only by a thin black line of grout, the same way tiles are connected on a bathroom floor. The workstations were so close together that if you extended both your arms you would touch your neighbors. The concept of "personal space" didn't seem to exist here, and I realized that if I ended up sitting next to an asshole—or worse, in between two—my days were going to be miserable.

I stared at the wall of computer monitors looming in front of everyone. Every single employee on the floor had at least three monitors at his workstation. Some traders had as many as six. In order to view them all, some were elevated above others on stacked reams of printer paper. It was hard to believe that there was enough information to look at on a daily basis to warrant multiple computer monitors, and I quickly began to worry that I wasn't going to be able to follow everything the way the other guys could. At the time I didn't realize that someone could sit directly behind you and you could be so busy you'd go months without ever actually speaking to that person, or even know his name. You could. I would.

I was nervous, adrenaline making me so jittery it was hard to stand still. I scanned the men sitting in the rows. They were all on their phones, some of them with their feet up, mindlessly tossing small rubber balls into the air while they spoke. The phones rang incessantly, multicolored lights blinking on an enormous switchboard. The desk was covered with coffee cups, soda cans, bottles of water, and newspapers. The place smelled like the short-order cook station at a diner—a combination of grease, sweat, strong coffee, and burned bacon. I gave a quick glance around and saw a huge box filled with bacon, egg, and cheese sandwiches lying on the floor. As I scanned the group, I noticed the one other woman on the desk. I made a mental note to introduce myself to her sooner rather than later.

Chick grabbed my shoulders and began to turn me in ten-degree clips as he pointed to other long counterlike rows filled with people conducting business. "Here's a brief layout of the floor." He spun me to the left and pointed to a square configuration in the corner of the room. "That's the emerging markets desk. They sell bonds issued by developing countries. Brazil, Mexico, Chile. Most of Latin America." He turned me another ten degrees so that I was facing the middle of the room. "Over to the left we have high yield, bonds issued by companies with lower credit ratings. That means the debt has a higher risk than say a high-grade bond, which is debt sold by larger, more well-established companies. Your Ford, IBM, Procter & Gamble, and most other big-name companies you can think of are traded off the high-grade desk, which sits directly to their left. Past them you have mortgages, which should be self-explanatory, and at the end of the room you have the money market team. They sell bonds that mature in one year or less. There's also some structured product teams over there," he said as he rotated me again and pointed to a bunch of nerdy-looking guys in the right far corner. "They do highly complicated structured trades that most people don't understand, and that includes a majority of the people in this room. You'll learn what they do eventually, because I'm training you and I don't have idiots working for me. Finally, around the corner is the foreign exchange desk. They trade global currencies. If you ever travel to Europe and have to change your dollars for sterling or euros, you'll have to know where those rates are trading. That's their job. Capiche? There are economists and strategists scattered all over the place. You won't have much cause to interact with anyone who doesn't work in rates to start off."

I tried to process everything he was saying, but my brain shut down somewhere around the time he mentioned Brazil. I was so screwed.

"Now, these rows over here," he said as he pointed to long rows that faced each other, the elevated monitors forming a wall in between the guys so they didn't have to stare at each other all day, "is the trading desk. These guys actually price and trade the bonds that we, the sales desk, buy and sell for our clients. It's our job as salespeople to solicit business and keep our clients informed and happy. Clients can pick up the phone and call any shop on the street to do trades; we need to make sure that they call *us*. How do we do that? By being good fucking salespeople, that's how. That's what we are going to teach you. How to be a good fucking salesperson. Capiche?" My head was spinning, and I could swear that I just heard one of the trader's computers cluck like a chicken for no apparent reason. *What the hell was going on here?*

"What's that noise?" I asked, afraid if I hadn't really just heard a clucking chicken I was about two minutes away from a stroke.

"What, the chicken?" he asked.

I was relieved he heard it, too, and yet startled that he didn't seem to think random barnyard animal noises needed explanation. I nodded. "Yes, the chicken."

"Some of the traders programmed their systems to make farm animal noises when they do a trade. They can't possibly keep their eyes on everything all the time so the sound effects help let them know where their positions are. So don't be surprised when you hear something moo, or bark, or oink. The junior guy's system rings a cowbell, but it's annoying so I might make him change it. I hear that fucking thing in my sleep."

Unless you saw it for yourself, you couldn't accurately imagine this scene if you took three tabs of acid and locked yourself in closet. I gulped.

"So are you ready to start?" Chick asked as he walked toward his chair on the desk, where he apparently spent most of his time, despite having a private office.

Ready to start? I couldn't remember anything he just said. I needed a map. And a finance-to-English dictionary. Pronto.

Before I could ask him to clarify a few things, he called everyone to attention.

"Listen up, team; this is Alex. She's our new analyst. Introduce yourselves and make her feel at home." A few people nodded; some of them raised their hands and waved. One guy actually got up and shook my hand, though he was on the phone when he did it so he didn't actually speak to me. I looked around and noticed that there were no empty workstations. I sure as hell wasn't going to sit on someone's lap, so I was sincerely hoping that Chick was going to tell me where I'd be sitting. When he sat down and started typing into a massive Excel sheet, I realized he wasn't.

I had no choice but to ask him, or else stand in the aisle all day like the team mascot.

"Excuse me, Chick. Where should I sit?" I asked, nervously.

"Here you go." Without taking his eyes off his spreadsheet, he reached behind him and grabbed a tiny metal folding chair that was leaning against the wall. It was kindergarten size. I took the chair from him and held it in front of me without unfolding it, clearly confused.

"You don't have a desk yet," he said, without trying to hide his irritation. "We have to figure out where to put you. In the meantime, just pull up the folding chair behind people and watch what they do. Rotate through the whole group."

My mind was racing. How could there be nowhere for me to sit? I didn't just show up unannounced. I got this job offer last October. It was July. In ten months' time they couldn't even find me a desk? A man in his late thirties walked over and grabbed Chicky's shoulder, staring at me like Sylvester the cat used to look at Tweety Bird. He was tall, well over six feet, with a platinum blond crew cut, broad shoulders, and huge biceps. He never took his eyes off me as he talked to Chick. It made me so uncomfortable I had to stare at the floor.

"Yo, Chicky, this is the new girl?" he asked in a thick southern drawl.

"Alex. Our new analyst."

"She's cute. Would I do her?"

"I get the feeling she's feisty, so yeah, probably. I doubt she'd do you, though."

"Give her time, Chick. Give her time." He then grabbed one of the last two sandwiches out of the box and offered it to me. "Hey, Alex. Welcome to Cromwell. Have a sandwich." His hands, like Chick's, were perfectly clean and smooth.

I answered him politely, "No, thank you, I'm fine."

"You don't like the swine?"

"Excuse me?"

"The swine. Bacon. You aren't Jewish, are you? If you aren't Jewish, then why don't you fancy the swine?"

"What? Umm, no, I ate already, thank you. But I don't have a problem with the swine, no."

"Suit yourself, newbie. It's probably better. If you start eating bacon every day, you'll lose that tight ass of yours, and nobody here wants to be stuck looking at a pretty girl with a fat ass. Remember, for girls, eating is cheating." With that he threw the sandwich back in the box and winked at me as he walked away.

I looked for Chick to say something, anything, to defend me, but he didn't. Instead, he removed his wallet and his BlackBerry from his drawer.

He smacked me on the back as he stood. "I have a golf outing, but I'll be in tomorrow," he said as he struggled with the sleeves on his blazer. I watched him leave, feeling as if I was watching my lifeboat turn around while I was still treading shark-infested waters. One hour as a full-time employee at Cromwell and, so far, it was nothing like I had imagined.

I STOOD HELPLESSLY CLUTCHING my chair like a security blanket, staring at my fellow team members, none of whom made a move to introduce themselves. I walked down the first row, feeling as if I was walking the plank, until a man who looked an awful lot like Andy Garcia intercepted me. He had the same tan skin, the same black hair, the same brooding eyes, and thankfully, a smile.

"Hey," he said as he shook my hand. "I'm Drew. Why don't you hang out with me today?"

"Oh really?" I was relieved, like a kid just saved from being picked last for dodgeball. "That would be great, thanks."

"Pull up a seat . . . well, a folding chair. Whatever."

He slid his chair to the left, to make room for me. I stared wide-eyed at all the numbers, the scrolling headlines, the modeling systems, the Excel sheets, the various colors flashing spastically on his monitors. Drew smiled and said, "Until you get your own desk—and, knowing this place, that could take a year—you'll just have to shadow people during the day. Here's what you need to know." I flipped open my spiral notebook and waited anxiously for my first sales lesson. "First, don't put the chair in the aisle, that's the fastest way to piss people off. Make sure your chair is pulled as close to the desk as possible."

"Okay, easy enough." Not exactly the kind of lesson I was hoping for, but it was better than nothing.

"Second, don't annoy people. When guys are busy, don't ask them questions. Don't try and make small talk with anyone. Until people get to know you, no one has any interest in talking to you. Sorry, but that's just the way it is."

"Don't talk to anyone. Got it."

"And whatever you do, avoid Kate Katz—a.k.a. Cruella—like the plague."

"Why?" I glanced at the woman on the phone at the end of the row. He had to be referring to her; she was the only other female on the government bond desk. She didn't look scary. She reminded me of my third-grade teacher, sort of. Only with more expensive clothes and a better haircut. Her short brown bob was tucked behind her ears, and her crisp white shirt was tucked into dark navy pants. She wore small diamond earrings, little makeup, and loafers. She wasn't exactly what I would classify as intimidating. She looked friendly enough, I thought.

"Just trust me on this one. Lastly, I assume you noticed the coffee stand in the hallway?"

"Yeah, I saw it when I got off the elevator."

"Good. We call it Papa's. I have no idea why. Make the guys who work there your friends. You will be spending a lot of time getting coffees there for the group, and the quicker you get there and back the better. If they like you, they will take care of you faster. Other than that, you'll figure things out as you go. You can hang with me today. I'll show you the screens we use, and get you used to following the markets. Cool?"

Very cool. If I could, I'd canonize Drew. "Thanks so much."

"No problem. Now, where's your calculator?"

I quickly produced the shiny new HR-issued calculator. "Right here. What can I do?"

He handed me a printout of a grid, filled with numbers in type so small they looked like newspaper print. "Give me the weighted average of these prices. Don't forget that these are in thirty-seconds, so you'll have to convert them to decimals before you average. Also check to see if any of the handles look bad. They should all be around par. If not, let me know and I'll double-check. There are probably a few errors in there."

"Sure, I can do that." And I could have, assuming someone had told me what a handle was, how to weighted average something, and how to turn something called thirty-seconds into decimals. As soon as I had those down, I could definitely do this.

He gave me a knowing smile. "You have no idea what I just said, do you?"

"I, ummm . . ." *Shit,* I thought. My business classes suddenly seemed like a complete waste of time. I might as well have majored in underwater basket weaving.

"Be honest, Alex. Pretending to know things you don't will only make it harder. Do yourself a favor and admit what you don't know."

"You might as well have been speaking Mandarin."

Drew laughed. "Here." He pointed to the first figure on the grid: 99–28. "The 99 part of the price is called the handle. If you booked this trade at 98–28, the trader will tell you that you have a 'bad handle.' It's clear at all times which handle bonds trade at, so a lot of times people won't refer to them. There's just no need and the less time you take relaying prices, the better. So if a trader gave me a price on this bond, he'd just say, twenty-eight. When I said to check for bad handles, I meant that if most of the bonds are trading around par–100, and you see a price that's say, in the seventies, the handle is probably bad."

"Ohh, okay, that makes sense." I pointed to the twenty-eight part of the price. "So then that's in thirty-seconds?"

"Right. Bond prices are quoted in thirty-seconds, so in order to change that to a decimal, you just divide 28 by 32."

I typed the numbers in my calculator. This was sixth-grade math; I had no problem with that. I entered 28, hit the divide sign, punched in 32, then pressed the equal button on my calculator. The screen flashed ERROR.

That didn't seem right. "Shoot, I think my calculator's broken." I showed Drew my screen.

"I take it you've never used a financial calculator before?"

"No, we used regular ones in school," I said.

"These don't work like normal calculators. After every input, you have to hit the enter button, and then the function at the end. So you type in 28, then enter. Then you input 32, hit enter again, and the divide key at the end. It's always that way. For example, if you needed to add two plus two, it's two, enter, two, enter, plus."

"Why couldn't the financial calculator people just leave it the same as every other calculator in the free world and not make things harder than they need to be?"

"Good question. I don't have the first goddamn clue. You'll get used to it though."

"If you say so."

"I have to make some calls. Are you cool now with getting this done for me?"

"I think so. I'll try."

"Good. Let me know if you have any questions, but use common sense. If I'm cursing at someone or losing money on a trade, telling me you can't figure out how to work the calculator probably won't go over well."

"Got it. Thanks for the help. I guess I have more to learn than I thought."

"Girlie, you have absolutely no idea." He chuckled as he grabbed his headset and hit a button on the phone board.

I grabbed my backward, nonsensical financial calculator and got to work on my first real assignment as a Cromwell employee.

Three

Girlie

I SPENT THE rest of the month working like a lunatic. I got to the office every morning by 6:15. I wanted to make a good impression, even if there wasn't much that I could do. During the day, I sat behind people on my folding chair and was mostly ignored. A few guys attempted to teach me how to look at any number of a dozen applications that scrolled numbers in a dizzying array of colors. I learned to discern which ones displayed the stock market, the Treasury bond market, derivatives and swaps; where you could see the calendar of economic indicators that were being released that day; foreign exchange rates; corporate spreads; and prices for futures contracts and for the European and Asian markets. I still didn't really understand what any of these things were, but I watched their prices flash like mini strobe lights on their computers. I was given little projects to do, which was a problem since they all involved having access to a workstation.

My solution was to stay late every night, using the models and various programs on someone else's desktop to solve the math equations I had to turn in the next morning. I usually got home around 8:00 P.M., ate whatever I could find in the refrigerator, and collapsed into bed from exhaustion. I was beginning to forget what Liv looked like, and so far, we had yet to take advantage of our cool apartment in the city because we were both too busy working. Every morning I was quizzed on the important news stories around the world, and I was asked what might have moved the market overnight during Asian trading. The sheer mass of material I was supposed to know was staggering. I still didn't know anyone's name except for Chick, Drew, Reese (swine guy), and Kate/Cruella. I don't think anyone knew mine. Instead, they called me "Girlie." Much to my horror, I answered to it.

On a particularly steamy day in August, I sat in my metal chair, listening to a large man with hands that looked like catchers' mitts explain bond market basics and tried very hard not to fall asleep. He had a scruffy beard and chocolate-colored eyes that were friendly despite the fact that he looked like he could crush my head like a walnut with his bare hands. His name was Billy Marchetti, but everyone called him Marchetti. As he playfully flicked rubber bands at me while he waited for me to finish the equation he had given me I heard some random guy on the floor scream "Pizza's in the lobby!" at the top of his lungs.

Without looking at my watch, I knew exactly what time it was. Every Friday for the last six weeks, some guy screamed "Pizza in the lobby!" across the floor at 10:30. And every Friday morning at 10:30, the floor erupted into applause that rivaled what was heard in Yankee Stadium when Jeter scored against the Red Sox. I had had a glimpse of trading floor eating habits my first day at Cromwell—hundreds of egg-and-cheese sandwiches dripping with grease being devoured as fast as humanly possible without choking to death. At the time, I disregarded it. That was before I understood the pivotal role that food plays in the finance industry. Every day there were bagels, or egg sandwiches, or Krispy Kreme doughnuts. The food was ceremoniously carried to various parts of the room in huge cardboard boxes that were dropped on the floor every thirty feet like paper land mines. Within seconds, dozens of grown men would descend on the offerings like angry bees swarming a honeycomb, grabbing whatever they could get their hands on. You wouldn't think that guys who earned seven-figure salaries would care so much about free doughnuts. You wouldn't think so, but they do.

Mealtime at Cromwell was like feeding time at the zoo; if you were fast and big, you ate first; if you were small and slow, you had better get out of the way. An example of Darwin's survival of the fittest, adapted for healthy, well-fed men. The delivery options weren't restricted to the usual Chinese or pizza joints. If someone felt like ordering $2,000 worth of penne alla vodka, veal parmigiana, and Caesar salad for lunch from an expensive restaurant that didn't have delivery service, the executive chef and the waiters would deliver the food themselves. Sometimes there were trays of fried chicken, ribs, and cornbread from a BBQ place in Midtown; kung pao chicken, lo mein, and anything else on the menu from the Chinese place; or cheeseburgers and fries. In the afternoons, when energy began to fade, someone would inevitably appear with three dozen milkshakes, ice cream sandwiches, or bags of candy from the drugstore. When it was someone's birthday, the secretaries ordered huge ice cream sheet cakes, and platters of chocolate chip cookies. I was pretty sure I was going to wind up weighing two hundred pounds. And I was single. This was not good.

Chick pressed the button on "the hoot," a microphone that broadcast his voice across the floor. "Copy that. We got this one, Frankie. Pizzas will be there in five, and if they're not, you have my permission to beat my analyst." He pointed to me with his right hand. "Girlie slave, go get the pizzas and bring them back up to Frankie. Go." Chick believed in figuring things out for yourself and being proactive. For the most part, I had managed to follow along without having to ask for clarification until now. Considering I didn't know how many pizzas I was supposed to pick up, or how I was supposed to pay for them, or who the hell Frankie was, I thought now it was appropriate to ask a few questions.

I stood nervously behind his desk. "I'm sorry, Chick. How many pizzas do you need me to get and how should I pay for them?" I asked, sweetly.

"Do my shoes need a shine?" he responded, as he examined his impeccably clean loafers. "Hey, Wash!" He called to the shoeshine guy roaming the floor. "Can I get a shine, buddy? My shoes are looking a little dull." The man with the shine box came over and set his tiny stool down and began shining Chick's shoes while he was still wearing them.

He looked up at me like I was a bothersome gnat. Then without answering me, he yelled over his shoulder, "Willy! You back there?" A guy in his mid to late twenties seated in the back row popped up from behind a computer monitor, sucking on a lollipop. I hadn't noticed him until now, which was strange since he was good-looking.

"Yeah, Chick?" he yelled back, a phone still held to his ear.

"Get over here and take Alex to pick up the pizzas." No please, no thank you, just the order. Get the pizzas.

Thirty seconds later, Will walked past Chick's desk and waved for me to follow him. He was wearing the standard blue button-down shirt under a dark gray Henley sweater. He had black hair and blue eyes and was fit without looking like he spent all his free time lifting weights in the gym while admiring himself in the mirror. He was handsome by anyone's standards but, for Cromwell, he was Movie Star Hot.

"Thanks for coming with me. I'm Alex," I said coolly as I shook his hand.

"I'm Will Patrick. Nice to meet you, Alex. You're Chick's new indentured servant, huh?"

"Basically, yeah. Chick just called you Willy. Which do you prefer to be called? The nicknames in this place are confusing."

He smiled, revealing a perfect set of white chompers. They could have used his mouth as an "after shot" in a toothpaste commercial.

"Will, if you want me to answer you. Chick's the only one who calls me Willy just so he can call me a dick every day without getting in trouble with compliance. Unfortunately, when I was in your shoes, I made the mistake of telling him I hated it when he called me that. Now, if Chick has it his way, it will be on my tombstone."

"So I should get used to being called Girlie?"

"Pretty much."

"Wonderful. So how many pizzas are we getting?" He smirked. When we reached the lobby, I froze in horror. There were five delivery guys waiting for us, stacks of pizzas at their feet. When Frankie had yelled "Pizza in the lobby," he meant pizzas, plural, as in one hundred of them. Will picked up one of the stacks and handed it to me.

"You can handle carrying ten at a clip, right?"

"Umm, I think so. I've never done it before."

"Get used to it, Girlie," he said, as he grabbed a second stack and flashed me a smile. "Let's go."

I have always had a contentious relationship with Murphy's Law. For some reason, at the most inopportune times, I seem to embarrass myself in a way that's completely out of character. I've always been a good athlete, but ask me to walk down the aisle in a bridesmaid dress and for some reason that I can't explain, I always end up tripping. I have had my heel catch in the hem of pants that I wear all the time as soon as I found myself in the presence of a good-looking guy and have landed on my butt on a crowded Midtown sidewalk for inexplicable reasons. I'm basically Murphy's bitch.

I was so definitely not the girl you wanted carrying multiple pizzas up two escalators, into an elevator, down a hallway, up a small flight of stairs, down a small flight of stairs, and then to wherever it is that Frankie sits. Slowly (did I forget to mention that I was wearing four-inch stilettos that hurt like hell and a pencil skirt that forced me to walk like a geisha?) I followed Will back to the trading floor. It was only 10:30. Why did we need eight hundred slices of pizza before lunch?

We found Frankie, a trader on the corporate bond desk, across the room. Will set his stack of pizzas down on the floor and I tried to do the same, except people started grabbing the boxes, and ripping them open before I could put them down. I turned and started back toward the elevators, and noticed Will heading back to his desk. I called after him, figuring he forgot that there were still eighty pies downstairs that we needed to deliver.

"Sorry there, Girlie, but I just went with you on the first trip to show you the ropes. The rest are up to you."

"You want me to make eight more trips? You won't help me? How do I pay for these?"

He chuckled, enjoying the latest in a seemingly endless string of hazing rituals. "I seriously will not be helping you, but I have faith in your ability to not fuck up carrying pizzas. Our brokers send them every week. The bill goes to them. I enjoyed our chat, Girlie. We should do it again sometime."

I watched his back as he walked away. Right, of course. They're a gift. The weekly hundred pizzas. Of course they are. How in God's name was I going to manage working here without gaining thirty pounds? Fifteen minutes and eight trips later I dropped off the last stack and returned to my chair, dodging empty boxes and pizza crusts along the way.

"Hey, A!" I heard a voice call from behind me. I turned to see Will, flashing his perfectly white teeth, holding a slice of pizza up in the air, as if toasting me. I couldn't help but smile. Chick had said that I couldn't date anyone in the office, but he never said anything about flirting. *Right?*

In September, after two months of being a nameless gofer, I found myself looking forward to the firm's annual analysts' boat cruise. The cruise was a Cromwell tradition. The firm rented a yacht for the new class and some of the senior employees for the alleged purpose of team bonding. It left from Chelsea Piers and cruised around the island of Manhattan. Oddly enough, a chance to share horror stories with my peers, others who understood how brutal it was to be the new person on the desk, sounded heavenly.

Since Chick would sooner gnaw off his own hand than spend an evening stuck on a boat with a bunch of insignificant kids, he was sending someone else as his representative.

"Boat cruise tonight?" Chick asked, as he chugged a soda.

"Yeah, I have to leave at five thirty. I hope that's okay."

"It's fine. Reese will be there. Have a good time."

Great. Swine Guy was coming. I had purposely avoided him since my first day. He scared me. "Thanks. I'm sure I will."

At the yacht, two waiters clad in white dinner jackets and black bow ties were standing on either side of the entrance ramp holding trays of wine. Not a bad greeting as far as I was concerned. There was a DJ spinning a bunch of pop radio classics loud enough for everyone else on the pier to stop and gawk. I saw a few familiar faces from my training class, but I didn't know any of the investment banking interns. There were probably fifty or sixty first-year analysts in the entire firm, but I decided to only talk to the ones in sales and trading because we would be able to discuss the difficulties of adjusting to life on a trading floor. At least we had that in common. I took a glass of white wine and approached my fellow freshman Cromwellites, all of us united in our inadequacy. Or so I hoped.

"Hi, guys!" I chirped as I joined a conversation. I meant "guys" literally. They were. Every single one of them.

"Hey," a few muttered, barely acknowledging my existence.

"What's up? It's been a bizarre two months, hasn't it? The folding chair is just crazy." The group shot me inquisitive looks, as if I had just confessed that I had been beamed up by an alien spacecraft.

"A folding chair?" one of the more vocal analysts asked. "You're joking, right?"

"No! Wait, you guys don't have to sit on folding chairs?"

"No. I have a desk. Don't you, Dan?" a guy named Adam asked.

"Of course," Dan responded. "How could you not have a desk, Alex? That's humiliating. What in God's name do you do all day if you don't even have a computer?"

I suddenly felt like I was in the middle of one of those dreams where you show up to class naked.

"There . . . well, the thing is, at the moment . . . there . . . wait. You guys seriously all have seats?" It never occurred to me that being deskless wasn't customary.

"Yeah, Alex, we really do. Clearly your group doesn't think you deserve one. Sucks to be you. So, anyway, are you guys going to the Yale-Harvard game this season?" Dan asked the others, none too subtly excluding me from the conversation. I skulked to the stern, leaned against the rail, and stared at the Statue of Liberty as we cruised up the Hudson River. I was isolated, an outcast among my peers. I overheard a few conversations other analysts were having, each trying to prove that he had a more important role, a better boss, a desk that made more money. I wasn't going to play that game, mostly because I was pretty sure I would lose. I decided a better course of action was to keep munching on appetizers at the railing with my good friend, Lady Liberty.

I was halfway through my third mini BLT when someone pulled my ponytail, yanking my head backward. I turned to see Reese with a big smile on his face, and a shrimp in his hand.

"This spot taken, Girlie?"

"Nope. No one else back here except for me and the swine."

"The what?" He leaned his elbows on the railing so that we were closer to eye level. Reese must have been six foot four, and it was hard to hear him what with the noise of the wind and the boat engine, not to mention the din from the idiots bragging about the many feats of intellectual strength they'd performed over the past two months.

"Remember the day I started? You asked me if I fancied the swine. I'm a big fan of the swine. I just wanted you to know." I held up the remaining half of my bacon lettuce and tomato sandwich.

Reese started laughing and patted me on the head. "I forgot about that! I like to unnerve the new kids right away. It's my idea of a personality test. If you had gotten all huffy on me, I never would have talked to you again, you see? With girls especially, you gotta know what you're dealing with if you want to stay out of trouble. Good job. So far, you're okay with me."

"Thank God! I'm Alex, but my friends call me Girlie," I said, as I extended my hand, feeling comfortable for the first time since stepping foot on the boat.

He laughed again. "Well, hello there, Girlie. You can call me Reese. How are you liking Cromwell so far?"

"I love it."

"Really? No one's given you a hard time?"

"Nope! I'm having a ball. Everything is great."

"Bullshit," he replied with a smirk. "Don't lie to me on the first date, sugar. I only have room in my life for one woman who lies to my face, and I've already got a wife." He held up his left hand and shook his ring-clad finger.

I didn't think complaining was a very good idea. So I stayed silent.

"I'm not letting you leave until you give me an honest answer, sugar. How are you liking Cromwell?"

He was serious.

"Well, I'm just worried that maybe I'm not doing enough or that people don't like me. I don't want to be annoying. I'm supposed to be asking everyone questions, but also staying out of the way. That's kind of hard to do considering I don't have my own desk yet." There, I said it. Now I probably should just throw myself overboard.

"Why do you think people don't like you?" Reese chuckled. "Let me tell you something. If people didn't like you, you'd know it. You should ask some of the other kids what their time at the firm has been like, and then you'll see how nice people are really being."

"I was just talking to some of the other analysts and I'm the only one who has to sit on a folding chair. It sounds like they have real work to do, and so far I really haven't been able to do anything except help Drew and a couple of others with a few things."

"Is that why you're standing over here by yourself instead of mingling with the other rookies?"

"Sort of."

"Ahhh. I see. And obviously, you believe everything they're saying."

"Well, yeah, why would they lie?"

"Because they're guys," he said, without hesitation. "I talked to one guy who's such a tool he doesn't even realize that his team is ripping on

him. I'd feel bad for him if I didn't think he was such a prick after talking to him for two minutes."

"Who?" I asked, eager to discover which Ivy Leaguer wasn't quite as
impressive as he claimed.

"That guy, the one in the orange shirt. You know him?" Reese
pointed to the gaggle of analysts.

I looked over and was not at all surprised to see Adam holding court.
Still.

"Oh yeah. I know him," I said. "He went to Princeton. And just in
case anyone doesn't know he went to Princeton, he name-drops about
his eating club, wears at least one orange item every day, and carries a
duffel bag with a giant tiger's head on it. He has a huge ego."

"Sugar, if you don't like big egos, you're in the wrong industry. I'm
going to cheer you up though. Watch this. Hey, Tony the Tiger! Come
over here." Reese waved to Adam, whose face lit up like a hundred-watt
bulb as he realized that Reese wanted to speak with him. He pulled his
shoulders back and adjusted the buckle on his belt, clearly thinking that
he was being summoned because he had made such a good impression
on a Cromwell managing director. I wasn't sure why Reese asked him
to join us, but I knew kudos were not on the menu. Adam smoothed the
collar on his tangerine Lacoste polo shirt before he shook Reese's hand,
while simultaneously patting him on the back.

"Hey, Reese, right? We spoke a little while ago about Greenspan and
the Federal Reserve." Adam flashed him a big smile before turning his
attention toward me. "Hey, Amber."

"My name's Alex."

"Right, sorry."

("No, you aren't." I didn't say that.) "No problem." Sounded better.

"Her friends call her Girlie, though." Reese was enjoying this. I
wondered if I could make it if I tried to swim to shore.

"Girlie?" Adam was confused, a new feeling for him.

"Only her friends, though. I mean, I call her Girlie. You should stick
with Alex."

Adam shrugged. "How long have you been at Cromwell, Reese?"

"Twenty-one years. How long have you been at Cromwell?"

"Two months. But I think I'm really adding value quickly."

Reese gave me a wink. "Yeah, you were saying that earlier. Why don't you tell my girlie friend here about your trade last week."

This caught my attention. He was allowed to do a trade? I wasn't even allowed to pick up the phone.

"It was great. I'm trading size already, you know? They want me to just hit the ground running."

"What does trading size mean?" I asked. Reese pretended to cough to muffle his laughter.

"You know, big trades. Moneymakers, not the little dinky trades that don't matter if you fuck them up."

"I sit on a folding chair. I guess I'm doing the opposite of trading size," I said.

"Adam, tell Alex how you did it. Teach her how to work the ropes. Tell her the whole story like you told me."

Adam was loving the attention. "So there's this company called Cox Communications, a major player. So this guy I'm working with is a fellow Tiger. He's a great guy and really lets me get involved—we were in the same eating club. He took the order from his client and then told me to shout out the order to the trader."

Here I had to interrupt, because I knew he was lying. "Adam, you haven't passed the Series 7 or the Series 63 yet. You aren't allowed to trade. There's no way they let you do that. It's illegal."

"Well, no, I didn't execute the actual trade, but his client wanted a big chunk of shares. I had to tell the trader to start building a position, but it wasn't an actual order."

Reese continued to prompt Adam to finish the story. "So, Adam, what exactly did he tell you to do?"

"I had to stand up and scream across the floor to the trader that I was a large buyer of Cox."

Reese started laughing and asked Adam to repeat what he'd said.

"You said what?"

"I said I was a large buyer of Cox. Everyone started clapping and cheering. It was awesome."

I'd heard it before, but now I saw it was true: book smarts and street smarts are *not* the same thing. As far as street smarts went, Adam was clearly a complete idiot.

Reese stood there, his arms folded across his chest, slowly nodding his head. Then he stepped forward and put one hand on each of Adam's shoulders. "Adam, we've got to teach this girlie how *real* men operate. So, one more time, show us how you yelled it on the floor."

"I'M A LARGE BUYER OF COX!" he yelled proudly.

Reese dropped his hands from Adam's shoulders. He tilted his head to one side, never losing eye contact with him, and said ever so slowly, "If I were you, Adam, I wouldn't be crowing about having announced that you're a pole smoker. I'm sure the guys in equities have been laughing their asses off at you ever since."

Adam's body went rigid. He turned bright red as the full force of his own stupidity hit him. He tried to pretend he was invisible. He wasn't. His brow furrowed like he was in pain, and quietly he said good-bye, this time getting my name right. He walked away slowly, his shoulders slumped forward, no longer pulled back in their arrogant Princeton posture.

I stood silent. I wanted to laugh, but he was my peer, my counterpart on the equity floor. If they could make Adam—undeniably smart and aware—humiliate himself that way, what on earth did my team have in store for me?

Reese patted my head again. "Still think we don't like you, sugar?"

"I can't believe they did that to him."

"See, that's what people will do when they don't like you. The more time you spend here, the more you'll see how badly we can torment someone when we want to make him miserable. If the worst thing that has happened to you is that you don't have a real desk, then you have nothing to worry about. Play the game, sugar, just play the game."

"I don't know how to play the game."

"You'll learn. Until then, just keep your head down and wear beige . . . you get what I'm saying?"

I did. It was the first thing I genuinely understood since I had started. That was something to be thankful for.

"I get it. And I should keep fancying the swine, right?"

"Always fancy the swine, sugar. Now, stop holding up the railing. Get over there and start mingling! You're in sales, for God's sake. We don't need any wallflowers in the group. Work the crowd, make people like you, and pretend to like the assholes you can't stand. That's all part of your new job."

"Thanks, Reese," I said as I followed him into the crowd with a renewed sense of confidence and enthusiasm. "For the advice, I appreciate it."

"You're one of us now, sugar. One thing about our desk: we always have each other's backs. It doesn't mean we won't fuck with you mercilessly, though."

"Sort of like older brothers?"

"Exactly. Forty of them."

Reese had given me my very first sales lesson, and it was probably the most important one that I would ever learn: if I wanted to be successful, then I needed to get really good at pretending to like people I didn't.

four

If I Wanted to Educate the Youth of America, I'd Have Been a Fucking Nursery School Teacher

THE FIRST WEEK of October, I celebrated a very important occasion with Annie and Liv at a sushi restaurant downtown named, ironically, Bond Street. I had passed all my exams. It was a Friday night and we were all in good moods, so we hit the downstairs lounge of the restaurant and threw back martinis, sushi, and Bloody Marys made with wasabi until two in the morning. It was a good thing we all had apartments to go home to or I have no doubt Liv and I would have fallen asleep on the train and ended up missing our stop on Metro North. Chick didn't register much when I proudly handed him the printouts proving my passing grades on all three exams. I don't know what I expected him to say. Maybe "Good job, Alex." Or, even, "Take the day off, Alex." But he didn't. He glanced at the paper, gave me a fist bump, and went into a meeting. I tried not to let it bother me.

I THOUGHT MAYBE I'd get my own desk after I passed my exams, but November arrived and I was still stuck in the folding chair. Someone had written "Girlie" on the back of it with a Wite-Out pen, so I never had any trouble finding my seat. I wish I knew whom to thank for that.

Every few days I'd move my chair along the row to sit in between two new salespeople. It was impossible to remember the names of my coworkers, because everyone had multiple aliases and was called by various combinations of first, surname, and/or nickname at any given point in time. I didn't know how I was ever going to keep them all straight. There were multiple Johns, Joes, Bobs, and Peters plus those who went by Murph, Sully, or Fitzie, and their names may or may not have also started with John or Joe or Bob or Peter. Then there were the guys with nicknames that replaced whatever their first names were, usually because of personal quirks or idiosyncrasies. There was "Loaf," named for his horrendously thick head of hair that looked like a loaf of bread; and there were "Tank," "Moose," and "Pigpen." There was a guy called "Mangia" because he ate a lot, and one called "Two-Bite" because he didn't. There was "Shrek," "Barney Rubble," and one tall guy with an unusually long neck called "Dino" after the brontosaurus on *The Flint-stones.* There was "Chewie," a hairy guy they compared to Chewbacca, and "Wet Baby Possum," the guy who sat in the back row who had arguably the worst hair I had ever seen. (Someone had once quipped that it looked like a wet baby possum crawled on his head and died there, and it stuck.) They all wore khakis, various patterned blue shirts, brown belts, and their egos on their sleeves. They laughed loudly and made fun of one another, and I found it virtually impossible to tell them apart. Just addressing someone was a panic-inducing event, because I learned the hard way calling someone Barney because you think that's his real name and not an insulting nickname assigned to him because he looked like Barney Rubble wasn't a good idea. At least Jarrett was pretty mad about it.

Every female on the floor had a name that the men used to reference her, and it was never her real name. Of course, there were only forty or so women, excluding the administrative assistants, among four hundred men, but still, that was a lot of code names to remember. There was

"Magda," so called because she had clearly spent too much time in the sun when she was younger, and "Pepper," a Brazilian girl with an olive complexion. There was "Busted Britney Spears," named for her resemblance to the pop star if you looked at her after consuming ten beers, and "Raggedy Ann," a redhead who looked disheveled more often than not. Darth Vader's assistant, Hannah, was qualified to do absolutely nothing, and the guys ripped on her mercilessly. The men in my group called her "Baby Gap" because they figured that was where she bought her shirts. Her wiry frame was thin enough to get lost behind a parking meter if not for the fact that she had an enormous set of fake boobs of which she was clearly proud. And then there was the other woman in my group, the one I had thought would be a friend of mine because we women should stick together. The desk at the end of the front row was occupied by Kate Katz, otherwise known as "Cruella," "The Puppy Skinner," and/or "The Black Widow."

Before I met Cruella, Drew and a few of the Bobs and Joes told me her story. She had been in the Business for twenty-five years. She was very smart, very driven, and very tough. In her younger days she was the cause of many a broken marriage, before finally settling down and having children in her late thirties. Her husband was a wildly successful equity trader who worked at another firm, so she wasn't in this business for the money anymore. From what the group could gather, the only reason that she worked from 6:30 A.M. until 6:00 P.M., traveling to and from Westchester on either end, was because she hated her husband and kids or, more likely, they hated her. Once upon a time I was sure she'd been beautiful, but she had suffered under the strain of the Business and its endless demands. Her middle-aged metabolism and sedentary lifestyle resulted in excess padding in her hips and thighs, no matter how many hours she may have logged with her personal trainer. But she appeared harmless, so I found it very hard to believe that the stories I heard were true.

"Wassup, sugar?" Reese asked, as he playfully kicked the legs of my chair. "Do you want to come hang with me today?"

"Thanks, Reese, but I was actually thinking of sitting with Kate today. You know, girl bonding."

"Are you insane? Have you not been paying attention? Don't do it." Reese pretended to shudder with fear.

"Listen to the man, Girlie. She's evil. Stay as far away from her as possible," Drew interjected.

"I've been here for four months now. I'm not as clueless as I used to be. I think it will be fine. Besides, Chick told me to sit with *everyone*. That includes Kate."

"Suit yourself, sugar. If you want to ignore my advice, you go right ahead. Don't say I didn't warn you," Reese said as he folded his arms across his chest.

"You're going to be sorry," Drew sang as I made my way down the row.

I unfolded my chair next to her without an ounce of fear. "Excuse me, Kate? I was wondering if I could sit with you this morning," I said in my most cheerful voice.

This was the closest I had ever been to her, and for the first time I noticed she had a diamond on her left hand that the Rangers could use as a practice rink. She wore very little makeup, and the dark blue circles under her eyes made her look older than her fifty years. It was like she had given up. For a second, I felt bad for her. Maybe she was overwhelmed with the pressure of balancing a successful career with a husband and children; or maybe she was exhausted from too much stress and too little sleep. She turned her chair to face me slowly, staring at my outstretched hand while hers remained tightly clasped in her lap.

Then she spoke. "I'm sorry, what was it about me sitting down here ignoring you that signaled you to come over and whine in my ear?"

Or maybe she was the true incarnation of evil and was too busy breaking kids' crayons in half to care about what she looked like. I waited for her to laugh and say she was kidding. She didn't.

"Let me tell you something, little girl. I don't get paid the money I do to educate the youth of America. If I wanted to educate the youth of America, I would have been a fucking nursery school teacher. Now, since you have been here for all of what, two days?"—correcting her didn't seem like a good idea—"I suggest you learn a few things before you attempt to talk to me again and waste my time with what I'm sure are questions that my twelve-year-old could answer. That being said, maybe the cluster fuck over there"—she waved her hand dismissively at Drew and Reese, who pretended they weren't listening to our conversation—"could have done you some good by actually giving you something to read, instead of trying to look down your shirt all day. Oh, and maybe I should be more specific. I mean read something that doesn't have big color pictures of Tom Cruise or shiny tubes of lip gloss. Those types of books actually exist and could probably help you since it is blatantly obvious you don't know the first fucking thing about the bond business."

She spun around and opened the bottom drawer of a large file cabinet positioned behind her desk, and one by one removed a massive collection of hardcover books and photocopied packets. She shoved them at me, piling them up in my arms one after the other until I could barely see over the top of the stack.

"Let's start with the basics. *Inside the Yield Curve, Mortgage Bond Basics, Modeling the Swap Curve, The Treasury Bond Basis, The Fabozzi Fixed Income Handbook, The Handbook of Economic Indicators, Understanding Option Market Volatility.* Read all of these. And when you're done, you can come back to me, and *maybe* I'll talk to you. From the looks of you, that should probably take you a good eight to ten years, so let's plan to chat again then. And do yourself a favor. If you want to work here, if you want to graduate off your pathetic little chair and into a big girl's desk, then other than these books, you shouldn't so much as glance at any other publication of any kind unless it's thrown at your front door every morning by a kid on a bicycle." (Again, probably not the best time to point out that I lived on the twelfth floor of an apartment building.) "Now, go bother someone else. I've reached my painful-conversations-with-idiots quota for the day."

My arms were starting to ache under the strain of the library she had just thrown into them. I had hoped that Cruella would take me under her wing, guide me through the testosterone maze that we both worked in. She had been in the Business forever, so obviously she had to be tough, but she was way more than tough; she was wicked. I caught myself wondering if maybe once upon a time she had been like me, ignorant, unsure of how to act like a lady when you spent your days surrounded by men. What if she had been, and the years on the trading floor had hardened her into something else, something vicious, vile, and well, scary? What if that was what happened to *all* women after a few years in this environment? Maybe that was what *needed* to happen to you if you were going to have a successful career on the Street. I made a silent promise to quit before I'd allow myself to follow in her angry, unattractive footsteps. I carried my library back to Drew's desk, Cruella's insults still ringing in my ears.

"I tried to warn you," Drew said as he removed the top half of the stack from my hands.

"Does the offer to sit with you today still stand, Reese? I'm not above begging," I asked him while he sat on the edge of Drew's desk clicking his stapler so that staples flew randomly all over the carpet.

"Sure, Girlie. Don't worry," Reese said as he wrapped his arm protectively around my shoulders. "Stick with me and you'll be just fine. Buckle your seat belt, baby. Today I'll teach you how to work the phones."

ON WEDNESDAY THE FOLLOWING WEEK Chick pointed at me early in the morning and said, "Girlie, you need to update these models for us. We need the new currents on the sheet, and remove any bonds that rolled out of the basket this cycle. I want them to be cleaner. Also, work in the forward drops for the swap curve. I want to see the three-month, six-month, and one-year forward rates as well as the spot rates. Why don't we have that?"

"I don't know, Chick," I replied honestly. If only because I had no idea what he was talking about. "I'll get to work on them. When do you want them by?"

"Tomorrow. I'm leaving for a golf tourney. Reese taught you how to use the phones, right?"

"Yeah. I know how to work them," I said. Which was true. I originally thought Reese's offer to give me a phone tutorial was a complete waste of time. I was a girl, for God's sake. I was well versed in phones and all their functions. Until I realized that the phone system at Cromwell was slightly more advanced than the cordless phone I'd had in my room in high school. The Cromwell phone system was more complicated than anything I had ever seen. It had various types of lines: inside-only; outside-only; direct-to-client; desk-to-desk (New York office and our desks in other cities in the United States and overseas). A few phone lines were labeled with abbreviations I didn't understand and that Reese told me not to "worry" about; I never touched those. They scared me. I had stayed late after my coaching session with Reese, calling my mom and Liv and seeing if I could, in fact, mute them, disconnect them, place them on hold, conference them, or transfer them to each other without accidentally hanging up on one of them. It took me two hours to get it right. Don't tell anyone that.

"Good. Sit at my desk while I'm gone. I left the models up on my screen so you can work on them from my desk. Touch my e-mail and I'll kill you, but the team will need help with the phones. There are a lot of people out today for some reason and without me they'll need an extra set of hands. Pick up the outside lights only. No client directs. Capiche?"

"Sure, Chick. No problem."

"Good. See you in the morning."

I slid into Chick's chair, closed down his e-mail, and looked at the models on his monitor. He wanted them fixed by tomorrow. Wonderful. I prayed that the day would be quiet and I'd be able to spend all twelve hours working on the models. I still didn't understand all the market jargon and my Excel skills sucked, so figuring out how to fix these formulas was going to be painful.

The morning was fairly quiet, and the rest of the team had no problem fielding occasional phone calls while I worked on Chick's models. I spent hours working on the sheet, dissecting each formula symbol by symbol, and I was beginning to make progress. Then, somewhere around 3:00 P.M., things went crazy.

Hit ringing line, I mentally instructed myself. The night I had stayed late at work calling my friends and family suddenly seemed worthwhile. I wish they had taught a class on it at UVA. I'd have felt a lot more confident.

"Cromwell, this is Alex."

"Alex, my car isn't here. I'm waiting outside the clubhouse with my clubs and my car isn't here. I look like a goddamn caddy. You ordered me a car, right?"

Oh shit. "Hey, Chick, yeah, I did. I'll call the car company right now and find out where it is. Give me one second, okay?"

"Grrrr," he grunted. I think that was a yes. *Press hold, press left headset, dial number on the Post-it stuck to the side of Chick's keyboard.*

"Hi, yes, I'm calling to check on a town car I ordered for a pickup at Baltusrol Country Club, confirmation number 8625 . . . Uh-huh, okay, ten minutes? How bad is the traffic though, because this is my boss and he has a very low tolerance for employees who lie to him. So if ten minutes is really twenty minutes, I need you to tell me. Okay, fine, ten minutes. Yes. Thanks." *Clear line, hit right headset, hit line.* "Hi, boss, I just spoke to them. They said there's some traffic, but the car will be there in ten minutes."

"Fine."

Click. Chick hung up. Another light flashed. *Hit ringing line.* "Cromwell, this is Alex."

"Oh Christ, it's you," an all-too-familiar voice said, agonized that she had the misfortune of speaking to me.

"Hi, Kate, can I help you with something?"

"You can try, although your being successful is a low probability event."

I energetically gave the receiver the finger. "I need a reservation at

Le Bernardin tonight for four people at 6:30. I'm going into a customer meeting in Midtown. Get me the reservation and e-mail my BlackBerry."

Le Bernardin? That's one of the most popular restaurants in the city. The freaking mayor can't get in there with three hours' notice. "Kate, I'll call, but I don't know if . . ." *Click.* Kate hung up.

I grabbed the *Zagat's* restaurant guide out of Chick's top drawer and looked up the number for the most popular restaurant in town.

Hit light, dial number. "Hi, I'm calling from Cromwell. I was wondering if it would be possible to get a reservation for tonight for four people at 6:30?"

The hostess laughed rudely. "I'm sorry, we are fully booked for the next four months. If you like, I can get you in at five thirty or ten o'clock on December twenty-ninth."

"I know, but this is for Kate Katz, who I doubt you know, but I assure you she is a very important person at Cromwell Pierce." (Read: psycho hose bitch.) "Is there anything you can do?"

"I'm sorry, no. Please hold."

Click. The hostess hung up. Le Bernardin must have the same phone system as Cromwell.

The phone rang again. *Hit flashing light.* "Alex, this is Cromwell." *Wait no, that's not right.* "I mean, Cromwell this . . ."

"My car still isn't here, Alex!" Chick yelled before I could finish clarifying that my name wasn't Cromwell and I didn't work at a firm named Alex. I checked my watch. It had only been five minutes, not ten.

"Okay, boss, umm, sorry. Hold, I'll call them back right now." *Clear line, hit left headset . . . oh shit. I was supposed to hit hold in there somewhere.*

I accidentally hung up on Chick. I'm dead. Another line rang.

"HELP ON THE LIGHTS!" I screamed in panic the way ER doctors yell for crash carts. Drew threw on his headset and picked up the phone.

I called back the car company. "Hi, I just called looking for a car. Confirmation number 8625? I really need to know where this car is. Okay, it's pulling in now? Great, thanks."

I dialed Chick's cell phone. "Yeah. It's here, see you back at the office." *Click.* He hung up.

"Alex," Drew yelled from down the row. Cruella says she doesn't want to go to Le Bernardin anymore. She wants a reservation at Per Se instead. Same time, same number of people. I hope you know what she's talking about."

I looked in the drawer for the *Zagat's* again, but it wasn't there. I rummaged through papers on Chick's desk looking for the little red restaurant bible, but I couldn't find it. My heart was beating so quickly I feared it might pop out of my chest. I stood, and the wayward book fell off my lap onto the floor. I found the number for Per Se. *Hit light, dial number.* "Hi, yes, I'd like to make a reservation for tonight at 6:30 for four people, and if you love me you will tell me that's possible. Yes, I know you don't know me, but you're talking to someone who is hanging on to her sanity by a thread and if you tell me there are no reservations, I might go postal . . . you can? Oh thank God, you are a nice, nice man, thank you. Yes. Katz, 6:30, four people. God bless you." *Click.* I hung up. It felt nice to be on the other end of the disconnect for once.

I threw my headset on the desk and rubbed my throbbing temples. The phone rang.

I screamed as I mentally gave myself the proper instructions to pick up the phones on the NASA-worthy phone board for the hundredth time in the last hour. *Hit right headset, hit ringing light.* "Cromwell, this is Alex . . . No, Susan, I'm sorry he's still not back but I promise you I'll give him the message. No, I actually have no idea if he has his cell phone on him but he's at a meeting so it's probably off anyway. Is it an emergency? Okay, good. Then I promise as soon as he returns to the office I'll have him call home. Okay, no problem." *Click.*

"What's up, Alex?" Will asked as he plopped himself down in an empty chair and wheeled over next to me.

"Seriously, why does that guy Chip's wife call thirty times a day? I have answered at least seven phone calls from her in the last two hours. What part of 'I will tell him you called' does she not understand?"

Riiiiing. Chip's line rang again.

"It can't be her again. It just can't be."

"Here," Will said as he picked up my phone receiver. "You want help? You got it." He hit the ringing light. "Hello? Sure, hold one second, please." He dialed a number, pressed transfer, and hung up.

"Did you just hang up on Susan?"

"I didn't hang up her. I transferred her, umm, elsewhere," he said, his eyes glinting mischievously.

"Where?"

"The Chinese place down the block."

"Please tell me you're kidding. Please tell me you didn't just transfer her to Szechuan Panda."

"Yup."

"How is that helping?"

"I bet she doesn't call back again! I subtly told her that she was being an annoying pain in the ass. I just solved your problem. Well, one of them at least."

I giggled. "I appreciate the help; you're a good friend." *Friend? Was that presumptuous? Nice going, Alex. Way to make yourself look like an idiot.*

Riiiiing. "OHMIGOD!" *Hit ringing line.*

A muffled voice in a strange accent on the other end of the line said, "Yeah, is this Fung Yoo dwy cleana? You mess up my shirt! My suede shirt, you ruined my shirt! You gonna pay for this!"

"What?" I asked in desperation. "Wait, sir, hold on, you have the wrong number; this isn't a dry cleaner. This is a trading floor."

"You stupid beetch, you ruin my suede shirt. You replace it. It cost five hundred dolla!"

"Sir, please, you have the wrong number!" I tried in vain to make him understand that his ruined suede shirt (who wears suede shirts?) was not my problem. I turned to my left to see if someone else could pick up the phone to help and found Drew, Will, and Marchetti listening in on the line from the end of the row, laughing with their phones on mute. I turned the other way and discovered Reese, standing in the corner with his headset, looking straight at me. "You stupid beetch, Girlie-san, you ruin my shirt! You pay me five hundred dolla!" They erupted into laughter as I dropped the phone on my desk. Prank called by your own teammates. Normal? Not so much.

"I'm done!" I said, laughing. "You guys want to screw with me? Fine, I'm waving the white flag, you win! Score is immature idiots, one; Alex, zero." I waved my arm back and forth, pretending to surrender to the enemy. "I can't answer another phone or I think my head will explode. What is going on here today? It's crazy!"

Marchetti came over and rubbed my tired shoulders, "It's okay, Girlie. Just trying to loosen you up a bit. You looked stressed. Relax. Are you coming out with us tonight?"

"Sorry, guys, I can't. I have to finish these sheets for Chick. Have fun, though."

"Okay. Good luck, Girlie," they said in unison.

When the phones finally stopped ringing, I turned my attention back to the spreadsheet and tried not to worry about what would happen if I didn't finish it.

I WAS EXHAUSTED AND FRUSTRATED by the end of the day. I still couldn't understand concepts that I was sure I should get by now, and I lived in fear every day that Chick would call me over for one of his infamous pop quizzes. I couldn't even handle ordering him a fucking car. How was I supposed to learn the markets when I couldn't master basic technology? I had a splitting headache and was dreaming of a hot shower and sweats when I got home at 8:00. When I entered my building, the doorman stopped me to deliver an envelope that had been dropped off earlier. Inside was a single sheet of paper, folded in thirds.

A—

I have a dinner tonight at Smith & Wollensky's. Meet me at Manchester's afterwards for a beer? I'll be there by 9:30.

—Will

I couldn't believe that he had come to my apartment. I couldn't believe Will knew where I lived. I couldn't believe that Will remembered my name. I wasn't sure if it was really sweet or stalkerish, but I decided not to worry about it. Suddenly, I caught a second wind. After a quick shower, a change of clothes, and a forty-minute battle with a blow-dryer, a hairbrush, and a straightening iron, I left my apartment and walked uptown.

Manchester's was a small British pub on Second Avenue at Forty-Ninth Street. They had a good selection of beers on tap, but you usually couldn't find two feet of clear space to enjoy them in.

When I entered, I found Will sitting at the end of the bar, next to a few rowdy European guys who were watching a soccer game. He was drinking a pint of beer and chatting with the bartender, who had three teeth and a Union Jack tattooed on his wrist. When Will saw me enter, he waved me over, and the soccer fans happily shifted down the bar to open up a seat for me.

"Glad you got my note. I was trying to decide how long I should wait before figuring that you weren't coming." He patted the wooden bar stool next to him, and I hopped up onto the seat.

"It's only nine thirty-five, and you're already planning your exit strategy?"

"I was going to give you until ten. I think a half hour is a perfectly respectable amount of time to wait."

"I'd say forty-five minutes, since you had no way of knowing when I got your note."

"Good point," he said, flashing that Ultra Brite smile. My stomach did a somersault. That was never a good sign.

"Well, I'm glad you waited, for what it's worth."

"You're welcome. I'm glad you proved your staying power so that I could finally hang out with you outside the office. I had to make sure you weren't going anywhere before I asked."

"What do you mean 'proved my staying power'? It's November. I've only been at Cromwell for five months. Hardly a record."

"For a girl it's not a small achievement. We had a girl on the desk last year. She seemed smart enough, but she quit after six weeks. Couldn't hack it. I don't bother getting to know new girls until I'm pretty sure they're going to stick around. Otherwise it's a waste of time."

"I'm not going anywhere anytime soon."

"I hope not."

I felt myself blush and decided to change the subject. "How was your dinner?"

"Good. I took out my biggest account and had to show them a good time, so we went to a cigar bar and then Smith and Wolly's for some porterhouses and a few bottles of wine. The maître d' has become a buddy of mine since I'm there so often, so he took good care of us."

"Sounds like fun," I said. Even though I was thinking that he sounded a bit like a stuck-up snob. The butterflies in my stomach calmed down.

"Look at you in your jeans. That's not business casual attire."

"This isn't a business meeting."

"True. You look nice."

I blushed as the butterflies returned with a vengeance. "Hey, how did you know where I lived anyway?"

"I got your address off the group master list. Nancy, Chick's secretary, will give you anything if you ask her nicely."

"So you're stalking me."

"Stalking implies the attention is unwanted. You're here, so clearly I'm not stalking."

"Fair enough." I smiled.

"So what were you planning on doing tonight if you hadn't met me for a drink?"

"I was debating going for a run, but otherwise nothing."

"Do you run a lot?"

"I do. I like it, it helps me relax. Truth be told, I used to run more often, but it's been hard to find the time since I get stuck working late so much. I don't know how anyone does this job and manages to stay in shape. When I do finally get to the gym, my lungs will probably explode."

"Yeah, you should try to find the time when you can. It makes a big difference."

"What does?"

"Working out. We eat a lot in the office, and especially for girls it's absurdly easy to put on weight."

"Proud Mary" blared from the jukebox. I like loud music, so normally it wouldn't have bothered me. But maybe it was time to ask the bartender to turn the volume down, because it sounded like Will had just called me fat, which clearly would be crazy. I mean, what guy invites a girl out for drinks and then tells her she's fat? Especially when said girl is a size 4. OK, fine, sometimes I'm a size 6. But I have two dresses from Diane von Furstenberg and a pair of pants from J. Crew that are a size 4. I wear those a lot.

"What?" I asked quizzically.

"Nothing! It happens to all of us when we start. It's impossible to work on the desk and not gain a little weight so I'm just saying you should try to keep exercising whenever you can. That's all."

I suddenly lost interest in my light beer. I wanted to leave the bar, go home, and do sit-ups. I put my glass down.

"Don't go getting all sensitive on me. You look great. I didn't mean to upset you. Forget I said anything."

I figured I had two options: I could be THAT girl, the girl who made an issue of every little thing and ruined a good time on purpose, or I could forget about it, move on, and be breezy. I thought it best to be breezy, drink my beer, and then tomorrow eat nothing but Saltines and strap myself to the treadmill until I threw up.

There was an awkward pause before he said, "I'm sorry if I just put my foot in my mouth. I didn't mean anything by it, honestly. Forgive me?"

"Yes, thank you." I conceded.

"Tell me a little about yourself. All I know so far is that you're really good at carrying pizzas."

"What do you want to know?"

"Let's start with the basics. Siblings?"

"One younger sister, Cat. She's been seeing the same guy since high school and will probably be engaged soon. We don't have much in common."

"You aren't dating anyone?"

"No. What about you?" *Please say no.*

"No one worth mentioning." I felt my stomach flip-flop again. Was having drinks with Will breaking Chick's rule about interoffice dating? No. This wasn't a date. It was more like team bonding. "How did you end up at Cromwell?" he asked.

"It's kind of the family business. My dad's an i-banker. I used to visit him at work when I was little and I thought it was the most unbelievable place in the world. All the energy, all the people, all the noise. All I ever wanted to do was work in the Business."

"And now here you are, Cromwell analyst extraordinaire."

"My mom isn't as psyched about it though. She didn't really want one of her daughters in the 'snake pit,' as she calls it."

"She sounds like a smart lady. I don't blame her. I wouldn't want my sister or daughter working on a trading floor. Don't get me wrong; I'm glad you're here because you seem like fun and you're nice to look at, but still I can understand where your mom's coming from. Sometimes the stuff that goes on, the things you must hear, aren't really appropriate. For lack of a better word."

I feigned outrage. "I'm something to look at? Bring in a poster and hang it up on the wall in front of your computer if you want something to look at."

"I could, but it would get boring. You don't bore me."

"Gee, thanks for the compliment."

Awkward silence lasted for a few seconds, but it felt like an hour. "What about you? What's your story?"

"I'm an only child. I grew up in northern Virginia, and I went to UPenn for undergrad. I've been with Chick for four years now. I'm a VP, I'm a Capricorn, and I live on the Upper West Side." Before I could ask him another question he continued. "Enough about me, though." He slowly reached into his pocket and handed me a wad of singles. "Should we play some songs on the jukebox? You can tell a lot about someone from their music choices, you know."

"So if I play Celine Dion or the Backstreet Boys, you're going to make a run for it?"

"You bet. There'll be a giant Will-shaped hole in the wall."

"That's a lot of pressure."

"You go put some tunes on. I'll get us another round of beers."

He elbowed my side to nudge me toward the jukebox. I was giddy. This was not good. I'd only met this guy a few months ago, and we had only interacted briefly in the office. I barely knew him, and I was already a smitten kitten.

I returned as the bartender slid two more Blue Moons in front of us. We chatted easily and, before I knew it, it was midnight, and we were both pretty buzzed. I still wasn't sure exactly what we were doing, but I knew I was a happy girl. We stepped outside and walked south, toward my apartment. The air was cooler, and I wished I had brought a coat with me instead of banking on the unseasonably warm temperatures continuing once the sun went down. It was freaking November. Who goes out without a coat? I crossed my arms in front of my chest and shivered.

"You're cold. I was going to walk you home, but why don't you just get a cab here?"

I hadn't realized he was planning on walking me home. Good-looking *and* a gentleman—not a bad combination.

"Thanks for the beers, this was fun," I said as I pushed a lock of hair behind my ear.

"It was. So I'll see you tomorrow."

"I'll be there, bright and early."

"You know, we should do this again soon."

"I'd like that."

"Great. It was nice hanging out with you tonight, Alex."

"Yeah, you too."

He closed the cab door behind me and turned to walk uptown.

five

Bonus Season

I DON'T CARE what anyone says: there's no place in the world better than New York City at Christmas. When we were little, my parents used to bring Cat and me to the city to see the Rockettes at Radio City Music Hall, the tree in Rockefeller Center, and the fantastic window displays on Fifth Avenue. Bundled up in our toggle coats, we'd walk from the tree at Forty-Ninth Street up to FAO Schwarz at Fifty-Eighth Street. Vendors peddled chestnuts and soft pretzels, and at night the Empire State Building was lit up in red and green. People like to say that Christmas is really a holiday for children but, as an adult, I still love it every bit as much as I did when I was a kid. I love the smells, the colors, even the crowds in the department stores. I love the garlands and wreaths and twinkling lights covering the trees that line the median down Park Avenue. December is a month of sensory overload in New York, and there's nothing like it anywhere else on earth.

That first year at Cromwell, I found it odd to work the entire month of December, with no winter break. I was wistful for the wonder of the

season, but I was trapped in my Girlie chair. The firm tried to bring a
bit of the holiday spirit indoors, sparing no expense in decorating the
building. There was a giant tree in the lobby, and huge sparkling snow-
flakes dangled from the ceiling. Cromwell got an A for effort, but it still
didn't come close to matching the spectacle of the real thing outside.

The mood on the trading floor was drastically different during the
month of December than it had been since I arrived. December 31 marked
not only the end of the calendar year, but also the end of our work year,
which, for everyone on the Street, meant one very specific thing: Bonus
Season, Wall Street's great unifier. When you work the way we work all year
long, you do it with the assumption that the first week in January you'll
receive a six- or seven-figure bonus check as a reward for the amount of
business you generated over the course of the year. The numbers had been
finalized by the beginning of the month, so any business done after the
first of December was essentially meaningless. Ergo, we basically stopped
working. There were holiday parties every night, and by the middle of the
month I was exhausted, looked like I had been run over by Santa's sleigh
and his eight reindeer, and I had gained a solid ten pounds.

One Friday, the fixed-income group threw a party for the whole
floor. At 4:00 P.M. kegs appeared and tables were adorned with cheese
platters and antipasti. Waiters and waitresses passed hors d'oeuvres
that men popped in their mouths like breath mints. Another night,
Chick rented out an entire restaurant just for the government bond
group, so we could have a year-end team bonding session over expensive bottles of wine and osso buco. The salesmen and traders had to take
our most important clients for drinks to say thank you for another year
of business, and those nights rarely ended before midnight. You weren't
allowed to opt out of the parties; it was considered political suicide. I
tried to turn down the invitation to one of the many fiestas held by upper
management (which they inevitably didn't even bother to attend), and
Chick told me in no uncertain terms that if I wasn't there, I shouldn't be
surprised if my ID didn't work the following morning. I prayed for New
Year's Eve to arrive so that the holiday bender would end and I could

regenerate some of the liver cells I had damaged over the course of the month. I hadn't seen the inside of the gym in a month, my clothes were tight, my eyes were puffy, and I was only twenty-two. I didn't know how some of the older guys did it and didn't drop dead.

Trading floors are frigid iceboxes year-round. In the winter, they are almost unbearable. It's a matter of necessity since the computers give off so much heat. If the room is heated as well, there is a fairly good chance the systems would get too hot and explode. So the floor was always freezing, and most people kept fleece jackets and scarves at their desks for days that were unusually bitter.

One morning in late December, Drew rubbed the palms of his hands together to warm them up. "Christ, it's cold in here today. What would you give to be on a beach somewhere right now?"

"I'd be happy to be in a third world country right now if it were near the equator," I said, the metal legs of my chair almost too cold to touch.

Chick returned from a meeting and shuddered as he removed his overcoat. "Well, A. Today's a big day for you. It's like Christmas came early."

"Why?" I asked.

"Today, you get a desk." He pointed at the desk next to Drew.

"That's Dave's desk."

"Correction, it *was* Dave's desk. Now, it's yours."

It was as if someone had given me a convertible, or a bag full of cash. It was the best Christmas present I could have hoped for. A desk of my very own. Good-bye, Girlie chair!

"Wow, Chick," I said as I folded up my chair and leaned it against the wall, resisting the urge to throw it in the garbage can. "I never thought I'd be so happy to have computers. And drawers!"

"It's the little things I do to keep my employees happy."

"What happened to Dave?"

"Dave's dead. I shot him this morning," he replied flatly.

"*What?*" I asked, confused.

"It's a metaphor, you nitwit. Dead. Shot. Axed. Eighty-sixed. No more. He's gone, so now you get his desk. Use his notepads until you get your own. I'll have Nancy order them tomorrow."

"Use his notepads?" I glanced at Dave's empty chair—my chair. And at the pictures of his kids still proudly displayed next to his headset. Chick seemed completely unfazed by the fact that he had just fired someone during the holiday season. Not exactly a shining example of Christmas spirit.

"Congrats, Alex. You're my new desk buddy," Drew said, as he swept Dave's personal belongings into a box. "Do you have any particularly annoying habits I should know about before you take up residence three feet from me?"

"I don't think so."

"Good to know. Welcome to the middle row, where the average temperature is thirty degrees and local time is now ten forty-five."

"It's only ten forty-five?" Chick said. "You could freeze ice cream in here today, it's so cold. I can't have a team with frostbite." He clapped his hands. "Everyone, Starbucks on me today, so give Alex your orders. Start with mine, Girlie-san. I want a venti hazelnut coffee, extra hot."

My new desk was immediately swarmed by team members shouting drink orders. The problem with specialty coffee places like Starbucks is that no one drinks plain coffee anymore. The odds of my getting all the orders for chai teas, mochas, lattes, and machiatos correct were low. Reese also mentioned that he wanted an M&M cookie to go with his cappuccino.

Chick handed me a hundred-dollar bill. "Take someone with you so you don't drop them and end up with third-degree burns." At least he realized that I wouldn't be able to balance dozens of hot beverages and a giant M&M cookie all by myself.

I hesitated a second before approaching Will, but then decided, what the hell.

"What's up, rookie?" Will asked as he closed his Internet application. "To what do I owe the pleasure of your visit to the back row?"

"Chick told me to nominate someone to help me carry the coffees.

Since you were nice enough to come with me for the pizza pickup, I was hoping you'd be willing to help me again."

"That was supposed to be a onetime thing," he said with a smirk that made me weak in the knees.

"You don't have to. I can ask Drew if you're too busy."

"I just want to be clear. You're sort of asking me on a date. Is that correct?" He raised a dark eyebrow, relishing the ability to embarrass me.

"A Starbucks date, yes," I specified.

"Am I destined to be the sucker that helps you carry food for the rest of my life?"

"It appears so, yeah. What do you say?"

"Sure, I'll come with you. I need a mocha pronto, and I'm freezing to death up here."

"You ordered a mocha?"

"With whip, yup."

"That's kind of a girlie coffee isn't it?"

"Real men like mochas with whip!"

"If you say so," I sang, unwilling to resist the urge to flirt.

"Let's go, before I change my mind and you have to make ten trips by yourself, smartass."

When we arrived the line was out the door, as usual. "We're going to be here for a while." I sighed. "If you need to get back to your desk, it's okay. I can make multiple trips."

"Nah, I'll wait with you. It's dead up there today. I've been ordering Christmas presents online for the last three hours. It's good to get off the floor for a while."

He gestured toward my cashmere turtleneck. "Black today? Better." He nodded approvingly.

Better? Had he been making mental notes on my clothing and my appearance this entire time? "Thanks," I said brightly. "Khakis today? Way to think outside the box."

"Well, unless you'd prefer plaid, I don't really have a lot of options. Is that what you girls do? Spend the day sizing up the guys on the floor?"

I laughed. "You wish! I assure you we don't, although there are only, what, forty of us on the entire floor? I don't really know any of the other *women* on the floor, so I have no idea what they do. But I doubt it."

"You should," he replied succinctly. "We do."

We were now fourth in line so, provided no one in front of us was also ordering for an entire desk, we would be helped shortly. Just when things had gotten very interesting.

"You do what?" My voice cracked.

"Rate the girls. One to five."

"Are you serious? Cromwell isn't a bar. Where do you guys get off?"

He smiled mischievously.

"You're telling me the guys I'm buying coffee for right now *rate* my looks?"

"Yeah, every day. You score better when your hair is down than you do when it's in a ponytail. Just FYI."

"We work in an office, not on a catwalk." *Right?*

"Oh, calm down, you're always in the top three. It's a compliment. I wouldn't have mentioned it otherwise."

"So I should be flattered?"

"Yes, I just paid you a very high compliment. It's a tough group."

"You are all pigs, you know that?"

"I plead the Fifth."

We reached the register, and I placed our order. Will and I packed up the coffees as they were placed on the counter and walked back to Cromwell in awkward silence. Once we reached the lobby elevators, Will baited me, obviously enjoying my discomfort.

"Do you want to know where you rank today? I'll tell you if you want. It's totally against the rules, but I will."

"No. I don't want to know, because I don't care."

"Yes, you do."

"No, I don't."

"Yes, you do. It's killing you, I can tell." We were staring straight ahead, watching the floor numbers light up one by one. I didn't reply.

When we got back to the desk, the guys attacked us as usual, reading the side of the cups to find their orders. Despite the chaos I heard a familiar voice shout, "Girlie! You better not have forgotten my cookie, baby!"

I looked down the row and saw Reese standing up with his headset on, clapping his hands together and then holding them out like he was about to catch a football. I pulled out the waxed paper bag holding the two-pound cookie and threw it at him like a Frisbee. "Thanks, Girlie!" he said, as he took a huge bite. When all the drinks were claimed, I realized I'd forgotten to order one for myself. I hate my life.

Will threw the empty bags in the trash can behind me and noticed that I was coffeeless.

"Why didn't you get one? It's freezing in here!"

I pulled my Burberry scarf out of my purse and wrapped it around my neck. "I forgot. I was too worried about getting everyone else's orders right."

"Wow, you're a mess."

Will removed the lid from his drink and poured half of it into an empty coffee mug sitting on Drew's desk.

"Here," he said as he handed me the steaming drink. "Bet my mocha with whip isn't sounding so prissy to you now, is it?"

I took a sip of the hot coffee and felt my feet begin to defrost. "Thank you, thank you, thank you. I'm sorry I made fun of your coffee."

"You're welcome." He patted my back and strolled back to his seat. When he was a solid ten feet away, he called to me, "Hey, Al?"

"Yeah?" I turned my chair around to face him, and he held up two fingers and grinned.

I held up my middle finger and said, "That's where you rank today, buddy." I wondered if I placed second to Baby Gap and her miniature shirts.

I heard him laugh. "Touché, Alex. Touché."

. . . .

THE NEXT DAY, CHICK SPUN my new chair in a circle while I was sitting in it. "Listen, Girlie, just because you have a desk now doesn't mean you're relieved of delivery duties. You're still responsible for the pizzas and milkshake patrol, too." He threw a wad of crisp twenty-dollar bills onto my desk. "We're getting lunch today from the sushi place across the street. I just ordered it. It'll be ready in twenty minutes. Go pick it up."

"No problem, Chick. Thanks so much for the desk."

"You're welcome. It's about time you had a real place to sit. Now, the real work begins."

I glanced out the windows behind me and noticed it had started snowing hard. And the snow was sticking. I looked down at my new herringbone Manolos. Somehow, telling Chick I couldn't pick up lunch because I didn't want water marks to ruin my new shoes didn't seem like a good idea.

Shit.

Twenty minutes later, I stepped outside into the blustery cold. There were two cabs in the street, swerving back and forth, their tires unable to gain traction on the snow. I wrapped my large pink pashmina around the top of my head like a cashmere kerchief. The sushi place was only a few hundred yards away, but it took me almost ten minutes to get there. The wind chapped my face, and I had clumps of snow and ice trapped in my eyelashes. By the time I arrived, I was soaking wet, my cheeks were bright red and burning from the cold, and my nose was running like a leaky faucet.

The small Japanese lady working the counter looked at me with pity as I entered and proceeded to stomp the snow off my feet and chip away the icicles that had formed on my earrings.

"Hello, I'm picking up an order for Ciccone, please?" I said.

She nodded and produced four large plastic bags from the floor behind her. "Very bad weather today, yes?"

"Yeah. It's cold outside."

She glanced at my feet. "Not good day for no socks. You get sick like that!"

I didn't feel like getting into a conversation with her about the pain we women must endure for beauty, or the fact that I was dressed like a moron, so I smiled in polite disinterest.

"I know, believe me. How much do I owe you?"

"That cost $196.00. You pay cash or charge?"

I pulled the twenty-dollar bills from my purse, paid the bill, and pocketed Chick's change. I had to lean my full weight on the restaurant's glass door to open it against the wind.

Back in the Cromwell Pierce lobby, elaborately wrapped and beribboned stacks of fake presents were arranged meticulously beneath the equally elaborately decorated tree, which loomed large in the high-ceilinged lobby. The carpet absorbed water and kept people from slipping, which was good as there are few surfaces I can think of more dangerous than a wet marble floor. Too bad I was rushing to get back upstairs to remove my water-marked shoes and deliver $200 worth of sushi. In retrospect, I should have walked the full length of the carpet, but you know what they say about hindsight.

I was no more than five feet inside the building when I decided to step off the carpet to circumvent the crowd that was slowing to gaze up at the tree. That was not one of my better ideas. (That hindsight thing again.) One minute I was walking tall in my nice shoes and fancy scarf, and a split second later I was water-skiing across the lobby. There was nothing for me to grab on to for balance. Nothing, that is, except for the enormous fir tree with its hundreds of glass ornaments. In a panic I dropped the sushi bags, reached out, and clutched one of the large branches, but it wasn't strong enough to keep me upright. I felt myself begin to fall, but I didn't let go of that freaking tree. Instead, I held on to the branch, causing the entire tree to bend over like a slingshot. When I finally did let go, it snapped back to its upright position, the sudden jolt causing dozens of ornaments to fall to the marble below, sending colorful glass shards flying in every direction. The next thing I knew I was sprawled out on the floor, facedown in the pile of fake presents under the tree. Fabulous.

Somehow, the sushi bags were standing upright, intact. The last thing I wanted was to have to explain to Chick what had happened; a semiprivate humiliation in the lobby among strangers was way better than a very public one among coworkers. I pushed myself up to a sitting position as a bunch of men came running over to help, and I felt my face burning with embarrassment. I held up one of my hands and shouted, "I'm fine. Completely fine, it's nothing. Really." They ignored me, intent in their quest to help the damsel in distress.

Two men in their midfifties bent down and grabbed my upper arms, pulling me up off the floor. "Are you okay, miss? Did you hurt yourself?" they asked.

"No, I'm fine. Nothing a few decades in therapy won't fix." One of the men brushed needles off my upper thigh, straddling the line between helpful and perverted, while the other retrieved a wayward Manolo. I picked up the bags of food, waved to everyone in the lobby, and, on a lark, curtsied. As the bystanders broke into whistles and applause, I laughed in spite of myself. I took some comfort in the fact that no one I knew had witnessed my cartoon-style fall. If I didn't say anything to anyone when I got back to my desk, then it would be like nothing had ever happened, right?

I put the bags down on Chick's desk and slithered back to my chair. *Deep breaths,* I told myself. *No one knows. It could have been much worse.* Had I sprained my ankle I would've had to resign from the humiliation. My breathing was starting to return to normal when an e-mail popped up in my in-box.

MSG FROM PATRICK, WILLIAM:

A—

Nice wipeout. I would give it a solid 8. You lost points with the Russian judge for not sticking the landing. On the other hand, thank you for providing me with one of the funniest visuals ever. I will replay that moment over and over in my head for years to come.

P.S. Congratulations on salvaging the food. I'm impressed.

So much for no one seeing me. It's official: God hates me.

MSG FROM GARRETT, ALEX:

W—

I never liked Communists so you can tell the Russian judge
what to do with his scorecard. Quick question: if you saw me
fall, how come you didn't help me? Please advise.

You had to admit, I had a point. Cinderella would never put up with
that shit.

MSG FROM PATRICK, WILLIAM:

A—

What did you want me to do, throw you over my shoulder
Tarzan-style and carry you back upstairs? You're a big girl
and you clearly were fine. Besides, somehow I don't think you
would have taken my help if I had offered it. True or false?

P.S. You're cute when you are mortified.

I am?

MSG FROM GARRETT, ALEX:

W—

Well, I guess now we'll never know, will we? I assume I'll see
you at the party tonight?

I never heard back.

Of all the holiday parties, the one that everyone looked forward to the most was the one the head of all fixed income at Cromwell threw for everyone in the division at a dive bar in Midtown. I'd heard it was a great time and I was excited to see for myself.

When the clock finally struck 5:30, the floor started emptying out as everyone headed outside to a long line of black cars that would take us all uptown. When the car dropped us off on the corner of Ninth Avenue and Fifty-First Street, I understood why everyone looked forward to this party. You could hear the band playing from the sidewalk. Men stood outside in their plaid Christmas pants and reindeer ties, smoking cigarettes and talking. As I approached the door, Drew and Marchetti appeared from across the street, eating slices of pizza.

"Hey, Alex," Drew said as he held out his hand to smack me five, a big smile on his face.

"Merry Christmas!" I said. "I thought they had food at this thing. Should I have eaten before we came?" There was no way I was going to hang out all night with nothing to eat. Not that I couldn't survive off the fat that had recently accumulated on my thighs, but that wasn't the point.

"No, don't worry, they have plenty of food inside. Marchetti just wanted to get a good base going before we started hitting the tequila."

Drew grabbed my hand and pulled me inside and directly up to the bar. Everyone was laughing, smiling, and grabbing free beers from the waitresses' trays. Every time I finished a beer, another one would appear as if by magic. The dance floor was packed with people jumping around like they were reliving their proms.

"Hey, hey, Girlie!" Reese and Marchetti joined Drew and me at the bar, and we clinked our beers together in holiday spirit.

"Hey, Reese!" I answered cheerily. "What's shaking?"

"Not a lot, Girlie, not a lot." Drew handed us all shots of Jack Daniel's.

We clinked glasses again and I downed the burning liquid with the guys, because I knew if I didn't, they'd never invite me to drink with them again.

They ordered another round and downed them. I politely asked if I could sit this round out, and they were nice enough to spare me.

Chick caught my eye from the corner of the room. He waved me over, so I left the guys behind to discuss what kind of wine they were having with Christmas dinner.

"Hi, boss, what's up?" I quickly became nervous, figuring the only reason he would want to talk to me at this moment would be if I'd done something wrong. I really didn't feel like being bitched out at the holiday party.

"I know this time of year all conversations revolve around bonuses, so I wanted to discuss your situation," he said.

"Oh," I said, relieved and more than a little surprised. "I know I'm not eligible for one since I haven't been at the firm for a full year."

"Technically, that's true. The *firm* won't pay you for a few months of work, but that doesn't mean that *we* can't." He pulled a white envelope from his inside jacket pocket. "Merry Christmas."

I opened it and for a second I thought my eyeballs were going to explode from their sockets. "Oh my God," I said.

"There's ten grand in there; I'll save you from getting paper cuts trying to count it all. The group took up a collection for you. Since it's cash, you don't have to worry about paying taxes, so in theory it's twenty grand."

"Oh my God," I repeated. Ten thousand dollars. Cash. "Chick, I don't know what to say. This is really incredible."

"Well, then this is going to really knock your socks off." He handed me a check for another ten thousand dollars. "This is from me. You passed all your exams and, so far, you've impressed me with your ability to adapt to life on the trading floor. Keep up the good work, Alex, and I have no doubt you have a bright future at the firm. Good job, kid."

"Is this for real? Twenty thousand dollars?"

"If only all my employees were as easy to please. Don't mention it to anyone. I don't want word getting out that I'm turning into a softie in my old age. Actually, give me the cash back. I'll hold it for you. A girl shouldn't be walking around Manhattan with that many bills on her." He chuckled as he beamed with an almost fatherly pride.

"I won't tell anyone, I promise!" I clutched the envelope to my chest. I had an irresistible urge to hug him, but somehow I didn't think he'd appreciate it. "I honestly don't know what to say. I have the greatest job on earth."

"One of them, no doubt. It probably ranks below professional athlete and rock star, but I think the Street has third place locked up." He squeezed my shoulder as he walked away.

I caught sight of Will on the far side of the dance floor, laughing and talking to some of his friends. I pretended not to notice him while checking myself in the mirror behind the bar to make sure that my hair was in place and that my eyeliner wasn't smudged. Will didn't so much as look in my direction. He was staring off in the distance behind me. I checked the mirror again and noticed a redheaded girl wearing a black dress leaning against the far wall by the dance floor, chatting with some guys from the high-yield desk. Odd, I didn't remember ever seeing her on the floor and, since there were only a handful of women in the office, I should have run into her in the ladies' room or something.

"Hey, Girlie, grab me three Buds, would ya?" I heard Reese call from behind me.

I nodded and flagged down a waitress. When I delivered the beers to Reese, he said, "I saw you talking to Chick. Did he give you your Christmas present?"

"Yes! I don't know how to thank you guys."

"You deserve it, Girlie. Don't spend it all in one place."

"I don't think I could if I tried."

"Give it a few more years and that twenty grand will look like chump change."

"No way, that'll never happen," I said, secretly hoping he was right. "Hey, who's that girl over there by the dance floor? I don't recognize her."

He took a long swig of beer as he spun on his heels to check her out.

"Oh, that girl. Yeah, I don't know her name. She works in the Boston office. Comes down for the Christmas parties and other random events. Why?"

"No reason. Just wondering," I lied.

I looked back toward Will who was still watching the redhead. *Grow up, Alex,* I told myself when I began to feel jealous. I couldn't stand there and stare at him, and I was afraid of rejoining the guys and being forced to consume yet another shot of Jack Daniel's. Instead, I weaved my way through the crowds of intoxicated men and went to look for a ladies' room.

There were three guys in line in front of me when I reached the solitary (unisex) bathroom. Ten minutes later we hadn't moved forward, and eight or nine guys had joined the line behind me. I was about two minutes away from going across the street and using the bathroom at the pizza place when suddenly the door opened and the redheaded girl from Boston emerged. Ten seconds later, a guy I had seen on the floor followed her. As she passed the men waiting on line, she received catcalls, snickers, and one very clear invitation to return in ten minutes. The guy got high fives and slaps on the back. I stared, openmouthed, in obvious shock, and in violation of one of the cardinal rules of being a woman on a trading floor: never lose your poker face.

"Uh-oh, I think Alex is mad!" a trader yelled from the end of the line. "Get off your high horse, Girlie. Last time I checked we were all adults here. Get over it." He laughed as he glanced at his buddies for approval.

In a tone that was completely disrespectful to someone senior to me, I replied, "What *you* are is completely disgusting." Tears were starting to well in my eyes for reasons I didn't really understand.

"What are you, Alex, jealous? Other girls are getting all the attention and you aren't? Don't get me wrong, little girl, you're hot and all, but there are some races you just can't run. At least not yet. Ask me again after a few more beers." The man heckling me appeared to be in his early forties. The skin on his neck was a shade pinker than his face, like he was about to drop dead from a massive coronary. I wouldn't mind if he did.

I snapped.

"Maybe so. But let me tell you something, if she and I ever ran a race, you wouldn't be worthy of standing on the sidelines to watch, you fat fuck." The second the words were out of my mouth, I regretted them.

Someone from the end of line yelled, "Holy shit, T.C., you just got your balls cut off by a skirt!" The entire line erupted into laughter. The fat man was not amused. I stormed out of the line, grabbed my coat from the chair, and headed for the front door. Drew was calling after me to stop, but I was pretty sure I was about to start crying and I wasn't about to make this night any worse by further humiliating myself in front of everyone. I ran around the corner, trying in vain to hail a cab. If you've ever tried to hail a cab in Midtown Manhattan in December, you know that I had a better shot of being beamed up by a spaceship. When Drew caught up to me, he found me leaning against a parked car wiping tears from my already frozen cheeks.

"Alex, wait. That guy is a huge loser; don't let him upset you. Do you really care what he thinks?"

"I can't believe he said that! I was under the assumption that grown men didn't belittle women half their age for kicks. I also was under the impression that grown men didn't hook up with colleagues in public bathrooms. What the hell is going on here?"

Drew leaned against the car next to me and buried his hands in his pants pockets. "Not everyone is like that. Unfortunately, the ones who are don't try to hide it. For every asshole there are a million good guys. It's just that the assholes get noticed."

"This just went from one of the best nights of my life to one of the worst in about ten minutes. I just want to go home."

Drew caught the attention of a cabdriver who had just come out of a coffee shop across Ninth Avenue. He held the door open as I climbed in the backseat.

"Merry Christmas, Alex. Get a good night's sleep. Tomorrow will be better. I promise."

The cab pulled away from the curb and headed toward the West Side Highway. *I had a managing director call me ugly, and in return I called him a fat fuck. Yeah, well, tomorrow certainly couldn't be much worse.*

six

Hotel Cromwell

I GOT UP extra early to go to work so that I could just get it over with. I dreaded going in like no other day I could remember. I logged into my computer and found a new e-mail.

MSG FROM PATRICK, WILLIAM:

A—

What the hell happened last night? I saw you jet out of the bar. Are you okay? There was a lot of chatter about you mouthing off to someone.

I was trying to figure out how to respond to Will's e-mail when I was interrupted by a very angry Chick pulling me out of my chair by my hair. "My office. Now" was all he said before walking away. This was not a good sign. He only used his office to welcome new employees, give year-end reviews, fire people, and talk in private. You only got called to

Chick's office if what was about to happen wasn't appropriate for every-one on the trading floor to hear.

I scanned the room to see if anyone had noticed that I was in trou-ble, but the team appeared focused on their morning tasks. Everyone except Will, who shrugged sympathetically.

When I entered Chick's office, a room I hadn't set foot in since my first day at the firm, I found him standing with his back to the door, staring out the window. I closed the door quietly behind me and sat down in the wooden chair facing his desk. I sat there for a solid three minutes before he even spoke, and when he did, he kept his back to me.

"What the hell did I tell you?"

Chick had told me a lot of things over the last six months. I had no idea which of those things he wanted me to repeat back to him, and I figured not saying anything was better than getting the answer wrong. I stayed silent.

"I said," Chick began, his voice continuing to escalate. I stole a glance at the panes of glass surrounding his door and wondered if they were soundproof. From the looks on the faces of the secretaries sitting in their cubicles outside, they were not. "What the hell did I tell you? When you got here, I told you that you should just quit on your first day if you couldn't handle working mostly with men. What possessed you, Alex, what in God's name possessed you to call Tim Collins a fat fuck? Who the hell do you think you are? Timmy Collins brings in fifty million a year for this firm. How much do you bring in, Alex, huh? Tell me. How much revenue have you produced for this group since you got here?"

"Nothing, Chick. I don't have any clients," I whispered, my voice so soft it was almost inaudible.

"Exactly, thank you. He produces fifty million a year and you're lucky I let you answer phones, but for some reason, some reason I will never, *ever*, understand, you thought it would be okay to call one of the highest producers on the entire fixed-income floor a fat fuck. Does that make sense to you? I hired you because you were supposed to be a smart girl, Alex, not a crazy fucking feminist with something to prove. The only person you have to prove anything to is me. And the only thing you have proven to me after last night is that you clearly don't care about your career. I just gave you twenty grand to show our appreciation and this is how you say thank you? Did my positive reinforcement go to your head? Make you think that everything I told you on your first day was no longer applicable?"

"No, Chick, no! I'm sorry. I just lost it. I shouldn't have. I spoke without thinking. What can I do to fix this?"

"To start, you're going to apologize to Timmy for disrespecting him and for forgetting that he's senior to you in every way possible. You hear me? You'll do it in person the second you leave this office, or I'll make sure that you don't pick up a phone here for the rest of your very short career. Capiche?"

Surely he was kidding. "You want me to do it in person? At his desk, in front of everyone?"

"That's what 'in person' means, Alex, yes."

I felt the need to explain what had happened. Chick knew me well enough to know that I wouldn't just curse out some guy for no reason. I wanted him to be on *my* side. "Chick, I think if you knew the whole story you would see that I wasn't really that out of line. He said . . ."

"Alex!" he screamed as he turned around to face me. I wished he had kept his back to me. "I don't care what he said to you. I don't care. You will apologize, because that's what I'm telling you to do. And if you want to work here, you will do as I say. I cannot believe I have already wasted ten minutes of my day dealing with this bullshit. That's all I have to say to you. You have five minutes to deliver the apology." He pointed to the door and picked up his phone, so I lowered my head and left his office.

Of all the things I had been expecting, having to apologize to Tim Collins wasn't one of them. Maybe I had been out of line, but the thought of having to face him and say that I was *sorry* nauseated me. I asked someone to direct me to his desk, which was located on the far side of the trading floor. My heart pounded as I approached. He was eating a bagel with butter, sucking the grease off his fingers. When he saw me, he folded his hands across his chest. "Come to beg forgiveness so that Chick doesn't can your ass?"

I held my hands behind my back so he couldn't see my clenched fists. "Umm," I stammered, "I came to say I'm sorry for speaking to you the way I did. I was out of line. I'd like to put it behind us and move forward."

Swallowing your pride sucks.

He snorted and turned to the man sitting next to him, "Hear this, Sam?" he asked. "This is the skirt that called me a fat fuck last night, and now she wants to 'move forward.'"

"Cut her some slack, T.C. You're lucky she doesn't sue you for sexual harassment."

"Oh please. I was just joking around. She's the one who took a harmless joke and turned it into a big deal."

A joke? You can't be serious.

"Well, I didn't know you were kidding and I guess I was being overly sensitive. I owe you an apology."

"Go," he ordered. "Forget it. Do yourself a favor and loosen up though, or you won't last a year here."

I returned to my desk, feeling like I needed to take a second shower. I was about to grab my notebook and get on with my day when I noticed a large Starbucks coffee sitting on top of it, the boxes on the side of the cup checked off for nonfat and mocha.

"Did you get me this?" I asked Drew, grateful for his silent sign of solidarity.

"No, I just got off a conference call."

When I checked my e-mail, I found a second message from Will.

MSG FROM PATRICK, WILLIAM:

A—

You seem like you could use a boost this morning. I hope this cheers you up. I heard what happened. Collins is an asshole, don't worry about it.

P.S. If the coffee doesn't help, maybe a drink sometime will. What's your cell number?

—W

I spent ten minutes trying to think of the perfect response, struggling with how to thank him without sounding too eager or interested. Tone is often difficult to convey in an e-mail. Anyone who has had a cyber relationship knows that. I decided that, in this case, simple was definitely better.

MSG FROM GARRETT, ALEX:

W

I'd like that. 203-555-5820.

Perfect.

Drew rolled his chair over next to mine. "How bad was it?"

"On a scale of one to ten? A nine. Chick made me apologize. I had to walk over there and say I was *sorry,* like I was the one who did something wrong. I shouldn't have gone off on him like that, but give me a break."

"ALEX!" Chick yelled as he returned to his station on the desk. I jumped up so fast I almost knocked over my chair.

Christ, what now? "Yes, boss?" I asked, terrified.

"The capital markets guys are rolling out a new deal. They're putting together the marketing presentations—the pitch books—for clients. You're responsible for getting them done. Today. Go over to the capital markets desk and work with the bankers to get them in order. When they're done, send them up to the copy center for our standard order. It should take them a few hours to get them all copied and bound. When they're ready, pick up the books, take them to the mailroom, and pack them all for FedEx. You'll remember this the next time you decide to mouth off to someone."

"Okay."

"The last pickup is at midnight. I don't care if you drink Red Bull for the next seven hours in order to get them done, but they go out tonight. Capiche?"

I nodded. "Sure. No problem."

I hurried over to the capital markets desk and introduced myself to a group of men standing around a bank of monitors at an empty computer station.

"Hi, I'm Alex. Chick told me to come down here and help you guys finish up the presentations."

One of the guys, a salt-and-pepper-haired man, shook my hand enthusiastically and said, "Ah! Yes, great, Alex, thanks! We need the help. Our associate is out and we aren't that well versed in PowerPoint. I take it you know your way around the application?"

"Yeah, no problem." I logged on to the empty computer and opened the file. You'd think that printing a few books would be simple, but when a group of high-strung bankers with type A personalities who are used to getting their way are forced to compromise on seemingly mindless decisions, it becomes exponentially more difficult.

"Let's see what we have here."

Banker Number One leaned over my shoulder and stared intently at the screen. "What size is that font? It looks like it's for blind people. Make it smaller, Alex," he instructed. I reduced the font from fourteen to twelve.

"Now it's too small," another commented. "And why are we using squares and not rectangles for the cash flow chart? The slide is rectangular; the boxes should be rectangular." Banker Number Two leaned over my shoulder and traced the square outline on the screen, just in case I needed a tutorial in basic shapes. He smelled of stale coffee, cigarettes, and Old Spice.

I put the mouse on the corner of the box and dragged it to the left, morphing the square into a rectangle and then recentered the text within the new form. "Better?" I asked, hopefully.

He scratched his head and looked pensively at the screen. Banker Number Three chimed in. "I don't like it. Why's it red? Red's bad luck. Red is associated with losses, with a down stock market. It's a negative color. We are trying to convince people to buy this deal. Having red in the presentation could send them subliminal messages. Change it."

I changed the color from red to green, which made sense to me. If I followed his logic, then green should be a positive color, associated with gains, profit, and money. He shook his head again.

"What the fuck, Alex? This isn't a Christmas card. Make it gray."

Gray, right. Obviously.

The first banker didn't like the way the boxes were aligned. They were too far apart, then too close together. The wording was wrong; it wasn't succinct enough. So I changed the banner sentence as the bankers volleyed back and forth between the words *can* and *will*.

"The disclaimer at the bottom of the page should be italicized. Legal wants to make sure that it's clear and highly visible," Banker Number Four commented.

"Italics look so—what's the word I'm looking for? Amateurish. Can't we bold it?"

Right, italics scream amateur hour, but bold somehow exemplifies professionalism. Does anyone even read these things?

Banker Number Two shook his head. "Bolding it makes it the focal point of the page. We can't let the disclaimer detract from the risk outline."

"Hmmmm." Banker Number Three nodded pensively. "I see what you mean."

Are you guys kidding me?

"What about underscoring it, but using regular type?" Banker Number Five suggested to Banker Number One as he rubbed the five o'clock shadow on his chin. The sandpaper-like sound made me cringe.

"That's it! That's perfect. Great job." They patted one another on the back in congratulations on their ability to propose such a staggering solution.

Underlining.

All of the times I thought about what my father did at work, I never pictured him obsessing over something as stupid as fonts and type color. I wondered if he was over at Sterling right now tormenting some poor analyst with such asinine and pointless work. I sincerely hoped not.

"Now, about these boxes . . ." Banker Number One mused.

Align it on the right, center justify it. Maybe it will look sexier with the boxes running down the center of the page? Make the boxes three-dimensional, shade them from light to dark, shade them from dark to light. The arrows aren't the same length, or thick enough, there are too many arrows, no, too few. The spacing is uneven, the page numbers are too prominent. Should we be using Times New Roman (classic and dependable) or Arial (modern and forward-thinking)?

And on and on and on.

Fifteen minutes later they had agreed on the first slide. I sat in my chair like a hunchback, every muscle in my back aching. I tried to arch my back in an effort to return my spinal column to its proper alignment, but that resulted in my chest jutting out like a porn star's. I noticed one of the guys raise an eyebrow in interest. I slouched again and resigned myself to a lonely future ringing church bells in a tower.

"Okay then," I said, pretending not to notice their wandering eyes. "Should we move on to page two?" I glanced quickly at the bottom of my monitor. "Slide 2 of 46."

Fabulous.

Hours went by and we weren't making much progress. I looked at my watch. Two thirty. No wonder bankers worked all night; these idiots obsessed over the smallest details.

"Don't we have a new pitch book format?" Banker Number One asked me. "One where the firm logo is on the top right and not the bottom left?"

"Yes, but we aren't required to use it."

Please don't say it, please don't say it.

"I think we should use the new format. This one's antiquated. Keep the font and characteristics consistent from slide to slide using the two we just corrected as a guide. Then you'll just have to have the books copied and stuff them in their overnight packs."

"I'll have to start over. I can't just cut and paste from this program to the new one."

"That's why I'm not offering to pull up a chair and wait for you. I need these to go out tonight so don't waste time. Leave one on Chick's desk, so he gets it first thing on Monday. Also have a messenger deliver one to my house in Connecticut tonight so I can read it over the weekend. Thanks a lot for the help."

"No problem," I mumbled as they walked away. I kicked my shoes off under the desk, rolled up my sleeves, and prepared for a long night of tedious pitch book revisions.

I sent the pitch books to the printer at 5:30 and was informed it would take roughly two hours to complete the order. I sat alone on the desk reading our economist's weekly update, the trading floor lights dimming, trying to make productive use of the quiet time before the manual labor portion of my punishment began.

At 7:00 my cell phone rang.

"What's up, where are you?" Liv asked, music and laughter echoing in the background.

"Work. I hate my life. Will you come down here, stab a pencil in my eye, and put me out of my misery, please?"

"Why the hell are you still at work at seven o'clock?"

"I'm working on pitch books. I fucked up and Chick is punishing me. I'll talk to you when I get home."

"You screwed up? What did you do?"

"It's a long and horrifying story. I'll tell you when I get home."

"I'll wait up for you. How late do you think you'll be?"

"I'm not even sure. I'm going to be here for a while. I have to organize an entire mailing."

"Your job sucks."

"Yes, I'm aware. I have to go. The books should be finished soon, and it's going to take me a while to drag them all downstairs."

"Okay, Hulk Hogan. See you later."

Click.

I stifled tears, an oddity for me. I'm not a crier. Especially not in public, so the realization that my eyes were watering for the second time in two days surprised me. This job was all I ever wanted up until yesterday. Today, well, today all I wanted was to get the hell out of the building and go home. That's all.

P ick up for Ciccone," I said as I signed the log in the copy center at 7:30. Only a half hour after I talked to Liv—it felt like twelve.

"Yup," the lady at the counter chirped as she pointed to a stack of at least a dozen boxes. "Those are all for you."

"You're kidding."

"Nope, four hundred books. Do you have anyone coming to help you?"

"No." I sighed. "No one is coming to help me."

I looked down at my patent leather ankle strap heels. Once again, I was wearing the most inappropriate footwear. Fuck my life.

I grabbed the first box, grunting like a bodybuilder under the strain of the weight, and slowly began my descent to the mail room. When I arrived ten minutes and a pint of sweat later, I dropped the box on the floor next to the work table and returned for the second box. By the time I finished, an hour later, my arm and back muscles ached and my hair was glued to the back of my neck with sweat. *Screw you, Chick,* I thought as I unceremoniously dropped the last box on the floor. *I don't need to put up with this shit.*

I constructed an envelope-stuffing assembly line on the long metal table in the middle of the room. At one end, I set up stacks of books, ten books per stack. Next to that, I laid out the express mail packs, all facing the same direction with the openings on the left so that the books could slide right in. Once the book was sealed in the pack, I smacked a self-adhering label on the package. The labels almost never went on straight, but last time I checked I wasn't getting any extra points for making the packages look pretty. I spent almost four hours in solitary mailroom confinement, finishing around 11:30. I had barely enough time to make the midnight deadline. I began to panic.

I called our main mail center in the basement to pick the packs up immediately, and I ran down to the floor to leave a copy on Chick's chair. As I made my way toward the elevator banks I heard giggling and singing coming from the conference room. Strange, since I would have sworn I was the only person left on the floor. Fergie's unmistakable voice punctuated the silence as she sang about her humps and lady lumps. *What the . . . ?*

When I walked in the room, I was shocked at the scene taking place. Air mattresses covered the floor, and a half-dozen random drunk girls danced around while swigging wine from paper cups stolen from the coffee counter in the hallway. The girls didn't seem fazed by my intrusion, all except for the ringleader—Baby Gap—who was dancing on the table in white cotton pajamas and pink bunny slippers. Literally, pink bunny slippers.

"What are you doing?" I asked, completely horrified.

"Hi, Alex! I have some girlfriends visiting from out of town and my apartment is too small to fit everyone so we decided to get a room at Hotel Cromwell! Not a bad idea, huh?"

"Have you completely lost your mind? You can't have a slumber party in the office. Where did you get this stuff?" I eyed the bottles of vodka and wine lined up on the floor.

"I keep it in the file cabinet behind Keith's desk."

"You turned the file cabinet into a wet bar?"

"Uh-huh, but I also keep some personal items in there. A hair dryer, a corkscrew, snacks, a change of clothes, and a dock for my iPod!"

"Hannah, you can't sleep here. What if someone sees you?"

"It's Friday. No one else is here."

"I'm here. I'm actually still working."

"Well, then you should join us!"

"No. In fact, don't tell anyone I saw this. Don't tell anyone I was here. Don't tell anyone you know me."

"Sure, Alex. No problem! You're more than welcome to help yourself to a drink, though. And if you want to stay, I have an extra toothbrush in the cabinet."

I left the room without saying a word and heard her turn her attention back to the other drunk bimbos. "Who wants to play flip cup, ladies?"

I stormed down to the lobby, wondering if Baby Gap would be able to keep her job if she bought her clothes at stores that catered to adults. I stopped in the car dispatcher's office, then dragged my weary, aching, carpal-tunnel-racked body outside to a black car, collapsed in the backseat, and sobbed from exhaustion. Eleven forty-five on a Friday meant I was allowed to take a car home for free, compliments of Cromwell.

Wasn't that nice of them.

seven

Sake Bombs

I F I WERE allowed to take vacation, I would have taken the following week off. But I was still too new, so I was forced to go back to work and suffer through the dead markets between Christmas and New Year. I managed to make it home for dinner on Christmas Eve with my family, but had to head back to the city the following night so that I could be at work on the twenty-sixth.

I was happy to see the year end on the calendar change. January meant the start of a lucrative new trading year, and everyone else was energized from their time away from the office. I was thoroughly exhausted, but determined to work even harder to regain Chick's respect. I ran all his models—complicated spreadsheets containing every bond and derivative we traded. They tracked trades his clients had put on so that he could monitor their performance and could advise them as to when they should book profits or cut losses. I stayed late to update spreadsheets and read every packet and book Cruella had given me. I wasn't going to let T.C. derail my career, and I certainly wasn't going to let him make me doubt my ability to do the job. I was tough, and there was no way I'd allow anyone to break me.

"Girlie, whatever plans you have tonight, cancel them," Chick ordered one bitterly cold Thursday in the middle of January.

"Okay, Chick, what do you need?" It was Thursday and I was really hoping he wasn't going to make me stay late doing something mindless. I had a happy hour to get to.

Chick tilted his head to the side and looked at me for a moment, as if trying to determine if he really wanted to say what he was about to say. "I finally heard the real story about what happened at the Christmas party."

I gulped. Please, not this again. "Yeah, I meant what I said, Chick. I'm really sorry about that whole thing."

"We've already gone over that, and you were wrong to say what you did. From what I hear though, he was also way out of line."

I was speechless. It sounded like Chick was apologizing.

"We're taking clients out for dinner tonight at Buddha Bar. You're coming with us. You'll be meeting a lot of very important guys. Make sure you brush your hair before we go. Don't fuck it up. Capiche?"

"Wow, that means a lot, Chick. Thanks!"

I hadn't been asked to join Chick on a night out since I started at Cromwell. The guys were constantly entertaining and indulged their clients with courtside tickets to the Knicks, seats behind home plate at the Yankees, and center ice tickets for the Rangers. They had front-row seats to the best concerts in town and often were out of the office playing golf in the Hamptons, California, and even Ireland. There were fishing trips in the Caribbean, box seats at football games, and dinner at some of the trendiest restaurants in town. I couldn't believe I was finally invited to join him. I felt recharged and reenergized, vindicated even. With one small gesture, Chick had restored my confidence.

"One more thing, Girlie slave."

Oh God, here comes the catch. I had to sit next to T.C. and make nice? What?

He handed me two tickets. "I was supposed to go to U2 this week-end, but one of my kids is sick so we can't make it. You take them."

U2 tickets? I was afraid he was messing with me. I stood there and stared at him, waiting for him to snatch them away and laugh at me for being gullible, yet again.

"What's the matter? Don't you like U2?"

"Are you kidding!" I said. "I love U2! You're really giving these to me?"

"Yup. Floor seats. Tell Bono I said hi."

"I really don't know how to thank you."

"Have a good time."

"Oh, I will!" Liv was going to die when I told her we would be rocking out with Bono and the Edge at Madison Square Garden this weekend.

I could barely focus for the rest of the day. I decided to shoot Will an e-mail.

MSG FROM GARRETT, ALEX:

W—

Chick just asked me to go to Buddha Bar tonight. If you're out later, maybe we can try and grab a drink afterwards?

—

I wouldn't normally have asked a guy to call me, but considering I had given him my phone number three weeks ago and he still hadn't used it, what harm could it do? I stared at my e-mail for the next twenty minutes waiting for a response, but there wasn't one. I strained my neck to see if Will was at his desk. He was, throwing a tennis ball up in the air.

I spent the rest of the day working on Chick's spreadsheet. He had told me to make sure I finished by the end of the week, and I decided I'd try to finish it before we left as a sign of my appreciation. At 5:00 I went into the ladies' room and emptied my purse onto the counter. I ran a

Kleenex underneath my eyes to remove the mascara that had migrated onto my skin, and I applied fresh lip gloss. I brushed my hair and took one last look at myself: I looked good, the stress of the Christmas season nowhere to be found on my face. As I turned to leave, Cruella entered and scanned my appearance.

"Well, don't we look pretty. I didn't realize that having your face fully painted makes it easier to sell bonds."

I had had very little contact with Cruella since our initial encounter, but every time I did it usually involved her hurling some kind of insult at me. After the mess with T.C., I figured taking on the Puppy Skinner was a very bad idea, so I usually pretended I didn't get that she was making fun of me. "Chick is taking me with him to a client dinner tonight," I said with a forced smile.

Cruella laughed. "Let me guess . . . Rick is going to be there. Why else would he bother dragging an analyst who knows nothing about the markets with him? It's not like you'll add anything to the conversation."

I stood there speechless, unable to comprehend why she needed to be such a bitch. I stuttered, "I . . . well, I . . . he . . ."

Good job, Alex. Way to show her you're not a total moron.

"You know, I used to be like you. I used to think that everyone was nice to me because I was smart, because they *respected* me. I hope you wise up, little girl, for your own sake. I really do." She disappeared into one of the stalls.

I used to be like you.

What if that were true?

I couldn't allow myself to worry about it, because the possibility that I was on a collision course with a bitter old woman was too much to bear. When I got back to my desk, I found Chick choosing one of the ten ties he left in the coat closet for client events. He whistled at me when I walked by, which made me smile. I had just sat down when Chick snapped his fingers, grabbed his blazer, and walked off the floor. I took one last look at my e-mail, but there was still no response from Will. I really wish Cromwell allowed analysts to have BlackBerrys so that I could check my e-mail during dinner. Oh well. *There will be other nights,* I reminded myself as I followed Chick outside. *It's probably better this way. You need to focus on making a good impression.*

When we got down to the valet, a dark sedan waited at the curb. The driver flashed the lights, and someone stuck his arm out of the front-seat window and waved. Chick opened the door for me. When I looked up to see who was sitting in the front seat, I almost choked. Will was talking to the driver about traffic and fiddling with the radio. He finally stopped on a one-hit wonder from the '80s. Then, he turned around to talk to Chick.

"Hey, Chicky, does this make you think of your college years or what? The eighties must have been a great time to be in college. Girls with big hair, guys with mullets. I bet you rocked a nice mullet, huh?"

"Bite me, Willy. You would have lasted ten minutes with us at Penn State. You wouldn't have been qualified to be our fucking water boy. I'm sure you were big man on campus at Wharton, but it's nowhere near the same thing."

"I hear the ladies liked short guys back then."

"I'm six fucking feet tall if I stand on my wallet. That's what the ladies like. Keep this up and I won't pay you enough to take your fat dates to the drive-through at McDonald's. Capiche?"

I was waiting for one of them to acknowledge the fact that I was in the car. Will hadn't even said hello. I knew he had read my e-mail because I had put a read receipt on it. (I admit, this is a little lame, but you can drive yourself crazy wondering if a message has been opened.) It had been two months since Will and I had drinks outside of work, and while we flirted in the office a fair amount—but not enough to register on Chick's radar—I was surprised that there had never been a follow-up. I was more surprised that now we were in the same car and he wasn't speaking to me at all. I didn't know what Will was trying to accomplish by ignoring me, but if it was to drive me insane, he was well on his way to succeeding.

Buddha Bar was dimly lit, the way that most hip restaurants in New

York are: candles covered the tables and banquettes, and the walls were painted a deep ruby red. Everyone who worked there was thin, fit, and clad in black, undoubtedly just killing time before their big break. Like most restaurants in the Meatpacking District, the bar and the lounge were already crowded with other bankers, lawyers, and traders when we arrived, everyone drinking and trying to talk over one another.

We headed over to the bar and joined a rowdy group of men swigging beers and throwing back scotch. They ranged in age from thirty to forty and were all impeccably dressed and immaculately groomed. When they saw us coming, they called in unison, *Chiccckkk-eeeeeeeee*, holding their glasses in the air. Chick walked around shaking hands and patting backs, while a pretty blond bartender took his drink order. No one said a word to me, although from the way they were looking at me, I might as well have been a peanut in the elephant pit at the zoo. Within two minutes, Will and Chick were both holding scotches, and I was standing off in the corner ignored by both the group and the waitress. Finally, one of the older men acknowledged me. He wore a navy blazer and a white shirt with too many buttons open. Clearly, he thought he was quite the stud.

"Now, you're too gorgeous to have just followed Chick in off the street. I assume you're actually supposed to be here?"

I nodded and smiled.

"I'm Rick Kieriakis." He smiled and extended his hand. Chick overheard him introduce himself. Until then, I was pretty sure he had completely forgotten I was there.

"Ah, sorry, Ricky. This is Alex Garrett, our analyst. She's been with the team for about six months now, and since you'll be talking to her I wanted you to meet in person." Chick introduced everyone to me, rattling off their names like items on a shopping list. I shook all of their hands and tried very hard to remember who was who. There was Kevin, Brian, Sal, Nate, Skip, Petey, and Rick. They were loud, well dressed, and impressed (with themselves). You could go anywhere in New York City and easily pick out the group of Wall Streeters. One of the negative side effects of life on the trading floor was that you got so used to shouting you lost your "inside voice" entirely. For anyone who wasn't used to it, it could be pretty obnoxious. Even if you were used to it, it was still pretty obnoxious.

"So, you're new at Cromwell?" Rick asked. He picked a wayward navy thread off his crisp white shirt and adjusted a silver cuff link. More than a few women stared at him. His perfect posture, impeccably tailored jacket, and peacockish nature screamed all they needed to know: *I'm rich.*

"Yes, I came right out of undergrad. I started in July. I'm sorry, Chick didn't mention where you worked."

"Rude for a sales manager, don't you think?" He laughed. "I'm a portfolio manager at AKS."

Shit. AKS was one of the largest and most well-respected hedge funds on the Street. I was basically talking to a Bond God as far as salespeople were concerned. I immediately felt self-conscious, insecure, and completely out of my league. Chick could have warned me I was speaking to someone who most guys bow down to on a regular basis. *Fuck.*

He must have sensed my fear and continued jovially. "You're on a good team," he said with a smile. "There's no one better to work with and learn from than Chick. He's the best."

"Yes, I'm very lucky. How long have you been at AKS?" *Good job, Alex. That's the best you can come up with? Just kill yourself now and get it over with.*

"About fifteen years. I started my career on the floor of the Chicago Board of Trade more years ago than I care to admit. Then I went back to business school at University of Chicago. When I graduated, I moved to New York and worked at a hedge fund doing much of the same stuff you're doing. Then I went over to AKS to run my own portfolio. Enjoy your time now, Alex. Before you know it, you'll be forty and married with kids, living in the 'burbs like me."

Since when is that a bad thing? I wondered where his house was, and if it had a hammock.

"It sounds like quite the life!" I wanted to endear myself to Rick. I knew if I didn't impress Chick's clients, I'd never be invited to another dinner. I figured stroking his ego was a safe bet. Innocently, I added, "I hope I'm able to have the same kind of success you've had. Do you have any advice for a young person starting out in the industry? Chick's an amazing mentor, but I'd love to get a client's perspective."

"Well, there are lots of ways to get to the top in this business. I guess it depends on how hard you want to work."

Rick reached up and fondled the blue topaz pendant that dangled from a silver chain around my neck. My parents had given it to me for my twenty-first birthday. "Beautiful necklace. Beautiful girl."

Ew. "Thank you," I replied, nervously. He released the pendant and ran his finger lightly along my clavicle, before returning his arm to his side. I suddenly felt sick to my stomach. I took a step back, to put a little more room in between us and cleared my throat. He was married and on his sixth scotch. Was it possible he didn't realize how creepy he was acting? Maybe he was just trying to be nice to the new girl? A lot of maybes raced through my mind as I tried to convince myself that I was here for a reason. That I wasn't just bait, and Cruella's comments weren't true.

"You know, after dinner we could go to the Gansevoort for a drink. I have a room there," he said.

Or maybe he was just an asshole. Plain and simple.

Rick reached over and began to rub my right shoulder with one of his huge paws. I took another step backward and looked around for Chick or Will. Chick was in the middle of the group, telling a story about a golf outing. He was swinging an imaginary club, and everyone around him was laughing. Will was nowhere to be seen. Swell. There clearly wasn't anyone coming to my rescue, and I wasn't going to risk my job again by doing something stupid. Like Reese said, Sales 101 was pretending to like people you didn't. I could do that. Easy.

"Thank you, but I have to be in early tomorrow so I'm going home after dinner." It was the only diplomatic thing I could think of to say. Before he could respond, Chick ushered us to our table. As the guys all sat down I realized the only empty seat at the table was in between Chick and Rick.

Fucking fabulous.

Chick waved down the closest waitress, an amazingly tall girl with a long blond ponytail and lips that could stand to see a little less of the collagen needle. "Okay, let's make sure we get at least two orders of the sea bass, a few orders of lettuce cups, three orders of edamame dumplings, three orders of the duck, two seared tuna filets, a side of the scallop fried rice, some ribs, and three or four of your steaks, medium rare. If we want more after that, I'll let you know. Also bring me three large bottles of your best cold sake. Thanks, doll."

The men raised their glasses and toasted to nothing in particular, unless they were just toasting themselves. No one spoke to me for the duration of the dinner; all anyone did was tell the person sitting next to him how great he was, how much money he was up on the year, and lament the collective incompetence of their assistants. The conversation moved at a rapid pace, and I felt like I was watching a tennis match; my head turning from side to side as if on a swivel. I couldn't remember anyone's name. Not that it mattered.

Guy Number One: "I'm thinking of buying a beach house in Southampton. Property values are coming down and I found this great fixer-upper for three million. It isn't on the ocean, but it's close enough."

Guy Number Two: "What's the point of buying a house in the Hamptons if you aren't even on the water? You don't have enough cash to buy a proper piece of real estate?"

Guy Number One: "Fuck off, I don't see you throwing down cash to buy anything. What happened? Did you spend all your money on porn again?"

Guy Number Two: "No, your wife stopped charging me for the live shows."

Guy Number Three: "What about you, Will? Any good stories for us lame married guys? What does a good-looking guy with some cash in the bank do to keep himself busy in New York these days?"

Chick: "Good-looking? How many sakes have you had, man?"

Will: "I have to keep that to myself. I wouldn't want to make you all jealous."

Rick: "Will, my friend, my advice for you is stay single. Being married is for the fucking birds. The women, they keep themselves up until you sign the marriage certificate, and then they let themselves go to hell. It's brutal. If I could do it all over again, I never would have pulled the trigger."

Me: Ummm, hi, my name is Alex, and in case it escaped your attention, I'm female, and I'm sitting at the table. Oh, and I'm not deaf. Although I'm beginning to wish I was.

Guy Number Four: "Tell me about it. I'm really starting to hate my wife."

Me: Guys? Anyone? Hi, lady at the table. Right here, see me?

Rick: "So why don't you find yourself an extracurricular activity? We all should try to be a little more well rounded if you ask me."

Suddenly I felt Rick's hand on my leg, causing me to jump and rattle the small cups filled with sake littering the table. I moved over to the edge of my chair, as far away from Rick and as close to Chick as I could possibly get without jumping in his lap. Chick moved his chair slightly to the right without question, so that I had room to slide my own away from Rick's tentacles. I wondered if maybe he knew what his buddy was doing.

Will: "Let's change the topic. I don't think Alex is too interested in this conversation."

Me: Thank you. Thank you, thank you, thank you.

Chick: "Nate, have you been to Pebble Beach this year?"

Guy Number Five: "I was out there last month. The greens were smooth as a bikini wax."

Me: And here we are again.

I kept trying to get Will's attention from across the table, but it was as if he was purposefully avoiding eye contact. Why a guy thinks the best way to show a girl he's interested is to ignore her in public I will never understand. The Board of Education should consider adding a class to the junior high curriculum on reasons *not* to do this. It would save women all over the world millions of dollars in therapy.

Two hours later, I was the only relatively sober person at a table full of belligerently drunk men doing sake bombs. They poised their shot glasses of sake on top of chopsticks balanced on the rim of a large glass of Sapporo. All at once, they yelled "Sake bomb!" and banged their fists on the table, knocking the sake into the beer before chugging the whole thing. As soon as the sake bottles were empty, the waitress would suddenly appear with another three. Plate after empty plate was cleared, only to be replaced by another. When our waitress finally delivered the check, Chick handed her his American Express card without even looking at the bill. While the men finished up their sake, Chick handed me a bunch of tickets for the coat check.

"Grab the coats, Girlie." It was the only time he spoke to me directly during the entire dinner.

"Sure, I'll meet you up there." Why I, the one girl in the group, was responsible for retrieving ten overcoats I wasn't sure, but this night had stopped going the way I wanted it to a few hours ago. I handed the supermodel/coat check girl the stubs and was surprised when I heard a familiar voice behind me.

"So you're the coat collector, too, huh?" Will had followed me out to the hallway.

"Yes, well, I don't like to brag but coat carrying is just another one of my many talents."

"What are some of the other ones?" Will had a goofy, hammered grin on his face. It may have been the only reason I was getting this attention, but, at this point, I really didn't care. After this dinner, the bar for making me happy was pretty low.

"That's not information that I give out to just anyone. You have to earn it."

"And how does a guy go about doing that?"

"You're smart. I have faith in your ability to figure it out." I wanted to ask him why he had ignored my e-mail, but before I had a chance, the rest of the group appeared. There was a large black limousine parked at the curb, and Chick walked right up to it and opened the back door.

"Everyone in, the party is continuing at an undisclosed location. Except you, A-Bone; you need to get a cab. The night ends here for you." I realized exactly why I wasn't invited to join the guys. Strip clubs were off-limits for client outings, and the only way they could get away with going to one was if there were no women in tow. My guess was that was where they were headed. I was just as happy to go straight home. The last time I saw a bunch of scantily clad chicks dancing on tables was my last week of college. Trust me, that was memory enough to last me a lifetime.

Everyone else piled into the car, nodding politely in my direction. Rick took my hand and kissed it before getting in.

"Pleasure to meet you, Alex. I hope I'll be seeing more of you in the future."

"Nice to meet you, too," I said politely. He then pulled a piece of paper from his jacket and placed it in my palm, closing my hand tightly around it.

Chick approached me and smiled. "Good night, Girlie; see you tomorrow."

Will waited for Chick to get into the limo before turning back to me.

"Are you going to be okay getting a cab?" I could hear the group in the car yelling at him to hurry up.

"I'll be fine. Another one of my talents is hailing cabs late at night on deserted city streets. Have fun." As I walked away I pulled out my phone and pretended to call someone. Maybe I had plans, too. Before I even made it to the corner a cab pulled up—a smelly, yellow gift from God. I unfolded Rick's note and used the light from my cell phone to read it. On the back of a $3,800 restaurant receipt, he'd written, *For a good time call Rick. 516-555-4827.* I crumpled it up and threw it out the window. Before I could put my phone back in my bag, it beeped. Christ. What now?

> *SMS from Patrick, Will:*
> *Let me know that you get home okay. It was good seeing you*
> tonight.

It had been the world's most disappointing business dinner, and I'd been hit on by a married man and ignored for the better part of three hours. Still, when I climbed under my comforter later that night, I couldn't help but smile.

Will had texted me.

I responded.

> *SMS from Garrett, Alex:*
> *Thanks for checking. I got home fine. Have fun tonight.*

Two minutes later it beeped again. I flipped it open with excitement, wondering what else Will had to say. Except, it wasn't from Will.

> *SMS from Kieriakis, Rick:*
> *Miss you already, xo Rick.*

How in God's name had he gotten my phone number?

eight

Go-Go Gadget Undies

I WAS BEGINNING to miss the days of being deskless; at least then I hadn't been under any real pressure. By March, Chick had made me his personal Excel slave, and I spent grueling hours trying to figure out how to work the countless number of models the desk used. Chick liked things done quickly. Sadly, I still didn't have enough Excel experience to keep up. It was going to end up being another late night.

I clicked on a cell and examined the formula that appeared in the text bar across the top of my spreadsheet. There were countless formulas that, to the trained eye, probably weren't that difficult to understand, but to mine read like hieroglyphics. As the hours went by, the floor emptied, until I was the only one left. I lost track of time, my vision blurring from the glare of the monitor and the strain of trying to read all the numbers.

I heard a low whistle from behind me. "Whoa, what are you still doing here?" I looked up and focused my weary eyes on Will. He cocked his head to the side and tapped the face of his watch. "It's after nine."

"Believe me, I know." I sighed, completely exhausted. "Chick asked me to clean up the model, which really shouldn't be taking this long. I can't figure out what I'm doing wrong, and I'm about to go blind from staring at these numbers."

I sank back into my chair and rubbed my aching shoulders, feeling my knotted muscles snap, crackle, and pop like a bowl of Rice Krispies. I added scoliosis to the list of medical ailments this job had inflicted upon me, right next to cirrhosis and advanced coronary artery disease.

"What are you doing here?"

"I forgot my keys," he replied as he opened the top drawer of his desk. "Thank God I noticed while I was still downstairs in the bar. If I had gotten all the way home without them, that would have sucked big time."

"Totally," I said, vaguely aware that I looked about as good as I felt.

"What's the problem?" Will asked as he pulled up Drew's chair.

"See here?" I pointed to the final column of numbers.

"Uh-huh."

"This formula looks right to me, but for some reason it's not working. I can't leave until I fix it, which means I'm going to have to move in to the office."

"Nah," he said. "You've just been looking at it too long. You're missing the easy answer. Slide over."

I gladly pushed my chair away from my desk and allowed him unfettered access to my keyboard. "All you have to do is subtract out the handles, multiply the decimal by thirty-two, and add the handle back in. Then control C to copy the formula, highlight the rest of the column, ALT E, S, F to paste the formulas over the remaining cells, and you're all set."

Of course. Why didn't I think of that?

"I didn't realize you were such an Excel whiz."

"I had your job once, too. There are a few tricks you don't forget."

"Thanks. You just saved me hours of torture."

"Good thing I forgot my keys, huh?"

"Yes. Next time Chick makes me stay here to finish something if you wouldn't mind leaving your wallet behind, I'd appreciate it."

"I'll see what I can do. All right, what's up for tonight, now that I've saved you from moving in to the office?"

"Oh God, nothing. I guess I'll just go home and crash on the couch. Still better than being here. What about you?"

"I'm not against having a few cocktails. If you're interested, I was going to grab takeout on my way home. Do you want to come over and join me? I assume you haven't eaten yet?"

"Not unless you count the stale cookie I had two hours ago."

"I don't."

"Then nope!"

"I figured. Are you a chicken and broccoli or a kung pao chicken kinda girl?"

"Both," I said as I readjusted my bag on my shoulder. "Throw in an egg roll and you've got yourself a deal." We strolled out of the building together, chatting as if we'd done it a thousand times before. For some reason, it felt like we had.

Twenty minutes later, we entered his apartment on the Upper West Side. It was neat, well assembled, and unfussy. The progression of this relationship—not that that's what this was—was very odd. We went out once four months ago, and now I was having takeout in his apartment, and he didn't seem to think that veered at all from the normal course of dating. But what did I know? My last boyfriend was a frat boy who could barely find his way to class. Not really a fair comparison.

I placed the plastic bag filled with greasy Chinese on the kitchen counter. "This place is great."

"Yeah, this building used to be a warehouse or something, so it has higher ceilings and bigger windows than most places." He set two plates on the coffee table in front of the TV and opened a bottle of wine he pulled from a small wine refrigerator in the hallway. I opened the cartons of food, the smell immediately reminding my brain that I was starving.

Will sat down next to me and served us both from the white cardboard containers.

"I didn't realize how hungry spreadsheets can make you. Thanks for inviting me over."

"No problem. I don't miss those days, staying late and doing all the menial tasks for everyone. How are you liking it so far?"

"Well . . ." I hesitated, fully aware that Will and Chick were friends. "Are you asking on or off the record?"

"You're sitting on my couch," he reminded me. "That makes this conversation entirely off the record."

"It's not bad. I mean, don't get me wrong, I'm still scared to death of Chick and Cruella and most of the other guys on the desk. I'm constantly afraid I'm going to mess up. Half the time I have no idea what I'm talking about, and it seems like I'm never going to learn enough to be a full salesperson. I've been on the desk for six months, and I still feel like a complete idiot. I just know what I know now, and it just seems so overwhelming when I think about all the things I don't know. Does that make sense?"

"Mmmm hmmm," he grunted as he chewed the kung pao and washed it down with a sip of red. "This isn't a job that you can pick up overnight. There's a lot to learn, and if you're smart, which you are, you'll get there. You just have to be patient."

"I just can't imagine being able to talk the markets the way you guys do. No matter how much I read, half the time I just sit there and think, how do they *know* that?"

"None of us had any idea what we were doing when we started. Trust me, you'll learn."

"How long did it take you to feel like you had a grip on everything and weren't worried about embarrassing yourself every day?"

"Any day now," he joked, as he threw the empty Chinese containers back in the plastic bag.

I stood and stretched as the food coma began to overtake my body. "Thanks for dinner, and for listening to me vent. I know you're right. It just sucks being low Girlie on the totem pole."

"Hang in there."

"Everyone keeps saying that."

"Then listen to us! We might just know what we're talking about." He leaned against the kitchen counter, fiddling with his watch band. "Do you want another drink?"

I checked my watch, it was 10:45, a little later than I liked to be out on a "school night," but what the hell. I nodded. "Sure. One more can't hurt."

T HE SUN STREAMED through the window and I strained to see the time on my alarm clock: 8:29 A.M. I exhaled deeply as I rolled over, buried my head under my pillows (which felt much firmer than normal), and reached back to pull my comforter up over my head. It felt scratchy, like Velcro.

Then I heard what no girl ever needs to hear the morning after she goes out for drinks with a coworker: his voice.

"You better get up. You're really late; Chick's going to kick your ass." *OHHHHHHHHMIIIIIIIIIIIIIIIIIEEEEEGAAAWWWWWWWDDDDD.*

Before I even allowed myself to process where I was, I glanced at the clock again: 8:31. At least I didn't have to worry about living with this embarrassment. Chick was going to kill me.

"Shit!" I shot up in bed. "Why didn't your alarm go off?" I cried in panic as I scrambled to get up and collect my things, somewhat grateful that being late gave me an excuse to get the hell out of there as quickly as possible. "Chick's going to kill you, too, you know."

"I wasn't expecting a houseguest." He laughed as I ran around like a Tasmanian devil. "I told Chick I was going to be in late today. I have to meet a client for coffee at nine thirty, so I'm in the clear. You, on the other hand, might have to go into witness protection." I grabbed my T-shirt, sweater, and pants from the floor in the corner of the room. Worst-case scenario, I'd be two and a half hours late for work. Best-case scenario, I'd be hit by a bus on the way there. "Are you acting like a lunatic because of me or because you're afraid of being late for work? I'd just like to know for the record what exactly is making you freak out. Oh, and don't steal my Giants jersey!"

I looked down at the jersey I was swimming in. At least I was clothed. I located a wayward sock balled up under the dresser and dashed toward the bathroom to get dressed, giving Will the finger as I left the room.

There was no time to shower, not here, and certainly not at my apartment on the other side of town. And there was no time to pick up a change of clothes either. I splashed water on my face and changed back into my clothes from the day before. I threw my underwear in the bottom of my purse. Not showering I could handle, but I refused to wear the same undies two days in a row. When I was dressed, I went out to the living room and sat down on a large leather chair to zip up my boots.

"Are you okay?" Will asked sincerely.

"Physically, I'm fine. I'll have to get back to you on my mental state."

"Good. I hate to mention this when you're so clearly on the brink of a nervous breakdown, but are you going to have to wear the same clothes to the office today?"

"Oddly enough, I didn't pack a change of clothes on the off chance I'd wake up on the Upper West Side two hours late this morning."

"Fair point," he replied. "You'd better get going. Hopefully when I get in I won't find you tied to a stake."

"That's supposed to be funny? What if he fires me?"

"He won't fire you," he assured me. "He'll enjoy torturing you too much to fire you."

"Oh joy."

"I'll call you on the desk when I'm on my way in."

"Sure, yeah. Call me, I'll hold my breath," I muttered.

But the door had already closed behind me.

I NEED TO GET DOWNTOWN to Wall Street as fast as humanly possible. Arriving in one piece is optional," I instructed the cabbie as I slammed the door behind me. I grabbed my phone to make the gut-wrenching call to the office, but when I dialed the number I was greeted with a familiar two-toned beep.

The battery was dead. I had slept at Will's. My clothes smelled like stale wine. My hair was greasy and knotted. I looked like . . . well . . . like I had just rolled out of bed.

I was a dead woman.

I took the escalator stairs two at a time, all but threw my ID at the security guard, and launched my bag onto the conveyor belt from five feet away as I ran through the metal detector. I tapped my foot anxiously as I waited for my purse to clear the x-ray machine and watched in horror as the belt stopped, then reversed, so that security could get a better look at the contents of my bag.

"What's the problem? There's nothing in there!" I yelled at the security guards, who didn't seem to care that I was going to be tarred and feathered as soon as I hit the trading floor.

"Just a second, there's something . . ." He pointed at the computer screen with the back of a ballpoint pen. "That's curious . . . Miss, we need to search your bag."

"It's the same freaking bag I put through the x-ray machine every morning!"

"Step aside, miss." A security guard pushed me away from the machine as two men with firearms holstered at their waists carefully donned white latex gloves.

"GREAT!" I screamed. "This is just great. You guys choose today to think I'm a security threat?"

"Miss," the guard, who was clearly losing patience, said, "step aside and let us search your bag. The sooner we clear this up, the faster you can get upstairs."

I stood by helplessly as they removed my wallet, my dead cell phone, my travel makeup bag, my day planner, and a brush: the contents of my life displayed like evidence from a crime scene on a cold metal slab in the Cromwell Pierce lobby.

My heart stopped.

Please don't tell me they're . . .

They couldn't possibly . . .

They wouldn't in front of . . .

My undies.

No sooner had I realized what was about to happen than the x-ray operator carefully removed my underwear from my bag and held them up for the security team to see. I shifted my weight back and forth as two more heavily armed guards approached the conveyor belt to see up close what they probably hadn't seen in person in their entire lives: a woman's thong. After a solid twenty seconds of watching a SWAT team manhandle my unmentionables, I snapped.

"What the hell are you looking at? Do you think they're go-go gadget undies? I say the magic word and they transform into a hand grenade or an Uzi that I'm going to use to take out a bunch of businessmen?"

They relented, aware that they were on the brink of a sexual harassment suit. When I had collected everything, I shot them all the most evil look I could muster, shoved my nose in the air, and declared, "Bite me."

I could handle humiliation at the hands of men who wrote my paychecks, but I drew the line at rent-a-cops who x-rayed briefcases for a living.

I'm sorry, but a girl has limits.

I reached my workstation three minutes later, to a round of applause from the rest of the desk. I collapsed in my chair. Drew chuckled first, then his laughter grew louder until he was roaring like a crazy person on his way to a padded room.

"Stop laughing at me. This isn't funny! Chick's going to kill me, Drew. What do I do?" I pleaded with him to give me advice.

"Sorry, you're screwed, my friend. You broke the proof-of-life policy."

"The proof of *what*?" I asked, terrified. How was it possible I'd never heard about this? It definitely wasn't in the handbook.

"The proof-of-life policy. Bad enough if you're going to be late and miss the economic data that comes out at eight thirty, but if you don't call in by eight fifteen or so and let him know that you're alive and on your way in, he'll kill you himself."

"No one ever told me about it!" I wailed.

"I guess everyone assumed you knew, or that you'd never be dumb enough to come in this late. One or the other."

"You're not helping!" I hissed. "Seriously, Drew, tell me what to do."

"I don't know what to tell you, A, but do me a favor and move over. I don't want to get caught in the cross fire."

I glanced at the clock on the wall. Nine twenty. *How did this happen?*

"Hey, wait a second," he said curiously, as he swirled his index finger in a circle referencing my upper body. "Isn't that the same sweater you wore yesterday?"

"No."

"Yes, it is," he countered, more confidently this time. "That's definitely the same fucking sweater you had on yesterday. I was calling you the Great Pumpkin all day. Don't tell me it's not the same sweater!"

I tried to think of something to say. "This is tangerine, not orange. It's a completely different shade." *Of all the days to do a walk of shame at work, it had to be the day I wore a bright orange cardigan. Couldn't have been one of the days I wore black, no. That would just be too convenient.*

"Bullshit!" Drew yelled as he erupted into laughter. "You didn't go home last night!"

"STOP!" I yelled. "It's not the same sweater. Yes, they're similar, but this is NOT the same one. Now drop it. I'm going to have a hard enough time today."

"Okay, Girlie, it's not the same sweater. You stick to that story," Drew said.

"Well, well, well. To what do I owe the honor of your presence?" Chick strolled down the row toward my desk, his hands in his pockets, his eyes intently focused on mine. I stood to apologize.

"Boss, I'm so sorry. I overslept, there's nothing I can say."

"It's not just that you're late, Alex. It's that you completely ignored my proof-of-life policy. I've been calling you, but every call has gone right to voice mail."

"My phone's dead," I whispered.

"Do you know what I think, Alex, when I have a young girl working for me who doesn't show up, doesn't call in, and can't be reached via cell phone for over two hours?"

I shook my head.

"I THINK YOU'RE DEAD!" he screamed, causing my body to go rigid and my breath to catch in my throat. "I think maybe you're lying in a morgue or in an ER and don't know your own name. This place"— he swept his arm in a wide arc, as if he were a *Price Is Right* girl modeling the first showcase in the showdown—"is the *first* place someone will notice if you don't show up. You could be missing for hours, even days, before your friends or your family notice, but if you aren't at your desk and we don't hear from you, we assume something's wrong. I was about an hour away from sending the cops to your apartment. I'm not a fucking babysitter, Alex. I have kids at home, I don't need them in my office!"

"I . . . I . . ." I struggled to find words but was too afraid my voice would crack.

"Don't say you're sorry. I don't want to hear it." He exhaled. "I'm happy you're okay, Alex, but now that you are, your ass is mine. Not that you don't belong to me every day. But today, ohhhh today you *really* belong to me. You seem to have forgotten my rules, Alex. Safe money is on you never forgetting again."

I breathed a sigh of relief when he returned to his desk.

"Well, that could have been worse," Drew said.

"Are you insane? How could this be worse?"

"He could've noticed your sweater."

I answered phones and kept myself busy, trying not to imagine what Chick was planning for me. At 10:30 I got an e-mail.

MSG FROM PATRICK, WILLIAM:
How bad was it?

MSG FROM GARRETT, ALEX:
It was a train wreck. This is your fault.

MSG FROM PATRICK, WILLIAM:
I'll take responsibility for the alarm clock, but I can't be held responsible for the fact that you find me irresistible.

MSG FROM GARRETT, ALEX:
Bite me.

From my desk I could hear him laughing, and a smile crept onto my face.

MSG FROM PATRICK, WILLIAM:
For what it's worth, I had a great time.

MSG FROM GARRETT, ALEX:
Me too.

I was so screwed.

An hour later Chick whistled in my direction. "Get over here, slave. Charge your phone?"

"Yes, it won't go dead ever again."

"Good answer. You're buying lunch today for the group, and we decided we want meatball parm and eggplant parm heroes."

Okay, I thought. *This I can handle.* It could have been way worse. Chick could have sent me to Chicago for deep dish pizza if he wanted to. Meatball parms, I could do. No problem. "Okay, where should I order from?"

"Arthur Avenue."

"In the Bronx?"

"Do you know of another Arthur Avenue famous for its Italian food?"

I shook my head. "How many am I getting?"

"Twenty-five or thirty of each. Will is taking the orders now, and he'll call it in."

"No problem."

"And one more thing, Alex."

A sudden sense of doom washed over me. "Sure boss, anything."

"I want a wheel of Parmesan."

"What? What do you mean, a wheel?"

"I mean, I want a fifty-pound wheel of cheese."

The expression on Chick's face assured me he was deadly serious. Picking up lunch wasn't my punishment; figuring out how to wrestle fifty pounds' worth of cheese from the Bronx to the southern tip of the island was my punishment. Lunch was just a bonus.

At least he was original.

"Leave. Now. The sandwiches should be ready by the time you get there." He handed me a Post-it note. "This is where you're going. You're picking up twenty-five meatball subs, twenty-five eggplant subs, and a fifty-pound wheel of cheese. And it better be fifty, Alex. I want to see the receipt. Capiche? Hope you have a credit card with room on it. You're going to need it."

I dropped my head in shame, grabbed my bag, and made my way down to a car. I sat in the backseat listening to 1010 WINS on the radio, staring at the East River as we snaked north on the FDR Drive. I had made a mess of my personal and professional lives in one shot. *Why do you do this to yourself?* So much for developing a healthy friendship with Will. That was clearly out of the question.

We reached the Bronx. I handed the driver the address and asked him to wait for me while I picked up a few things.

"Sure, no problem. Just this stop and then we're going to head back to Cromwell?"

"Yeah, I just have to pick up some food, and umm, a cheese wheel."

The driver turned and looked at me over his shoulder as we were stopped at a red light. "A what?"

"A cheese wheel," I repeated sullenly.

"I've been driving cars for Cromwell for ten years and, believe me, I've seen some strange stuff, but this one might top the list."

Joy.

We pulled over in front of a deli and I walked up to the counter. A small heavyset Italian man with a jovial face, and a belly that suggested a life well fed, smiled at me.

"Yes, miss, what can we do for ya?" he asked, with an accent as thick as the tomato sauce smothering the veal cutlets in the glass case next to me.

"I'm here to pick up an order for Ciccone, please."

"Chic-cooo-nayyy," he repeated to make sure he understood my pathetic Americanized pronunciation of an authentic Italian surname. He scanned boxes of sandwiches and platters of meats and cheeses that awaited pickup. "Ahh, va bene," he said as he picked up two large cardboard boxes filled with foot-long subs tightly wrapped in foil and slid them across the counter. He ripped a green order slip from one of the boxes and read it out loud. "Twenty-five-a meatbawls, and twenty-five-a eggplant parmigiana. Va bene?"

I nodded.

"That's $227.00. You pay cash or card?" I removed my American Express from my wallet and placed it gently on the counter.

"Credit, but I actually need one more thing." I nervously fidgeted with the leather band of my watch. "I need a large wheel of Parmesan."

He nodded, unfazed. "Okay sure, how much-a you need?" He moved behind the glass case and removed a large wedge of the cheese from a display. "You show me what size and I slice it for you."

"No, actually, I need an entire wheel. A fifty-pound wheel if you have one."

"Fifty-a pound?" he squawked, his mouth gaping in surprise. "Mamma mia, how you gonna carry fifty pounds of parmigiana?"

"I have a car outside. Maybe you can help me get it in the backseat?"

"You gonna put the parmigiana inna that car?"

"I hope to, yes."

"That going to not be so cheap, fifty pounds of parmigiana."

I motioned to the card still lying on the counter, about to be stressed to within an inch of its life.

"I know." I sighed. "Just add it to the bill."

The man picked up a calculator and began to punch numbers, adding fifty pounds' worth of curdled milk to my tab. "Okay, $984.61, signorina, and I give you a break because you cute, eh?"

"Nine hundred and eighty-four dollars?" *That's an entire new wardrobe! That's at least nine really nice dinners out in Manhattan! That's almost half a month's rent!*

"That's-a how much it cost to buy fifty pounds of parmigiana. Don't forget you have the meat-a-bawls and the eggplant heroes, too." He swiped my card. I did quick addition in my head. The heroes and the cheese combined cost over $1,200. I thought I was going to throw up. "Me and Gino, we bring-a the cheese outside for you."

"Great, thanks," I all but cried as I grabbed the two huge boxes of heroes off the counter and walked outside to the sidewalk.

"How much did it run ya?" the driver yelled out the window as he popped the trunk.

"Almost a grand, not including the sandwiches," I replied, placing the cardboard boxes of heroes carefully on the floor of the trunk. I stood on the sidewalk and waited for the wheel of cheese to be rolled out. *I have no one to blame for this but myself. This is what you get for being the biggest idiot on earth,* I thought to myself.

He whistled long and low. "That's gonna leave a mark."

Before I could reply, the two Italians approached the car from a side alley, carefully holding the cheese as if it were a ticking time bomb. I opened the car door and slid across the seat, reaching out to help maneuver the cheese through the door as they carefully placed the wheel next to me. Well, not so much next to me as on me.

The backseat wasn't large enough for the cheese and me to fit comfortably, so I was forced to rest part of it on my lap. The Italians waved good-bye, and we began the drive south back to Manhattan.

Riiiing. I fished my phone out of my bag, no easy task since half my body was incapacitated by cheese. I glanced at the number. *Now what?*

"Hello?"

"Hey, Girlie," Marchetti said. "How's the Bronx?"

"Swell. What's up?"

"Did you confirm the three hundred million Feb elevens I did this morning? The back office said they aren't instructing on them yet."

"I confirmed it with Tracey in the back office. Tell Reggie to call her."

"Will do. How long until you get back? We're hungry."

"Half hour if traffic is okay."

"Cool. Hey, wait, Kate needs to talk to you." He added in a whisper before she picked up the line, "This should be interesting."

"Alex, did you type up the trades I did this morning with Colony Capital? I'm checking my messages and I don't see them. How harrrrd is it to type up a confirm? I'm not asking you to execute the trades, just take your little fingers and type up the details."

I felt like telling Cruella that she was the only salesperson who didn't type up her own trade confirmations, that no one else saw it as an optional part of his job. "Yes, Cru, I mean Kate. I sent them to the client and to your e-mail." *You high-maintenance prima donna, I'll show you something else I can do with my finger.* I waited in silence as she searched her messages.

"Found them." *Click.*

I dropped my phone in my lap and closed my eyes. *You just have to pay your dues,* I reminded myself. *Everyone has to pay their dues.*

The phone rang again. "Yes?" I said, trying desperately to not sound irritated considering I was two hours late for work.

"Hi, sweetie."

"Hi, Mom." *Thank God,* I thought. Someone who doesn't want me to do anything for her.

"Are you okay? I just called the desk, and some man told me you were on a scavenger hunt for cheese in the Bronx! What does that even mean? Are you in the Bronx by yourself?"

"Not anymore; it's a long story. Chick just made me spend a thousand dollars on a cheese wheel and some meatballs."

"What?" she said in disbelief. "On *cheese*? Please tell me you're joking."

"I couldn't make this up if I tried."

"That's just insane. You should tell your boss to go to you know where."

"Because that's the way to advance my career."

"Some career, cruising all over New York City with a thousand dollars' worth of cheese. It's not too late to go to law school."

"I'm NOT quitting, Mom! I like my job. Maybe not today, but usually."

"You know, Alex, pride is one of the seven deadly sins."

"Trust me, pride won't be the sin that kills me."

"Do me a favor. Call your father at work. He wants to hear how you're doing. Maybe leave out the pilgrimage for the cheese."

"Count on it." *Click.* I hung up. There was no way I was going to call my dad right now. He would ask why I wasn't on the desk, and then I would have to lie to him, or risk having to explain what happened to bring on the cheese punishment. I had enough issues to deal with at the moment. Lying to my father wasn't something I needed to add to "Alex's list of shame" for the day. It was long enough as it was.

I closed my eyes and tried to imagine the next leg of the ordeal, where Chick sent me to a hardware store to buy an industrial-sized cheese grater. *Why, why, why did I have to be so late?* "Oh Christ." I sighed as I drummed my fingers on top of the wheel, thinking out loud. "How the hell am I going to get this thing up to the floor?"

"That's easy," the driver said over his shoulder. "Just get a dolly and take it upstairs in the service elevator."

Genius.

I dialed the firm's main number and asked to be connected to building maintenance. I told them I needed a dolly and use of the service elevator, which they said was no problem. They offered to have someone meet me at the curb to help. When we pulled up in front of the building, there was a tall man wearing a blue jumpsuit waiting patiently with the dolly.

"Thanks for the ride," I said to the driver after he deposited me, the cheese, and the boxes of heroes on the sidewalk.

"No, thank YOU. I can't wait to get home and tell my wife this story."

I turned to the maintenance man and said as calmly as possible, "This is why I need your help."

"Whoaaaaa," he said as he stared wide-eyed at the giant yellow block. "Is that parm?"

"Yup, Arthur Ave.'s finest."

He shook his head in disbelief and said pointedly, "You guys have way too much time on your hands."

No arguments there.

We loaded the wheel on the dolly, and I rested the two boxes of subs on top as he escorted me to the service elevator. When we reached the trading floor, I pushed the cart down the hall and called out, "Make way, coming through," as seemingly unfazed coworkers weaved to the right and left, avoiding my path. Two guys from emerging markets were walking in the hallway and offered to help. They ceremoniously carried the cheese over to Chick's desk.

And they say chivalry is dead.

Chick knocked on the wheel. "How much? All in?" he asked.

"About twelve hundred," I said. "One thousand for the cheese and about two hundred for the sandwiches."

"I pay you more than twelve hundred a year, don't I?"

"Yes," I whispered.

"So really, you're lucky I didn't fire you, which in essence would cost you a lot more than twelve hundred bucks. I assume you learned your lesson and will never be this late again?"

I slowly nodded my head.

"Okay then. My job here is done." He reached under his desk and removed a large, imposing cleaver.

"Where did you get that?" I asked. He smiled, as if it was perfectly normal for him to have a potential murder weapon resting on his briefcase. My thong couldn't clear security, but he somehow managed to smuggle a knife through x-ray. Bastard rent-a-cops.

He silently circled the cheese like an animal entrapping its prey. When he found what he deemed to be the perfect spot, he hacked into the giant wheel, barely penetrating the thick outer layer as the blade sliced the rind.

"Now, we eat."

nine

You're Going to Eat the Vending Machine for $28,000?

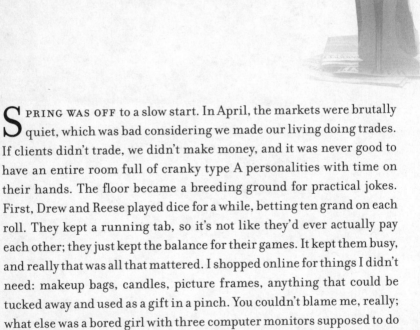

S PRING WAS OFF to a slow start. In April, the markets were brutally quiet, which was bad considering we made our living doing trades. If clients didn't trade, we didn't make money, and it was never good to have an entire room full of cranky type A personalities with time on their hands. The floor became a breeding ground for practical jokes. First, Drew and Reese played dice for a while, betting ten grand on each roll. They kept a running tab, so it's not like they'd ever actually pay each other; they just kept the balance for their games. It kept them busy, and really that was all that mattered. I shopped online for things I didn't need: makeup bags, candles, picture frames, anything that could be tucked away and used as a gift in a pinch. You couldn't blame me, really; what else was a bored girl with three computer monitors supposed to do when there was nothing going on? We played basketball with Nerf balls and garbage cans, and golf using baseball hats as makeshift holes and putters that were stashed in closets, and we messed with each other's desks, stealing extra shoes or favorite trinkets.

Quiet markets also provided opportunities to exact retribution for past offenses. Earlier in the month, a trader named Biff (yes, there really are people called "Biff") completely ripped me to shreds for a mistake I made booking a trade. His reaction was completely disproportionate to the seriousness of the crime (believe me), and Reese was furious at him for attacking one of his teammates so vigorously. As payback, he stole a stuffed bear Biff kept on his desk, one of his prized possessions for reasons no one understood. While the trader was in a meeting, Reese carefully constructed a ransom note with letters cut out of magazines and old copies of the *Wall Street Journal*. The note stated very clearly that unless Biff bought lunch for the entire sales desk, and apologized, he'd never see his teddy bear again. As word spread, clients began calling in saying things like, "I saw your bear in the back of a van on the West Side Highway; it was bleeding," or "I found a bear head in a garbage can in Battery Park. I really hope it's not yours." Reese bought a disposable camera and took pictures of the bear all over the building: at the coffee stand, on the Xerox machine, in the mailroom, hanging from the lamppost outside, holding the front page of the *Journal* with the date visible. He developed them at a one-hour photo shop and left them on Biff's desk every time he stepped away. Reese was merciless; he tucked ransom notes in Biff's briefcase, in his desk drawers. This went on for a week. When Biff couldn't take it anymore, he shot me a half-assed apology e-mail and had buckets of fried chicken delivered to our desk. The next morning, Reese came to work at 6:00 and returned the bear, which had an Ace bandage wrapped around its head and was covered with Band-Aids.

Marchetti messed with Reese's computer so that it translated the alphabet to Japanese characters. It took tech support an hour to figure out how to change it back to English. When Chick discovered the fried chicken came with dozens of mini corn muffins, he decided to mess with me. He scattered minimuffins everywhere. He lined them along the perimeter of my keyboard, a veritable minimuffin army. He hid them in my drawers, in the extra pair of shoes I kept under my desk. I found them in my makeup bag, at the bottom of my purse, and in my coat pockets. Every day, I removed corn muffins from any number of bizarre places, never knowing when I would smoosh one in my stiletto or find crumbs stuck in the wand of my mascara. I prayed that the markets would pick up so that the practical jokes would abate. If I missed a muffin, we'd end up with mice.

Drew stole Will's credit card, and shipped bizarre things to his apartment. Leather chaps, a whip, a case of body lube, nose hair clippers, jumper cables. Will called a hotel that Chick was staying at in Boston and informed them that he had back problems and needed to sleep on the floor, so they should remove the bed. When Chick arrived at his suite at midnight, the bedroom was empty, save for two pillows on the floor. He didn't find it funny, but we sure as hell did.

One of our traders had a well-documented aversion to pickles, refusing to eat anything that had come in contact with one. Early one morning, Drew removed the mouthpiece from the trader's phone while he was getting coffee and poured pickle juice into the receiver. As soon as the trader returned and sat down in his seat, Drew dialed his number. When the trader answered, the juice ran all over his chin and his shirt, and he puked. He held that one against Drew for a long time. On the other hand, downtime did have its advantages. There was more time to pursue extracurricular activities.

My relationship with Will was anything but normal. First off, I had no business as a sane person to call it a relationship. Since the night we hung out last month that had resulted in a $1,200 lunch tab, I had seen him only once outside of work. We went to a dive bar in the village and played pool for a few hours and then he put me in a cab and sent me home. That was fine; I was all for backtracking and approaching this completely irresponsible relationship with a colleague with caution. But hanging out only once after spending an indiscriminate night together seemed to be taking caution to the extreme. Normally, I would've just figured he wasn't interested, swallowed my pride, and moved on. But that was hard to do when I sat a few feet away from him and he flirted with me mercilessly on e-mail. I was beginning to wish that technology wasn't so advanced. If we didn't have unfettered access to each other via e-mail all day long, it would be way easier to stay detached. Carrier pigeons no longer seemed like a dumb way of communicating. It probably kept people a lot more sane.

First thing in the morning one sunny late April day, Marchetti waved a white order form in front of my face. "It's time for the annual ordering of the Girl Scout cookies," he said cheerfully.

"The what?" I asked as Drew snatched the form and filled in his name and address.

"Girl Scout cookie time—awesome," Drew said. "His daughter's in third grade, and if she sells the most cookies in her troop, she wins a scooter or something. Marchetti passes the form around and everyone buys some, and by the time we're done she's sold enough to win a freaking BMW, never mind the scooter. It's the little things we do to help make the lives of little girls that much nicer."

"If she wants a scooter, why doesn't Marchetti just buy her one?"

"It's the *principle* of the thing. You know, teaching the youth of America that they have to work for what they really want."

"That's great in theory, but you realize that she isn't exactly selling any of these cookies herself, right?"

"Why are you raining on the Girl Scout parade?"

"I'm not! I'm just pointing out that your theory is flawed."

"How about this theory? I like Samoas and won't get any unless the form is dropped on my desk. Is that reason enough to enthusiastically support the Girl Scouts?"

"Touché. I do like me a good Samoa." I opened my wallet and noticed that it contained only a ten-dollar bill and a gum wrapper. I gulped. "Do I have to pay now or later?"

"You pay up when Marchetti delivers the goods. For now, just write your name and your order on the form."

"What would I do without you, Drew?"

"You'd be lost." Drew finished filling out his cookie request. "Go to town," he said as he dropped the cookie form on my desk, but Will snatched it up before I had a chance to even look at it.

"Umm, what are you doing?" I asked.

"I'm ordering cookies. What does it look like I'm doing? Was there a reason you couldn't wait until I was done with it?"

"You don't have to order cookies if you don't want to, Alex. After the cheese thing, if you'd rather not light your money on fire, we'd understand."

"No, we wouldn't," Drew said.

"See, no they wouldn't. And I love how you think I'm so poor I can't afford a few boxes of cookies. I think I can manage!" I said.

"Do you need a loan?"

"No!"

"Are you sure?"

"You're annoying me, Will. Fill out the form and hand it over."

"Fine. If you need a loan though, you know where to find me." He finished scribbling, tossed me the form, and returned to his desk.

Then I had an idea—a way to get back at Will for making me late and therefore responsible for my being out $1,200. I scrutinized the form, wrote on it, and returned it to Marchetti at his desk. I stifled a laugh.

"How long does it take for the cookies to arrive?" I felt like a kid anticipating Christmas. I didn't know how I'd be able to wait.

"A couple of months," he answered succinctly.

"Perfect."

Marchetti's Girl Scout cookies prompted a conversation about cookies in general, and that morphed into a conversation about the cookies in the vending machine, and *that* somehow instigated one of the largest trading floor bets in Cromwell history.

"There's no way, Marchetti. There's no way you can take the whole thing down by four P.M." Chick laughed as he threw down the gauntlet to Marchetti. They were standing in a group that included Will, Drew, and Reese. It was early in the morning and it already promised to be a slow day.

Marchetti was confident. "How much do you want to bet I can do it during market hours? How much you wanna bet I can do it *today*?"

"You might be one crazy guinea, Billy, but there's no way. Your stomach would explode. Didn't you see the movie *Seven*? Where that fat guy eats himself to death? That will be you, and I'm not calling your wife to tell her you're not coming home tonight because we made you eat the vending machine and you're dead."

I rolled my chair down the row and joined in. "Wait," I interrupted. "You're going to eat everything in the vending machine? There are ten different kinds of gum in there that no one has eaten since 1989. There's no way you can swallow that much gum and not throw up. No way."

"My indentured Girlie makes a good point," Chick said. "I didn't think about the gum. Gum doesn't count as real food anyway. So if you're going to do this, you have to eat *one* of everything in the vending machine, not *everything* in the vending machine, excluding gum, starting today at nine thirty and finishing before the closing bell rings at four P.M. You can use my office if you don't want to be distracted, but Alex has to sit in the room with you to make sure you don't throw anything out or give anything away. You'll be supervised at all times. If you go to take a leak, you let me know and someone will go with you. Ten thousand dollars is the current pot, but I imagine once word gets out it will be higher. If you throw up at any point during the day, game over. Do you agree to these terms?"

The rest of the team had heard what was going on and formed a large circle around Billy and Chick, chanting "Bil-ly, Bil-ly, Bil-ly" and pumping their fists in the air. Billy stuck his chest out, pounded it with his fists, and shouted, "Bring it on! Mangia, mangia!"

And with that, Billy Marchetti agreed to eat the vending machine for $10,000.

Chick instructed everyone to remove all their singles from their wallets. Within seconds we were all holding up large wads of cash, waving them in the air like little green geisha fans.

Chick turned to me and said, "Girlie, collect the singles, get a box, and then go get one of everything in the vending machine, including the breath mints but excluding the gum. It's now eight thirty. Billy, you have an hour to prepare. Make sure you call your clients and tell them that Drew is covering them today. Alex, he doesn't go anywhere except the men's room without you watching him, and if he tries to cheat in any way, you come right to me. Now go."

As I walked by the trading desk, one of the younger traders saw the stack of cash I was holding and made a joke about me having had a good night dancing tables. Typical.

Without question, there were items in the machine that had been there for over a decade. The top row held the usual assortment of chips and salty snacks: Sun Chips, hard pretzels, Fritos, sour cream and onion potato chips, Doritos, Cheetos, and Funyuns (definitely there since the '80s). The second shelf held all the Hostess products: Twinkies, Cupcakes, Devil Dogs, Ho Hos, Yodels, and Snow Balls. There were bags of chocolate chip cookies, Vienna Fingers, Oreos, and Snackwells (for those health-conscious vending machine visitors). There were Snickers, Milky Ways, Butterfingers, M&Ms both plain and peanut, Skor Bars, and Almond Joys. The bottom row had the gum and a variety of breath mints. I put the box on the floor and one by one started running dollar bills through the machine.

Word traveled quickly and by the time I returned to Marchetti's desk with all thirty-two items, the pool was up to $20,000. Of course, everyone wanted to know the rules and what safeguards were in place to make sure that he won it honestly. This was Wall Street after all. No one parted with his money without being fully aware of the risks and well versed on the details of the deal.

Chick stood and grabbed the hoot off his desk. He pressed the button and blew into the microphone to get the floor's attention. "Everyone, listen up. If anyone else wants in on the vending machine bet, have your money to me by nine twenty-five."

The floor erupted in applause and cheers. Chick's desk was mobbed with people. Will recorded all the names and wagers alphabetically in a spreadsheet.

"Well, this won't be a normal workday for you, huh?" Will said as I dropped the box of junk food on the floor. "This is going to be fun."

Fun? This is the most ridiculous thing I've ever seen in my life, I thought to myself. Drew went through the items for me and created an inventory so that there would be no confusion as to whether or not an item was consumed. Will double-checked the list, and once everyone was satisfied that the inventory was complete and accurate, Chick fetched Old Faithful, my folding chair, from the closet and placed it right behind Billy. My mission seemed clear: watch him eat, check the item off the list, and hold on to the wrapper, which would serve as proof each item had been consumed.

Billy pretended to stretch out his quads and his hamstrings. The group was pretty evenly split between those who thought he was insane enough to actually do it, and those who bet that he would puke by noon. Will poked my back with his notebook.

"You ready? You know if you mess this up, they'll probably burn you at the stake."

The scary thing was, I sort of believed him.

As the opening bell rang on the floor of the Stock Exchange a few blocks away, Billy Marchetti ripped open a package of Twinkies.

One by one, he consumed the heavier items: the pretzels and most of the Hostess shelf. Random people passed by calling out "Mangia, baby!," "You're an animal!," and "I hope you took your Lipitor." I diligently collected wrappers and marked time. Twinkies, 9:30; cupcakes, 9:35; Ho Hos, 9:38. When Cuban sandwiches arrived around noon, Billy started to get nauseated. According to my list, I couldn't blame him. He had worked his way through all the Hostess cakes, half the row of chips, and both bags of M&Ms. Seventeen items. He decided to take Chick up on his offer to use his office. I followed him. As he high-fived guys in the hallway with one hand, he unbuttoned his pants with the other. I piled the remaining items on the desk, sat down in a chair, and stared at Chick's fish tank, grateful to have something else to look at. It was clear that Billy had no intention of losing his focus by talking to me anyway. I still couldn't believe that this was my job.

Eventually, Billy began to have trouble breathing and started sweating profusely. I asked him if he was okay, and he nodded, emptying an entire bag of Fritos into his mouth and spewing Frito dust all over Chick's carpet. One of the rules was that he could drink as much water as he wanted, but nothing else, and empty bottles of Poland Spring littered the floor around the desk. The sweating worsened. Considering that his pants were also unbuttoned, it dawned on me that if someone saw us leaving this office who didn't know what exactly was going on, I would become the star of a very juicy trading floor rumor. I had a feeling that being half dressed in an office with a coworker was probably included in the handbook as grounds for dismissal. I really needed to read that thing.

Drew burst into the room.

"Chick told me to come back here and check on your progress." He took one look at Billy—his shirt drenched with sweat, his pants open, his breathing labored—and started laughing hysterically.

"Dude, Marchetti, you're fucked. Look at yourself, you're lucky if you don't have a heart attack. I didn't realize we paid you so badly you're willing to put yourself through this for a measly $20,000. Do we have those electroshock paddles for when you keel over?" Drew pretended to hold two paddles in his hands and rubbed them together while shouting "Charging. Clear!" He then tensed his arms and pretended to shock Billy's chest. I laughed.

"I'm going to finish this, and when I do, I'm going to kick your ass, Drew. Alex, bounce him out of here. You're supposed to be my security guard."

I nodded in Drew's direction. "Drew, sorry, but you have to leave. This office is reserved for private bingeing until four o'clock."

"Actually that's what I'm here to tell you. You don't have until four. Chick wants you back on the floor for the last half hour so that everyone can see you through the finish line. You're going to be a legend if you pull this off. Of course, if you fail, you're going to have to move to Nebraska and become a bank teller."

"Fuck off, Drew. I mean it!" Billy snapped.

"Wait." I grabbed Drew's arm as he was about to leave the room. "Can you sit here for five minutes? I'm starving. All you have to do is make sure he doesn't throw up in Chick's office and hold any additional wrappers until I get back. Whatever you do, don't touch my list. You'll screw up my system."

"You bet, I'll keep an eye on fat bastard here."

"Thanks."

"Wait!" Billy snapped through bites of a king-sized Almond Joy. "When you go to the coffee stand, tell Jashim you want to borrow a blender."

"Why do you want a blender?"

"Just bring me the blender!"

"Okay. I'll ask."

When I got to the coffee stand, I grabbed a diet Snapple and a bagel.

"Hello, Ms. Alex!" Jashim, the guy working at the counter greeted me with his usual enthusiasm. "What can I get you? Do you want a special milkshake?"

"No, thanks, Jashim, no milkshakes for me today. Just the Snapple, bagel, oh yeah, and a blender, please."

"That will be $3.50," he said. "Did you say you also need a blender, Ms. Alex? I don't think we sell those."

"No, I just need to borrow one."

Jashim shrugged his shoulders. "Whatever you need, Ms. Alex, I will give you." He reached under the counter and produced a blender with the plug wrapped neatly around the base. I flashed Jashim a smile.

"Thanks. I'll take good care of it."

"No problemo."

When I got back to Chick's office, I found Drew leaning against the wall shaking his head in disbelief as Billy continued to eat. He had unbuttoned the top three buttons on his shirt. In addition, his plaid boxers were now exposed. It was starting to make me a little uncomfortable. We still had an hour to go, and if things continued this way, he'd be naked by the closing bell. I placed the blender on the floor next to the couch and took three wrappers from Drew. Billy had eaten the Almond Joy and two rolls of breath mints while I was gone, but his pace had slowed dramatically. My poor friend was toast.

We left the office and headed back to the desk at 3:30. According to my list, there was still a Reese's Peanut Butter Cup triple-pack, the Doritos, two rolls of mints, a bag of Oreos, the Butterfinger, and a package of Animal Crackers left. There was no way in hell Marchetti was going to be able to finish in thirty minutes. I wasn't sure why he needed the blender until about 3:50, when he plugged it in behind his desk. He threw the remaining candy bars, the mints, cookies, and chips into the blender with a bottle of water and I realized what he planned to do in order to win.

Oh he wouldn't . . .

He's seriously not going to . . .

Marchetti pressed a button and the machine began to whirl. He pureed the mixture until it was the texture of half-melted ice cream, partially liquid but with lumps of candy still large enough to chew. As the crowd gasped, cheered, and marveled, he chugged the entire thing finishing at exactly 3:59.

Then, he turned green.

As the group gathered around him congratulating him on his epic achievement, Chick collected the empty wrappers and bags from me and counted them off one by one against the list. When he was satisfied that every last item had been consumed, he jumped on the hoot again.

"Everyone who bet that our crazy Billy wouldn't be able to eat the vending machine during market hours is out cash. The judges have gone over the rules and regulations and everything is copacetic. The final tally on the pot is $28,000. Way to go, Billy!" He then held his iPod earphones up to the hoot and played Queen's "We Are the Champions" while the floor rewarded him with a thunderous standing ovation. I am sure Billy would have loved to hear it, but I don't think he did. He was too busy making a mad dash for the bathroom. Despite his best efforts, he failed. He threw up all over the carpet on the way to the men's room, and then needed help getting home to his apartment. But he had $28,000 in his pocket.

Just another day at the office.

B Y THE END OF MAY, the time had finally come for Liv and me to have our own places. After a year together in Murray Hill, our lease was up, and I finally had enough money to get my own apartment. I wanted to move downtown, so that I was closer to work. I couldn't stand commuting from Midtown to the financial district anymore. I never managed to get up on time to take the subway, and instead I ended up taking a cab to the office for twenty bucks a trip. It just wasn't worth it anymore to live above Fourteenth Street. I found a great apartment in the West Village that would probably bankrupt me and decided I would rather live in a cool apartment and be in debt up to my eyeballs than save money by living in another part of town. Liv decided to keep the Murray Hill place and was staying in our apartment by herself, and she was happy she could take down the fake wall, have a normal size living room, and move into the real bedroom. Liv thought I was crazy to pay what I was paying to live across the street from a firehouse, on one of the noisier streets in the city, but I didn't care. I was so tired most nights from work I could probably sleep through an earthquake. I was excited to be on my own, but I was definitely going to miss the companionship that a roommate provided. Liv always kept things interesting, and with the craziness at work, I was afraid I was never going to see her.

Our last night together in the apartment was fun and bittersweet. We ordered a pizza and cracked open a few beers while packing my belongings into cardboard boxes and stacking them against the wall for the movers who were coming in the morning.

"Right about now is when having a guy to help out would be very handy," I said as I hefted another box.

"No shit! Why didn't you ask Work Will to come help?"

"Asking someone to pack your apartment assumes a level of intimacy that we are nowhere near attaining."

"I don't get what you're doing then, since you don't seem to be getting any of the benefits of having a guy around. Actually, when I think about it, he's never actually around. After six months of seeing each other, shouldn't you have progressed past the weekly drink and random hook-up routine? I mean, what are you guys even doing? It's not like you can say you're dating. I haven't even met the guy, and you're lucky if he places an outgoing phone call. I don't get it. Don't you want more from a guy in your life? I would."

"Like to kill mice and pack boxes?"

"Yes. And change lightbulbs. And take out the garbage. I need a guy if for no other reason than dealing with the garbage. I'm so over that."

"Come on, Liv. Girl power!" I said with more enthusiasm than I felt. The truth was, I had told Will that I was moving and that Liv and I had to get everything packed in one night. I'd hoped he'd offer to come over and help. We'd been seeing each other—and calling it that was a stretch—for six months and he still hadn't met Liv or Annie, and truth be told, it bugged me. I was beginning to wonder if he was lazy, clueless, or just plain stupid. And then I figured that I would just go with stupid, because my experience told me that most guys were, and it was just easier to assume that was the reason rather than worry about the other explanations. He probably just didn't want to be in the way and figured I'd see him on Monday. I'm sure that was it. But the truth was, I was annoyed. Fuck girl power. My back hurt.

At 10:30 we took another beer break and collapsed on the floor in front of the TV because the couch was covered with packing materials. I heard my phone beep but couldn't tell where it was coming from, as I had lost it in the chaos that was now the living room. Liv pushed aside a roll of bubble wrap and held my phone up triumphantly.

"Found it!" she said, checking the display. "Whoa!" she said, shock clearly registering on her face. "Who the hell is Rick? Is that why you

wanted to move? Are you seeing someone and not telling me? What
happened to Work Will?"

Oh God. Not again.

"You've got to be kidding me," I moaned. "I'm going to have to
change my phone number."

"Wait, this isn't that sketchy client, is it?"

"Yup."

"You have to put a stop to this, especially now that you'll be living
alone. Did you tell Chick?"

"No!" I screamed. "I don't know what I'm supposed to do about it,
other than *not* complain to Chick. So far I've taken the path of least
resistance, just ignoring him as much as possible."

"Bad idea. Guys love a challenge."

"I know, or at least, now I do. All it's done is make him more per-
sistent. It's becoming pretty clear that he's going to be a real problem."

"I'll say. Listen to this." Liv proceeded to read Rick's message out
loud: ' "Staying in the city tonight, don't make me stay alone.' I don't see
how that qualifies in any way as professional communication. I can't
imagine Chick would be cool with one of his buddies harassing one of
his employees. It would open the firm up to a lawsuit."

She was probably right, and I had thought about it a few times, but
after the mess with Tim Collins, there was no way I was going to complain about another guy, especially not one of Chick's top clients. I had
dealt with sketchy guys before; I had faith in my ability to handle one
married math geek with a wild imagination.

"Have you gone out alone with him?" she asked, skeptically.

"No!"

"Do you want to?"

"No!"

"Have you ever thought about it?"

"No! And I resent that, Liv, come on. I think I'm dating Will anyway."

"Well, I think you need to kill this now before it grows into a beast

that you can't control. You've already got your hands full with one amazingly screwed-up work relationship."

"I have it under control."

"What you *have* is a corporate stalker."

"You're right. I'll take care of it. I promise."

And I meant it, really, I did. I just had to figure out how.

"Will you do me a favor, please?" Liv asked.

"On our last night together, sure. What?"

"Call Will and ask him to help us stack boxes? I'm going to throw my
back out."

"No fucking way."

"Alex, you're being ridiculous. You guys are friends with benefits,
and even without the benefits, you're still friends. How big a deal is it to
ask him to help?"

"He's a *work* friend. It's not like he's some guy from college I've
known for years."

"Please! Seriously, my back is killing me; just call him. Don't ask
specifically if he'll come over. Just mention you're packing and see if he
offers. There's nothing wrong with that. And for the record, I think you
lost the right to call him a 'work friend' when you started hooking up
with him."

"Fine, I'll call him, but I'm *not* asking him to come over."

"That's all I want. My deltoids thank you."

I dialed his phone number and held my breath in anticipation. As
usual, it went to voice mail. I always answered the phone when he called,
but for some reason, he never had his phone with him when I did. It was
more than a little annoying.

"Hey, Will," I said after the beep. "It's Alex. I'm just calling to see
what's up. I'm home packing so give me a ring when you get this."

"Shit. Voice mail?" Liv whined at the thought of having to finish
packing on our own.

I surveyed the mess that was our—now Liv's—apartment and sighed.
I took my pictures off the wall and wrapped them in towels. I went

through all the cabinets and cupboards and pulled out my pots, pans, glasses, mugs, dishes, silverware, and utensils. As we worked, we came across items that triggered memories of our time together, and I realized how much I was going to miss her. Two hours later we had all of my stuff packed, labeled, and ready to go.

Liv stretched her hands above her head and arched her back. Her yellow zip-up sweatshirt was coated in dust bunnies and her hands were covered with newspaper print.

As she collapsed on the couch, my phone beeped.

"Typical," she sighed. "Watch, that's Will. He could probably sense that we didn't need his help anymore so he decided to call you back. How do guys do that? It's like they can sense when they're needed and go underground."

I pulled the phone from between the couch cushions and flipped it open.

> *SMS from Kieriakis, Rick:*
> *I like a girl that plays hard to get.*

"It's not Will. It's Rick again."

"Psycho," she said as she twirled a piece of her hair around her index finger.

"Yeah. Clearly. Well, on that note, I'm going to bed."

I placed my phone on the nightstand next to my bed and, with a surprising feeling of sadness and loss, went to sleep for the last time in our converted one-bedroom apartment in Murray Hill.

ten

Charity Begins at Home

AS THE BREEZY New York spring turned into a hazy New York summer, Will and I began sneaking around outside of the office so that Chick wouldn't find out that we were seeing each other. I was beginning to think one of the reasons Will had never wanted to come over before was because I had a roommate. Once I got my own place, we started hanging out more after work and things seemed to become somewhat more consistent. Of course, that's not saying much since originally there was no consistency whatsoever, but I like to see the glass as half full. It had taken seven months, but I felt like things were finally going in the right direction. We took separate cabs in the morning, never left the office at the same time, and tried to keep office flirting to a minimum. We kept things casual, mostly because I was afraid to ask him to define our relationship. We had quiet dinners, drank beers at every bar on the Upper West Side, bet on the ponies at Belmont, and spent rainy afternoons at the movies. While I was happy that we seemed to be getting on a more normal track, Will was still hard to read. He preferred to hang out during the week and he always seemed a bit distant, but I chalked it up to his being nervous about Chick busting us. I was nervous about that, too, but it wasn't like Chick hung out in the city on the weekends, so that didn't explain why Will was never around then. It was like from Friday night until Monday morning he fell off the grid, and I didn't really understand why. I mean, I had friends, and a life of my own, too. It wasn't like I was sitting at home waiting for his phone call. Still, that didn't mean he couldn't make one—ever. I was trying hard not to let it bug me. Will was a quirky guy; it was one of the things I liked about him. So I decided to live with his quirks. I didn't really have much of a choice.

Soon it was July, and we started having waterside cocktails after work, always careful to travel far from the office. It made my personal life a bit complicated, but I was handling it. Of course, at work, it was business as usual.

One of the firm's time-honored traditions was the annual trading floor charity auction, mind-blowing in its fund raising capabilities. The donated items ranged from the perfectly normal to the absolutely outrageous, and there was no way of telling how high the bidding would go. The auction itself took place at the end of the day, on the floor, and was followed by a massive party at an off site venue. It was without a doubt one of the best days of the year.

"Look at this. This is funny. Twenty-five hundred dollars to play golf with Darth Vader at Shinnecock. Who the hell would pay money for that?" I asked Drew.

"A lot of people if Baby Gap is the caddy," Drew said as he snatched the pamphlet from my hands. "There's some good stuff in here. Giants tickets on the fifty-yard line, a trip to Bermuda, a round of golf at Maidstone, a spa package at the Mandarin."

"What are we talking about?" Chick asked as he buried his hand in a bag of potato chips.

"The auction," Drew answered.

"Good stuff in there this year. I'm going to bid on the trip to Ber-

muda, but I've got something to do this afternoon and won't be here for
bidding. Girlie, I'll call in from my cell. You bid for me."

"Me? Seriously?"

"Yes, you. You have a problem with that?"

"No, of course not." I didn't have a problem with it, but everyone
else on the floor probably would. Chick was forcing me to break one
of Cromwell's most sacred unwritten rules: women don't bid in the
auction. The auction was a male ritual, a socially acceptable way to
discover who made more money than whom. The very senior Cromwellites took great pride in being able to shut down a colleague's bid,
of proving that one was Master of the Bond Universe. Richer. More
powerful. Better looking (in their heads at least). No woman had ever
bid in the auction, not even Cruella. It might have even been in the
handbook.

"See you guys on the roof tonight," he said, as he grabbed his briefcase and ran off the floor.

"Noooooooooooooooooooooooooooooooo." I pretended to sob as I
grabbed Drew's forearm. "Why is he doing this to me? Why can't *you*
bid for him?"

"That wouldn't be nearly as funny."

A T 3:00 THE FLOOR BUZZED even more than usual as we prepared
to begin the auction.

"All right, gentlemen!" Vinny, the auctioneer, boomed over the
loudspeakers that were set up like a giant sound system all over the floor.
He stood at a podium at the head of the center aisle, holding a microphone, and wearing a baseball hat etched with the firm's logo. "This is
my favorite day of the year at Cromwell. It's time for us to remember that
not everyone is as fortunate as we are, and to give back. Last year this
floor raised $286,000, but this year we can do better!"

The room shook as everyone cheered, loving Vinny's pep talk. A
resounding "YES!" rang out from the crowd.

"Are we going to raise even more money this year?"

"YES!"

"Are we ready to show everyone why Cromwell is the greatest shop on the Street?"

"YES!" The thought of eliciting envy from our competitors was enough to make Cromwellites donate their kids if Vinny asked them to. A few guys chest bumped. I still had a hard time getting used to that.

"Then let's get this party started! First up, we have a helmet signed by the Forty-Niners. The whole team!"

"Giants!" some yelled, offended that a football helmet from San Francisco was for sale.

"I know, I know. This hurts me, too. But some of you must be closet Forty-Niners fans. For this one day only, it's allowed. Opening bid is two grand!"

"Three thousand!" one trader shouted.

"Three thousand five hundred!" another countered.

"Four thousand!" someone screamed.

"Sold!" Vinny yelled as he slammed his gavel on the podium.

Will appeared at my desk. "I'm going to hang here with you. I want a front-row seat for when you start bidding."

"I can't believe he's making me do this. He could at least let me bid on the spa package if he's going to make me humiliate myself. I'd cut off my arm for a full day of pampering at the Mandarin."

"Why don't you bid on it if you want it?"

"Sadly, I can't afford to spend thousands of dollars on a massage and a pedicure."

"Suit yourself."

We turned our attention back to Vinny.

"Now this one, fellas, this should go for top dollar. This is a bonus item. It's not even on the list! I'm personally bidding on this one, so who's ready to take me on?"

"You're going down, Vin!" an anonymous voice yelled. "I'm going to make you pay through the nose!" The room was so crowded there was no way to decipher who was challenging Vinny, but it didn't matter.

"Every day, he gets your coffee, makes your milkshakes, and sells you cookies. Now it's time to say thank you for his years of hard work. You know who he is, the unsung hero of the floor, our very own Jashim! Who wants to pay to take Jashim to lunch?"

Jashim, the coffee-stand guy, ran onto the floor, soaking up every second of his five minutes of fame. He waved to everyone as the room exploded into screaming cheers, and the theme from *Rocky* played over the hoot.

"He's going to auction Jashim?" I asked Will.

"This is hysterical."

"Vinny can't auction a *person*!"

"Why not? Cattle sells at auctions."

"Jashim's not a cow!"

"No shit. Thanks for clarifying."

Jashim stood on a chair and waved to his adoring fans, reveling in his newfound status as a trading floor celebrity.

I didn't hear the phone ring, but I saw the light blinking on my board. I grabbed my headset. "Cromwell," I said loudly. I pushed the earpiece tightly against my ear, hoping that I'd be able to hear the caller over the din.

"Where are we?"

"Hi, Chick."

"Are we almost there?"

I looked at the brochure. "Bermuda's number thirteen. Right now they're bidding on Jashim."

"What? Jashim wasn't on the list!"

"Sold to your favorite vending machine eater and mine, big Billy Marchetti! Way to go, Bill!"

"Marchetti just spent fifteen thousand to take Jashim to lunch."

"I paid Billy last year. Believe me, he won't miss the cash. What's next?"

"The spa package. I'm so jealous of whoever ends up with it."

"Then buy it for yourself."

"I can't afford it."

"It's for charity, A. Haven't you ever heard that charity begins at home?"

"I'm all for charity, but I don't care how rich I am, I'm never spending that much money on a backrub."

"Talk to me when you're rich."

"Fair enough."

"SOLD!" Vinny declared as someone forked over ten Gs for a day of pampering at the Mandarin for his wife. Lucky bitch.

"Boss, you're up." I breathed deeply and prepared myself for total humiliation.

"Item number thirteen. A four-day trip to Bermuda. Sun, sand, and more important, four days out of the office. Let's start the bidding at a very social ten thousand dollars. Do I hear ten?"

I gripped the microphone attached to my headset tightly, making sure that Chick would hear me clearly. I couldn't screw this up. I didn't want to go back to the mailroom.

"Starting bid is ten grand, Chick," I said calmly.

"Bid ten."

"Ten grand!" I yelled.

Simultaneously, everyone turned to face me, their mouths agape in shock. It was almost as if I could see the thought balloons floating above their heads: *Did she just . . . bid?*

I stood frozen, as eight hundred eyeballs focused on me. I stared back. Slowly, a smile crept onto Vinny's face. "Well, then! I've got a ten grand bid from Alex in the back. Do I hear twelve?"

"Twelve!" A hand shot up on the far side of the room.

"Twelve grand! Let's go, everyone. Open your wallets! Sixteen, anyone, do I hear sixteen?" Vinny's eyes darted around the room ensuring he wouldn't miss a hand in the corner.

"It's going at sixteen now, boss."

"Go sixteen."

"Sixteen!" I screamed.

Will chuckled. "Holy shit. I didn't think it was possible for a human being to turn as red as you are right now."

"Shut up! Don't distract me." My head throbbed.

"Eighteen!" someone else yelled as the standing room only crowd cheered and applauded. "Eighteen now," I murmured into the headset.

"Twenty. I want this trip, Girlie!"

"Twenty!" My voice cracked.

"Twenty from Alex. The little lady wants to hit the beach! Let's go twenty-three everyone. Twenty-three!" *Please make this end, please make this end.*

"TWENTY-FIVE!" a baritone boomed.

Twenty-five? We were only at twenty-three, who just upped the price to twenty-five? I pushed Will out of my way and strained to see who had bid for the trip. *Oh please tell me this isn't happening.*

Vinny was pointing to Doug Hanlon. Doug was Chick's boss. Maybe Chick's boss's boss.

"Chick," I hissed. "Doug Hanlon just bid twenty-five. You're not going to make me . . ."

"Bid thirty!" Chick was not about to be slighted by someone just because he was on the executive committee.

People pounded on their desks causing the room to shake. I cupped my hands around my mouth and bellowed back, "THIRTY!"

Reese came running over to my desk, shadowboxing. "Give it to 'em, sugar! Give it to 'em! Take no prisoners!"

I boxed back, delivering a phantom uppercut to his jaw. Reese immediately collapsed on the floor, pretending to be knocked out.

"The little lady has thirty, fellas!" Vinny beamed in my direction from the podium. "Does anyone want to go thirty-five? Anyone? Thirty thousand dollars going once, going twice, and Alex takes down the trip for thirty Gs!" The guys applauded, whistled, and cheered while I tried to crawl under my desk and hide.

"Did I get it?" Chick hissed over the phone.

"Sold to you, boss, for thirty."

"Good job, Alex. I'll bring you back a magnet for your refrigerator."

Click.

I collapsed in my chair and waited for the throbbing in my head to subside. I was worried I was about to have an aneurysm.

Will rubbed my shoulders. "Good thing the party at the Gansevoort is tonight. Looks like you could use a drink."

"Or twelve. I'm looking forward to it; I hear the view from the roof is insane."

"So what? It's the same skyline you've seen a million times. I thought only tourists were impressed by rooftop views of Manhattan."

"What can I say, I have a thing for skylines."

"Really? That's interesting."

"It is? How come?"

"No reason. Are you going to the bar for late night? I think Chick is organizing something after the rooftop."

"Nah, I'm planning on leaving by ten thirty at the latest. I guess I'll see you up there."

"You bet. Hey, I have something for you." Almost slyly, Will placed an envelope on my desk.

"What's this?"

"Open it." He smiled.

I removed a brochure from the envelope. It was a gift certificate for a full day of pampering at the Mandarin. My heart stopped.

"You bought this?"

"For you. It's basically your one-year anniversary here, right? Plus, I figured you could use a massage after all the pizzas we make you carry."

"Oh my God. I can't believe you did this for me. I really wish I could kiss you right now, you know, and not get fired."

He laughed. "You wanted it, and the money goes to charity anyway. Enjoy it. I'll figure out a way for you to thank me later."

He winked before he returned to his desk and I returned to my work, counting down the minutes until we could leave for the client party, and staring at the gift Will had just given me.

. . . .

THE ROOFTOP WAS ROCKING by the time I arrived. I grabbed a drink at the bar and made my way outside to find people. I caught sight of Will standing in the corner talking to a hedge fund manager, and he nodded in my direction when I stepped onto the patio. Chick was off talking to Rick, one person I wanted to avoid, but, much to my horror, Chick waved me over. I had no interest in speaking to Rick, in person or via text. I would do a lot of things for Chick—he was my boss, my mentor, and my friend—but I was not about to let him pimp me out to his clients as eye candy or as anything else. I plastered a grossly exaggerated smile on my face and obeyed Chick's order.

"Hey, boss," I sang happily as Chick fist-bumped me. I turned toward Rick. *Stop texting me, you crazy fucking lunatic.* Or maybe I said politely, "Good to see you, Rick."

"It's been a while, Alex. You look very nice tonight." He leered as he gave me elevator eyes.

"Thanks." I knew I looked good, because I had carefully prepared my party outfit since I knew Will would be there. The fact that my friendly married stalker had noticed the dress, too, was an unwelcome side effect, kind of like when you take aspirin for a headache and end up having to have your spleen removed.

"So how long am I going to have to wait until Alex can cover me, Chick? She can cut her teeth on me a little . . . as long as she doesn't bite."

"Take it easy there, Rick! She needs more experience before she's ready to cover anyone, let alone you guys. Sorry, buddy, but for the time being you're stuck with me."

"That's a shame. Brains and a body, the Holy Grail of saleswomen. You can't blame a guy for trying."

Chick squeezed my shoulder and said in a fatherly manner, "Cool it, Rick. Don't make my girl here uncomfortable."

Rick placed his hand on my lower back and pulled me toward him. "She can handle it, Chick. Alex isn't shy, from what I can tell." Chick pulled me back toward him like a chew toy. I was grateful.

"No, she's not. But that doesn't mean it's open season for you," he said as he wrapped his arm around my back. I slugged down the contents of my glass in two large gulps.

"Fine. I'll lay off. I'm going to go refresh my drink. It was good to see you, Alex. Keep working hard and maybe one day I'll convince Chick to let me have you."

I wanted to tell him that if he hit on me again I would break his legs, but I had to keep quiet. Sales had a lot to do with knowing what to say and what not to say. Chick handed me another glass of wine.

"Head inside and tell the girls from event planning to close it up and go home. We don't need them here anymore. I sure as hell don't want to be paying for their drinks when they're supposed to be working." Chick was a generous guy to the people who worked for him, but if you weren't on our team, you had to fend for yourself.

I made my way back to the hallway outside the elevators, and the girls were already packing up their things. I popped into the ladies' room to fix my makeup and my hair. I was getting ready to go talk to Will. That plan was quickly derailed when I discovered Rick leaning against the wall in the hallway, chewing on a toothpick.

"Oh hey, Rick." I tried to make my way past him, but Rick held his arm straight out in front of me, forcing me to stop or risk having his hand come in direct contact with my chest. I froze: trapped in a small space of hallway between the elevator and the bathroom.

I smiled, despite the urge to punch him in the face. "Are you leaving?" *Please say yes.*

"No."

Damn.

He waved the toothpick in the air like he was conducting some kind of invisible orchestra. "I just wanted to talk to you privately."

There are two hundred people on this roof. The concept of privacy doesn't exist. Thank God.

"Chick shot me down pretty quickly when I asked if you could cover me. I think he wants to keep you all to himself. Not that I blame him."

Jesus Christ, what did I do to deserve this?

"I appreciate the offer." I was pretty sure Rick needed medication—or a higher dosage, whichever applied.

"Mark my words, one day you'll cover me. I think we'd make a great pair. I'd love to hear your thoughts on the markets—or on me. One or the other."

You want to hear my thoughts on you? Sure. One day, I promise to give them to you.

He gently smacked my ass, causing my body to burn with disgust. I closed my eyes and tried to will my breathing back to normal. Rick had crossed the line, but just barely. Not enough to complain. After all, guys smacked each other on the ass all the time; so did pro athletes.

I went back outside and roamed the rooftop, chatting happily with people. I introduced myself to some of Drew's clients, the ones I spoke to when he was unavailable. I scanned the crowd for Will and spotted him chatting with Baby Gap in the corner. Swell. I worked my way through the crowd, mingling the way a salesperson should. Chick found me at the bar an hour later talking to a few of the traders and tweaked my nose.

"Sorry about Rick, Alex. Just ignore him; he's a good guy, but for some reason he likes to toy with you. He thinks you're funny, and he likes a girl with spunk. You've got that in spades."

"Thanks. I think."

I checked my watch. Ten thirty. Time for me to go. "I think I'm going to head home."

"Okay. Get home safely." I scanned the crowd for Will to say goodbye, but I couldn't find him in the sea of guys in khakis. I gave up and began to weave my way toward the elevators when my phone rang.

"Hello?"

"Alex, hi. It's Hannah."

"Hannah? Aren't you here at the party?"

"Yeah, I'm right behind you."

"Why the hell are you calling me?" I turned and saw her standing in the middle of the room. She waved. "You're standing twenty feet away." I said.

"I need you to talk to me for a minute."

"On the phone?"

"Yes! There's this really cute client, and he's ignoring me. I want him to think that I'm important so he'll talk to me."

"You're not important."

"He doesn't know that."

"I wouldn't bet on that." I hung up on her and left her chatting to a dead line. Assuming, of course, that she realized that I was no longer there.

I limped out of the hotel, my feet throbbing from standing in heels all night. I was about to hobble west to grab a cab when a window lowered on a town car a few feet from the entrance.

Will leaned out the window and asked, "What took you so long?"

"You make it sound like I knew you were waiting." I laughed. "I looked for you upstairs. If you told me you were down here, I might have bailed sooner."

"I snuck out. I didn't want Chick to see us leave anywhere near the same time. I've been down here for about fifteen minutes now. I'm bored."

"That's because you have the attention span of a gnat. Thanks for waiting. Good idea leaving early but next time maybe you could, you know—and I'm going out on a limb here—tell me you're waiting for me, and you might not get stuck hanging out in a town car for fifteen minutes. Just a thought," I teased.

"Shut up and get in the car," he said with a laugh. "You're such a wiseass sometimes, you know that?"

"I thought that was one of the things you liked about me."

"One of many," Will said.

I climbed in the back of the car as my legs squeaked against the leather seat. "Now this is what I call courteous door-to-door service."

"I'm happy to take you home, but actually, I want to make a stop first."

"Where are we going?"

"I want to show you something. Trust me."

"The last time you told me to trust you I woke up in your apartment two hours late for work." He laughed as the car pulled over in front of a loft building in TriBeCa. "Where are we?"

"Come inside." We rode the elevator to the top floor and then exited a small door. We climbed a flight of stairs and walked onto the empty roof, the balmy air tickling my face as I looked up and saw what I didn't think existed in Manhattan: stars.

We walked to the low wall that lined the perimeter of the roof. "*This* is a skyline."

We had a perfect view of the entire city. The expanse of Midtown, the Empire State Building, both the Hudson and the East rivers, and the glittering lights of the bridges to the east. Cars inched along northbound in traffic, their taillights forming blinking red snakes of color on the roads like Christmas tree lights before they're wrapped around the tree. I'd never seen something as incredible in my entire life—and that includes the previous month's limbo contest at work.

"How'd you get the keys to get up here?" I gasped as I spun 360 degrees, reveling in the opportunity to be alone in a city that rarely ever gives you the chance.

"A buddy lives in the building. He gave me his keys after work today. When you said you liked skylines, I figured I'd take you to see the view from up here."

"You're full of surprises today. I feel spoiled."

Will pulled out a chair from a small table in the corner for me. He pulled another chair next to me and stretched his long legs out in front of him. For a moment we sat in silence, facing north, staring at the lights, the buildings rising like giant stalagmites from the bedrock below. "I like spoiling you. I told you the Gansevoort wasn't that impressive."

"It's nothing compared to this. It almost makes you forget that the city is actually a total shit show."

"Almost. You really appreciate the simple things, don't you?"

"I guess. There's so much excess around our business, sometimes it's nice to take a step back and just enjoy. I guess I don't really think that just because something's expensive means it's special. For my money it doesn't really get any more special than this, and this roof is free."

"Not exactly: my buddy pays out the ass for his apartment."

I laughed. "Well, free for us!"

"Ain't that the truth. Did you have fun at the party?"

"I got cornered by Rick Kieriakis, and that kind of put a damper on things."

"He has a way of doing that."

"He's been hitting on me. Hard. Do you know how he got my phone number? Did you give it to him?" I prayed he would say no.

"Of course not. He calls you? Why is this the first time I'm hearing about this?" he asked, seemingly shocked. Maybe I should have mentioned this sooner, but saying it out loud meant that I could no longer deny it was a problem. And it was. A big one.

"No, he texts me. It's not really an easy thing to bring up in conversation, though maybe if you picked up your phone when I called you, it would have come up." I bit my lip as soon as the words came out of my mouth. I sounded like one of those insecure girls I hate. The ones who are possessive and needy and whiny.

Will smirked. "Well, you have me here now. So what is going on? When did this start?"

"It started that night at Buddha Bar. I couldn't figure out how he got my number, but if you didn't give it to him, then I guess Chick did."

"There's no way he'd do that. You know about Rick and Cruella, right?"

"No. What?" I asked, flustered at hearing their names in the same sentence. It was like an axis of evil.

"She and Rick used to hook up when she was single. Rumor has it she liked him a lot, and he totally dicked her over. I don't know the whole story, but apparently he fucked up her head pretty badly."

"How'd I not know this?" I asked. "I thought I'd heard all the dirt on her."

"It was before your time, years ago. Reese once said that her Rick saga flipped a switch and morphed her into an angry bitter shrew. There's no way Chick would willingly let him contact you and destroy another female on his team."

"So you're saying that Rick is responsible for her being so evil?"

"Apparently. I don't think she was always like that, although it's hard to imagine her any other way, isn't it?"

I nodded. "Yeah, it is." The comment she made to me in the ladies' room that day suddenly registered. *What the hell did he do to her to make her so angry?* And then, an even more disturbing thought: *Now he's turned his attention to me.* I had to change the topic, because I couldn't handle thinking about Rick anymore. He occupied enough of my time—too much—as it was. "What do you think Chick would do if he knew you and I were seeing each other?" I asked as my mind flashed horrifying images of what Chick would do to me if he knew I had blatantly ignored one of his rules. Fuck.

"Probably strap you to the folding chair and lock you in the closet."

"The sad thing is, I believe that." I didn't want to get ahead of myself, but worrying about Chick finding out about us was becoming a full-time job, and I already had one of those. I figured it couldn't hurt to ask. "So what happens then?"

"What do you mean?"

"If we keep seeing each other. How does this work? It's odd pretending I hardly know you when we're in the office, but it can't stay like this forever, can it? Not that I think this is forever, I just . . . you know what I mean."

"I think we just take it one day at a time. For now, why don't we just have fun tonight and worry about the rest of it later?"

"You're right," I said, even though I didn't agree with him.

"What's up for the weekend?" he asked.

"I was going to ask you that. Are you around?" I figured since I had already fallen into the abyss with my "you don't call me on weekends" complaint, I might as well just suck it up and ask him if he wanted to hang out. We really should be at a point where that wasn't a strange question to ask. Best-case scenario, we could do something on Sunday. Worst-case scenario, I'd kill myself.

"Unfortunately, no. I'm going to Boston."

I felt my shoulders slump in disappointment, but I tried to stay cheery. "What's in Boston?"

"I have a meeting Monday morning, but one of my buddies from school lives there so I'm going to go hang with him for the weekend. I'll take the shuttle back on Monday night."

"I didn't know you covered anyone in Boston."

"I just picked up a hedge fund," he said casually.

"Ahh, well, that's good; at least you'll get to mix some business with pleasure."

"I thought we were already doing that."

"Good point."

My phone beeped. A text message. I looked at my watch. It was almost midnight. I knew it would be from Rick before I even read it. No one else would be texting me this late on a weeknight.

> *SMS from Kieriakis, Rick:*
> *Why didn't you say good-bye before you left?*

Original. Christ, Heidi Fleiss got more professional text messages than I did. I threw my phone back in my bag without saying a word.

Will smiled. "It's getting late," he said reluctantly as he ran his hand through his windblown hair.

"I hate to leave." I sighed.

"We can come back another time."

"Good. Tell your friend he's forbidden from moving."

"I'll do that."

"Do you mind dropping me off at home?"

"I wasn't kidding, I really am coming to your place."

"Okay. Just remember that I don't have a view."

"The firehouse isn't bad if you don't mind being woken up by sirens at three A.M. when a bodega's on fire. I don't know how you stand it every night."

"Yeah, I should have thought that through a little better. Sometimes I just get so into something I ignore all the pitfalls. Apartments in the Village being one of them apparently." *Guys being another,* I caught myself thinking.

Will smiled and wrapped his arm around my waist as we descended the stairs.

eleven

The Petting Zoo

I T TOOK ME two months to finally unpack everything and feel settled in my apartment in the West Village. Liv was right. If you were going to have a guy in your life, he really should be able to help you move. Will had definitely dropped the ball in helping me pack, but he was a huge help in the *un*packing process. He hooked up all my electronics, hung pictures, and assembled a new TV stand for me. I appreciated the help and was especially happy that Will was becoming a bigger part of my life. By August, the place finally felt like home, and I was sure I had made the right decision in stretching myself a bit in rent to move downtown. My commute was shorter, my apartment was bigger, and I was getting more sleep once I adjusted to the fire engines. I saw my friends less than I had when Liv and I lived together, but I was happy. For a few reasons.

"Oh good, you're both here," Chick said to Will and me as we stood chatting by my desk. "Are you guys free this weekend?"

"I'm around. Why, what's up?" I said. It was the dead of summer, and I should have had some fun weekend plans to look forward to, but

I didn't. Annie and Liv were in the Hamptons for the weekend, and I had opted not to go so that I could enjoy some quality time with my new apartment. And I hoped, some quality time with Will, too.

"Me too," Will said. "I have plans on Friday night but otherwise I'm free. Unless, you want me to work, in which case I'm booked solid." I wondered who he had plans with. I wanted to kick myself for not making it sound like I, too, was busy.

"Saturday afternoon we're having a birthday party for my three-year-old, Gracie. The wife is getting a petting zoo and some other bullshit. Both of you should come. Get the address of my house in Westchester from Nancy, and get her to book you a town car, too. The party starts at one."

Before I could think of a reason why I couldn't go, I heard Will answer for both of us. "Great, we'll be there." Now, *that* was interesting. Since when did we become a "we"?

"Are any of the other guys going?" Will asked.

"I invited a few of them, and their families. Most of them can't come because they have things to do with their kids this weekend. I know you don't have any kids of your own, at least not any that you recognize, but there will be a bar so you should be fine." Will laughed and went back to his desk.

"Looking forward to it, boss." I said. The truth was that I couldn't think of anything I'd rather do less than spend my Saturday watching a bunch of toddlers pet goats in Westchester. But there was no way I could miss it. Plus, it was a chance to be with Will on a weekend, which wasn't a bad thing. Although I could have done without the goats.

MSG FROM PATRICK, WILLIAM:

A—

I'll pick you up at 12:30. I don't know what you're supposed to buy for a three-year-old girl so I'll leave that up to you. Just make sure you sign my name on the card and let me know how much I owe you.

Two hours alone in a car with Will wouldn't be the worst way to spend an afternoon. I figured I'd better do some online research on what was hot on the three-year-old circuit. The last thing I wanted was to give Chick's daughter a lame birthday present.

As I opened the Toys "R" Us website I heard Marchetti's voice boom behind me. "The cookies are in! Sorry, I know they were due in July but it took me a month to get them in here."

The cookies! It had been four months and I had completely forgotten about them. I watched in amusement as Billy and three other colleagues approached Will's desk carrying huge stacks of cookies, dozens of boxes.

"Okay, boys, drop them here. Willy, you're the top purchaser this year. My daughter, Sarah, thanks you for your help. She loves her scooter."

Will stared at the cookies, completely bewildered. "Wait, Billy, there has to be a mistake. These aren't all mine. I only ordered eight boxes!" Marchetti's helpers continued to drop stacks of cookies at Will's feet. Exasperated, he asked bluntly, "What the hell is going on?"

"What do you mean? Of course they're yours. I have the form right here."

Will snatched the order form from his hand. "Someone's fucking dead. Who did this?" he asked as he waved the form in the air. "Own up to it; who did this? Reese! This has your name all over it!"

Reese strolled over. "What are you bitching about? I didn't do anything."

"Someone turned my order for eight boxes into an order for eighty boxes! What the fuck am I going to do with eighty boxes of cookies?" Billy dropped the last two stacks on the floor.

"You owe me $346. You can write me a check, cool?"

"No. Not cool. Uncool. I want to know who's responsible for me being out $346 on cookies!"

I stayed silent, pretending to examine my nails.

Reese was the first one to catch on. "Holy shit, sugar!" He laughed. "Did you do that? That's fucking classic!"

"You didn't!" Will ran over to my desk. "You didn't do this!"

"The student has become the master," Reese said as he bowed in reverence. "You're my hero." My whole body trembled with laughter. It felt good to be on the other side of the joke for once.

"You're so dead, Alex! What the hell am I supposed to do with mountains of Thin Mints and twenty boxes of peanut butter sandwich cookies that I don't even like?"

"It's official, Girlie-san: you're now my favorite person on the floor. Why haven't I ever thought of doing that?" Drew asked as he chewed a Samoa.

"I seriously have to pay for these?" Will asked.

"It's not the Girl Scouts' fault that Alex screwed you like a ten-dollar hooker. Pay up! Oh man, wait until everyone hears about this," Chick said as he beamed.

"Be afraid, Alex. Be very afraid. I'm going to get you for this!"

"I look forward to it," I said flirtatiously. "Can I have a box of Thin Mints? You seem to have some to spare."

He tossed a box at my head. "Choke on them!"

MSG FROM PATRICK, WILLIAM:
I can't believe you had the balls to do that! It's a good thing I like you or I'd ruin your life.

MSG FROM GARRETT, ALEX:
I couldn't resist. Can we still be friends?

MSG FROM PATRICK, WILLIAM:
I'll think about it. I might have to come up with a way for you to make it up to me.

I hope so, I thought to myself. That was the point.

. . . .

"WHAT DID WE GET HER anyway?" Will read messages on his BlackBerry as we sat in the back of the town car on our way to Gracie Ciccone's birthday party. I hadn't been sure what to wear for the occasion, the guest of honor wearing Huggies Pull-Ups and all. I decided on black pants and a pink silk top. Will pushed the sleeves of his yellow Polo shirt up to his elbows and smoothed his hands across his faded jeans.

"We got her a princess trunk with a bunch of dresses and shoes and wigs and stuff inside, so she can dress up like any Disney princess she wants."

"What the hell is a Disney princess?"

"You know, Snow White, Sleeping Beauty, Belle from *Beauty and the Beast*?"

"Ahhh, gotcha. I was always a Tigger fan myself."

"Hey, I called you last night. I left you a voice mail. Did you get it?" I tried not to sound annoyed, but the truth was his phone habits—or lack thereof—were driving me crazy. Picking up a phone was not difficult. We did it hundreds of times during the day.

"Sorry, yeah. I had it on silent, so I didn't see it until this morning. What did you want?"

"Nothing really. I just wanted to let you know that I got a card." And then, I couldn't help myself. "You never answer your phone."

Without missing a beat, Will said, "Thanks for dealing with the gift. Sorry I didn't call you back."

"No biggie," I lied. *You never call me back.*

I looked out the window as we drove past the beautiful suburban homes. Two kids who looked to be about twelve or thirteen walked on the sidewalk, each of them with a shiny Dalmatian on a leash. It occurred to me that these dogs probably lived better lives than most people. Then, a different thought occurred to me.

"Oh God," I gasped, squeezing Will's leg in fear. I was prepared to deal with Rick. I had been preparing myself since Chick's invitation, figuring he would be there. I wasn't prepared for Cruella. "Is Cruella going to be here, too? Am I going to have to spend the next few hours dodging both her *and* Rick in Chick's backyard?"

"No way. She and Chick don't socialize. You only have one asshole to worry about this afternoon. Don't worry."

I breathed a sigh of relief. There was no way I could handle both of them without my brain exploding. The driver slowed in front of a large Tudor-style home on multiple acres of property. Two valets directed our driver to a makeshift parking field a few blocks away. Pink balloons bounced against each other from the black mailbox at the bottom of the walk, and the children's squeals were audible from the street.

"Whatever happened to simple birthday parties? I had pin the tail on the donkey and ice cream cake. I got screwed."

"I don't think I even had birthday parties. But this is Chick, and he doesn't do anything half-assed."

"Good point."

Will pinched my elbow as we walked up the flagstone path and rang the doorbell. A young Hispanic woman answered the door. She took the gift from Will and instructed us to follow her as she led us through the foyer and into a mammoth kitchen, which was bustling with caterers, servers, and nannies. There were stainless steel Viking appliances everywhere and side-by-side dishwashers, which I'm sure came in handy when the Ciccones entertained. Pots and pans in every size possible hung from a brass rack suspended over the center island, and two large KitchenAid mixers were visible through glass-doored cabinets. French doors opened out onto a patio and an expansive backyard.

We stepped outside, into the mass of people mingling on the patio, and the housekeeper added our gift to a pile of presents on a rectangular table. We followed her onto the lawn, where we were immediately met by a waitress offering us champagne. I gladly accepted.

"I'll wait for a beer, thanks," Will replied politely. "Is it just me, or is there something effeminate about a man drinking champagne in the middle of the afternoon?"

"You're right. Chick would probably make some comment about you drinking a girlie drink. Beer's a safer choice."

Will quickly grabbed a beer out of a cooler as I scanned the crowd of men standing at the bar and spotted a few familiar faces. T.C. was there, working the crowd. I wondered which one of the ladies on the lawn was unfortunate enough to be his wife. Rick was mingling with a heavyset blond woman who once upon a time had probably been quite beautiful but who hadn't aged well. I tried to figure out which one of the preppy twin-set-clad women was Mrs. Ciccone, but it was impossible—they all looked alike.

Swell.

Scattered across the lawn were large round tables covered in alternating pink and white tablecloths with giant pastel centerpieces. As Will returned to my side, Chick spotted us and came over to say hello. I caught him subtly check his reflection in the French doors, smoothing his white shirt into the waistband of his khakis and recentering the buckle on his brown leather belt.

"Guys!" he yelled, a big grin on his face. He reached out and shook Will's hand, then planted a kiss on my cheek. "Thanks for coming. Are you all set with drinks?" Will and I both raised our glasses and assured him we were okay on the beverage front.

"You have a beautiful home, Chick. Where's the guest of honor?" I asked.

"Oh, the kids are at the petting zoo. We kept that separate because Maggie can't stand the noise the goats make." I made a mental note that Mrs. Chick's name was Maggie.

He waved for us to follow him. "Come say hello to Maggie. She wants to meet you, Alex."

Will and I followed Chick around to the side of the house. About fifty yards away was a wooden pen that contained two goats and two lambs, and a large cage that held three white rabbits. Animal handlers were helping kids pet the goats or hold the bunnies, and each kid seemed to be followed around by his or her own babysitter. It was like a little circus for three-year-olds, and it all went on without interfering with the parents' fun on the other side of the house. Chick sure did know how to throw a party.

We walked over to a cluster of tables and a petite blond woman stood when she saw us approaching. Her navy blue sheath dress swayed in the wind and blue-and-white polka dot flats were barely visible in the lush grass. She was arguably the most pulled-together woman I had ever seen in my life. Maggie removed her enormous Chanel sunglasses, revealing bright green eyes, and came to stand at her husband's side.

"Mags, you know Willy," Chick said. Will kissed her on the cheek while holding one of her hands in his.

"Great to see you, Maggie. This is some party!"

She gently hugged Will's shoulders. "Great to see you, Will. How are things with you? You still breaking hearts all over Manhattan?"

"Not on purpose, I promise."

"Now somehow I don't think that's true." She turned her attention toward me as Chick continued with the introductions.

"And this is Alex."

Maggie extended her perfectly manicured hand. "So nice to meet you, Alex! I've heard so much about you. How are you liking Cromwell?"

"It's great. Thanks for inviting us today. You have a beautiful home."

"Of course! I'm delighted to meet you, and I want you to enjoy yourself." Maggie put a hand on my arm and motioned toward the tables. "Here, Alex, why don't you come sit with us girls?" She eyed my almost empty glass of champagne. "We'll get you another drink, and you can meet some of the other ladies."

Chick seemed fine leaving me in the company of the other women, a luxury he didn't have at the office. "Great idea. Will, I want to show you my new Harley. It's in the garage."

"You ride Harleys, Chick?" I tried to picture my preppy, smart, powerful boss clad in leather chaps and a T-shirt that said IF YOU CAN READ THIS THE BITCH FELL OFF while straddling a hog. Chick promptly pointed his stubby index finger in my face.

"Don't laugh at me! Riding a motorcycle is extremely cathartic. I've had one for over ten years, but I just upgraded."

Mrs. Ciccone piped up. "We might as well have lit that money on fire for how often you're going to ride that thing."

"When you go out and make the money, Mags, you can have a say. Until then, I'll buy myself a *fleet* of motorcycles if I feel like it." Chick was smiling. Nice to know that he treated his wife the same way he treated us. At least he was consistent. "Come on, Willy." Will and Chick walked off toward the five-car garage on the other side of the house.

"Come sit, Alex." Maggie gestured kindly, so I followed her to her table. She immediately handed me a glass of white wine and offered me a seat next to her. I really liked Maggie. The three other women sitting around the table peered at me curiously.

"Ladies, this is Alex. She works for Ed."

"Hi," I said. I took a long swig of the wine. For some reason, I felt about as welcome as one of the goats in the petting zoo.

"This is Cindy Collins. You might know her husband, Tim." I shook Cindy's hand. She was a pretty woman, with hazel eyes and wavy black hair. She had freckles running across the bridge of her nose and perfectly straight white teeth. She was much prettier than he was good-looking, but that was always the case when women married for money.

"We met briefly not long after I started but I don't have much interaction with him. It's very nice to meet you," I replied, honestly. *Your husband is an asshole.*

"And this," Maggie motioned to a tall blond woman, probably in her late thirties, with legs that came up to my neck and big blue eyes that looked like sapphires embedded in her head, "is Tina Kieriakis. Her husband, Rick, works at AKS. He's been a friend and client of Chick's for years."

Ohhhh—your husband is the guy who texts me at all hours of the night to meet up with him? Another fine specimen of the male species. I gave her a wave and smiled. "Yes, Rick and I have met at a few client events. Very nice to meet you, Tina." She was stunning.

"You too, Alex. I give you a lot of credit. I swear I don't know how you do that job. I think it sounds awful. Eating lunch at your desk isn't civilized." Her voice was low and velvety. Why the hell was her husband hitting on me when he had *her* at home?

"And this lovely lady," Maggie said as she pointed at a petite brunette with light eyes and a perky nose, "is Tina's friend Bridget. Her husband is an executive at Sony and they still live in the city, in Gramercy Park."

"Nice to meet you," she said as she swirled the wine in her glass.

"Likewise." I scanned the driveway for any sign of Will and Chick, but they were nowhere to be seen. I tried to make conversation about something other than their husbands and what I heard or saw at work.

I picked neutral territory and also the only neutral person at the table. "Bridget, do you like living in Gramercy? I love that area. It's so convenient to everything and you have the subway right there."

"Oh sweetie, the subway? I haven't been on the subway in years!"

"Me neither," Tina chimed in. "Last time I was in the city, it was pouring rain, and I thought about taking it because I knew trying to get a cab outside of Grand Central would be a nightmare. But it's just so dirty and crowded, and there are always homeless people down there. It's vile."

"It isn't so bad," Maggie said brightly. I looked again toward the driveway. No Will. No Chick. It must have been one hell of a bike.

"So you came here with Will, Alex?" Maggie asked suggestively. *Oh shit.*

"Yes, we shared a car from the city," I answered.

She lowered her voice. "Is that all you're sharing? He's very cute."

Okay no, I was not going to have this discussion. Not with Maggie. Definitely not in Chick's backyard.

"We're just friends," I replied flatly. I said a silent prayer that one of the rabbits would escape so we could end this conversation.

Tina chimed in. "I used to say that, too, honey. Me and my sociology professor in college? Just friends. Me and my sister's boyfriend in high school? Just friends. I admire your modesty, but come on, you aren't fooling anyone."

Mental note, Tina's a slut, which probably explained why Rick married her. She continued probing like she was my long-lost sorority sister. "I saw the way he looked at you."

I shifted in my chair. "Sorry to disappoint you all but I promise we're just friends!" But maybe if they noticed that he liked me, then Chick had, too. *Shit.*

Tina threw her hands up in the air. "If you insist."

Maggie gently put her hand on my forearm and said, "Don't listen to her, Alex. She just loves to gossip, any way she can get it. I think we all miss the dating scene a little bit."

"Oh God, I don't miss that scene at all," Bridget said. "All the stress about who should call whom, is he seeing other people, the three-day rule, all that nonsense. Plus, I was constantly stressed out because I always double-booked and could never keep anyone's name straight. It was a full-time job dating in Manhattan! I couldn't be more thankful that those days are behind me. Honestly, Alex, how do you stand it?"

I wasn't looking forward to explaining to her that I actually didn't date much, because I was too busy with work, and I certainly wasn't going to mention Will. Thankfully, Chick and Will reappeared just then. I inadvertently exhaled a deep long breath. They must have been gone for fifteen minutes, but it felt like an hour.

Chick put his hands on Maggie's bony shoulders and asked her sweetly, "Are you all getting acquainted with Alex?"

"Oh yes, absolutely. We're having a great time," she replied.

Chick nodded. "Good."

I felt a hand on my shoulder and a familiar voice say, "Good to see you again, Alex. It's been a while." Rick grabbed a chair from a nearby table and pulled it up right next to me. "I see you've met my wife and the rest of the ladies. This is some house Chick has here, huh?"

I felt like the other woman, like I was doing something wrong just by virtue of sitting next to Tina's husband in front of her. I smiled innocently and said, "Yes, it's lovely. How have you been, Rick?" Not that I cared.

"I've been good, sweetheart. Thanks for asking. Business is good;

I'm not complaining. So, Chick, how is Alex doing? Are you teaching her everything you know?"

Chick smiled. "She's doing great, but she's still got a lot to learn."

"I could help train her if you want," Rick said with a wink. No one seemed to think that was strange, including Tina—except, thank God, for Chick, who shot Rick a look warning him to back off.

Rick rubbed his hands together and stood suavely. "Well, excuse me, ladies. I'm going to run inside, but I'll be back in a few minutes. Can I get anyone anything while I'm in there?"

"We have waiters, dumbass," Chick said.

Rick chuckled. "Indeed you do." He stood and headed back toward the kitchen. Chick motioned toward the house. "I'm going to go check on the caterers, but why don't you two come scope out my wine cellar? Or would you rather stay here, Alex?" I almost knocked my chair over I jumped up so fast.

"No, I'd love to see it. Thanks so much for introducing me to everyone, Maggie. It was so nice to meet you all." The ladies waved as we left them and headed for the house.

"It's right down that staircase in there," Chick said as we stepped into the kitchen. He pointed to a small room off the kitchen, which, on closer inspection, turned out to be a butler's pantry. "Don't try to take anything though, Willy; I know exactly what's down there. Girlie, keep an eye on him for me. If something goes missing, I'm going to blame you."

"Consider it done," I said.

We descended the staircase to the wine cellar. The room was covered from floor to ceiling with hundreds of bottles of wine, and there was a thermostat-like contraption on the wall by the door. I didn't know much about wine other than the fact that I liked it, but Will was very impressed by the selection.

I removed a bottle from its rack to see if I recognized the label.

"Don't touch those! If you break one, Chick will kick your ass," Will said as he took the bottle from my hand and replaced it in its slot.

"I'm not going to start juggling the Brunello. Chill out, old man."

"Old man?" He replaced the bottle and turned to face me, somewhat within my personal space. Not that I minded.

"Well, honestly, you're twenty-seven. I mean you're way older than I am, in case you didn't know."

"And how do you feel about older men?" He took a step closer and I stepped back. However, the wine cellar was, well, an *intimate* space, and I couldn't move much farther without disturbing the collection of saucy cabernets. My back was already flush against the section of wine from France.

"It depends. Some of them I don't mind." He put his hands on my hips and kissed me. My mind was racing. It wasn't that it was weird for us to be kissing—I mean we were seeing each other—but somehow making out in Chick's wine cellar didn't seem like a good idea (though part of me felt it could be kinda fun, blatantly breaking Chick's rules in his own house). Still, I didn't think we needed to tempt fate and have someone catch us. Trading floors are the most efficient distribution of gossip in the free world. If anyone saw us, Chick would find out about it, and I really didn't want to go back to the mailroom.

"Chick would kill us if he found out you kissed me in his wine cellar. It probably raises the air temperature or something," I said. It certainly was raising mine. I'd have given my left arm to not be at Chick's house at this moment. But, sadly, I was.

"You're scared of the big bad boss? He's not a tyrant," he said as he reluctantly released me.

"Let's go back upstairs before he comes looking and I have to tell him you stole a bottle." He leaned in and kissed me again, and for a few seconds I couldn't have cared less if Chick came down here and saw us himself. I needed to get out of the wine cellar. We were interrupted by a creak on the staircase. Probably a good thing.

"Well, what are you guys doing down here?" I turned to see Rick standing in the doorway and immediately felt every synapse in my brain begin to fire. Being trapped in a small room in the basement with Rick was not my idea of a good time.

"Alex and I are trying to figure out if Chick would notice if we rearranged some of his bottles." Will smacked Rick on his back. "What do you think? How much trouble would I be in if I just swapped a few?"

Rick chuckled. "I think you'd get fired, Will. I wouldn't recommend fucking with your boss's wine cellar."

"Yeah, Alex didn't think so either." Will clapped his hands together as if it would somehow eradicate the awkward tension in the room. "What brings you down here?"

"Chick sent me down here to grab a bottle of Barbaresco for Maggie, and he asked me to send you back upstairs, Will. He wants to introduce you to someone."

"Let's go, Alex," Will said as he headed for the stairs.

"Actually, Alex, why don't you stay here and help me find the wine for Maggie? Go ahead, Will; I won't let her get lost, I promise."

"In the wine cellar? I think that's unlikely," I said as my stomach flip-flopped with anxiety.

"See you back outside." Will shot me a concerned look as he reluctantly left me alone with Rick and hundreds of bottles of wine. If I drank all of them, it wouldn't put me at ease.

Rick began to pull bottles from their slots, checking the labels. "Alex, you never respond to my text messages."

I smiled a tight-lipped smile. "Oh, I don't check my phone all that often. Sorry about that."

"Really? I don't know too many single twentysomething girls who don't have their phones glued to their hand at all times."

"How many single twentysomething girls do you know?" I asked.

"Not enough."

"Your wife is very nice." I thought maybe shifting the focus to the gorgeous woman sitting in the backyard would bring this conversation back to more neutral territory.

"She is very nice. She lacks something though."

Yeah, a clue.

"Not from where I'm standing."

"You're spunky. I like that. Most girls are boring, or in this industry, brutish. There's not a lot of femininity to women in finance. You're an anomaly."

"Thanks. I try."

"Why won't you have dinner with me?" he asked as he circled the room.

"I . . . don't think that's a very good idea. Chick wouldn't like it." I wondered if it would be poor form to push past him and run upstairs. Probably. "I think we should go back upstairs. Did you find the wine yet?"

Rick smirked and nodded as he removed a bottle and hefted it in his hand. "Sure, you can go back upstairs. But, Alex, going forward, keep your phone on you. Don't forget, I'm the client. You never know when I might need you."

I nodded and left the wine cellar and practically sprinted up the stairs.

I hurried through the kitchen and found Will outside on the patio. I tugged on his arm and whispered, "I think it's time to go."

"Are you all right? He didn't do anything stupid, did he?"

"No. But I want to leave."

"Okay. I'm sorry I left you down there, but I didn't really have a choice. Let's start making the rounds."

After we had said good-bye to the Stepford wives, Chick, and T.C., Will and I collected our car from the valet. Will held my hand in the car on the way back and talked more to the driver than he did to me, but that was okay. I didn't know what to say anyway, so silence was fine by me. When we reached the Triboro Bridge, Will told the driver that we would only be making one stop, and then gave him his address. He squeezed my hand and I looked out the window, trying to remember if I had bothered to shave my legs that morning. The car pulled over on the corner of Seventy-Ninth Street and Columbus Avenue, and Will held my hand tightly as we strolled south. I still couldn't remember if I had shaved my legs, but I figured I'd take my chances.

twelve

I'm Responsible for the Destruction of Corporate Feminism

W ILL WAS MAKING it very hard for me to focus. I found I spent all of my spare time and most of the time that wasn't spare thinking about him and, more important, wondering if he was thinking about me. September was busy, and I was expected to pull my weight. Today especially, wasn't a good time to be preoccupied since the Federal Open Market Committee was meeting. Every six to eight weeks the FOMC, a committee within the Federal Reserve made up of really smart people who serve as Federal Reserve governors and the presidents of the Federal Reserve banks (read: supergeeks), met to decide what to do with interest rates. The day they released their rate announcement to the public was one of the most important days on the Street. Most people didn't know this committee existed or think that it mattered. But whether or not people knew it, it did. Every time someone discovered they could refinance a mortgage and save themselves money in monthly payments, they could thank the FOMC. Every time they tried to get a loan for a car, a business, or a credit card, and discovered the interest rate had risen, they could blame the FOMC. There wasn't a person in

America who wasn't affected by the decisions made in that meeting, except most Americans had no idea. If they did, they'd probably spend a little more time watching CNBC in lieu of the Home Shopping Network. Wall Street people cared about every single word of the one-page statement issued by the FOMC. We cared if they used a comma instead of the semicolon they used in the previous statement. We cared if they replaced the word *should* with the word *could,* or the word *growth* with the word *stability.* We cared. About everything.

"Alex," Drew snapped one morning as he waved his hand in front of my face. "Earth to Girlie! Hello? What the hell is wrong with you lately? Daydreaming isn't allowed on this desk."

"Sorry, Drew. I'm just a little distracted, that's all."

"Distracted? Of all days to be distracted Alex, today is not it. The FOMC decision is in a half hour."

"I know. I'm sorry." I needed to get Will out of my head before he cost me my job.

"Don't be sorry, just focus. Charlie's out today so I need your help."

"How could he not come in today? I was under the impression that missing the rate announcement was an offense punishable by death."

"His wife's in labor with their fifth or sixth kid or something. She could be in labor for twenty-four hours for all he knows. And if he wants to afford to send his five or six kids to school in Manhattan, he really should get his priorities straight."

"You know, if I was married, and in labor, and my husband wasn't there because he was worried that the Fed might change the funds rate, I think I'd divorce him."

"Then don't marry a guy from the Street. Are you cool to help on his lights?"

"Of course," I said, glancing down at the rows of phone extensions on Charlie's board. They were dormant now, but I knew that in half an hour or so they'd be flashing like Christmas lights. I had to rise to the occasion and keep calm, cool, and collected. I knew that today would be a day I could prove myself with the guys. I had to pass this test with flying colors or I was screwed. Even though I couldn't yet handle direct client calls, I could field the other non-trade-related phone calls, no problem. I was practically an expert at that by this point.

"Thanks." Drew put his headset back on and hit a light on his phone board. Conversation over. I followed suit and put on my headset.

I still wasn't supposed to answer the direct client-to-desk lines. If you answered one of those lines, you usually ended up talking to some angry guy barking a buy or a sell order into your ear. There's an urban finance legend about an analyst who worked here a long time ago who picked up one of the direct lines and ended up talking to a portfolio manager who gave him an order to buy some futures contracts. Since he hadn't passed all of his exams, the SEC could've thrown his ass in jail for violating securities law. When the boss found out he executed the trade, he was fired, and the SEC fined the desk a *lot* of money for failing to properly supervise employees. Last anyone heard, that guy was working a hot dog cart on the corner of Seventh Avenue and Thirty-Eighth Street; whatever he was up to, he sure as hell wasn't working in the industry.

When I wasn't focusing on the markets or thinking about Will, I was worrying about Rick and his incessant text messages and phone calls. Over the last few weeks I'd been getting a lot more of them. Maybe eight or nine a day. And that didn't include weekends, when sometimes they started as early as 7:00 A.M. Since Rick was a client, I couldn't exactly write back something like, "You're gross, old, and married, and those are the three very unattractive qualities," or "Fuck off." I had thought about it, though. The Will situation wasn't much better as he continued to confuse me by being attentive and fun one minute and then suddenly totally MIA the next. I didn't know what to do about either of them. Since I couldn't manage to come up with any solutions on my own, I decided to seek answers from a higher power: astrology. In retrospect, that was a mistake. A big one.

I probably should have waited until after the FOMC announcement to replace my trading systems with the astrology website. But I figured it would only take a minute or two to check out "Aries Lucky Love Days." Hell, I figured, glancing down at the still-quiet phone board, it'll take three, five minutes, *tops*.

Oops. You'd be surprised how much information you can get on your love life from astrology websites.

Fifteen minutes later, when the committee surprised the market by lowering the target interest rate, the market went crazy. Instantly, phones started ringing. All of them. Simultaneously.

Every salesperson was on the phone, shouting orders at the traders, scribbling in their notebooks and ordering me to book all the trades. When one of the outside lines started ringing, Chick gesticulated wildly at me to pick it up.

"Cromwell," I said cheerfully.

"Is Charlie there?" some angry-sounding guy snapped.

"Umm, no, Charlie's wife is in labor so he's not . . ."

"Offer a hundred million five-year notes," he ordered.

Uh-oh. This was not supposed to happen. I had answered a normal line. This was the line that the guys' wives call, and the line delivery people use when they're in the lobby with pizza. What the hell was this guy doing, asking me to offer a hundred million five-year notes? I didn't know how to do that. I knew who traded five-year notes—a really scary guy across the floor who always yelled and threw his phone at people. He was someone I planned on avoiding for as long as humanly possible.

"Excuse me?" I already knew this wasn't going well. The market could move a lot in a split second. Delaying the trade to ask someone to repeat something was bad. Very, very bad.

"Offer me a hundred million fucking five-year notes!"

Fine! You don't have to yell. Jeez.

I knew that I was supposed to have the trading platforms on my screens at all times, but I had taken that screen down when I pulled up my horoscope. When I glanced at my computer to try to see what price I should expect to hear back from the trading desk, I saw that Aries' lucky love days were the eighth and the twenty-third. *Shit.*

"Offer a hundred million five-year notes!" I screamed frantically. Everything happened so fast I didn't have time to be scared, or to second-guess myself. My first trade! I felt every nerve ending on my body tingling with adrenaline.

I heard the scary trader scream, "Four!" At least, that's what I thought he said.

"Four!" I relayed curtly to the client. The client who would have been talking to Charlie had Charlie not knocked up his wife for the fifth—or sixth—time.

"Done."

"Done at four!" I screamed back to the trader. I'm a rock star. I not only just did my first trade, I did my first trade with a really scary trader, and a big trade. If Adam, the smug analyst from the boat cruise, were here I would have turned to him and said, now THAT is trading size! How do you like me now Princeton, huh?

It was a good thing that Adam wasn't there.

"What the hell are you talking about done at four? The market's at ten! I said *who's* it *for!*" the trader screamed. "You don't tell me when I'm done, I tell YOU when YOU'RE done!"

Oh shit. I had just sold bonds at a ridiculously low price; if the trade went through, quick math told me I had just cost the desk roughly $200,000. Fuck me.

Immediately, Chick came running, screaming and waving his hands the way an umpire does when he calls an out at the plate. "Say nothing done! Say nothing done, no trade! No trade!" Chick dove across the desk like he was on a slip and slide, knocking papers, pens, notebooks, and one BlackBerry onto the floor as he ripped the phone out of my hand. "Who the fuck is this?" he screamed, demanding a response. "Pete, what the hell are you doing trying to get something done at four? You know the market isn't there. You're trying to fuck us over and take advantage of a junior person? Come on, man, what are you doing?"

Drew sprinted past me toward the trading desk to try to calm the trader and assure him that we were taking care of the mistake, that he wouldn't lose money as a result of my stupidity. I sat frozen in the chair, afraid to breathe. I was pretty sure I was going to be fired, provided that Chick didn't have a massive coronary or a stroke and drop dead first. He called down to the trader and told him to get on the line and help with damage control. They were on the phone for another five minutes and when they hung up, Chick threw his pen down on my desk.

"Do you want to know how much you just cost us? And you were lucky, Alex. You were really lucky that the client was willing to meet us halfway because he knew I caught him being a slimy bastard by taking advantage of your inexperience." He paused for effect as I stared at him, fighting back my tears.

"Ninety-three thousand dollars." He snapped his fingers. "Gone. Just like that. Why the hell didn't you know where the market was? Where were your screens? If you knew the market was trading at ten or eleven, you would have known he didn't say four. What the hell were you looking at? I taught you better than that!"

"Ninety-three thousand?" That was more than what most people made in a year. I just lost someone's annual income because I was reading my horoscope. I am too stupid to live.

"I'm so sorry, Chick. I panicked. I wasn't expecting anyone to trade on that line. He caught me off guard and I didn't know what to do. I'm sorry."

"Sorry isn't going to begin to fix this mess. The trader wants you fired for being an idiot, and now I look like I haven't taught you a damn thing since you started."

Fired? I can't get fired. Not when I've already dealt with so much shit in an effort to reach this point! I just did my first trade! Granted, I fucked it up. Royally. But this was the moment I had been working toward since the day I started.

"Chick, I . . . I don't know what to say." I could feel the rest of the group staring at me. He should have just dragged me to Times Square and flogged me like they did in the old days.

"There's nothing you *can* say. Get your head out of your ass, and start paying attention. You don't want the reputation of being an idiot, and right now that's what the trading desk thinks you are. We'll talk about this later when things slow down. Get back to your desk and book some trades. No more phones for you today."

I slithered back to my chair, wishing I could will myself to become invisible.

Scary trader stood when he saw Chick approach and threw his hands up in the air. "What the fuck was that, Chick? Is she kidding me?" The rest of the trading desk kept their eyes on their own screens, but the trader was screaming so loud I was pretty sure Jashim could hear him out in the hallway.

"I know, man. She fucked up. I'll take care of it."

"How? Are you going to eat my loss? Fuck!" The trader banged his fist on his desk as he fell back in his chair.

An hour later, when things had quieted down, Reese strolled over.

"Rough one, sugar, huh? How are you holding up?" he asked, as he set a cookie on my desk.

"I'm screwed, Reese. I made myself look like an imbecile, and I made Chick look like he hasn't taught me a single thing since I started. Why the hell didn't Charlie come in today? I really think his wife can manage without him. That's why God invented nurses and epidurals." I was so embarrassed, I just wanted to go home. Which was a problem, since it was only 3:30.

"Nah, don't worry. Back in the day when we had to wear ties, whenever a young guy fucked up his first trade, we would cut his tie off and tack it to the wall. The wall of fame—or shame, depending on how you looked at it. Every guy here had his tie up on that wall. Now, I'm not sure what the hell we would cut off you to put on the wall that wouldn't get us fired. But, the point is, everyone makes mistakes. Learn from them and move on. You don't know it now, but today is the greatest day of your career."

"Are you insane?"

"I mean it! How the hell do you think you learn? No one remembers their really good days. Everyone remembers the ones that made them want to off themselves. Today's yours. Congratulations. You'll be a much better salesperson going forward after having fucked up so badly today."

I was starting to feel marginally better. He was right. I guess everyone was going to screw up at some point, and unfortunately, when you screwed up in this business, you lost money. It was simply an occupational hazard. "You think Chick will be okay with it then?"

"Fuck no!" Reese burst into hysterics. "Chick's going to shred you like a chicken, and I don't want to be anywhere near you when that happens. But, just remember, we've all been there. Just relax, refocus, and get back to work."

Easy for him to say.

Thankfully, the rest of the afternoon was hectic and I think Chick was too tired to have a meaningful conversation with me. When most of the group went to the bar for post FOMC cocktails, I skulked down to the lobby, uninterested in anything except going to bed. Surprisingly, Will fell into step with me as I hurried to the exit. He grabbed my arm just before I entered a revolving door.

"Not a good day for you, huh, Alex?" He leaned in close and whispered, "Don't worry about it. Chick will fix it. I promise."

"Screw you," I barked. "It's your fault."

"My fault?" he said, surprised. "How do you figure that?"

"You distracted me, and because of you, I was checking my horoscope instead of paying attention to the market. What happened to me today is a perfect example of why some people think that a woman can't be president."

He looked at me like I had just sprouted five heads. "You've lost it. It's official."

"No, I haven't! You know exactly what I'm talking about. The people who think that women are too emotional and therefore a woman can't be trusted to have her hand on the button. You know, in case one day her husband pisses her off and she responds by blowing up the universe. I did that today. I let my emotions completely distract me, and I blew up my universe."

"You were thinking about me? Well, I guess I'm flattered."

Okay no, that wasn't my point. "Don't flatter yourself. I was thinking about how you never answer my calls on weekends, and how I have no idea what we're doing from one day to the next. Or if there's even a 'we'—um, I mean 'us.' I was thinking about how much of an idiot you are." I ended our conversation when Cruella stepped off the escalator and headed our way. I was hoping she wouldn't notice me. Just in case my day hadn't sucked enough, she did.

"Alex!" she chirped shrilly. "Nice job today. Really. You know, next time some poor girl's résumé comes in front of management, they'll consider hiring her, and then someone will remember you, and the mess you made today. And even if that girl is bright, talented, and motivated, it won't matter, because they'll take her résumé and throw it in the trash. Instead they'll hire some guy from a no-name school from nowhere, who probably doesn't know his ass from his elbow, but will have enough common sense to not read tarot cards on the desk in the middle of the day. Congratulations on killing the futures of innumerable women on Wall Street. Well done."

Will was pretending to check his BlackBerry and said nothing in my defense. Nice. With a sniff of her nose and a hitch of her briefcase, Cruella stomped past us through the revolving doors and into the backseat of her waiting town car. Apparently she was in a rush—probably on her way to steal toys from orphans.

"Don't let her get to you. She's a bitch." Will put his hand on the small of my back in a futile attempt to make me feel better. It didn't. As we exited the building, I wondered if the market for hot dog carts on Seventh Avenue was saturated. I was pretty sure that's where I was headed.

I APOLOGIZED TO THE TRADER at the end of the week, telling him how sorry I was and how stupid I was and how I would never be so ill-prepared on the desk again. He asked me if I had learned something from it, and he thanked me for being Girlie enough to admit my mistake and beg forgiveness. All things considered, it could have been much worse. Reese was right. I was a member of the team, and as such, most things would be forgiven once the person you pissed off berated you and made you feel like the biggest idiot on earth. In this case, it was hard to argue that I didn't deserve it. Quite frankly, sometimes you just need to get your ass kicked.

After my disastrous performance on FOMC day, it took me a month before I felt comfortable answering phones again, and six weeks before Reese stopped yelling "Fore!" as he pretended to swing a golf club every time I walked by. Slowly though, the humiliation faded, a tenuous confidence returned, and I was able to refocus on my career.

People had started to chatter about problems in the markets, low rumblings about some of the structured products that Chick told me most people didn't understand. After he had pointed out the really smart guys who traded them on my first day, I didn't think much about them. I was way too busy learning my own bizarre products to worry about what other people were doing. Now it seemed that understanding what they did for a living was going to become more important. We had a sense of it, although none of us knew then what we know now. In fact, the markets going crazy the day of the FOMC debacle was, in retrospect, an early sign of trouble.

Indian summer ended and the tables at the bars outside were packed up and moved inside for winter, and so did we. You could see the first signs of extreme stress start to manifest on the faces of a few traders across the floor, but we didn't worry too much about it. Whatever happened in other areas of the floor didn't concern us too much. The end of the year was looming, only a few months away. Since we were paid at the end of the year based on how much money our individual group made, and our group, the government bond sales desk, was doing very well, there didn't seem to be much cause for concern.

At least, not yet.

thirteen

Eat My Dust, Tony the Tiger

T HE FALL FLEW by, and I found myself thrown into the party season once again. The dreaded December ten pounds had returned,
but this year, I managed to make it through the entire season without
calling any managers fat fucks, so that was good. It was hard to believe
another year had gone by.

Bonus day was tense and emotionally charged, and I sat quietly
while Chick handed out compensation to each member of the group
from his office. When it was my turn, I began to sweat and tremble.
I prayed he didn't hold my trade error against me. I had worked hard
since then. Hopefully, it was hard enough.

"Sit down," Chick said as he sprinkled fish food in his tank.

I nudged the chair closer to his desk. Considering I received twenty
grand last year for only four months of work, I was hoping for sixty for
the full year. Since I still didn't have my own accounts, it seemed like a
lot, and since I had lost more than that on my botched trade, it was probably unlikely.

"As you know, today is bonus communication day. The group had a good year as a whole, and the firm had a good year, too, so we're able to pay people well for their performance. Now, that being said, you're still relatively new and don't cover any accounts yourself. So your pay is adjusted to reflect that."

"Of course. I understand."

Shit.

He held a single piece of white paper in his hands. It took all of my willpower to not jump over his desk and snatch it from him.

"Expectations in this business can often get out of hand, so I hope you won't be disappointed with your bonus. Remember that you're still young, and there's lots of room for growth."

Shit.

"It's not a problem, Chick. I just want to keep learning. I want to cover my own accounts. The extra cash is great—don't get me wrong—but I'll appreciate anything."

"That's the right attitude to have. That's why I've decided to promote you to associate."

"Promote?" A promotion after a year and a half at the firm was unheard of. Standard practice was to spend three years as an analyst.

Eat my dust, Tony the Tiger, buyer of Cox.

"A promotion means that for 2008 you'll have a fifteen-thousand-dollar increase in your base salary."

"Does a promotion mean that I don't have to get the Friday pizzas anymore?"

"Just like a woman. Never satisfied." He grinned.

"I don't know what to say. You won't be disappointed, I promise."

"Good. Here you go." He slid the piece of paper across his desk as I struggled to locate the only line item I was interested in reading.

My eyes scanned the numbers before finally focusing on the sum at the bottom of the page. Damn secretaries. They had messed up my form. "Umm, Chick? I think this is a typo. See right here?" I pointed a finger at the offending number, which elicited a chuckle from Chick.

"That's not a typo."

"It's not a typo?"

"It's not a typo."

"It says $110,000."

"Correct."

"Plus you're increasing my base salary to the associate level?"

"Correct."

"So, just so we're clear, you're paying me $175,000 for the year?"

"It's nice to know my new associate can add."

"Holy shit," I said, as I struggled to regain control of my poker face. "I just wasn't expecting anything near this. I thought the number would be in the mid-five-figure range."

"You're welcome, but we aren't done yet. It's not quite that simple."

"Oh." I reluctantly remained in the chair, hoping that there wasn't a "but" following my windfall of cash.

"If you notice, a portion of your bonus is allocated in Cromwell stock that's restricted."

"That means I can't sell it for a certain amount of time, right?"

"Correct. The vesting schedule is 20 percent a year. In five years, you'll be able to sell all your shares at the market price."

"Cool." I didn't really see the problem. A little annoying that it wasn't all in cash, but in the future the Cromwell stock price could be twice what it is now. I could double my money! You've got to love finance.

"However, if you quit or leave the firm, or God forbid are fired for cause, you forfeit all of your unvested stock. Do you understand what that means?"

"It means from here on out, if I quit or get fired, it's going to cost me money."

"Essentially. You're now a Cromwell shareholder, which should make you work even harder for the firm. Capiche?"

"Capiche. Is that what people mean when they talk about golden handcuffs?"

"Precisely. I just made it much harder for you to leave and go somewhere else."

"I don't want to work anywhere else. I love it here!"

"Good."

"One more question? How much of my total bonus is in stock?"

"Fifty-five thousand dollars. The markets are going to be a lot harder in the immediate future, so an increased portion of pay is going to be in stock. It might look good on paper, but people are going to have a lot less cash this year. Keep your mouth shut and don't advertise you're happy with your pay. Not everyone will be."

"I promise I won't." If there had been room, and I wasn't worried about accidentally kicking Chick in the face, I would have done cartwheels.

"One more thing, Girlie." Chick said slowly, clearly enjoying dragging out the conversation. I held my breath. "Despite the colossal trade fuckup, you seem to be grasping things quickly, and I know the rest of the team believes in your ability. We have some small accounts that people want off their plates, and I think maybe you're ready to cover them. They are high maintenance and can be difficult at times, but they'll be a great learning experience for you. If you need help or have any questions, come to me or anyone else on the desk. Congratulations, Al. From folding chair to sales babe in a little over a year. I must be one hell of a mentor."

"You are!" I said.

"Stop sucking up. I hate brownnosers. Now, we start all over. Everyone begins the year with a big fat zero next to his name. And you'll be happy to know, we have a new kid starting in January. You have less than a month left being the new chick. Congrats, and go get 'em."

"I will, boss!"

I skipped out of Chick's office, the sheet of paper discreetly tucked away in my pocket. I couldn't help but smile when I returned to my desk. The guys were all used to hiding their emotions on bonus day, unwilling to alert someone to the fact that they thought they were underpaid. I had no clue how to conceal my excitement. $110,000. That was more money than I had dreamed of this year. It was more money than a lot of people dreamed of in a lifetime—even if half of it wasn't really money.

"Wow, someone's happy. I heard Chick was planning to promote you. Did he?" Drew asked as I spun my chair in circles.

"He did! How great is that! I'm an associate now. Do you know what that means?"

"You're still keeping your subtitle of pizza bitch until there's someone more junior than you around here. You realize that, right? The good news is, he hired a new analyst, I think, so there might be a light at the end of your gofer tunnel."

"Yeah, fine. I can carry pizzas for a while longer if that's what I need to do. That's not what I was talking about. I'm getting my own accounts! He said that there are some small ones people want to get rid of. I'm at least a full year ahead of schedule!"

"Congrats, Alex. I'm happy for you. Going shopping after work?"

"Yup! Today is one of those days I just really love my job."

"Everyone loves their job on bonus day. Enjoy it. There will be lean years. Two thousand eight is going to be tough with this mortgage mess. Trust me."

"Impossible," I said smugly. "What could possibly happen?"

A FTER WORK I WENT SHOPPING in Midtown and picked up a new bag I'd been coveting and two new pairs of shoes. It was, quite simply, a perfect day. When I got home, I felt like I was floating through the lobby, and I couldn't wait to get up to my apartment and open a bottle of wine. The doorman stopped me on my way to the elevator and handed me an enormous bouquet of white roses. Things just kept getting better.

When I entered my apartment, I dropped the bags on the floor, placed the vase on my coffee table, and fished the card from in between the blooms, fully expecting it to say "Congratulations. Love, Mom and Dad."

No such luck.

Congratulations. I had no doubt your skills were advanced for your age. I'd imagine that's true out of the office, too. XO Rick

The flowers suddenly seemed more menacing than cheerful.

How does he know where I live? I glanced at the door to make sure I'd remembered to dead-bolt it behind me. I took the flowers and threw them in the garbage can, because they were ruining my good mood. I decided that if the unwanted attention didn't abate, I'd talk to Chick about it. I knew he noticed it, so I convinced myself that he wouldn't be surprised. Chick would look out for me, I knew it. So I tried instead to focus on the positive and the things that were going well in my life. Which at the moment was just about everything. Wall Street and I may have gotten off to a bit of a rocky start, but now all I wanted to do was get back to work and kick off 2008.

THE DIFFICULT THING about having my own clients was that with them came expectations above and beyond what I was used to. I spent most of January entertaining. I introduced myself to everyone over lunches, dinners, and in-office meetings all over the East Coast. I was exhausted, but so intent on proving myself that adrenaline was compensating for the ridiculous lack of sleep. For the most part, all my accounts were friendly and wanted to give me a chance to prove myself. I wasn't going to let anyone down: not the clients, not Chick, and not myself. I spent hours studying the markets, economics, and current trends in the market. Before I knew it, it was February. January had come and gone, and I think I spent a total of twenty waking hours actually home in New York, doing non-work-related stuff. I wasn't able to see Will as much as I wanted due to my new workload. Thankfully, he understood, and while I missed spending time with him, I was sure eventually things would return to normal. Whatever "normal" was.

One bitterly cold morning I heard Reese chuckling from the end of the row. I checked the clock on the wall. Ten o'clock. "Whoa, Chick, what the hell happened to you? You look like you were dragged in here by a garbage truck," Reese said as he strolled over with his swine sandwich.

"Please tell me you have more of those, Reesey?" Chick groaned.

Reese grabbed one out of a box on the floor and threw it on his desk. "Rough night?"

"Rougher morning. I was in AC last night. Won twelve grand."

Atlantic City is two hours away. He left the office at a normal time last night, so he couldn't have gotten there before 9:00 with traffic. Why would anyone go all the way to Atlantic City for a few hours in the middle of the week?

"Traffic bad this morning?"

"Traffic? Come on, Reese. I didn't take a car, I took a chopper from the Wall Street pad. Me, Rick, and a bunch of the guys from AKS. One of the young kids Rick works with just broke up with his girlfriend, or rather, his girlfriend broke up with him, so I thought he could use some cheering up. We picked up some beers and took the helicopter down after the close, gambled all night, and flew back this morning. Worked out great for me. I won twelve Gs, but the kid lost three, so now he's out a girlfriend and three grand. Tough morning for him."

Chick emptied his bottle of Advil into his palm and swallowed them dry. He turned to me. "Alex, go take the new girl and get me a Gatorade from your boyfriend at the coffee stand."

"My boyfriend?"

"Jashim. Every time I'm up there he asks me about you. 'Oh, how's Alex doing today? Oh, bring Alex her special coffee for me, the way she likes it.' "

"You have never brought me a coffee from him."

"What the fuck do I look like, Alex, a barista?"

T HANK GOD FOR THE NEW GIRL. No matter how long you spend on a desk, you're always the new kid until you're not. Patty was the new analyst Chick hired after she graduated from college. Typically, she

would have started in July like I did, but the markets were getting difficult, and a lot of firms were delaying start dates until after the end of the
year, to keep payroll count constant. She started in January, and while
she didn't know it yet, she was immensely lucky to have me as a supe-
rior. I could've used someone like me when I started. The fact that Chick
hired another girl made me especially happy, because it was proof that
Cruella was wrong about me.

I glanced at Patty, sitting demurely in the folding chair, clutching
a notebook. She'd been here a month, but she still looked terrified. I
didn't miss those days, and I didn't miss that freaking folding chair. So
I did what I would've wanted Cruella to do for me when I started, you
know, if she had a soul.

"Come. Let's walk," I ordered as I approached her chair. She dutifully followed me off the floor.

"Where are we going?"

"I want coffee, and Chick needs a Gatorade. He wants me to take you
with me. I also need to go to the ATM in the lobby."

"Chick scares the hell out of me," she said.

"Yeah, he has that effect on new people."

I bought Patty a coffee and grabbed Chick's Gatorade from the
refrigerator. Patty seemed nice, smart, and completely clueless as to
how things worked on the floor. She reminded me a lot of myself; at
least, the way I used to be.

"Don't worry about Chick," I said. "He and some guys went out partying last night and he's a little hungover this morning. Just stay out of
his way today and you should be fine. Oh, and make sure you keep the
folding chair out of the aisle. The guys hate when they trip over it. It
sounds stupid, but trust me it's not."

"Okay, thanks for the advice," she said as we made our way down to
the lobby.

As soon as we had cleared the turnstiles in the lobby Patty said,
"Can I ask you something? Off the record?"

"Sure."

She looked behind her to make sure no one was near enough to hear our conversation. "There's a cute guy in the back row, what's his name?"

My blood ran cold. "His name's Will," I said curtly.

"He's really cute. Is he single?"

"Technically."

"What does that mean?"

"It means we're sort of seeing each other, but we don't advertise it, so please don't say anything to anyone, or I'll have no choice but to make your life miserable."

Her cheeks flushed and she stammered, clearly afraid that she'd just alienated the only person who had bothered to get to know her. "I'm soooo sorry," she assured me. "I won't say anything, I promise. Wow, that must make work a lot more fun, huh?" She elbowed me, which made me smile. I had a female friend at work. Cool.

"You'd think so, but it doesn't exactly work that way." I sighed. "Not a word to anyone, capiche?"

"Capiche." We headed back to the floor talking about normal girlie things: where she got her sweater (J. Crew), if I knew of any good wine bars on the east side (Fig & Olive, across the street from Blooming-dales), where you can get the best eyebrow wax for under twenty bucks (nowhere that cheap on the island of Manhattan, assuming you want to have eyebrows left when you're finished). When we got back to the desk, she grabbed her chair and set it up right next to Chick, ignoring the advice I had just given her. It's as if I taught her nothing.

"Where the fuck did you and Alex go? When I said to get me a Gatorade, I meant from the hallway, not from Midtown," he growled.

"I'm sorry, I hope I didn't miss anything," she said, apologetically.

I had just taken my seat when Chick whistled to get the group's attention. "Guys!" He clapped his hands together the way most people do to their dogs when they want them to stop digging in the backyard. "I'm hungry, who's hungry?" The group whistled and cheered—as per usual, everyone was hungry. Nothing new there.

"Hands up if you want cheesesteaks for lunch. Leave 'em up so I can count them." Hands shot up everywhere, as everyone resumed their conversations and went back to conducting business as usual. Chick counted the hands in sales before he turned his attention to the trading desk. While the traders didn't report to Chick, he liked to buy lunch for them, because a happy trading desk would be more likely to go easy on salespeople when they screwed up (say for example, when they lost ninety-three grand).

"So, Patty, where are you from?" Chick asked, already knowing the answer.

"Philadelphia," Patty replied, without missing a beat.

"I assume you've eaten your fair share of cheesesteaks over the years?"

"Absolutely! There's nothing better than a Philly cheesesteak."

"What's your favorite cheesesteak place in Philly?" he asked.

"Well, the two best places are Pat's and Geno's. They're across the street from each other. I like Geno's better, but they're both great."

Slowly, Chick reached into his jacket and removed a set of keys that he tossed onto Patty's lap. "Then let's do that. We'll decide which we like better. I'm ordering one hundred cheesesteaks, fifty from Pat's and fifty from Geno's. You know how to get to Philly, I assume, since you lived there your whole life? Go get them."

Patty didn't move, but I could see the skin on the back of her neck turn bright red. "I don't understand, you . . . you want me to drive to Philadelphia and pick up one hundred cheesesteaks?"

"Yes. And make sure you get a cooler or something down there so that they stay warm." Chick pointed to the clock on the wall, revealing a massively wrinkled shirt sleeve that was missing a cuff link. "It's eight thirty. Leave now and you should be back here no later than one. My Benz is in the garage downstairs. The gas tank is full, and I expect it to be full when I get it back. Make sure you use premium. Go. Now." Patty didn't move. Chick, used to his orders being followed immediately, barked, "Why are you still here?"

"You . . . you want me to drive your Mercedes?" she stammered.

"Yes."

"To Philadelphia?"

"Yes," he muttered. A little more brusque this time.

Oh Jesus, Patty, stop talking and just go.

"To pick up cheesesteaks, and then come back?"

Chick looked at Reese, "Did we hire Rain Man? Are you confused, Reese? I thought my directions were pretty clear."

"One hundred cheesesteaks. You had me at hello," Reese agreed.

"See, Patty? This isn't difficult. How are we going to trust you to handle hundreds of millions of dollars if you can't grasp the concept of a round trip to Pennsylvania?"

"No," she insisted. "I can go now. I'll call in on the way back."

"Why? I don't care where the fuck you are. As long as you don't end up in Ohio, there's no reason for you to call on the way back. Just get back here by one. And if you fuck up my car, I'll make sure you spend the next year grinding coffee with Jashim in the hallway. Got it?"

Patty ran off the floor, knocking her chair over in the process. The clanging noise made Chick wince in pain.

"Girlie, look up the numbers for these cheesesteak joints and order lunch. Tell them pickup will be in about an hour and a half."

"Sure, boss."

After I ordered the sandwiches, I called one of my clients, a hedge fund in Massachusetts. The client wanted me to run some scenario analyses for a trade he was looking at. He wanted me to show how a bond would perform if the market rallied fifty basis points, and what would happen if the market sold off fifty basis points. What would the cash flows look like; how would the bond's duration change? I was deep in thought for well over an hour, but my concentration was broken when my personal line rang. It was a private line that I gave to friends and family, and the receptionist at Bliss for when she needed to confirm my facial appointments. I answered the phone the same way I always do, "Cromwell."

"Alex?" It was Patty.

"What's wrong?" I hissed in a whisper so that no one would over-hear me. "Please tell me the car's okay."

"The car's fine, but the second batch of sandwiches isn't ready! They said they need another twenty minutes and if I have to wait here twenty minutes, I won't get back on time. What do I do?"

There was only one thing to do. "Well, then you're going to have to make up the time on the way home. Drive at least eighty-five on the turnpike. If you floor it, you should make it back on time."

"You're seriously telling me to drive Chick's car at eighty-five miles per hour? What if I get pulled over?"

"If given the choice between having to face an angry Chick or an angry state trooper, I'd take the trooper every time. Tell the cheesesteak guys to light a fire under it. How hard is it to throw some Cheese Whiz on a steak anyway?"

"A lot of love goes into these, Alex."

"It's a *sandwich*. Tell them to hurry up, and wear your seat belt on the way back."

I hung up on her. Great. If she ended up wrapped around a telephone pole, I was going to feel somewhat responsible.

I turned around to see what Will and the rest of the guys in the back row were up to. They were playing one of their favorite games, the one where they randomly threw pennies on the floor and counted how many one of the salesmen picked up when he walked by. The guy made a ton of money, but was one of the cheapest people on the planet. Will and the guys he sat with got a huge kick out of watching the salesman stop and shove pennies into his pocket, seemingly unconcerned with why they were on the floor to begin with.

Nice to know that the back row was working as hard as I was.

I spun my chair forward and continued with my spreadsheet. I used to hate running Excel models for Chick, but for some reason, when you're running them for your own clients, they aren't nearly as painful. I felt pretty confident in the figures, and was getting ready to call the client back with my findings, when the phone rang again. I liked Patty, but she was quickly getting on my nerves. I grabbed the receiver. "What now?" I said.

"Chick lets you answer the phone like that? A pretty young thing like you really should be nicer to people."

Shit. I recognized the voice.

"I'm sorry, I was expecting someone else. How are you, Rick?"

He chuckled. "I guess I'm not the only client calling you on an outside line to say hello. I'm a little disappointed you don't know who I am, and even more disappointed that you haven't returned any of my text messages."

I felt my body tense. "Can I help you with something?"

"How're you doing?"

"Fine, thanks. How are you?" Not that I cared.

"I'm good. Better now that I'm talking to you."

I laughed nervously and tried to get him off the phone as fast as possible. "Can I get Chick for you?"

"I didn't call to talk to Chick. This isn't Chick's line, is it?"

"No, it isn't. What can I do for you?"

"I was hoping you'd join me for a drink tonight at the Bull and Bear. I thought it'd be a good chance for us to spend some time together."

What in the hell is wrong with this guy?

"Oh, thanks, but I can't make it tonight. I'm going to be working late."

"All work and no play makes Alex a dull girl and Rick a very unhappy boy."

Ick.

"I'm sorry, I really can't. Maybe another night." *Fuck.* I shouldn't have said that.

"Another night it is. I'm holding you to that, Alex. You don't want to disappoint one of Chick's best clients, do you? That wouldn't bode well for your career."

I laughed again. He was kidding, right? That was a joke. An amazingly unfunny, sick, and twisted joke. "It was nice talking with you, Rick."

"You, too. If you change your mind, you know where to find me." With that, he hung up.

I returned my focus to my spreadsheet, and the clients who didn't make me feel like a corporate concubine.

A half hour later as the clock struck 1:00, Chick shook his head in disapproval. "Where the fuck is Patty?" he asked, as he banged his fist on his desk. "How long has she been gone?" Just then, Patty appeared, dragging a large blue-and-white cooler behind her.

"I'm back," she proudly exclaimed. "Everything's fine."

Chick opened the cooler, releasing the tantalizing odor of grilled onions and synthetic cheese into the air. "Everything isn't fine if the sandwiches are cold. Are they cold, Patty?"

"No, Chick, they're still warm. I promise."

"Good. Now sit, Patty." In ten seconds flat the cooler was empty. I didn't eat one. I felt my ass expand just smelling them.

"Why is it so hard to get good cheesesteaks in New York?" Reese asked as he examined his sandwich. "New York has the best of everything, but for some reason, we can't master the cheesesteak. Why is that?"

"Who knows? If the only thing New York can't master is the cheesesteak, I'm okay with that," Drew answered, tossing his wrapper in the trash.

"Good job, Patty," Chick said as he downed his tenth Advil of the day. "Next time you have to go get us sammies from Philly, you only have to go to one spot. You're right: Geno's *is* better."

Patty whispered in my ear, "Is it always like this? Am I going to be crossing state lines for lunch on a regular basis?"

"Anything's possible," I answered, nonchalantly.

"Christ. I don't think I really understood what I was signing up for when I took this job."

"There's no way you could have."

I gave Will a quick wave as I walked out at the end of the day, well aware of the fact that I had left an e-mail from him unopened in my inbox. I decided I was going to play hard to get. Or at least, not really, *really* easy to get. At least not today.

fourteen

Buyer of That Babe in Size

Patty seemed to be adjusting to folding chair life about as well as could be expected. I let her leave her purse under my desk so she didn't have to worry about anyone stuffing it with corn muffins or programming pictures in her iPhone. I figured since she had replaced me as Chick's Excel bitch it was the least I could do to thank her. By March we had become good friends, and I didn't realize how badly I missed having a girlfriend at work until she arrived. It was like we had known each other forever, our bond suggesting a friendship much longer than two months. But trading desks have a way of moving everything at an unusually fast pace: your concept of time, your friendships, your life span. To name a few.

Patty was smart, thank God, which meant she was capable of taking over for me as Chick's financial slave and needed only minimal guidance. This made me happy. It left me more time to pursue way more interesting endeavors.

MSG FROM PATRICK, WILLIAM:
You busy this week?

MSG FROM GARRETT, ALEX:
I'll have to check my schedule. I'm a very busy girl these days.

MSG FROM PATRICK, WILLIAM:
See if you are free on Thursday. I have a reservation at Nobu at
8:00. I'd hate to have to bring Marchetti. I'll go broke paying to
feed him.

MSG FROM GARRETT, ALEX:
I'll try to clear some time. Maybe two hours or so.

MSG FROM PATRICK, WILLIAM:
You'll clear the whole night and you know it . . . and if you
won't, I'll just pour sake down your throat until you change
your mind.

Fair point.

Nobu was one of the hottest reservations in town. The restaurant
was small and elegant, with tightly packed tables. The noise level ranged
from average to crazy loud, depending on the clientele on any given
night. It was popular among celebrities and models, because it was one
of the few restaurants in Manhattan where they'd actually allow themselves to eat the food—raw fish being figure-friendly and all. It was also
popular with the members of the New York Social Register who hoped
to end up on "Page Six," and with Wall Streeters who carried corporate
cards. I didn't know how Will managed to get a reservation, and frankly
I didn't care. I had been dying to go.

I decided to wear jeans, a gray Vince T-shirt with a boat neck and
long sleeves, and a pair of black pointy-toe stilettos that looked really
hot but hurt like a bitch. Sometimes, you just had to suffer to be beauti-

ful. And beautiful, I would have been. I paid over $100 for a blowout at
the John Barrett salon after work. My long hair was shiny and bouncy,
shampoo-commercial quality hair. But nothing will ruin a great hair
day faster than a nor'easter. Ten minutes after I arrived home to change,
it started to monsoon. An instant after stepping out on the sidewalk to
hail a cab, I looked like a Chia Pet.

When I entered the restaurant, Will was already there. He stood
and gave me a sloppy kiss hello. He was still wearing his work clothes
and he was definitely buzzed. My guess was that he'd never gone home
and instead had passed the time before dinner slugging beers with his
friends at one of the bars near the office. Maybe guys don't think about
their appearance much, and don't get me wrong, I didn't want a boyfriend who was vain and spent more time looking in the mirror than I
did, but it did make me feel silly that I was having a panic attack because
my hair was frizzing and he hadn't even bothered to change his shirt.
Will was already drinking a beer, but after examining the cocktail
menu, I decided on a martini.

"I'll have a lychee martini, please," I said to the waiter.

Will was intrigued by my order. "Since when do you drink martinis?"

"I don't usually, but I wanted to try it. You can get sake anywhere.
Any idea what a lychee is?"

He laughed. "Sorry, can't help you with that one. I'm sure it's good,
though. Everything here is good." He flashed a smile. "I'll take care of
ordering. There are a few things that you have to try. The food's off the
charts. You'll love it."

"Great!" I chirped like a stupid teenager. "One caveat, though: I
don't do fish eggs. Other than that, order whatever you want." I flashed
my most dazzling smile and batted my eyelashes shamelessly.

"Understood," he said. "Seller of fish eggs, got it." Wall Street people
had a very annoying tendency to introduce market jargon into everyday
life. If you liked something, you were a buyer. If you didn't like something, you were a seller. If you liked or disliked something a lot you just

added "in size" on the end. Once a pretty girl walked by our table at the bar and Marchetti whistled as he announced, "Buyer of that babe in size."

"Seller," Reese had countered. "Fat ass."

All the poor girl did was walk by the table and she immediately became an available-for-sale asset.

My phone beeped in my bag next to me, interrupting our conversation.

"Popular girl," Will said.

"Well, obviously, I turned down quite a few guys to have dinner with you tonight."

He smirked. I removed my phone from my bag to check my messages and immediately felt my good mood evaporate into the night air.

> SMS from Kieriakis, Rick:
> I miss you, do you miss me? Call me.

My frustration must have been obvious.

"What's wrong?"

"Rick."

Will looked angry. "Is there something you're not telling me?"

"No. I just don't know why he won't leave me alone," I said, honestly.

"You don't? I do."

"You do?"

"There are three kinds of women on the Street."

"This should be interesting."

"The first is the group who will sleep with anyone to make more money or advance their careers. The second is the group who works twice as hard as the first group to advance their careers and make money, because they refuse to sleep their way up the ladder."

"And the third?"

"The third is the group who can't handle being in one of the other two groups and quits. Rick doesn't know which group you're in, so he's testing you. Being a woman on the Street can be a disadvantage, no question, but there are some who use it to their advantage, too. Turn a negative into a positive if you will."

"That's vile. I'd *never* do that."

"I know that, but he doesn't. He probably thinks you're just another slut on the Street."

Our waiter returned and set a cloudy pale pink cocktail down in front of me. There was a toothpick floating in it that would've held olives in a regular martini, but in the lychee martini, speared some sort of plump, fleshy-looking object. Note to self: next time, order beer. I hesitantly took a sip of the cocktail. It was strong and fruity. I had found my new favorite beverage.

"This is great!" I said. "Why don't I drink these all the time?"

"At eighteen dollars a pop, it's probably better if you don't."

"This thing is eighteen dollars? Jesus, is there liquid gold in here?" Will smiled as he took the last sip of his beer and motioned to the waiter to bring another round.

"Better catch up," he said. I looked at my martini glass, which was still full, and took a large gulp in order to finish it before my refill arrived. Will's eyes were glassy, and while I'd happily suck down another martini, there was no way I was going to be able to catch up to him, especially since he had been drinking for three hours while I was trying to decide between my dark-wash and my extra-dark-wash jeans. I finished the drink quickly. I would've sucked the lychee off the toothpick if I was sure that I was supposed to do that, but when in doubt, I figured it was better to let a sleeping lychee lie.

"Sorry, I should have checked the price before I ordered. I think this might be one of the most expensive drinks on the menu. Do you maybe want to order some wine after this?"

"Are you kidding? I make a ton of money, and I asked you to dinner. You can order whatever you want. Don't worry about the bill." As if to prove his point, he flagged the waiter down again and ordered our food.

"We'll have an order of the yellowtail and jalapeno, an order of the rock shrimp tempura, an order of the miso cod, an order of the wagyu beef, and six pieces of sushi, whatever the chef thinks is best, but not, what was it again that you won't eat?"

Will pointed his right index finger at me and rolled it in a clockwise circle in midair while he tried to remember my request.

"No fish eggs, please," I said.

Will handed the menus to the waiter and ran his hand through his hair. "Right. Whatever the lady wants. Or doesn't want." The waiter smiled, then went back to the kitchen to place our ridiculously large order. Will suddenly produced a small bag from under his chair.

"I got you something. Open it."

I removed a wad of green tissue paper from the bag and found a thin Burberry headband nestled in the middle. "You bought me a headband?" *Random.*

"Yeah. You wear your hair down a lot, or in one of those messy ponytails. I thought you might like something nice to keep your hair off your face at work."

I wasn't much of a Burberry headband kind of girl, but it was a nice gesture and I didn't want to be rude. "Thanks. It's sweet of you to think of me."

"Put it on."

I felt silly following instructions on how to wear my hair, but I put it on and smiled. I knew he gave it to me to be nice, but I couldn't help feeling like it was a slippery slope—who knew how long it would be before he told me what I should wear or who I could talk to. I had no interest in ending up in a corporate version of *Sleeping with the Enemy*.

"What do you think?" I asked nervously as I ignored the warning bells going off in my brain. I reminded myself to stop watching so many movies.

"You look great."

I was buzzed and strangely happy, with both the restaurant and the company. I was planning to talk to Will about something important, but I was distracted when the waiter delivered a plate of thinly sliced yellowtail with a sliver of jalapeño, swimming in soy and sprinkled with cilantro.

"You'll love this. Taste it." Will picked up his chopsticks, which were resting on an elegant shiny black stone. After that, in rapid succession, we had fried shrimp, miso cod, the single best steak I have ever had in my life, and a few pieces of unidentifiable raw fish. I lost track of my drinks, too, because the waiter was constantly refreshing them if he noticed our glasses getting low. You really can't put a price on good service.

"Can I ask you a question?" I was finding it increasingly difficult to focus.

"Shoot," he said, his eyes bloodshot and bleary.

"You never seem to be around when I call you on the weekends. It's not a big deal," I quickly added. "I'm just wondering why you don't ever return my calls. I always answer when you call."

"I don't know; sometimes I don't like phones. We're on them so much at work, on the weekends I like to just have peace and quiet, you know?"

I thought about it for a second. It seemed to make sense. We did spend an inordinate amount of time on the phone.

"I'll give you the phone thing. But how come you won't meet any of my friends? It's not like they don't know that we hang out, but I'm pretty sure they're beginning to wonder if you're an imaginary friend. Why don't we ever go out with other people? It's like you're embarrassed to be seen with me." This was an exaggeration. I knew that wasn't the case, but the headband was making me say things I wouldn't usually say. I felt the need to stick up for myself to compensate for the plaid-fabric-wrapped vise clamped around my skull.

He chuckled under his breath. "We're in one of the most popular restaurants in the city. If I were embarrassed to be seen with you, we'd be in some hole-in-the-wall place in the East Village where no one would ever think to go. I think you're being a little crazy."

"No, I'm not!" Having a guy think you're crazy is the kiss of death.

"I like spending time alone with you. Is that so bad?"

"No, but you could at least meet my friends. They're fun girls. You'd like them."

"How do you know that we won't hate one another? Girls are tough."

"Well, you like me, don't you? They're just like me, so if you like me, you'll like them."

"It's not that simple. Once I meet your friends, they'll feel like they have the right to voice their opinions about everything, including me. I've found it's better to not involve them at all."

"Let me guess: your ex-girlfriend's friends couldn't stand you, and you blame them for your breakup."

"I didn't say that," he answered, perhaps a little too quickly.

"You didn't have to. Listen, they're a big part of my life, and if you want to be involved with me in any way other than as my e-mail pen pal, you're going to have to meet them. They don't bite, I promise. Well, Liv did once, but there were extenuating circumstances."

He exhaled loudly and twirled his chopsticks nervously in his hands. "Fine. We'll figure out a night to all go out. I'll meet them if it's a big deal to you." He reached for my hand as the waiter placed the check on the edge of the table.

"Great. I'm supposed to meet my friend Liv tomorrow. Why don't you have a drink with us? You don't have to stay long; just come and meet her. What do you say?" My foot was shaking back and forth under the table as I waited for his answer.

"The biter? You want me to meet the biter first?"

"Forget I said that. Long story."

"I can't tomorrow. I have plans. We'll all go out soon, I promise."

He let go of my hand to grab his wallet and fumbled with his cards as he struggled to remove his Amex, his lack of dexterity a pretty clear indication he was wasted. He threw his card on the bill and returned it to the waiter without even looking at the total.

Show-off.

"I wanted to ask you something," he said.

"What?"

"Your birthday's coming up, isn't it?"

"Next month. April 16. How'd you know that?"

"I told you, Nancy will tell you anything if you're nice to her."

I swear I blushed. It must have been the lychees.

"Anyway," he continued, "I was wondering if you'd let me take you out on your birthday. I assume you're free?" Will was smooth, but he still could use some pointers in the art of seduction. Telling a girl you assume she has no plans on her birthday isn't flattering. Even if it was a month in advance.

"Really? Why do you *assume* that?"

"Bad choice of words. What I meant to say is: to the best of your knowledge, are you available to go out with me on your birthday? I want to book you early."

"Much better. Well, I'm supposed to have dinner with my friends, but I can cancel. What do you want to do?"

"No intel. It's a surprise."

Will signed the check, and we made our way toward the exit. It was still pouring, so we huddled under an awning at the deli next door. He jumped into the street to hail a cab, and I quickly followed him into the backseat. The rain pounded against the window so hard it sounded like someone was throwing handfuls of gravel at the taxi from the sidewalk. My hair, and the headband, were dripping wet. I shivered. He pulled me next to him so I was almost sitting on his lap.

"Thanks for dinner. I had a really nice time." I sighed, the alcohol and endorphins making me feel like I was floating.

Will was quiet, a weighted silence that felt like an eternity. The only sound I could hear was the golfball-sized rain pounding on the roof of the cab. I was pretty sure when we got out that the top of the car was going to look like an English muffin.

"Listen, I need to talk to you about something," he said as he shifted in the seat.

"What?" I was starting to get cold. If it weren't for the six lychee martinis, I was pretty sure I'd be hypothermic.

"I'm not ready to have a serious relationship. We have fun together, and I like hanging out with you, but I think we should keep it casual."

"What?" I said sharply as I pulled away from him.

"If it ain't broke, don't fix it. It's been great hanging out with you this past year. But things could get pretty ugly for both of us if we started, you know, 'dating' and it didn't work out. So let's not go there."

"You're joking, right?" I worried that the headband was constricting the blood flow to my brain and that I hallucinated that he had just asked me out on my birthday—next month—and then told me he didn't want a girlfriend.

And women are supposed to be crazy?

"I don't want you to take it personally. I'm just being honest."

He hiccuped, and I realized that trying to have a serious conversation would be a waste of time. What was the big deal, really? Tonight, he learned I don't like fish eggs, and I learned he doesn't want a girlfriend. Fair trade. Sorta.

"So, just so I'm . . . clear. You don't want to date me, but you want to keep hanging out and doing what we're doing. And you want to take me out for my birthday."

"Yeah," he said.

I pulled back and looked at his face. His eyes were bloodshot and cloudy from too much alcohol and too little sleep. Figuring that status quo was better than nothing, I smiled and said the only thing that I could think of to say: "Well, okay."

Lucky for him, I didn't care about labels. All I cared about was my birthday surprise. Sometimes, I am way too easy to please.

fifteen

Wet My Lips Wednesday

WEIRD THINGS WERE happening at work. March and April were scary as some well-known funds collapsed and the markets stopped operating smoothly. I had taken a lot of things for granted, I realized. One of those was my belief that Wall Street firms would always have enough money to stay in business. Apparently, that wasn't necessarily the case. I tried to learn as much as I could about what was happening, and what could possibly happen in the future, and before I knew it, it was mid-April and my twenty-fourth birthday was looming.

On my birthday, thankfully a Saturday, I woke to my ringing doorbell. My alarm clock read 8:45.

"Happy birthday!" Liv said when I opened the door to find her and Annie standing there with a huge bouquet of flowers and a bottle of Veuve Clicquot. "How does it feel to be one year closer to thirty? I want to know, so I can spend the next eight months preparing for when I'm your age." She loved the fact that I was a few months older than her. It meant that I would hit all the ages women didn't want to hit first, namely thirty. Whatever. She had been really jealous of me ages sixteen to twenty-one.

"It feels great, you pain in the ass." I yawned. "Twenty-four doesn't feel a whole hell of a lot different than twenty-three did yesterday. What are you guys doing here so early?"

"We came to wish you a happy birthday before your hot date, you know, the one you're blowing us off for," Annie said.

"Very funny."

The truth was, I didn't mind getting up early. I had spent the week primping for my mystery date. I spent more than $500 on personal maintenance: a manicure, pedicure, wax, a triple oxygen facial, a haircut, highlights, body scrub, body wrap, and a massage. The seaweed wrap might have been a little excessive, but the ladies at the spa swore it would detoxify and firm my skin, and I saw no reason to skimp.

"Happy birthday, Alex," Annie said as she opened the bottle of champagne. We clinked our glasses together, the bubbles making my eyes water. "So what are you and Mr. Will going to do tonight? Maybe the big surprise is that he finally agrees to meet at least one of your friends, you think?" she asked.

"He hasn't said. I figure he'll call or text me later with more info. Honestly, I'm just happy he wants to spend my birthday with me. We never hang out on weekends, so I'm considering this a small victory."

Liv handed me a little gift bag stuffed with white tissue paper in an unsuccessful attempt to cover up a very obvious pink feather-topped object. Oh Lord. When I pulled the feathers out of the bag I found that they were attached to a clear plastic tube that held I didn't know what— socks? Whatever they were, they came in various colors: I could see red, pink, purple, and black.

"Go ahead, open it up!" Annie said, as her cheeks blushed a deep crimson. I pulled out the first tightly rolled cotton ball and shook it out. It took me a few seconds to figure out that I was holding the first of seven teeny-tiny pairs of days-of-the-week thong underwear. (And there were actually seven of them, so clearly Meg Ryan was incorrect when she told Billy Crystal in *When Harry Met Sally* that there are no Sunday undies because of God.) But these were not your normal days-of-the-week underwear; these were, hmm, how does one say this delicately? These were slutty-girl-every-day-of-the-freakin'-week underwear.

"Where . . . in the hell . . . did you guys get these?"

"I had nothing to do with it! I left Liv in charge of getting the gift. I would've gotten you a gift certificate for a spa or something!" Annie said in a rush.

"I think they're funny. It's not like anyone else will have them!" Liv countered defensively.

"No, certainly not," I agreed. "If I had these when I was little, my mom wouldn't have had to write my name on my Jockeys before I went to camp."

"These are my favorites," Liv announced as she held up a white pair with the phrase "Wet My Lips Wednesday" emblazoned in hot pink above an even hotter pink lip print. "Come on, tell me these aren't the greatest things you've ever seen? Maybe you can wear a pair out tonight with Will, you think? Let me find Saturday." I ripped the plastic sleeve out of her hand.

"Let's leave Saturday where it is, okay?" I said, through my laughter.

"Whatever he has planned, I hope you guys have an amazing time. I can't wait to hear about it tomorrow. If he manages to not screw the whole thing up, it will be like a scene from one of the movies on Lifetime," Annie said dreamily. "I can see it now, it'll be called *Foreign Love Exchange*, you know, alluding to the fact that you met and then fell in love while trading on the stock exchange."

"I hate to ruin your fairy tale, Annie, but I don't work on the stock exchange."

"Who cares? You know what I mean. A big floor with lots of rowdy people is a big floor with lots of rowdy people."

"Ahhh yes, big floors with rowdy people are where all good love stories begin, Annie. I'd also like to point out that there is no love story here. We aren't even dating."

"If it looks like a duck and quacks like a duck . . ."

"Hey, what are you going to wear?" Liv asked as she threw open the door to my closet. "You need to look hot."

I showed them the outfit I had in mind as we finished the bottle of champagne. The day was off to a great start and was only going to get better.

I'VE ALWAYS PRIDED MYSELF on being the type of girl who can handle just about anything. I'm not easily rattled. I'm not clingy or dependent. I am, however, just a little bit, and I mean a teensy bit, neurotic. By the time 7:00 P.M. rolled around and I was still sitting on my couch watching TV, I started to get upset. I had already sent Will two text messages, one at 6:00 and one at 6:30, both of them breezy and perfectly acceptable little notes asking what time he was picking me up or if I should meet him somewhere. But an hour later he still hadn't responded, so naturally my mind flashed to the only two possible scenarios that made any sense: he was dead or he was unconscious. In which case, how selfish was I to get upset over something as stupid as a birthday dinner as he lay bleeding from a massive head wound in some crowded inner-city emergency room? By 8:30, I had sent him three more text messages, progressing in tone from concern to mild pique to outright anger.

Text 1 (7:30):

> SMS from Garrett, Alex:
> Are you okay? Please call me. I'm getting nervous I haven't heard from you.

Text 2 (8:00):

> SMS from Garrett, Alex:
> If this is your idea of a birthday joke, running over my childhood pet would be more amusing. Call me.

Text 3 (8:30):

> SMS from Garrett, Alex:
> *You better be dead.*

Text 4 (an hour later):

> SMS from Garrett, Alex:
> *Seriously it's 9:30. This isn't funny where are you?*

I tried to calm myself. *Do not panic. Do not panic. There is an explanation for this. No one would intentionally do this to someone. I have seen episodes of* Jerry Springer *where people showed more compassion. There's an explanation; you just have to give him the benefit of the doubt until you hear it. The important thing here is to definitely, not, panic.*

By 10:00, I had been reduced to tears, sitting on my windowsill, smoking cigarettes and biting my nails until my manicure was ruined. I stared at my phone, waiting for it to ring, but it remained silent. My brain still couldn't wrap itself around the possibility that Will had blown me off.

At 10:45, my phone finally beeped. Maybe I should have felt honored that he finally took the time to answer one of the numerous messages I'd sent him, in addition to a handful of phone calls that went right to voice mail. I opened my phone with the same fear and excitement I'd had when I opened up my response letter from UVA. Until I read it; then I just felt sick.

> SMS from Patrick, William:
> *Really sorry, but not feeling well. Can't make it tonight. My bad,*
> *happy birthday.*

Happy birthday? My bad? Seriously? This had quickly become the most disappointing, insulting, depressing birthday of my life. I washed my carefully applied makeup off my face, the water mixing with my tears. I threw my new clothes on the floor, shuffled into bed, and planned on staying there until I had to go to work on Monday. When Annie sent me a text message at eleven asking if I was having a blast, I replied:

Home. Asshole.

I buried my tearstained face under my pillows and silently cursed the day he was born. There was some small comfort in knowing that when you're at your lowest point, there's nowhere to go but up.

That is, until you sink so low you might as well be sitting in a noodle shop in China.

I TRIED TO IGNORE MY doorman buzzing me the next morning, but when my phone started ringing incessantly, too, I finally forced myself to answer. Annie was in my lobby, and she wasn't going to leave. I opened the door in my pajamas, and judging from the look on Annie's face, I knew I looked as bad as I felt. So far, twenty-four was off to a fantastic start.

"Christ," she said as she threw her arms around my neck and squeezed like she was trying to juice me. "He should be shot, Al. With a rifle . . . at close range . . . in the face."

I nodded.

"What was his excuse?"

"He said he didn't feel well."

"What do you mean he said he didn't feel well? Does he have anthrax? Bubonic plague? Anything else is completely unacceptable."

"I know." I sobbed.

She glanced at my hands. "What did you do to your manicure?"

I stared at my nails, which I had gnawed down to the cuticles. "I don't know," I whimpered. "I guess I bit them off last night. It could be worse. I could have tried to slit my wrists with my corkscrew."

"First thing: we're going to fix those hands. Come on, my treat. I need a mani anyway."

I didn't want to leave my apartment. "I don't want a manicure. Of all the things about myself I need to fix, nail polish is really not high on the list." I sat down on my couch and pulled a blanket up over my legs. Despite my best efforts not to, I began to sob. Annie sat down next to me.

"I'm so sorry, Alex. I know how much you were looking forward to last night. He's not worth it. You can do sooooooooooo much better."

"All evidence to the contrary," I wailed. "I think I give off some kind of signal that only seriously delusional guys, and dogs, can hear. Everyone I date is an asshole, Annie, every last one. Why can't I ever like the nice guys?"

"You're attracted to the wrong things. You think the nice guys are sissies."

"I've been fighting so hard to make sure I don't end up a doormat later in life, I didn't even realize I am one now. The irony is sickening."

"You're not a doormat, and you haven't done anything wrong. He's been giving you just enough encouragement to keep you interested. This isn't about you, it's about him. *You* are just fine."

"I have one foot in the loony bin and the other on a banana peel. I'm *not* fine. And I can't have a nervous breakdown on the trading floor. How am I going to go back there and deal with him and not lose my mind? How am I supposed to work with him after this?"

"We'll figure it out. Don't worry about that now."

Good advice, except I could do nothing *except* think about it. "I'm going to have to quit my job. How can I go in and look at him every day after he did this to me? Chick was right; interoffice dating is a horrible idea. This is a disaster," I moaned as I wiped my hands across my eyes.

"You're not going to quit your job; don't let him force you out of your career. You'll go in there and be the strong, determined Alex you've always been. Let's go, girl. Throw on some jeans."

It was 12:30 when Annie and I entered the crowded salon and approached the polish carousel.

"Do you see 'Ballet Slippers'?" she asked as she picked up bottle after bottle of pink polish to examine the labels. "I can't find it."

"Have you ever thought about how stupid the names of these nail polishes are?" I asked, my foul mood rearing its ugly head. "I mean look at this: 'East Hampton Cottage,' 'Montauk Highway,' 'Marshmallow,' 'Blushing Bride.' Who comes up with this crap?" I picked up a bottle of dark brown polish and turned it upside down. "This one's called 'Chocolate Kisses.' It's *brown*, Annie. 'Chocolate Kisses'? Give me a break! It should be called 'Shit Kicker.'"

"I don't think women would be eager to paint their nails a color called 'Shit Kicker,'" she said, laughing.

I scowled. "Maybe that's what I'll do. I'll start my own line of nail polishes with better names. Names for the bitter women's circuit. I'll call it Angry Girl."

"Okay," she said, humoring me. "What's your idea of a better name for nail polish?"

"I'd replace 'Montauk Highway' with 'Jersey Turnpike.' Let's see, there could be 'Overworked and Underpaid,' 'Lying Cheating Bastard,' 'Blood Sucker.' That would make a nice red, I think."

"How about, 'Prenup'? Or 'Left at the Altar,'" she suggested eagerly.

I made a fist and raised it in a mock cheer. "Excellent, yes! Hey, how about 'Trailer Park.' That's a good one; I'd nuke 'East Hampton Cottage' in favor of 'Trailer Park.' There could be a market for this. Just think about how many women are doing this very same thing at this very same moment and more than half of them are probably depressed or pissed off like me. And if you're depressed or pissed off when you get your nails done, you really should be able to choose a color that reflects your mood. Is that really too much to ask?" I began to gesticulate wildly and my voice rose as I began talking in one long stream of consciousness. "You know, for example, let's say the guy you've been seeing stands you up on your birthday, you may not feel like putting a color called 'A-list' on your nails. I'm not A-list, Annie. I'm at the very best B-list and there's no B-list polish here! Fucking Idiot. That's the color I want, Annie. Help me find 'Fucking Idiot'; do you think it's in here somewhere?" I caught a glimpse of my reflection in the mirror behind the nail polish display. My eyes were wild, my cheeks flushed, my hair mussed. I looked like a lunatic.

Annie slowly pushed me onto the red velour couch lining the wall. "You're losing it," she said as her eyes darted around the room.

Annie and I sat in silence while we got our nails done, and my blood pressure slowly returned to normal. We moved to the dryers and only then, when Annie felt certain that I had calmed down enough to talk rationally, did we speak.

"Look," she said gently. "There's nothing I can say to make you feel better and I know that. The only thing that I *can* do is point out what an awful person he is. You don't deserve to be treated like this."

I didn't say anything. I noticed a piece of fuzz stuck in the wet polish on my thumb.

Fantastic.

"Do you want to go for a walk?" she asked hopefully. "Let's get some air. Come shopping with me. I don't want you to go home alone."

"I won't be alone. I have my buddies in the wine rack to keep me company."

I glanced at my phone sitting on the counter next to the dryer. I'm a masochist. I know.

"Alex, he's not going to call you. The sooner you accept it, the better off you'll be."

"Maybe he's really sick," I cried.

"He's not."

"I know."

I really hated crying in public. Even if "public" meant two manicurists and one friend. That was still three people too many.

Beep. My head snapped forward. I looked over at my phone, its flashing red light taunting me. I pounced on it. And then, I felt my chest tighten as the all-too-familiar feelings of hope and disappointment collided at the center of my rib cage.

> *SMS from Kieriakis, Rick:*
> *I heard it was your birthday. I'd love to help you celebrate. Meet me for dinner this week.*

Annie read the message and turned my phone off. "That's it. You're not going to stare at this thing for another minute. The only person on earth who is a bigger asshole than Will is Rick."

I shrugged my shoulders in response. I refused to accept the fact that I was somehow complicit in the tragedy of my own life. My voice cracked as I whispered, "I can't go to work tomorrow."

"Yes, you can. If you let him know how hurt you are, it will be one hundred times worse."

"Look at me, Annie! All he has to do is lay eyes on me and he'll be able to tell how upset I am. I'm a mess! Do you have any painkillers?" I begged.

"Sorry, no narcotics."

"Some friend you are. Can we go for cocktails?"

"Drinking is a bad idea. No booze."

It didn't seem like I had much of a choice. "Yes, Mom."

I WOKE UP FEELING ONLY one thing: anger. I was planning on telling Will exactly what I thought of him the first chance I had, and if anyone overheard me, so be it.

I pretended to be very busy reading the finance section of the paper as I stepped onto the floor, careful to avert my eyes from Will's desk. As I turned the corner and headed down the long aisle toward my desk, Patty jumped up from her seat and ran toward me. I'd forgotten I'd told Patty that Will and I were going out on Saturday. I tried to muster a smile and pretend I didn't feel like someone had thrown my insides into a Cuisinart and hit "puree." Patty linked her arm in mine and spun me around. Without breaking stride she said cheerily, "Hi, we are walking the other way now."

"Yes, I realize that. Why?"

"We need to talk."

"Where are we going?" I asked. She didn't answer. "Patty, just leave me alone. Honestly, if you knew the weekend I had, you'd get why I simply can't handle any drama this morning. I'm telling you right now, I'll lose it. Whatever this is about, it can wait," I said.

"I think I do have an idea about your weekend. Trust me here, Alex. We're going to the ladies' room on the sixth floor. There's never anyone in there."

Panic overwhelmed me. If she thought we needed to leave the floor, she was about to tell me something very, very bad and didn't want anyone else to witness my impending meltdown.

She stated matter-of-factly, "You don't look good."

"No shit."

"Seriously, Alex."

"Seriously, Patty. No shit."

"I'm sorry this happened. I hate him!" she said through gritted teeth.

I immediately dug my heels into the carpet and pulled backward like a stubborn dog that didn't want to be dragged from the park by its leash. "Wait, how do you know what happened?"

"I don't think *you* know what happened. If you did, I doubt you'd be here."

Whatever fear I had in anticipation of what Patty was going to tell me was immediately replaced by shock at what we witnessed when we entered the ladies' room. Standing in front of us, in all of her silicone glory, was Baby Gap. She had a small portable blow-dryer plugged into the socket above the sink and was drying her hair in the mirror. Since it was 7:00 A.M., and there were no showers in the building, it would've been weird enough to find her in the ladies' room with a wet head and a hair dryer. What was *really* shocking was that she was practically naked. Her red lace bra, which barely contained her surgically enhanced bust, and a matching red thong revealed more than I ever needed to see. She was barefoot (gross!) and had lotions, cosmetics, perfume, and a razor laid out on the counter in front of her. Apparently, we weren't the only ones escaping to the sixth floor for privacy. I didn't know where to focus my eyes, on her naked torso or her face. Despite my best efforts, there was nowhere to look except her cups, which runnethed over.

"Good morning, ladies!" Hannah said cheerfully.

Patty gasped. "What are you doing?"

"Oh God," I said as I averted my eyes. "You didn't sleep in the conference room again, did you?"

"What?" Patty asked.

Hannah laughed. "Oh! No, I just had a really late night last night. I was at Cipriani with a bunch of the guys from emerging markets and then we went to Marquee and then to some diner. Those guys are so much fun! I had a blast!"

"I bet they were nice to you," Patty said flatly, clearly annoyed that her plan was thrown off track by a half-naked bimbo. "So you didn't go home?"

"Well, not to *my* home. You guys know how it is."

We stared at her, and without saying a word left the room. I heard her call sweetly as the door closed behind us, "Do me a favor, don't tell anyone, okay?"

I guess I knew which one of the three groups of women on Wall Street Baby Gap fell into.

Patty covered her mouth but managed to mumble, "Did that really just happen? Alex, she's naked! With a full overnight kit! I think if you spend enough time in this building, you start to completely lose your marbles."

Sounded about right.

Plan B, Patty informed me, was to try the bathroom on the fourth floor. I leaned against the sinks and finally noticed that she had the *Boston Globe* tucked under her arm. Weird.

She took a deep breath and exhaled loudly, blowing a lock of hair that had fallen in front of her eyes off her face. "I need to show you something. And you're not going to want to see it, but it's being passed around to everyone on the desk, and if I don't show it to you here, you're going to see it up there, and I think it's better this way."

"What could possibly be in a Boston paper that would require we come all the way down here? Why do you even have a newspaper from Boston? You're scaring me." My chest constricted as I was overcome with an impending sense of dread.

"One of the traders from the Boston office sent it to Chick via FedEx. It's bad, Alex." She opened the paper and pointed to a picture with a small blurb written underneath. Once the receptors in my brain processed what I was looking at, I ran into a stall and threw up.

"Alex, I'm so sorry. I didn't want you to see it in front of everyone."

I thought I felt sick before, but no. *That* wasn't sick. *This* was sick. *Ms. Vanessa Manerro of Wellesley, Massachusetts, to marry Mr. William Patrick of New York.* There was a picture. Saturday night, while I was sitting at home waiting for Will to pick me up for our date, he was with his fiancée. While I was sending him text messages and worrying if something had happened to him, he was probably drinking a bottle of champagne with this oddly familiar-looking girl. She was wearing a Burberry headband. The same one Will had given me. I dropped the newspaper on the floor.

"I'm sorry. I must have just had a stroke or something. That really looked like the engagement announcements from the *Boston Globe*." I laughed out loud the way people do right before a big white van pulls up and someone throws a straitjacket on them. "I mean, could you imagine that? If he was engaged?" I was still laughing. When I looked at Patty, she wasn't. It was real. It was in the newspaper.

"He's . . . *engaged*?" I sobbed, as self-hatred overwhelmed me. "How could he be engaged without me knowing? I must be the dumbest human being on earth!" I picked the paper up off the floor and scanned the article . . . *to be married in Boston . . . career in finance . . . secretary at Cromwell Pierce.*

Cromwell Pierce? She works here. We both work at Cromwell. Well, techni-cally I work; she files other people's work. How did he manage to date two girls at the same firm at the same time? How did I manage to be one of them? I felt light-headed.

"Alex, say something."

I drew my hands in tight little fists and felt my nails dig into my palms as the tears began to flow. "She works HERE?" I said, my voice barely recognizable as my own. I started to shake with anger; unrelent-ing, all-consuming, mind-blowing anger. "Patty!" My voice reverber-ated off the ceramic tiles. "How did I not *know*?"

"She works in the Boston office! How the hell *could* you have known?"

Boston. Will told me he was going to Boston. For business. The night he took me to see the skyline from his friend's roof. I'm too stupid to live.

I threw the paper in the garbage can as hard as I could. It landed with a giant *thud* on top of balled-up paper towels and tissues. I stared at Patty blankly . . . engaged . . . as in . . . to be married.

"What did he say to you on Saturday?" she asked. "He must have known this was going to run. Did he honestly think you wouldn't see it? It's in the *Boston Globe,* for God's sake! Fine, it's not the *New York Times,* but it's still a major newspaper!"

"He said he was sick," I sobbed.

"Oh yeah, he's sick all right. He's fucking insane is what he is."

"Patty," I wailed. "How the hell am I supposed to go back up there and pretend like nothing is wrong?"

"You won't. I'm going to tell Chick I ran into you in the bathroom and you were getting sick and went home," she said, banging her hand on the counter.

I wiped my mouth and my eyes and tried once again to compose myself. Patty gave me a hug, and when we separated, the entire shoulder of her light blue sweater was stained with my makeup and tears. Great.

"Thanks," I whispered as I tried to pull myself together enough to make it out of the building without anyone noticing me. "If I had seen

222

erin duffy

this in front of him . . ." I trailed off because the thought of it was so horrifying I couldn't even manage to finish my sentence.

"Go home," she said. "It could be worse. You could be her. As bad as
this is, at least you know the truth."

"Yeah, I've got that going for me."

Chick was right. Dating a colleague wasn't just a bad idea. It was the
single worst decision I had ever made in my life.

sixteen

The Sugar Sweetie

T HE RING OF my phone woke me from my fitful, sedative-induced sleep later that afternoon. It was Liv, but I didn't answer. I couldn't bring myself to talk about it. I was never going to read a newspaper again. From now on I'd get my news the same way the majority of Americans do—by watching "Weekend Update" on *Saturday Night Live*.

I listened to Liv's message. She told me that if it made me feel any better she thought the girl looked terrible in the picture that ran online. (It didn't.) And she reminded me that I was better off than the poor girl in the picture who had no idea her fiancé was carrying on another relationship in New York while she was picking out china patterns in Boston. (She may have had a point.)

I decided to go for a walk, thinking that maybe the fresh air would help combat my depression. I threw on jeans and a zip-up sweatshirt. I walked south on Sixth Avenue, but I had no idea where I was going. I wandered aimlessly, so self-absorbed with my own misery I wasn't paying attention to anything going on around me. How could I? My entire life had just been destroyed. It made it hard to focus on anything, I was running on autopilot. I made the mistake of taking my eyes off the traffic light in front of me. As I stepped into the street, looking up at the blue sky and diaphanous clouds, I was immediately knocked on my ass by a delivery man on a bicycle. He tried to ring his bell to warn me to get back on the sidewalk, but it was too late. He had two choices: take out the girl stepping off the curb or swerve into traffic and become roadkill himself.

He barely slowed down as he took me out, although he did make time to turn and scream at me what I can only imagine were really offensive and unoriginal obscenities in a foreign language. I grabbed my purse, which thankfully hadn't exploded all over the street, and examined myself for injuries. My jeans had ripped, my left knee was bloodied, and the palm of my left hand was scraped raw. I was so frazzled I did the only thing a self-respecting, bleeding, depressed New Yorker could do: I went into a restaurant and sat at the bar.

The bartender, a burly guy with bone structure that looked like it had been chiseled out of granite, greeted me. "Hey, wow, are you okay?" he asked, looking at my bloody knee.

"Oh yeah, I'm fine. I was just hoping I could get a glass of pinot grigio. A big one."

He checked the clock on the wall. "Sure. We're in between services right now so the kitchen is closed. But the bar is open, and even if it wasn't, I don't think I'd have the heart to turn out a girl who so obviously needs a cocktail."

"Thanks, I appreciate it." He filled a glass and placed it on a napkin in front of me. Then he turned away and tended to something at the sink. I took a sip of my wine. Just what the doctor ordered.

"Here," he said, turning back toward me with an outstretched arm. He handed me a makeshift ice pack—cubes in a white bar rag—and I placed it on my knee.

"Thanks," I said, touched at the unexpected kindness from a total stranger. "I'm Alex, nice to meet you."

"Matt Matthews," he said as he shook my hand. "Nice to meet you, too. Truth be told I'm happy you came in. This time of day is boring, and I'm happy to have the company. Daytime bartending is a lonely gig." Matt was good-looking in the sort of way that your contractor or the guy who works in the corner hardware store is good-looking: he looked like he had lived a little. His arms—or every bit of them I could see—were covered in ornate tattoos. He looked like he had lots of stories to tell, and like he could fix things. And that was *never* unattractive.

"I can imagine," I said. "So how long have you been bartending here?"

"Six months. I'm actually training to be a chef."

"A chef? That's cool."

"Thanks, I think so. So what happened to you? Not too many girls come wandering in here in the middle of the afternoon bleeding and looking for a drink. If they did, this job would be a lot more fun."

"You wouldn't believe me if I told you," I said.

"I'm a bartender. You'd be surprised what I believe."

"I got run over by a delivery guy on a bike. He didn't even stop. It was like I was his own personal speed bump." I dabbed my scraped-up hand with a cocktail napkin.

"You know, I'm always surprised that doesn't happen more often. I've almost been mowed down on more than one occasion. I've never met anyone who actually got run over though."

"Today's your lucky day."

"Apparently so. Got time for another round? Or do you have to get back to work?"

I checked my watch. Four thirty. I was feeling pretty good for 4:30, but there was no harm in having just one more, right?

I nodded. "Another round, Matt Matthews, thanks."

I considered clarifying why I wasn't at work, and for a second I thought telling him would fall under the category of Too Much Information. But, then I decided, why not? Or maybe the wine decided for me. Either way, I continued. "No, no job that I have to get back to. I'm actually taking the day off for mental health purposes. Hence, my being able to sit at a bar in the middle of the day."

"Mental health day, huh? What happened?" he asked.

"This is going to be one of those questions you asked that you wished you hadn't."

"I want to hear it," he assured me. "Let's have it."

"Well, I was pseudo-dating a guy I worked with, but no one else in the office knew about it. At least, I don't think they knew, or at least, I pray to God they didn't."

"And what do you do exactly?"

"Finance."

"Wall Street. Figures. There's not a lot of love for you guys out there these days."

"Yeah, I know. Anyway, he said he didn't want a serious relationship, which I respected, so we kept it casual. He was supposed to take me to dinner on Saturday night for my birthday, but then he didn't call me or answer any of my messages and I didn't hear from him until almost eleven o'clock when he sent me a text message telling me he was sick. Then when I got to work this morning, ready to kill him, I discovered that his engagement announcement was in yesterday's *Boston Globe*. So, in an attempt to not go completely insane, I'm taking a day or two off."

Matt crossed his arms in front of his chest and looked at me skeptically.

"Did that really happen?"

"Scout's honor."

"Wow. Well, if it makes you feel better, it sounds like you're better off without him." He waited a minute and when I didn't say anything he continued. "I was engaged once. When I was twenty-two, I proposed to my high school girlfriend."

"Really? What happened?"

Matt opened a fresh bottle of pinot and poured one for himself. "Well, she was being all weird about a month before the wedding. She stopped returning calls and when I was with her she always seemed like she wasn't really paying attention to me, you know? So one day, I went to her house, and I sat her down and I asked her what was going on."

"And?"

"Turns out, she'd decided she was too young to get married. She wanted to 'experience life' before she was 'tied down'; she wanted to go to Los Angeles and try to be an actress. And she wanted to go alone. I was heartbroken, but I let her go. Now she's doing soft-core porn to pay the bills and living with some guy named Blade. And I'm here, going to culinary school and talking to you. So see, things tend to work out for the best. Even if you don't think so now, eventually you'll see you're better off." He pointed to my half-full wineglass. "This one's on the house. Happy birthday. The year can only get better from here."

"I hope that's true." I sighed. "So Matt Matthews, interesting name. Your parents weren't very original, were they?"

"Not particularly. One of the reasons I left Pittsburgh and came here was because everything there was so boring. I needed to be around some exciting people. You know, like people who are run over by delivery guys in the middle of the afternoon."

"Tell me about cooking school. What made you want to be a chef?"

"After my ex went to L.A., I moved here and spent a few years busing tables and peeling potatoes at a bunch of different places to save money for tuition. Then I enrolled in the Manhattan Culinary Institute. One day I'd like to own my own restaurant, so I want to try and learn as much about the business as I can."

"That sounds awesome. I like to cook. I watched someone on TV cook a chicken and make brownies yesterday, and she looked really happy. Is it hard to get in?"

"The application process is easy. You just go online and fill out a form, give them your uniform size, and a deposit. If you go full-time, in six months you're certified. If you go part-time like me, it takes nine months, but that's good because then you can keep working. Less money to have to take out in loans."

"What happens if there's stuff you don't like to eat, never mind cook? I don't like mayonnaise. I don't think I could cook with that. Would that be a problem?"

Matt laughed. "Yes. But there's a pastry arts section, too. Do you have an aversion to sugar?"

"Never met a sweetener I didn't like."

"Well, if you're looking for a fresh start . . ." Matt pulled one of the cocktail napkins off the top of the stack at the end of the bar and wrote a web address on it, " . . . here you go. Check it out. You meet a ton of fun people and are taught by some of the most famous chefs around."

I folded the napkin in half and stuck it in the pocket of my purse. It was 6:00 now, and I was definitely not sober. "I should probably go before I drink too much and get hit by a bus on my way home." I wobbled as I stood, and my knee buckled from the alcohol and throbbing pain. "Thanks for the company today. This was fun. I hope your ex-fiancée comes back a wrinkled, bleached-blond prune when she's thirty, crying to you about how Blade left her for a twenty-one-year-old butt-double."

"Ha! Thanks, Alex! I hope the jerk at your office goes prematurely bald and gets the clap. Look both ways when you cross the street from now on, okay?"

While I walked home, I thought about what Matt had said. Alex Garrett, Pastry Chef. That sounded much better than Alex Garrett, Bond Girl. Everyone says do what you love, and money and happiness will follow. Sure, I might have just downed a bottle of wine on an empty stomach, but I really thought this was something for me to consider. I could be a cake decorator. That would be a satisfying profession. I'd be a part of the happiest day in a person's life. For the first time since I found out Will was engaged, I felt optimistic. *I have direction. I have found my calling; I have found my way out of this mess.* I will be the Cupcake Queen, the Pastry Princess, the Sugar Sweetie (Reese would like that one).

Half an hour later, I snuggled under a blanket on my couch and reluctantly turned on the news to see what had been going on in the markets. Things were not good. This was not the time to be out of the office. I resigned myself to the fact that I was going to have to go in tomorrow, or I wouldn't have a job to go back to at all.

I ADMIT IT. I have woken up on my couch on more than one occasion. Tuesday morning I eyed the empty bottle of wine on the coffee table next to my laptop, and immediately checked my sent items to make sure that I hadn't done something stupid like resign to Chick over e-mail. Fortunately, I hadn't. Unfortunately, I had done something equally stupid. I stared at the conspicuous message in my in-box and clicked on it.

MSG FROM MCI

Dear Ms. Garrett,

Thank you very much for your application to the Manhattan Culinary Institute Pastry Arts Program. We have received your deposit of $6,000 and will be expecting monthly installments of $6,000 for the next six months for a total of $42,000. You will receive a schedule of classes as well as the appropriate medical forms shortly. You will need to have this information returned to the Admissions Office before the first day of class on 4/30/08 to be eligible for the summer semester. Thank you again for your interest in the Pastry Arts Program and we look forward to meeting you.

Regards,
Betty Blum, Admissions Officer

Oh my God. I had spent $6,000 on pastry school. Starting in two weeks. I doubted they had a refund policy for drunk enrollers. If there

was one thing my "mental health day" had proven, it was that I was certifiably insane. It was definitely time to reenter the real world.

A   s soon as I logged in when I got back to work Will sent me an
        e-mail that said, "I'm sorry, please let me explain."

I replied with an equally succinct message: "Fuck you." The only
problem was that writing that particular four-letter expletive flagged
the compliance department, and Chick received a very angry phone call
from the e-mail police about the language his employees were using in
interoffice communication.

"Stop writing 'fuck' in your e-mails, Girlie. I have compliance on
my ass now because of you."

"I'm sorry, Chick. I didn't mean it," I said with remorse.

"I don't really care one way or the other, but you can get fired for
stuff like this. Are you feeling better?"

"A little."

"Good. Get to work."

MSG FROM PATRICK, WILLIAM:
Alex, please talk to me . . .

MSG FROM GARRETT, ALEX:
FU&K YOU!

Compliance couldn't complain about that.

My personal life wasn't the only thing falling apart. March 2008
had marked the beginning of the market implosion and things had
only gotten worse since then. People had bought houses they couldn't
afford and spent money they didn't have. Wall Street had sold their debt
to investors, making a lot of people very wealthy along the way, but now
it was causing a lot of problems. The bonds were defaulting. Investment
banks, Wall Street powerhouses, were losing money on the trades. Some

of them went bankrupt—overnight. People were being laid off. People were being evicted. The entire country blamed us. Our jobs, stressful and high pressured under the best of circumstances, had become intolerable. The funny thing is, no one asked us if we should be risking all our money on these trades. No one asked me if I was comfortable with leveraging America to the hilt. No one recognized the fact that the CEO didn't come down here and ask us what we thought before he committed our money and our stock and risked the firm that we loved. The way the public saw it, we were responsible for everything that was wrong with America. I was waiting to open the paper one day and read that Wall Street had killed Kennedy *and* framed Roger Rabbit.

The craziest side effect of the turmoil was that Will was no longer my biggest problem, and I was no longer his. It was hard for me to believe, but the spring and summer of 2008 wouldn't go down in the history books as the end of Alex Garrett's personal life—it would go down as the end of life as we all knew it.

The rest of April was so busy I couldn't possibly worry about Will and what an asshole he turned out to be. I forfeited five hundred bucks to disenroll from pastry school and buckled down. I had to focus on my job, learn as much as I could about what was happening, and try not to let my face register the fear that I felt. By the time the first week of May rolled around, the group was so beaten down and exhausted we needed something to cheer us up. As always, the answer lay in lunch.

"Viva May-heee-co!" Marchetti sang as he approached my desk. "Alex, did you give Patty your lunch order? We're getting burritos today in honor of Cinco de Mayo."

"Patty!" I yelled down the row. "Put me down for a burrito."

"Sure," she said as she came over and leaned on the back of my chair. Since Patty had rescued me from abject humiliation the Monday following my birthday, she'd become a good friend. My loyal sidekick. As difficult as it was to believe, the "new girl" looked up to me for guidance, and she kept a protective eye out. She was one cool chick.

"Will's staring at you again. Are you even going to talk to him?"

"Nope. He's dead to me."

"Me too," she said. "I've already 'forgotten' his enchilada order."

"I appreciate that. I'd prefer you have him killed." She laughed.

After lunch I was tired, so I headed out to get an iced tea at the coffee stand and stretch my legs. As soon as I hit the hallway, I saw Will exiting the elevator and walking toward me. There was nothing I could do to avoid him. I took longer than necessary to extract two dollars from my wallet, because it kept my eyes focused on something other than him. Jashim had decorated the counter for Cinco de Mayo. There was a donkey piñata hanging from the ceiling, and a little wooden bat rested on the counter.

"Miss Alex, happy Cinco de Mayo!" Jashim kissed the back of my hand. *Take that, Will. Maybe you don't want to date me, but the Bangladeshi coffee guy knows a good thing when he sees it.*

"Thanks, Jashim. I like what you've done with the place." Will patiently waited for me to finish stalling. It was obvious I was ignoring him. He didn't seem to care.

Jashim gestured to a small toy dog sitting on the counter. "Did you squeeze the little dog? Go ahead, squeeze him!" I obediently squeezed his back. The dog's mouth started to move and in a Spanish accent it said, "Drop the chalupa." I laughed and turned to leave.

Will was standing there, wearing khaki pants and a short-sleeved green-and-yellow button-down shirt. I hate those shirts. Unless you're responsible for delivering mail or milk, button-down shirts should have long sleeves.

Will cleared his throat before he spoke. "You can't ignore me forever. We sit twenty feet apart." I realized I was still holding the stuffed dog, and so I squeezed it over and over and over again, so that as Will started talking, I was able to drown him out with "Drop the chalupa, drop the chalupa, drop the chalupa." Finally, Will snatched the dog from me.

"I'm sorry, Alex. I wanted to tell you, but I didn't know what to say. I was so wrapped up in my own fucked-up life, I didn't realize . . ."

I snapped. I wanted to punch him in the stomach, but I'm sure that's grounds for dismissal according to the Cromwell handbook.

"You'll have to be more specific as to what, exactly, you *wanted* to tell me. The list of things you *should* have told me but didn't is long, Will. It is really fucking long. Did you *want* to tell me that you were seeing someone else at the same time that you were seeing me? Or did you *want* to tell me that she works here also? Or maybe you *wanted* to tell me that the real reason you never answered my phone calls, and were never around on weekends, or stood me up on my birthday was because you were with your fiancée? Exactly which part rendered you speechless?"

"Alex." He tried to put his hand on mine, but I snatched it away and crossed my arms over my chest. "I should've done a lot of things differently."

"Deep thoughts, Will. I'm so happy we had this conversation."

"No, I mean I'm not happy with myself for the way I handled everything. I . . ."

"You probably shouldn't be happy with the way things turned out. From where I stand, you gained a fiancée who files papers for a living and probably only likes you for your money, and lost a friend whose stomach now turns at the sight of you. If I were you, I'd be unhappy with the way things turned out, too."

"Can't we talk about it? Alex, come on, we have to work together. We have to figure out a way to coexist here five days a week. You aren't very good at hiding the fact that you hate me."

I stared at him in disbelief.

"There was a way for that to happen. But it went out the window the day you allowed that announcement to run in the paper without talking to me first." Without thinking, I picked up the bat from the counter and with two hands, swung as hard as I could at the donkey piñata, hitting it with such force that the hook ripped out of the ceiling. The donkey flew toward the back wall of the coffee stand, forcing Jashim to duck. It ricocheted off the wall and split in half, sending pieces of candy raining down like sugary shrapnel. The Chihuahua was knocked off the counter, landing with a thud and a "Drop the chalupa." Jashim and Will both gawked at me like I was nuts and, for those few seconds, I probably was. I threw the bat on the counter, picked up my Snapple and turned toward Will. "Be happy that the donkey was there, because otherwise I would have swung at your head. We will never, ever be friends, and you have no one but yourself to blame for that."

I left Will to help Jashim pick up the candy and headed back to the floor. When I looked up, I saw Patty frozen in the hallway, holding three singles in her hand—an eyewitness to the piñata massacre. Great.

I stormed back to my desk. I felt Chick's eyes follow me as I passed, but I refused to look at him, knowing for sure that I had left my poker face in the hallway with my pride and most of my sanity. Suddenly, two hands landed on my shoulders. I jumped before I realized who they belonged to. Chick squeezed and whispered in my ear, "You're the best thing that ever could have happened to him. He will *never* do better than you, and he knows it." He patted my head and went back to his desk. For a second I was shocked by what Chick had said, and then even more so when I realized that he'd known the whole time that Will and I were seeing each other. I guess it wasn't the well-kept secret I had thought it was. I figured I'd add it to the list of things that I was oblivious to.

I LOOKED AT THE CLOCK. Three thirty. Two more hours. Only two more hours standing between me and some much-needed margaritas.

Patty and I burst out of the office at 5:30 on the dot and squeezed into a small booth at Tortilla Flats with Annie and Liv. As soon as we were seated Patty poured margaritas into our glasses and placed the empty pitcher down on the floor. Annie leaned forward on her elbows and narrowed her eyes. "Alex, what happened? You went berserk in the office?"

"Berserk is a strong word," Patty said as she reapplied her lip gloss. "But I think it's best if in the future we keep Alex away from blunt objects and baseball bats."

"I wasn't really going to swing at him. And that's what you're supposed to do with a piñata, for the record."

"Hit the piñata? Yes. Smack it into the next decade? Maybe not," Patty pointed out.

"I had to vent. You know how hard it is to sit on the floor with a smile plastered on my face and listen to his voice all day long? It's agonizing. I'm sorry, but I think I'm allowed to be just a little irritated."

Patty was laughing. "Absolutely. Poor piñata."

"You know who he is?" Annie asked as she played with the salt crystals on the rim of her glass. "He's a leave-her-at-the-altar kind of guy. He's the guy who does whatever he wants because, at the end of the day, he doesn't care about anyone else but himself. Just because that poor girl is wearing a ring doesn't actually mean they'll get married. If he bailed on her, it wouldn't surprise me."

"Wow, Annie." Liv nodded in approval. "That's actually a great point." They clinked their glasses together and I drank the rest of my margarita just as the waitress dropped another pitcher in the middle of the table.

"How are things otherwise? Things at work going okay?" Liv asked.

"Not really. Work's a shit show. The markets are in really bad shape, the housing market is getting crushed, our earnings are abysmal, and everyone's worried about getting paid at the end of the year."

"Who cares about the housing market? We rent," Annie said.

"Oh Annie, my dear little grad student. It's not as simple as that. It's all connected. Seven guys were fired yesterday. One minute they were at their desks, and then poof, gone. There's more coming."

"That's awful! Tonight is just what you need to take your mind off everything," Annie said.

"Amen to that. Pass the margos," I said as I reached for the pitcher.

An hour later we had drunk three pitchers of margaritas. Between the alcohol and the sugar content, the entire table was very drunk and very rowdy. A dangerous combination.

Annie clapped, "Ohhhh, I have such a good idea. Gimme your phone, gimme your phone."

"Why?" I asked as I moved it out of her reach on the table.

"Just gimme it. Is his number still in there?"

"Yeah, why? Oh, no, we are NOT calling him, Annie!"

She snatched my phone and scrolled through the address book. "Shhhhhh," she said, her buzz making her braver than she would normally be. "Don't worry, I star-six-sevened. He won't know it's us."

"He's not gonna answer. He never answers his phone, so this is pointless! What are you planning on saying?"

"SHHHHHHHHHHHHHHHHHHHH," she said as she frantically waved her hand in my face. "Perfect. Voice mail!"

"Told you, so hang up!" (Shit like this is why guys think girls are crazy.)

But she didn't. "Hey, Will, it's Kimmy. I just wanted to tell you that I had a really good time, but I still haven't found my underwear, so if you wouldn't mind checking your pockets, I'd appreciate it. I'm looking forward to next week!"

She closed the phone and burst into hysterics.

"I can't believe you just did that," Liv scolded.

"Annie!" I cried, horrified. "He's so going to know that was me!"

"Oh puh-leeeze," she said dramatically. "He's probably cheated on his fiancée with a lot of girls. I bet you he has to think about it. He won't know it's you."

I just stared at my phone, horrified.

"You know what you could do to drive him crazy?" Liv said. "Date someone else in the office."

"Bad idea!" Patty pointed her finger at me from across the table and started talking about me like I wasn't even there. "She can't do that, because, you know, what's the word I'm looking for? She can't be, a . . . ummmmm . . . come on, what's the word?"

"An office tramp?" Annie offered.

"A financial floozy?" Liv dragged out the word *floozy* so that it sounded more like fluuuuu-hooooo-zeeeeee.

"Guys? I'm here, you know that, right? I might be very, very drunk, but I can still hear you."

Patty ignored me and kept going. "The feeee-awwwwn-saaaay, I heard she's the floor whore in Boston. At least she was. Maybe now she's not, since Will is going to make an honest slut out of her." Now this caught my attention. I grabbed Patty's wrist from across the table.

"What do you mean? She's the *floor whore*? She's hooked up with other guys?"

"Apparently. From what I hear, she's made out with guys at more than one Cromwell party. And I don't mean that she dated these guys; I mean she hooked up with them once or twice—and that was that."

"How is it possible that you know this and I don't? I thought I was up on all of the floor gossip!"

"I don't know. One night at drinks people were talking about it and I happened to be there. They were ripping her to shreds."

"He's marrying the office slut?" I just might have found it funny if I wasn't having a horrifying flashback. The Christmas party. I knew she looked familiar! It was her. That was right when Will and I started our e-mail relationship. Oh my God. He was marrying the bathroom slut. Which meant they got together *after* he started seeing me, because there is no way that would have happened if he was already with her. Holy shit.

I received a text message. Will. Perfect timing as always.

SMS from Patrick, William:
Can we please talk? Violence is never the answer.

I held my phone up for them all to read. Exasperated, I wailed, "See? Do you see what I'm dealing with? How . . ." I had something I wanted to say, but I was drunk and I lost my train of thought.

"How what?" they all slurred in unison.

"How am I supposed to respond to this?" I tapped the screen violently with my left index finger, just to make sure that everyone knew what *this* referred to. Before anyone could answer, the phone beeped in my hand again, prompting everyone to become silent, like it was a ticking time bomb or something, which I guess, in some sense, it was.

Annie screamed, "Read it! Actually no, gimme it. I'll read it. I wonder if he got my voice mail?" She reached across the table for my phone. "Come on, give it to me!"

"Read them!" Liv barked. So, I did.

> *SMS from Patrick, William:*
> *I know you're there, stop screening me*

> *SMS from Patrick, William:*
> *Did you just prank call me?*

Shit.

Liv ripped the phone from my hand and tossed it into the pitcher in the middle of the table.

"What are you doing?" I screamed. "Why did you do that? That phone was expensive!" Not only had she ruined my phone but she had ruined our drinks as well. I wasn't sure which was worse.

"I'm sorry, but I can't stand listening to this anymore. Screw him! You're getting a new phone number."

"I think she could have kept the phone and just changed the number, Liv," Annie said as she tried to fish my phone out of the lime-green liquid with a fork.

"Well, I . . . I hadn't thought of that. But it doesn't matter. New phone, new number, new start."

"That I will drink to!" Patty did a tequila shot. Just in case she wasn't drunk enough.

Before I could say anything, from behind me an oddly familiar voice said, "I thought that was you." I turned around to find Matt Matthews, my friendly neighborhood bartender, smiling broadly.

"Well, hello there," I said cheerfully as I excused myself from the table. "I almost didn't recognize you with your arms covered."

"And I almost didn't recognize you without the bloody leg."

He smiled again, revealing a dimple in his cheek that I hadn't noticed before. I could feel the girls' stares boring into my back. *Who is this?* they no doubt wanted to know.

"Things any better than the last time I saw you?" he asked.

I shrugged, noncommittally.

"Come on, I gave you free wine once upon a time. You owe me."

I couldn't help but smile. He had me there. "Turns out the fiancée is the office slut."

"You have an office slut?"

"We do. And she is now engaged to my ex-not-boyfriend."

"Sounds like it was a nice miss. Are you still working in finance?"

"Yep."

"Did you ever check out pastry school?"

"That's a long story."

"You seem to have a lot of long stories."

"More than you know."

I liked Matt. He seemed honest, forthright, uncomplicated (in a good way). I remembered what Will said to me once about enjoying the simple things in life. *When did my life get so complicated?*

"I'm going to start as a chef at a new place in the West Village in a few weeks. I'd love it if you'd stop by sometime and check it out."

Did he just ask me on a date? No, definitely not. A date has a specified place and time. And besides, he was asking me to drop by his place of work. Nevertheless, I felt an oddly familiar twang in my stomach. Nerves?

"Congrats! I'd love to come. If you cook anywhere near as well as you pour cocktails, you'll be amazing."

He removed his phone from the breast pocket of his shirt. "What's your number?"

I programmed my office number in his phone, and he dropped it back in his pocket. "It was great seeing you, Alex. Enjoy the rest of your night. I'll call you."

"Great. I look forward to it." I meant it. The girls barely waited until he was out of earshot before they started shouting questions at me.

"Who was that?" Liv asked as they stared at me with raised eyebrows. I told them what I knew, which wasn't a lot.

"He seems nice," Annie said. "See, there *are* nice guys out there. We just met one."

He did seem nice, didn't he?

I turned and saw Matt chatting with a bunch of guys in jeans; laughing, drinking Coronas, not talking about money, or finance, or themselves. They looked truly happy and relaxed. Two things I hadn't been in far too long. Somewhere along the way, I had got caught up in the glamour of the industry and forgot how to have fun swigging eight-dollar beers instead of two-hundred-dollar bottles of wine. I envied him. He caught me glancing over and smiled. I gave him a small wave good-bye as we grabbed our bags and wobbled out of the bar, marveling at how one small conversation with a virtual stranger could be responsible for a complete shift in my mental state.

When I climbed into bed later that night, my mind was clear. I had great friends. I had a good job. I didn't need a guy dragging me down. For the first night in a while, I didn't drift off to sleep thinking about Will and his fiancée.

I didn't think about him at all.

I was back.

I wish I could say the same for the market.

seventeen

Financial Armageddon

I YAWNED AS I stood against the wall, away from the clutter of people buzzing in between the rows of chairs facing the podium. Every year, Cromwell gave target presentations on elite college campuses, sending alumni to help recruit fresh meat. Mid-May was late in the year to be giving the presentation to the rising juniors and seniors, but considering what was going on at work, we couldn't get away from the office before then. Chick sent me to UVA to trick some new kids into joining the business, despite the fact that the entire financial system was about to collapse. I didn't care. I was just happy to be out of Will's orbit.

"Long week, huh? Don't worry, at least tomorrow's Friday," Laurie, the HR co-coordinator said. I nodded, my eyes closed, and I stifled yet another yawn.

"I'm exhausted. How long is this presentation again?"

"The film's only about ten minutes but then we have an hour reserved for cocktails and I'm sure some eager beavers will linger so we probably won't be out of here for at least an hour and a half."

"I'll be a zombie when I get back to the office."

"I hear you," she said as she checked her watch and determined it was time to start her presentation. "Here." She handed me a familiar-looking laminated name tag.

Christ.

Laurie scurried off to the podium and quieted the frenzied room full of eager undergraduates. I took my seat in the front row with the three other Cromwell UVA alumni, all of us impeccably groomed, wearing expensive suits, and sitting perfectly straight, a shining example of what the students could one day hope to become if they were lucky enough to work at our firm.

What they didn't know couldn't hurt them. Yet.

Laurie leaned into the microphone, "Hello! Welcome to the Cromwell Pierce presentation. We have a brief film overview of life at Cromwell, and after that there will be cocktails and you'll have a chance to ask some UVA graduates what life at Cromwell has been like for them. Please direct your attention to the screen."

Oh good . . . Movie night. Maybe I'd catch a glimpse of Chick in one of the shots.

I stared at the screen as it flashed our firm name and logo in bold letters. I realized that some analyst somewhere probably spent two weeks in the office trying to figure out which shade of yellow to use on the letters, and that analyst would be happy to know that absolutely no one noticed or cared. Pictures of good-looking, well-built, smiling young professionals flashed on the screen as they shook hands with each other, transacted in a calm and friendly manner with traders who no doubt said "please" and "thank you" and sat in convivial circles discussing one another's ideas and opinions in an open forum. There were slides showing energetic, ethnically diverse employees sitting at polished tables in gleaming conference rooms with stunning views, displayed through windows flooded with sunlight. There were scenes of meetings in boardrooms, stretch limousines, and dinners at expensive restaurants with white tablecloths and roaring fireplaces.

It was one step removed from Nazi war propaganda.

Where were the sake bombs?

Where were the people screaming obscenities?

Where was this alleged "trading floor" with the shiny clutter-free desks and carpeting unstained by Marchetti's vending machine vomit?

And who the hell were the people in the film?

Those people didn't work at Cromwell. They were actors. Someone clearly was smart enough to realize that if they filmed an actual trading floor, the college kids would run screaming for the exits.

At least our marketing department earned their paychecks; I'll give them that.

When the first part of the brainwashing session was completed, Laurie returned to the podium and smiled proudly at the masses. "That," she said, "was just a brief glimpse into the life you could have as one of the lucky few selected to join the Cromwell family. At this time, you're invited to join us for cocktails and meet some of your former schoolmates. Use them as a resource. They're here to help!"

I moved quickly toward the exit, wanting to get a drink before the seniors descended on the alcohol like pigeons on New York City sidewalks. I unexpectedly caught a glimpse of myself in the mirror behind the bartender. Alex Garrett, back on campus, drinking a glass of wine.

Wearing a pin-striped suit, a silk blouse, and a name tag.

What did you do to yourself? I asked my reflection in horror.

She didn't have an answer.

When I turned from the bar, students immediately accosted me. They stared at my name tag and extended their hands.

"Hi, Ms. Garrett."

"Nice to meet you, Ms. Garrett."

"Can I ask you a few questions, Ms. Garrett?"

I nodded. "Sure."

A guy with a bright red tie that was entirely too large for his geeky thin frame fired first. "What do you think are some of the most important qualities one must possess to succeed on Wall Street?"

The ability to throw your pride out the window and become a human doormat was the first response that came to mind.

I couldn't say that.

I turned my attention to a small blond girl with a perky demeanor and a southern accent.

"Do you find it difficult being a woman on the desk?"

Difficult? Nah . . . I've had no problem in discovering that I hooked up with an engaged coworker. And now that I think about it, I enjoyed being called ugly after witnessing a blatant act of adultery, and I've had absolutely no problem with being the target of a psycho client stalker. All in a day's work. You should try it, Blondie. I'm sure they'd just loooooove you.

I shouldn't say that.

"What drove you to the Business originally? Why did you choose Cromwell over other firms?" asked a guy whom I could tell immediately was a future Will-in-training by the fact that he oozed cockiness for no apparent reason.

The ignorance of youth. I chose Cromwell because I didn't have to wear a suit. Choosing by any other criterion is a waste. They're all the same.

Probably shouldn't say that, either. "I chose Cromwell because of the diversity of opportunities it offered and, of course, for its sterling reputation."

"So you'd recommend applying for a job in finance?"

"Absolutely."

Liar.

"Have you ever struggled with your decision to go to Wall Street?"

"Never."

Liar, liar, days-of-the-week panties on fire.

"And you're really happy with your career path and your life at the firm?"

"Couldn't be happier."

Shameless. Pathological. Liar.

I had never been more ashamed of myself in my life. I excused myself and walked over toward the window and stared out at the students strolling across campus, blissfully unaware of how much their lives would change once they joined the working world. I felt an overwhelming sense of guilt for lying to the kids who were expecting me to give them straight answers, to serve as an example, to help them navigate their way into their professional lives.

And I lied to their faces.

I overheard a group of students talking nervously about the interviews they had endured earlier in the day.

"He asked me which end I squeezed the toothpaste from," a brighteyed brunette announced as she regaled her friends with the details of her interview. "What do you think he wanted me to say? What's the right answer?"

"He probably wanted you to say that you squeeze from the bottom to make sure you get every last bit out. You know, finance people want to know that you don't waste anything."

A blond-haired, surfer type better suited to Hollywood than to a life in finance seemed impressed with himself for breaking the cryptic code: "Yeah, they have a name for it on Wall Street. Leaving money on the table. That's when you don't keep every cent you can."

"Ohhh, I bet you're right. That's soooooooooo what he wanted me to say! Shoot! Now I'm not going to get the job!"

Starfish Ted really needed to come up with new interview questions.

Fuck it.

I was no Starfish Ted.

I had made my decision a long time ago, but I wasn't comfortable with encouraging anyone else to come to the Street unless they really knew what they were in for. "Hey, guys, do you mind if I give it another whirl?" I said as I walked back over to them. The gaggle of students gathered round, and I began to tell them what no salesperson on the Street should ever tell recruits. The truth.

. . . .

WHEN I GOT BACK to work the following morning, I walked into utter chaos. Summers tended to be a little slow on Wall Street, especially Fridays. People went on vacation, people left early to play golf, no one could seem to focus when the weather was so blissfully beautiful. Not this summer.

Just when you thought things couldn't possibly get worse, they did. Coming to work felt like being on an elevator in free fall. I reviewed the week's data. Confidence: down. Jobless claims: up. Manufacturing: down. Equity markets: down. Credit spreads: out. Treasury yields: down. It was financial Armageddon.

I glanced at my screen, every single number flashing red. Maybe the bankers I put that presentation together for when I was the new girl had been right. Red was definitely not a comforting color.

"Did they fire anyone today?" I asked Drew as he glanced at the headlines running across the newswires.

"Not today. I hear there's another round coming on Monday. Apparently they're going to whack a few guys in corporates."

"Are they going to cut our group? What if I get fired?"

"You're not getting fired. Relax. Chick loves you. We aren't going to get paid a freaking dime, but we'll have jobs."

"Don't joke like that, Drew. I count on that bonus."

"No shit, we all do. But it's going to be bad this year, Al, really bad. If I were you, I'd put a serious halt on my spending. No more shoes. Bear markets can last a long time. You need to have money in savings."

Great, and I'd blown a few hundred bucks on a fancy, new state-of-the-art phone that had powers I hadn't even yet begun to understand.

Chick walked into the middle of the group. Everyone stopped what they were doing, expecting bad news. It was the only kind of news we got lately.

"Okay, guys, listen up. I know things have been tough around here lately and morale isn't great, so we're going to have a team dinner next Thursday. And just in case anyone is wondering, your attendance is mandatory. I may or may not organize an after-party but I'll let you know about that later." He looked tired and old. Not like the usual confident, arrogant boss I'd grown to love and respect. He looked *scared*.

We sat in uneasy silence for a few seconds. After Chick returned to his seat, I turned toward Drew. "Chick's been weird. What do you think is going on?" I asked, concerned.

"He's stressed out, Alex. I don't think we have any idea how bad it actually is, but you couldn't pay me enough to be in management right now."

"What should we do?"

"Just keep your mouth shut and stay off the radar. The less people that notice you exist in times like this, the better." Drew grabbed his backpack from under his desk. "I'm heading out. Have a good weekend."

"You're leaving now? It's only four thirty! Not really the time to be leaving work early, Drew." I grabbed the new economics report and a highlighter and began to read. I figured looking busy couldn't be a bad thing, even if it was all for show.

"It's Friday, and we got completely beat up this week. I'm leaving. Don't stay too late. The weeks are only going to get longer from here on out."

I watched Drew leave and tried to reassure myself that he was right about us being safe. Our group was making money. In down markets, our group always made money. The only place people wanted to put their cash when the world was exploding was in Treasury debt. I shut down my system and practically ran off the floor at 5:01. I was a block away from the office when I heard Will's voice behind me.

"Alex, stop. You can't avoid me forever."

"Wanna bet? I've managed so far."

Good one, Alex.

"Please. Stop." He had caught up to me, and unfortunately there weren't any cabs for me to hail.

Or push him in front of.

"I'm not interested in hearing anything you have to say to me, Will," I said.

"I'm so sorry. I didn't mean to hurt you."

"You lied to my face. Forgive me if I'm not interested in listening to any more of your bullshit."

"I didn't lie to you, I just . . . left some things out."

"You told me you didn't want a girlfriend!" I wailed.

He put his hands in his pockets. "I fucked up. I get it. I fucked up, and I'm sorry. But I miss you. I miss talking to you and hanging out with you, and joking around with you . . . and there are some things I want to tell you, Alex. I don't want it to be like this."

"Are you still engaged?" I asked as the familiar wave of nausea overcame me.

He looked down at his loafers and choked out a barely audible "Yes."

I put both of my hands on his chest and pushed him as hard as I could, which really didn't have the effect I wanted since he was six inches taller than me. He took a step backward to put more room in between us, but I stepped closer and pushed him again. This time he grabbed my wrists.

"Stop."

"Will, what do you want from me?" I asked on the brink of hysteria. "Here I am. What the hell do you want?"

He ran his hands through his hair and continued to stare at the dirty cement sidewalk. I finally realized why he wasn't answering: he didn't know the answer himself.

There was one thing I needed to know, or else I was destined to beat piñatas with baseball bats for the rest of my life. "I asked you at Nobu why you never answered my calls, and you gave me some bullshit excuse about not liking the phone. I asked you why you were never around on the weekends, and you didn't tell me the truth. You had an out, right then, and you didn't take it. You're so interested in being friends now, why not just do the right thing then, instead of backpedaling and trying to make yourself feel better by telling me that you didn't want a serious girlfriend? No shit you didn't want a serious girlfriend. You already had one!"

"I was confused. She lived in Boston. I never saw her during the week. I'd see you during the day, and we'd hang out and I found myself liking you, too, and I didn't want that to end. I like you, Alex. I know I hurt you and I know you hate me, and if I could go back and do things differently, I would. But this hasn't been easy for me, either."

Well, now that was probably the one version of the answer I wasn't expecting.

"Why not break up with her then?" Tears welled in my eyes, despite my best efforts to stop them. I had promised myself I was done crying over him. I had lied to me.

"That night at Nobu, I didn't know which one of you . . ."

"Which one of us what?"

He cringed, knowing his answer was going to hurt. "Which one of you I wanted to be with. And I was drunk. So were you!"

"Don't you dare put this on me," I said. Wasn't that just like a man. It's your fault, even when it's not. I'm joining a convent.

He looked disheveled. In the last ten minutes on this sidewalk, he'd completely lost his composure. Now he knew how I felt. "Listen, there's something else I want to tell you."

"What? You're registered at Crate&Barrel? Don't expect me to send you a set of stemware."

"Just listen to me."

I shrugged.

"I'm miserable," he admitted. "I wish I could go back and do things differently. I don't want to go through with the wedding. I don't know what I was thinking. I want . . . I want for us . . ."

If he was going where I thought he was going, I didn't want to hear the rest of it. I was so done with this situation it was funny. Except it wasn't. Not even a little.

I snapped.

"No one forced you to propose. What the hell possessed you to ask her to marry you if you didn't want to marry her?"

"It's complicated."

"Is she pregnant?"

"No."

"Does she need a green card?"

"No."

"Then I really don't see how it could be complicated."

"Her father is the CFO of a major firm in Boston. The amount of money I could make off him is staggering."

You've. Got. To. Be. Kidding. Me.

"You can't be serious. You asked her to marry you *for her father's money*?"

He didn't answer.

"Wow. I guess women aren't the only ones who can sleep their way to the top, huh? You two deserve each other. You certainly don't deserve me. Fuck off."

The conversation, like our relationship, like our friendship, was over. And it hurt.

I hailed a cab and left him standing alone on the sidewalk.

JUNE 2008 WAS A DISASTER. It was getting to the point where I was afraid to tell people what I did for a living. Where I had once felt pride I now felt fear. Phones rang nonstop, the group unable to keep up with the endless demand for information. Clients wanted to know what was going on: Would things rebound? Should they be selling as the market traded down, or buying in the hopes that it would rebound? Where did we think unemployment would end up? Did we think it could hit 10 percent? The one thing all the clients had in common was that they were panicked. The traders were frazzled, cursing, breaking things, unable to clot their bleeding P&Ls.

One Monday morning there was an unexpected lull in the incessant ringing phones. I took a few minutes to collect myself and take stock of the situation. As soon as I looked up, I could sense that something was very wrong. No one was hungry, and that was never a good sign.

Drew read the news headlines scrolling across his computer. He raised his eyebrows at me as I rolled my chair over toward him.

"What's going on? Something's wrong," I said.

Drew looked over conspiratorially and said in a low voice, "A lot of meetings going on with senior management. Too many people behind closed doors, a lot of whispering in the hallways. No one has seen Chick yet. It isn't good."

"Maybe he's in a meeting?" I asked, panicked.

"Maybe *he's* the reason for the meeting."

Oh shit.

This was bad. A new desk head meant you had to interview for your own job, and if the new boss didn't like you, for whatever reason, you'd be fired and replaced by one of his friends. You had to be very careful not to make any enemies on the Street, because there was a good chance you would end up working with everyone again somewhere along the way. (Apparently Cruella missed that memo.)

"You think Chick is leaving? Who's going to run the group? Where's he going? Does he have an offer somewhere else?"

"Do I look like a Magic Eight Ball? I don't think it's his choice to leave, if that's what's even happening."

"What are we supposed to do?"

"Wait."

We didn't have to wait long.

Reese stood up five minutes later and announced that we were wanted in the conference room. We looked at one another and hesitantly followed him. No one spoke. I took a seat in one of the chairs against the wall. The rules of hierarchy weren't suspended just because you were in a conference room; if you weren't at least a vice president, you had better not even think of sitting at the table.

Not long after we all were seated, Darth Vader entered the room.

Darth sat at the head of the table. Chick's chair. I held my breath, waiting for Chick to walk in, kick Darth out of his seat, fold his hands behind his head, and throw his Gucci loafers on the table.

Any minute now.

"As of this morning, Ed Ciccone is no longer with the firm," Darth said matter-of-factly. He was unemotional, apathetic, uninterested. He was the anti-Chick.

Oh shit.

"I know this is a shock for all of you, but we're trying to make this transition as smooth as possible. I'll be running the group going forward."

Oh shit.

"I just want to make one thing clear up front. I don't run things the way Chick did. I'll be making some changes."

Oh shit.

"One thing you can count on is that this place will look very different a few months from now. Does anyone have any questions?"

No one raised a hand. Everyone was too busy thinking: *Oh shit.*

"One more thing. I think you all know my assistant, Hannah. She's joining the group as well. I trust you'll make her feel welcome."

Just when you thought things couldn't get any worse, we get Baby Gap, too.

"That's it. Everyone back to work."

I was about to leave the room when Darth called out to me.

"Alex, hang back a second. I need to talk to you."

Was he going to fire me right now? On his first day?

"Yes, Keith?"

"I called the focus clients this morning to let them know that Chick wasn't running the group anymore, and I spoke with Rick Kieriakis at AKS."

Oh God, please don't say what I think you're going to say.

"He had some very positive things to say about you. I have to admit, I was surprised to discover that such a big client would have such a strong view on a junior salesperson. You've made quite an impression on him. He asked that you cover him going forward. I wasn't particularly thrilled with the idea since there are far more experienced salespeople who should be in charge of that account, but he was adamant in his request. As of today, you're responsible for AKS."

No. AKS was Chick's account.

I wanted to tell him that I couldn't cover the account. But AKS could make a salesperson's career. Of course, they could also break a career if they wanted, and I now had no choice but to put up with the inappropri-ate notes, messages, and comments. If I didn't, Rick wouldn't have any problem telling Darth that I sucked as a salesperson. Not only would I lose a thirty-million-dollar account, but I'd also lose my job. Getting on the *Titanic* originally sounded like a really good thing, too, and look how that turned out.

I panicked, adrenaline flooding my central nervous system, caus-ing my entire body to quake. *Run,* every fiber in my body instructed. *Run and don't look back.*

I couldn't. What if I could win him over? What if I could make it work? Then the more likely possibility: What if he never stopped harassing me, and instead, was simply given carte blanche to do it?

Oh shit.

Run, my body pleaded with my brain. *Run!*

"Thanks, Keith. I appreciate the opportunity. I won't let you down." My mother was right. Pride was going to be my undoing.

"We'll see about that. Get back to work."

It was official: redheads were ruining my life.

P LEASE DON'T TELL ME you got canned the first five minutes he's been in charge," Drew said when I got back to my desk.

"No, Drew. Although that might have been better."

"What happened?"

"He wants me to cover Rick. This is either the worst or the best day of my life. I'm not sure which yet."

"Oh shit," he said. "Well, if you can make this work, you can write your ticket anywhere you want on the Street. People will be throwing money at you. It's a really phenomenal opportunity."

"And the downside? What about that?"

"I don't know what to tell you there, Girlie. You have to run with it, and do the best you can. That's your only option. Make lemonade out of lemons, if you will."

"That lemonade better be spiked. I need a drink. I'm dreading this phone call."

"Just suck it up and get it over with. The longer you wait, the worse it will be. He's expecting to hear from you."

I hit the light. Rick answered on the first ring.

"Well, well. Alex Garrett calling *me*. It must be my lucky day."

"Hey, Rick. I guess you know the reason I'm calling. I spoke to Keith. Thanks for the recommendation."

"What did I tell you, Alex? Back on the roof, remember? I told you that one day you'd end up covering me. I'd imagine there are more than a few guys on your desk seething with jealousy. You just leapfrogged over at least half a dozen guys in line for this account. You can thank me later. I'm sure I'll come up with something. From now on, I expect you to be all over me. I want you on me like a hungry dog on a bone." Then he growled—actually *growled*—which I guess he thought sounded sexy. FYI: It didn't.

"Do you have a few minutes to review your strategy and some of the positions you currently have on?" I asked as I nervously twisted my phone cord.

"At the moment, I don't. You can understand, of course, with the markets being the way they are. I don't really have the time to get you up to speed. Why don't you meet me tonight after work and we'll talk? Say, six o'clock at the Tribeca Grand Hotel?"

Shocker, a hotel bar.

"Sure, that works. I'll see you there."

"I'm looking forward to it. The conversation might take a while. Why don't we plan on getting dinner, too?"

Joy.

I headed toward the coffee stand and passed Baby Gap as she unpacked her things and placed them on her new desk. As I barreled by she stopped me. Her striped button-down shirt gaped so massively between the buttons on her chest I couldn't believe they didn't pop off from the strain.

"Hey, Alex?" she asked with her usual vocal inflection, the kind that ends every sentence on an up note as if her life was filled with only questions. Which it was. "What's the name of the country next to Spain? You know, the one where they speak Portuguese?"

"Germany," I replied. In that instant, a button exploded from her shirt, and ricocheted like a pinball off her computer monitor before disappearing beneath a desk.

"Alex, hellllllllp," she shrieked, as she grabbed her shirt placket and attempted to stretch the fabric over her silicone mammaries.

"Go find a safety pin!" I yelled as Hannah proceeded to run off the floor in search of a makeshift fastener. As she made her way to the ladies' room, half the men on our trading desk gave her a standing ovation. I looked back at Drew, shocked.

Drew rocked in his chair and laughed hysterically. "Shit, you just can't make this stuff up."

"Drew! I'm lucky I didn't just lose an eye! Honestly, how hard is it to buy clothes that fit?"

"I don't know, but I hope she never figures it out. I still have fond memories of last Tuesday, when she wore those sweet white pants with the hot pink thong. You should see the pictures I got of her ass with my phone."

"You guys are all hopeless, you know that?"

"Hey, don't fault me for having perfect vision."

When I arrived at the coffee stand, I found Reese and Marchetti getting lattes. Marchetti put me in a headlock and mussed my hair.

"So you got Rick, Girlie?"

"Yeah, it's great," I lied. "I'm a little nervous though. I hope I don't screw up." *Understatement of the century.*

"You won't screw up. Just don't execute any trades at four if the market's at ten," Marchetti said without missing a beat, once again reminding me that mistakes on this floor were never forgotten.

"Aww, cut sugar some slack! That was a long time ago. Has he set up drinks with you yet? It's been what, an hour?" Reese asked.

"Tonight at the Tribeca Grand."

"You better bring a stun gun or something with you, Girlie," Reese said as we waited for our coffees.

"Has anyone talked to Chick?" I asked.

"Not yet . . ." Reese answered. "I'm going to call him tonight. I don't know how the hell this happened. Chick must have pissed someone off pretty bad for him to get fired. It doesn't make a whole lot of sense."

"Nothing makes sense here anymore," Marchetti reminded us. "For fuck's sake, Baby Gap's on our team now. If I could start selling my stock right this second, I would."

Reese and I nodded in agreement. Then we looked at one another in silent, mutual despair and returned to the floor.

eighteen

Golden Handcuffs

I ENTERED THE dimly lit hotel bar on Sixth Avenue. It was only 6:00 but happy hour was already in full swing, New Yorkers having elevated postwork cocktails into an art form. The bar was more crowded than usual, but that was true of most places in Manhattan. Whenever the stock market was down, the bars were full. You could count on it.

Rick was chatting with the bartender when I approached him. "Alex! My new sales coverage, and the prettiest of them all. I'm a lucky guy. Of course, you're a lucky girl, too. Six months from now you'll be buying yourself an apartment with the money you make off me."

That could very well be true, but what would it cost me in return? I put on my game face. "I'm looking forward to it. You'll have to provide me with some insight into the inner workings of AKS. You have a lot of smart guys at the fund, some of the best on the Street."

"That's absolutely true, and we'll get to that. How are you holding up with the transition?"

I sighed. "It's been a hard day, obviously."

"It's too bad about Chick, but he'll land on his feet. He's a talented guy."

I nodded.

"Let's move on to the reason we're here. We're going to have to develop a closer personal relationship now that we have a working relationship. Don't you agree?"

Not really. None of my other clients hit on me; why should I have to put up with it from you? But, once more, dollar signs flashed in front of my eyes, so I held my tongue and said nothing. It sucked.

"Can I get you a drink?" he asked.

"Sure. I'll have a glass of white wine, please." If I was going to have this conversation, I was going to need my good friends Pinot and Grigio.

Rick ordered himself a scotch. We moved from the bar to a small cocktail table by the windows.

"Alex, let me ask you something. I get the distinct feeling that you don't like me. Why is that? Do you have any idea how many people would kill their mothers to cover me?"

Are you for real?

"I don't dislike you, Rick. I don't even know you."

"Ahh, good salesmanship. Pretend to like the people you don't. You've had some good mentors along the way."

I wish Reese was here right now. He'd kick your ass through the window.

"You never thanked me for the flowers I sent you. I took that to mean you didn't like them."

"Oh, no, they were fine. Do you mind if I ask how you got my address? Did Chick give it to you?"

He laughed. "Chick wouldn't have given me your personal information if I threatened to set him on fire. His secretary, on the other hand, is so starved for attention she'll tell you anything you want to know if you're nice to her. She even helped me out when your cell phone stopped taking messages; luckily you gave Chick the new number right away in case he needed to be in touch with you. Not that he's going to need to talk to you anymore."

Nancy. I should have known.

"You look surprised."

"No. I'm just . . . thinking." I said. And I was.

"You know, I used to believe that women didn't belong on Wall Street, other than as secretaries, of course. I truly didn't think one could be qualified to do what we do every day. Handle the pressure, do math in her head, maintain composure."

I smirked. "Sorry to prove your theory wrong."

He took off his jacket and laid it down on the cocktail table next to his highball. "I'm all for women in the workforce, I really am."

"That's a good thing since you just asked Keith if one could cover you," I said, before I could stop myself. I had to watch the attitude. It wasn't in the job description.

"I don't know that they should be in this specific industry though, what with the grueling hours and the stress. It's a tough environment, not really suited for the fairer sex if you ask me."

I didn't.

He gulped down his drink and shook the glass so that the cubes rattled back and forth against the crystal, a little ice bell for the waitress. "Take you, for example," he said as he reached out and lightly tapped the end of my nose with his index finger.

Oh great. Let's use me as an example.

"You aren't married."

"No."

Not that there's anything wrong with that.

"You're smart, beautiful, and yet, you aren't married. Do you want to know why?"

I suddenly felt like my skin was on fire. I knew why; because I had wasted the scarce amount of free time I had on a lying Wall Street bastard, that's why. Before I got too caught up in that train of thought, I returned my attention to Rick, who was midpontification: " . . . deterioration of family values, deterioration of gender roles. Women don't want to be treated like women anymore. They want to prove that they can make their own money, buy their own dinner, hell, even fix their own cars."

"The nerve of us!" I was losing my patience.

"Women are so busy working, they're getting married later and having fewer children. You're wasting time just because you think you've got something to prove. *That's* why you aren't married yet."

"Silly me, I assumed it was because I hadn't met the right guy."

"You probably have met the right guy. You've just been too busy to notice."

"Well, lucky for you then. Otherwise you wouldn't have coverage at Cromwell right now."

"That's unlikely, sweetheart." He leaned in closer and I could smell his stale, warm breath. It took all of my willpower not to puke all over the table. "You know, I can make you a very rich girl."

Yes, I was aware. Otherwise, I wouldn't have been talking to him. I sure as hell wasn't meeting him because I enjoyed the view. I pulled away and sat ramrod straight in my chair. "And I can make you a very rich man. I'll make sure that you have full access to everything we have at Cromwell. Meetings with traders, economists, all our research and trade ideas. I'm confident I can do a really good job for you."

He laughed a deep guttural laugh. "I'm sure you can do a really good job for me, and I expect you to. But, sweetie, I don't need you to set up my meetings. If I want to talk to a trader, I'll call him myself. And I don't plan on taking investment advice from a skirt. I doubt that's why Chick hired you either. There are a million smart guys out there he could have given your job to. Why do you think he picked you?"

I knew if I told him to go play Frogger with oncoming traffic that Keith would have my head. Still, I refused to let him defame Chick's character now that he was gone.

"He picked me because I'm smart, and I worked my ass off for him."

"And I'm sure the guys on the desk have loved watching that ass while it worked."

God, I've so had enough of this.

"I don't think your wife would appreciate you talking to me like that.

I know you've had a few drinks so I'll let it go, but I think we should probably just end this conversation now before you say something you regret." I smiled diplomatically.

"I know exactly what I'm saying, and I mean every word."

"Rick. Look. I don't know what kind of agreement you and your wife have worked out, and it's none of my business. So why don't we discuss your account in a professional manner, and stop with all this game playing?"

I could teach a course on how to attract highly dysfunctional people.

"Come on, Alex," he said menacingly. "You still don't understand how this business works, do you?"

"Yes, I do."

"Men like variety. *I* like variety. I don't want to go home to my wife every single night, especially when this city is filled with girls like you. And not all of them are in the position to make money from me. At least, not legally."

"Can I ask you a question?"

"I'd love for you to ask me a question." He raised a lone eyebrow.

"Tina is gorgeous, and she seems very nice. Why do you bother with me when you have her at home? She's most guys' dream woman."

"Tina," he murmured as he scratched his head. "I'll tell you about Tina, Alex. Tina and I got married when we were young. Too young. We got married because she was pregnant and it was the right thing to do. Back then I was just starting out. We didn't have any money or any idea what we were doing. We didn't get a prenup. You don't think I've thought about divorcing her? I've thought about divorcing her, no, check that, I've *dreamed* about divorcing her, for the last ten years. Except her family is from Atlanta, and she made it very clear that if I ever filed for divorce she'd be on the next midnight train to Georgia with my kids *and* half of my money. HALF of my money. Do you have any idea what it's like to be trapped in a marriage because you got married when you were too young to know any better? Can you even imagine what it's like to be held prisoner by your own bank account?"

Oddly enough, I did. We were both tethered to lives the younger versions of ourselves had decided we should have. We both wore golden handcuffs, and we both suffered the consequences of allowing the lure of money trump our chances for happiness. Of course, I didn't go around banging anything that walked to get back at Cromwell for the loveless marriage we were in.

But everyone had their own coping mechanisms, I guess.

I made my decision, although it might not have been a good one. "I don't think that I should cover you, Rick. I'll talk to Keith about it in the morning. Maybe he'll fire me, but hopefully he will just reassign you to someone else. It might be the biggest mistake of my career to pass up the chance to work with AKS, but I don't see any other option at this point."

"I'm handing you a golden opportunity to make some really easy money, and if you don't want to take me up on it, that's fine. But you're not reassigning coverage, and you're *not* mentioning this to Keith. You want to play with the big guys, little girl? I'll treat you the way you want to be treated. But remember, you asked for it. And when I call Cromwell in the morning, you better be the one answering the phone. You're playing in the big leagues now."

"Thank you," I said, well aware that his statement wasn't meant to be reassuring.

"You won't be thanking me tomorrow. Let's see how well you do now without Chick watching your back, sweetheart." He abruptly stood, swept his jacket off the table, and stormed out of the bar.

I leaned back in my chair and closed my eyes, convincing myself that everything was fine. Except I knew it wasn't. Tomorrow morning I was going to have to deal with him all over again: and the day after that, and the day after that, and the day after that, without Chick to protect me. The all-too-familiar weight returned to my chest. I counted backward from ten until the giant elephant compressing my rib cage went back to the circus or wherever it was elephants went when they weren't suffocating me in the Tribeca Grand Hotel.

· · · ·

T HE NEXT MORNING the phone rang at exactly 7:02. I hadn't even
     logged into my system yet.

Here we go.

"Good morning," I said cheerily.

"What the fuck took you so long?" he barked in my ear.

"I'm sorry?"

"I want my line answered on the first ring. The first fucking ring, do you hear me? I don't care who you have to hang up on. You got that?" He was so loud, I flinched.

"I apologize. It won't happen again." Sales 101. It was my fault, even if it wasn't.

"I want to know how the trading desk is positioned, and then I want to see where the on-the-run repos have averaged overnight for the past week. I want to see the 3s–5s–7s butterfly regressed against the outright level of five-year rates over the last ten years when the Fed has been in an easing cycle. Then I want to see range accrual notes on three-month LIBOR with a floor at zero and a 6 percent cap, and a list of what kind of accounts have been involved in the trade."

Now? It would take me two hours to get all this together. I wasn't even sure what half of this stuff meant, and none of my other accounts had even called in yet. "I'll get on it right away."

He cut me off. "I'm having a team meeting today. I want you to bring your head of North American Economics, Bob Keating, to meet with us, and I want steaks from the Palm ordered in for lunch. Call my assistant for our orders. The meeting's at noon. Don't fuck it up."

Click.

I looked at my watch, 7:15. How in God's name was I going to be able to get all this information together by 11:30? Fear, as it turns out, is one hell of a motivator. I immediately shot off a note to the repo desk, telling them I needed a grid for all the on-the-run bonds and their overnight averages for the last seven trading days. When Rick said he wanted the rates for the past week did he mean calendar week (seven days) or business week (five days)? I decided that it was better to bring too much information rather than too little. Task number one, complete.

I ran over to one of the traders on the structured notes desk and grabbed his shoulders as he stared at his screens.

"I need help," I said as I rubbed his shoulders.

"Ohhh, a little to the left," he said, without turning around. "What can I do for you?"

"AKS wants to see a bunch of stuff." *Stuff* was all I could come up with to encompass the mass of material Rick wanted. I showed him my notebook, where I had written down Rick's requests verbatim. Hopefully, he knew what it all meant.

"That's a lot of analysis, Alex. When do you need it by?" he asked.

"In about three hours," I said, waiting for him to tell me to go fuck myself.

He spun around in his chair. "*Three hours?* I've got live orders working here. I don't know if I'll be able to get all that to you in only three hours."

"Try please. He's in a pissy mood and I have to go up his office in Midtown at noon for a meeting. Is there any way you can get it to me in time? I'm drowning. I've got a new boss, a new client that hates me, and I'm about a week away from ending up in an asylum."

"I'll try my best. I'll send you whatever I have around eleven, okay?"

"Thanks," I said. "I owe you."

"Damn right you do!" he yelled as I ran back to my desk.

I rang up our chief economist's office, reaching his plucky secretary. By some kind of finance miracle, he was free for a lunch meeting and his secretary offered to order the car. I pulled up our internal analytical system and began to upload graphs and bar charts. I summoned everything Chick had ever taught me, threw it all into a few additional charts, making sure that both the X and Y axes were labeled properly and that the colors would be easily distinguishable from one another. One thing I had learned from the bankers was to never underestimate the importance of color coordination. I saved the file, uploaded it onto an e-mail, and looked at the clock.

Ten thirty.

I checked my e-mail. There was a file from the repo desk. I uploaded
it on to a spreadsheet, and waited for the file from the structured notes
desk. At 11:02 I received an e-mail with the subject line, "You owe me."
I dumped that data into a spreadsheet, sent the whole thing to the copy
center with the subject header, "Life or death, need ten copies. Pick up
in 20 minutes."

Send.

I stopped by the trading desk to find out how they were positioned
before sprinting up to the copy center to grab my books, still warm from
the machines.

"Where are you heading?" Drew asked as I grabbed my bag.

"AKS. He wanted me to bring Bob up there for a lunch meeting . . ."
As soon as I said the L-word, I froze.

Lunch.

Shit.

I had forgotten to order the steaks. I grabbed a *Zagat's Guide* from
my desk and typed the number into my phone memory as I ran off the
floor holding a stack of pitch books under my arm like a football. Then I
punched in the digits for AKS.

Mercifully, Rick's secretary answered on the first ring. I fished a
pen from the bottom of my purse and, as she dictated, I scribbled the
order on the back of the opposite hand.

I lost service while I rode the elevator, so I had to wait until I reached
the lobby to dial the number for the Palm.

"Hi, yes, I need to place an order for delivery and I should've called
sooner and I know it's short notice but if this food is late, I'm dead."

"We'll try our best," the man said. I saw Bob, our Very Important
Economist, waiting impatiently at the bottom of the escalator. I tried to
wave but I couldn't with the books occupying one hand and the phone in
the other, especially since I needed to be able to read the order off the
back of my hand carrying the books. I wobbled off the escalator, nodded
in Bob's direction, and ran up to the car dispatcher's desk. I threw the

Zagat's and my books on the counter and repeated the lunch order into my phone.

"Six strips medium rare, two medium strips, two orders of fries, a dozen bottles of Pellegrino, two Caesar salads, and one shrimp cocktail." The car dispatcher looked at me inquiringly.

"Confirmation number 9912," I said.

"What's that about 9912?" the Palm guy asked.

"No, that wasn't for you, sorry. Did you get the order?"

"Your car's out front, with instructions to wait," the car dispatcher said. I nodded and mouthed a thank-you to the dispatcher, grabbed the pitch books off the counter, and sprinted back toward Bob. I dumped the books in his hands, which he didn't appreciate, and pushed through the revolving doors without saying a word.

"Credit card number?" the Palm guy asked. The phone was lodged between my ear and my shoulder.

"Car 9912!" I yelled to yet another dispatcher waiting on the curb.

"Okay, 9912, next four digits?"

"No, what? That's not for you, sorry. Hold on one second. That's not the card number." I slid into the backseat of the car and Bob climbed in behind me, still holding my presentations, and not hiding the fact that he didn't consider serving as my lackey a part of his job description.

I dug my American Express card out of my wallet and read off the number.

The driver turned and looked at us. "Where to?"

"Fifty-Eighth and Sixth."

The Palm guy asked, "What about fifty-eight?"

"No, NO. That's not for you either."

"You're confusing me, miss. Can we go over the order again?" I held my hand over the mouthpiece of my phone and repeated the AKS address to the driver. I turned my attention back to the lunch order, well aware of the fact that if I screwed up lunch, it wouldn't matter how much information I brought with me to the meeting. I'd be dead.

"Okay, let's confirm," I said. I reviewed my hand and mentally crossed off each item as the Palm guy read the order back to me. "That's right. I need it in twenty-five minutes. *Please.*"

He must have heard the panic in my voice because I thought I heard a note of compassion in his voice as the Palm guy assured me, "We'll try, miss. We'll really try."

I hung up, panting. Bob shoved the books into my lap. "Are you okay?" he asked.

"Yes. I'm so, so, so sorry. Today has just been a mess and this meeting popped up last minute and I wasn't really prepared. But now I am. I think."

"Well, pull it together before we get up there. Rick is an important client. I've known him for years. I don't usually attend meetings with salespeople so out of sorts. It's not the Cromwell way."

I laughed to myself. *Let me tell you a thing or two about the Cromwell way . . .*

We arrived at the AKS office and I literally ran into two delivery guys in the lobby. They were holding large cardboard boxes and plastic bags, waiting to check in at the security desk. "Follow me," I said, leading the way.

Rick met us in the hallway outside the conference room. He greeted Bob warmly—like they were about to start a round of golf—before turning to me.

"Alex, how are you?" he asked as he kissed me on my cheek, letting his lips linger a little longer than was necessary. "Do you have everything I asked for?"

"I do," I said triumphantly.

"We'll see," he said, sounding none too pleased. "Right this way, everyone is waiting in the conference room."

We followed him into a large room containing a massive mahogany table surrounded by buttery leather chairs. A large flat-screen TV dominated one wall. I placed the food in the middle of the table and set up the waters on a side console by an ice bucket and crystal glasses. Rick and his colleagues attacked the food, piling their plates high. Bob and I sat at the head of the table, without so much as a glass of tap water. This wasn't a lunch meeting for *us*. We were here to work.

I sat back in my chair and listened intently as we flipped through the data I'd collected and Bob walked us through the collapse of the financial markets. It scared me. If Bob was right, things were a lot worse than I had thought. Bob fielded questions for over an hour once he had finished, and I took notes so that I would have something smart and different to tell my other clients when I called them later. As much as this meeting was for Rick and his minions, it was for me, too. I had been extremely lucky to gain access to Bob who, as Very Important Economist, was in high demand throughout the company and, increasingly, around the world. When the caucus had concluded, we shook hands with the AKS traders and strategists, and Rick walked us back to the elevators. I looked at my watch, 2:30. *That was a long-ass lunch meeting.*

"Thanks, Bob," Rick said genuinely as he shook his hand. "It was really a pleasure to hear your views on the current situation."

"No problem, Rick. Great to see you. Let me know if there's anything else I can do for you."

Bob stepped into the elevator and I turned to say good-bye to my tormentor.

"Let me know if you have any questions on any of the material I brought for you. Thanks again for the meeting. I'm glad it was productive," I said.

"It was." He leaned in close to me and whispered in a low tone, "It was quite the feather in your cap getting Bob up here on such short notice. What *did* you have to promise him to get him to agree?"

I rolled my eyes. "Nothing; I just told him that you were the client and he jumped at the chance to come see you guys." Sucking up is a skill I have mastered.

"You always have an answer, Alex. It's really amazing."

"I'll take that as a compliment," I said sarcastically.

Rick glanced at the Very Important Economist, still standing in the elevator, and said, "You go on down, Bob. Alex will meet you in a minute.

I just want to give her a few last-minute instructions before you guys head back downtown." He leaned in the elevator car, punched the Close Doors button, and turned to face me as my final safeguard vanished.

"Okay, listen up," Rick said, a fake smile plastered on his smug face. "You can make this easy on yourself if you want to. You know that. But if you continue to be a bitch, I'm going to treat you like one. You've been covering me for one day so far. *One day.* How much longer do you think you can handle me like this? When Chick was here I had to play nice, out of respect for him. But Chick's gone. It's a whole new ball game now."

He left me standing alone in the hallway, wondering how the hell I had ended up there.

We got back to the office at 3:00, and I spent the rest of the afternoon reviewing everything I had missed while I was in Midtown. When 5:30 rolled around and everyone made their daily trek down to the bar, I jumped to join them. As I chased after Drew and Reese, my brain finally was able to focus on what had happened.

Chick was gone. He wasn't coming back. What did that mean for me?

Everyone from our desk was at the tables set up on the sidewalk outside the restaurant next door to the Cromwell building. The place was unusually crowded, even for a sweltering day in June. This was our new normal: drinks after work. Every single day. On days when no one got let go, we drank to celebrate that. On days when our friends were fired, we drank to lament that. Today was a Tuesday, so we drank. We were out every night, all of us drinking to relieve the pressure and pretend somehow it would all be okay. Lately, no matter how much we drank, it wasn't enough.

Tonight the usual bucket of beers and plate of sliders were in the middle of the table; no one was touching the burgers. Which said a lot.

"This is bullshit. Now we have to start over with Darth of all people?" Drew said.

"What happens now?" Patty asked as she stuffed a lime into the neck of her Corona.

"I'm fucked." I was not in the mood to mince words. "Darth hates me, you guys. I don't even know why—it's not like I ever had anything to do with him, but he absolutely hates me. He's going to fire me, mark my words." I looked around the table at Reese, Marchetti, Drew, and Patty. None of them had any idea what I was talking about.

"You're losing it, sugar. Stop overreacting. You've got Rick now. You're untouchable," Reese said.

"If Rick is supposed to be what saves me, then I'm really screwed. The only reason Rick wanted me to cover him was so that he could make my life a living hell. By the way, he's succeeding."

"What are you talking about?" Marchetti asked. I hadn't had a chance to tell anyone about what was going on with Rick, but Drew knew some of it since he sat next to me all day.

"No. She's right. That guy is toxic. He hit on her and told her he would do a ton of trades with her if she went out with him. Now he's using business as leverage to try to make her sleep with him."

"Thanks for explaining, Drew."

"No problem, killer."

"You have got to be kidding me!" Patty cried. I couldn't tell if she was outraged on my behalf or simply offended that I hadn't confided in her. "Why don't you just tell Darth you want off the account?"

"I can't tell Darth I want off the account. If I give up AKS, I'm admitting that I can't handle him. It would be career suicide. I'm hoping he gets tired of being such a huge asshole and loosens up. He can't go on like this forever. Can he?"

Reese seemed to think about it for a minute, his brow furrowed while he looked up at the clear blue sky. "Yes, he can. That guy's a dick, always has been and always will be. He loves making the Street beg for his business. He'll fuck you either way and have fun doing it."

"Thanks. That makes me feel so much better."

"Just telling you how it is, sugar. I'm sorry. I wish it weren't true, but he's one of the biggest pricks I've ever met in this business, and I've been doing this a long time."

Oh shit.

"Reese, did you call Chick last night?" I asked.

"Yeah, I did. He's pissed off, obviously. Sounds like he got caught up in some political bullshit. Upper management is scrambling to control the damage on the floor, and I guess Chick didn't suck up to them as much as Darth did. So the powers that be fired him and moved Darth into our group. Just another day on the Street."

"Is he okay, though?" I worried about Chick being out of work in this economy. He was an expensive hire. It wasn't going to be easy for him to find another place to work anytime soon.

"He'll be fine. He's a smart guy. As soon as things settle down some-one will hire him and be very lucky to get him. Hell, hopefully he can get a job in management somewhere and hire us all out of this hellhole. This place is a sinking ship," Reese said.

I sighed. I hoped he was right. I scanned the faces of my friends sit-ting at the table and sensed they were all thinking the same thing.

The two beers left in the bucket were now floating in water, a sight no Wall Streeter likes to see. Reese ordered another dozen from the waitress and put them on his card. Marchetti offered to buy the round, but Reese pointed out that if things went the way he expected them to, we would be spending a lot of time in bars together after work and there would be plenty of opportunities for him to pick up a check. Which, in theory, was true. So we drank in honor of Chick and out of fear for ourselves.

Two DAYS LATER, on Thursday, Darth called Marchetti into his office to review his account list, and then fired him, so he never did have a chance to pick up a check. Darth's office became a metaphoric gas chamber, and we spent every day in fear of being summoned to it. We were in the bar again that night, getting bombed in honor of Marchetti, and out of even greater fear for ourselves, and what it meant to work at Cromwell.

"You know what's really screwed up?" Patty put her hair in a pony-tail and reached for her sunglasses on the table.

"There's only *one* thing?" I asked.

"Baby Gap."

"Ahh, yes. What's her real name again?" Drew asked.

"Hannah," I said.

"Whatever, who cares what her real name is," Patty scoffed. "Why in God's name does she still have a seat when she does nothing all day? Marchetti produced how much last year for the desk?"

Reese answered immediately. "Forty million, give or take. *And* he ate the vending machine."

"Forty million dollars. And he gets fired, but Life-Size Barbie gets to stay when she has no idea what she's doing? Do you know what she asked me the other day?"

"If the recession had resulted in the reduced price of cosmetic procedures?" Drew offered.

"If her size extrasmall shirt looked too baggy on her?" Reese chimed in.

"If she could have the afternoon off to get highlights?" I added.

"She asked me when she was going to be allowed to start trading stocks. Stocks!" Patty declared.

I snorted in disgust. "Did you explain to her that stocks and bonds are not the same thing? And that we don't do both?"

"I tried, but she was too busy shopping for velour sweat suits online."

"Shut the fuck up," Drew yelled. "She was *shopping* while people were getting fired?"

"Yes! That's why I want to know how she still has a job."

"One word: morale," Reese said. "It went to hell when the Dow broke eleven thousand. They can't fire her. She's the only thing getting half the floor into work in the morning. What else are people supposed to do all day to keep their minds off the fact that we're all broke and getting broker?"

Drew nodded. "Yup. You'll know things are really bad when they start firing the hot chicks."

nineteen

Payback's a Bitch

I DON'T REMEMBER much of July. It was a blur of alcohol, antacids, flashing red lights, screaming, cursing, and sleep deprivation. And that was just the weekends. By midsummer we were all functioning on autopilot, our bodies lunging relentlessly forward long after our brains had been damaged from stress and shock. Having a front-row seat to watch the destruction of the American economy wasn't really what I thought I was signing up for back in 2006. Then again, I hadn't had a fucking clue *what* I was signing up for back in the day, so maybe I shouldn't have been surprised.

My nonfinancial-sector friends were once again spending the weekends in the Hamptons, unconcerned with the fact that another Depression was looming. I wanted desperately to join them, to sit on a beach and read a novel purely for fun, or curl up with a stack of glossy magazines about fashion, beauty products, or the perils of online dating. But I was working too much on weekends to join them. Ironically, having my weekends free was one of the main reasons I had gone into sales to begin with, because in a normal economy, salespeople weren't needed to hold their clients' hands 24/7. So clearly my logic had been majorly flawed. Again.

It was really starting to bug me.

When I had started at Cromwell, Chick told me that there were a million other kids who wanted a job on Wall Street and failed to get one, so I should feel lucky. I didn't feel so lucky anymore, and these days I doubted the youth of America were lining up to work for the industry that was single-handedly responsible for crushing the American dream. Rick refused to trade with me, despite the fact that he kept me busy all day long modeling new trades, creating graphs and charts, and digging up historical pricing information from every database in the free world. When Chick had covered Rick and AKS, he brought in $30 million to $32 million annually. My production with him, so far, was way down. Actually, it was zero. My blood pressure, on the other hand, was way up. Which was also not good for me.

I was called in to "interview for your job" with Darth on a Friday during the first week of August. When I entered the room, he was sitting in Chick's chair at the head of the table; his Coke-bottle glasses were perched on the tip of his scaly nose as he skimmed a stack of papers in front of him. He pretended to read while I sat in the room in uncomfortable silence, staring at the horns on the top of his head.

Or something like that.

Finally, he spoke.

"How are you doing?" he asked, completely disinterested.

Fine, Darth. Except for the fact that you replaced my boss, fired my friend, and are now making me audition for a role I've killed myself for. "I'm great, thanks."

"What's going on with Rick Kieriakis?"

"You assigned him to me a few weeks ago at his request." Never hurt to remind the boss that you were in high demand from some very important people.

"Right," he said skeptically. "See, what's interesting to me, though, is that you haven't done any business with him since you started covering him."

True, but he berates me on a regular basis. Does that win me any bonus points?

"The market's been difficult. I'm sure once things settle down he will start trading again."

"That's all well and good, but the problem is, he's been trading a lot with a friend of mine who covers him at another shop. So why is it the market conditions make it difficult for *you* to trade with him, and yet he has no problem trading with other people?"

Somehow, trying to fill Darth in on the details surrounding the transfer of coverage from Chick to me didn't seem like a good idea. Darth wouldn't believe anything I told him; he'd just think it was a pathetic attempt by a female employee to explain away her incompetence. Whatever shred of pride I had left, I was keeping. At least while I was in this conference room.

"I don't have an answer for that."

"Well, it's a problem. So I called Rick this morning to get his thoughts on how things were working out between you, and if you were giving him the level of service he expected."

I could tell him right now Rick wasn't getting the level of "service" he expected; but if that's what he was looking for, he could find any number of girls in Times Square who would be more than happy to oblige him for a twenty-dollar bill or a MetroCard.

Darth opened a manila folder and consulted its contents. "He told me that you're doing okay, considering your inexperience, but that he isn't satisfied with the quality of attention you are giving him."

Oh shit.

"I talk to him at least ten times a day."

Darth closed the folder and spoke very slowly, as if normal pentameter would somehow confuse me. "I don't care how many times you call him. He's unhappy; that's all I care about. Things are tough here, Alex, and if you can't keep your clients happy, I don't see you being here much longer. How can I defend your presence when you have clients—important clients—who are unhappy with your work?"

He clasped his hands together on the table, interlocking his pale freckly fingers. Tufts of red hair grew out of his knuckles, the veins on the back of his hands made a blue roadmap across his skin. I imagined his childhood had been pretty miserable, and realized I was probably part of some *Revenge of the Nerds*–like plan he had for the group. Fantastic.

"I expect you to start making some headway with AKS soon," he said. "I don't care what you have to do. He's too big a client to be inactive." His voice was flat and vacant. Unlike Chick, who did everything with passion and emotion, this guy was a robot.

"Okay."

"Go," he said sternly as he pointed at the door.

I went back to the desk and took a few minutes to compose myself before placing the phone call. I put on my headset, cleared runway nine for landing, and hit the light for the seventh circle of hell.

"What the fuck do you want?" he answered.

The muscles in my calf began to shake. "Hey, Rick. I just had a meeting with Keith and I'd like to talk to you for just a minute if you can spare it."

"Sixty seconds. Go."

"Keith mentioned that you said you weren't happy with my coverage."

"That shouldn't be news to you."

"I don't know what else I can do, Rick. I'm trying the best I can to get you what you want, but if this is because you aren't happy with our personal relationship, then please, ask Keith to assign someone else. I'm afraid I'm going to lose my job over this. Please."

"You aren't going to lose your job."

"I'm not? You'll help me?"

"Absolutely fucking not. But I won't let Keith fire you. Then you could just disappear and what fun would that be for me? The only way you'll be rid of me, Alex, is if you quit. And considering you have a better shot of being hit by a bus than getting another job on Wall Street right now, I'd say that puts you in a bit of a bind, doesn't it?"

Click.

I dropped my headset on the floor and went to the empty ladies' room on the sixth floor, and for the next ten minutes, I sobbed uncontrollably.

I SPENT SATURDAY CLEANING my apartment and watching a *Law and Order* marathon on TV. I was so tired of being yelled at. All I wanted was to be left alone. On Sunday I picked up two bottles of red wine to help curb my depression at the expense of my waistline. I debated picking up a pack of smokes because I found lately that a single drag of a Parliament beat an hour of yoga any day, but I really wanted to quit, so I bypassed the bodega. Sundays sucked. The sun slowly began to set and shadows filled my apartment. I poured myself a glass of wine and lay down on the sofa. I hated that my job was driving me to drink. I hated lots of things.

My phone beeped.

> *SMS from Kieriakis, Rick:*
> *It doesn't have to be like this. I can make things easier on you.*
> *You should reconsider.*

Jesus Christ, even God rested on Sunday.

I spun my phone around and around in my hand, trying to decide if I should respond to Rick, and if so, what I should say. This wasn't the same job I had worked so hard for anymore. This job was turning me into someone I didn't even recognize. I wiped a tear from my eye before burrowing back under the blanket with another large glass of red.

It was the only coping mechanism I had left.

I STEPPED OFF THE ELEVATOR, my head still foggy and throbbing, leaving the guys to talk about fairways and lacrosse games, and repeated my personal pep talk for the second time since waking up. *You can do it, Alex. You can handle it. You will not let him break you.*

I logged in to my computer with my new password, killmenow. One word.

"Do I look as bad as I think I do?" I asked Drew.

He sighed. "I'm afraid so, my friend. You look . . . well, actually, you look like you're still drunk, if you want the honest truth."

I was afraid of that.

My phone rang, and if the firm didn't pay me to pick it up, I wouldn't have. I knew whoever was on the other end was only going to make me miserable. That's all anyone did lately. "Good morning, Cromwell Pierce."

"Alex Garrett, please."

I tried to summon enough saliva to speak, but my mouth was so dry it was like a cat died on my tongue. Nothing good was going to come from this conversation. "Oh, good morning, Keith. It's me."

"Can you please come meet me in my office?"

It's not your office. It's Chick's office, you asshole. I hung up the phone and turned to Drew. "I was just summoned to Darth's lair," I said with a sigh.

"I'm sure you're fine," he said.

"See, that's where you're wrong, Drew," I moaned, the stress weighing on me like a wet wool coat. "I haven't been fine in a very long time."

I slowly made my way through the hordes of screaming traders and salespeople and remembered my first day on this floor, when I had first glimpsed one of Wall Street's biggest powerhouses. I was both overwhelmed and disappointed. It was the first of many things at Cromwell that didn't end up being the way I imagined them to be.

I knocked softly on the door before I entered the office for the second time in three days.

"Take a seat, Alex."

Darth's piercing blue eyes and freckle-covered skin reminded me of a kid who lived down the block from me when I was little. He had a stutter and perpetual allergies. My friends and I used to torment him at recess for no other reason, really, than we could. My mother warned me to treat others the same way I wanted to be treated or it would come back to haunt me.

Payback's a bitch.

"Alex, there are two reasons for this meeting. The first thing I want to talk to you about is the annual Bond Market Association conference in Scottsdale. I assume you're familiar with it?"

"Sure, Chick used to go. It's a weeklong event where speakers from different shops give presentations. Great for networking, from what I understand."

"Precisely. I can't go this year because I have to be in London on business. Someone from Cromwell needs to attend as a lot of our clients will be there. I was going to send Reese in my place, but Rick called this morning and asked if I could send you instead."

"Me?"

"You."

"In Scottsdale? With Rick? For a week."

You've got to be fucking kidding me.

"You seem just as shocked as I was when he asked. It's not standard practice to send anyone but managers to this event, but then again, I've never had a high-profile client make a personal request for a salesperson. Rick gets what Rick wants, so pack your bags."

My chest heaved as I struggled to breathe. There was no way in hell I was going to this conference. I could just picture five days of Rick chasing me from cactus to canyon like Wile E. Coyote after the Road Runner. Forced to stay in the same hotel. Forced to spend twelve hours a day together. Forced to wear shorts and sleeveless tops in the desert heat. No way.

"Keith, I think it would be better if Reese went."

"Rick wants you."

This wasn't just an awkward night out at a Midtown restaurant or drinks in a hotel bar. This was a business trip that Rick no doubt intended to turn into a romantic getaway. I no longer had a choice.

"I didn't want to say anything Keith, but when Rick says he 'wants' me, I think he means it in the . . . umm . . . *biblical* sense."

Darth snorted with laughter. "Are you insane, Alex?"

"No."

"Rick's married. He's wealthy, powerful, and well known along the entire Street, and you're seriously going to tell me that he's interested in *you*? No offense, Alex, but if he wanted to cheat, he could do much better."

"None taken." *You colossal asshole.* "However, I think he has taken an unhealthy interest in me for the last year. I've been struggling to handle this on my own. I wouldn't have brought it to your attention, but there's no way I can go to Arizona with him."

"I'm sure you misunderstood, but why don't you give me some examples and we will see if there's any merit to your complaint."

"He sent me flowers at my apartment after I was promoted."

"He and Chick were good friends. He was trying to be nice to his new analyst. You should've written him a thank-you note instead of using it against him a year later."

"He texts me all the time. He constantly asks me to meet him for drinks after work."

"You're in *sales,* Alex. You're supposed to be meeting clients for drinks after work multiple times a week. Are all your clients hitting on you? Or is it just Rick?"

"When my other clients ask me to meet them, they don't reference their wives being away."

"It's all part of normal conversation. You're being way too sensitive. My wife's going to Palm Beach to see her parents next weekend. There you go. For the record, I was not just hitting on you."

"This is pointless." I sighed, aware that I shouldn't have shown such brazen disrespect. But I had stopped caring the day Chick had to turn in his ID. *Fuck this clown.*

"Yes. It is. You leave next Monday. That's all there is to it. This is a fantastic opportunity for you, and you're bitching about it. I'd rather you just say thank you and save the whining for someone else."

"I'm not whining. I'm really uncomfortable going to Arizona with him. Considering you're my boss, I don't really understand why you want to put me in such an awkward position." This was a last-ditch appeal to Darth's almighty, powerful, benevolent boss persona.

"You're going."

So much for that.

"Now moving on to the second reason I asked you in here."

Great.

"Something quite curious has been brought to my attention, and I was hoping you could help clear it up for me."

"Sure."

"I got a call from Human Resources this morning. For the first time in the history of the Cromwell recruiting program, we extended offers to three kids from UVA. That's your alma mater, is it not?"

"Yes."

"What's even more unusual is that *all three* of our offers were declined. That has never happened before and clearly it's cause for concern. Obviously, campus recruiting is an important part of our firm's future growth and as such we take it very seriously."

"I know. I attended the presentation."

"I'm aware of that. Do you want to know how I know?"

I shrugged. I assumed that Satan's powers were limitless, but I doubted that was the answer he was looking for. I met his steely gaze with my own, refusing to flinch. I had learned a few things in my time here, and as much as I hated Darth, he didn't scare me nearly as much as Chick had back in the day. *Bring it on, you smug bastard.*

"I instructed HR to contact the kids and find out why they decided to go to the competition instead of working here. We were all pretty shocked to hear the answers."

"What were they?" I asked, feigning interest and still trying to figure out a way to miss the Arizona conference. Maybe I could throw myself down a flight of stairs and end up in a body cast.

"You."

"Me?"

"You."

Suddenly, I remembered.

Oh shit.

"It seems that they were very impressed with your 'honest' answers to their questions. Which, of course, made us wonder what exactly they were talking about."

Oh shit.

"Did you tell the students that Wall Street was not like they saw in the movies?"

"Yes."

"Did you tell them that it can be difficult for women?"

"Yes."

"Did you tell them that the atmosphere and the pressure can be brutal, and that money alone is not a sufficient reason to take the job?"

"Yes."

"What the hell were you thinking, Alex? You were there as an ambassador for the firm! You were supposed to *sell* Cromwell to those kids. You're in sales, so regardless of whether you're selling the firm's image, or bonds that aren't worth the paper they're printed on, you SELL it. That's what I pay you to do."

You've got to love this business.

"Keith, they asked me questions and I answered them honestly. If we can't manage to recruit talent with an honest depiction of life on the Street and at this firm, then those kids weren't the right kids for the job."

"It's not your job to determine which kids have what it takes to make it here. It's not your job to give them your 'insight' into life at this firm. It most certainly is not your job to argue with me! I don't know what has happened to you, Alex. Honestly, it's like you just don't care anymore."

"What do you mean, what has happened to me?"

"You used to be smart, I think. Granted, you were an Ed Ciccone hire and there's a reason he doesn't have this job anymore, but that's a story for another day. In the beginning, it was funny watching you ingratiate yourself with the group, and—I have to give you credit—somehow you managed to pull it off. You worked hard. You didn't question your superiors. What happened to that girl? Now I have a girl who all of a sudden *forgot* that sales isn't about telling everyone the truth when they ask for it. I don't know where along the way you decided that you don't have to play the game anymore. If anything, you need to play it even more now. In case you haven't noticed, Wall Street is being turned into a bunch of pariahs by the media. Morale is a fraction of what it used to be and we're hemorrhaging money every single day. It's bad enough for the guys who have been doing this for twenty years and been through just about every shit storm imaginable, but then you decide to make it even *more* difficult by exercising your First Amendment right to free speech with a bunch of fucking kids who would—should—believe this place looked like Candy Land if that's what we told them. Does that make any sense to you?"

I remained motionless, unable to defend myself when theoretically he was right. Except, it didn't *feel* right. I'd given up a lot for this life, some of it willingly. But there were still some things I wouldn't give up for Darth, or Will, or Rick, or the Street in general. I refused to give up *me*. And screw this guy for expecting me to.

"What do you have to say for yourself?" he asked smugly as he smoothed his blue tie over his white shirt.

"Nothing," I said nonchalantly.

"Nothing?"

"Nope."

He sighed. "You've tried my patience today, Alex. I'll chalk it up to PMS. But you better pull it together and fast. The way you're acting now, it's like you don't even want to be here."

For the first time, Darth and I agreed on something.

I smiled broadly as I exited his office and headed for the elevators, wondering how long it would take him to realize that I had left my ID on his desk.

twenty

Capiche?

WHEN I GOT to the bar on Warren Street later that afternoon, Patty, Annie, and Liv were already waiting for me at a small table upstairs near the bar. After leaving Darth's office, I'd gone straight to HR and given notice. Then I'd walked out the Cromwell Pierce building. I didn't look back. I couldn't; I was shaking so badly my legs would only move forward. I walked home and kicked off my heels. Then I made a few phone calls. Then I cried like a five-year-old. Then I smoked a pack of cigarettes. Then I decided I needed a drink. Or ten. So, I came here to meet my friends. I collapsed onto an empty stool as Annie filled a glass with wine. Patty handed me a box filled with personal items from my desk: flip-flops, extra shoes, eyeglasses, a string of Mardi Gras beads Marchetti bought me not long after I started, a bottle of Advil, a stuffed pig that squealed when you squeezed it that had been left on my desk by an anonymous admirer, and the souvenir magnet Chick had brought me from Bermuda. I may just have walked away from all my restricted stock, but I did get a few consolation prizes. Little inside joke gifts from my friends. They were worth way more than the stock was as far as I was concerned. Especially these days.

"You just quit? You woke up this morning and went off to work just like every day, and in an instant, you decided to quit?" Liv asked, dumbstruck.

"It wasn't quite that simple but pretty much, yeah."

"I can't believe you just walked out!" Patty was waving her arms all over the place as she spoke, and if it wasn't for the fact that she wore a business suit, I was pretty sure people would have thought she was a complete lunatic. "I'm so pissed at you I don't even know what to say!"

"You're pissed? Patty, I'm sitting here holding a cardboard box and I don't have a job. You really should try to be a bit more sympathetic. Plus, I just lost my medical insurance, and I forfeited upward of $50,000 in stock when I walked out those doors. Do you really think that being mad at me is appropriate?"

"What about *me*? How am I going to deal with Darth Vader by myself? If anything, this is the worst day of *my* life. I'm going to have to get lunch by myself now, or even worse, go with Baby Gap. Have you even thought about that?"

"Good point. It does sort of suck to be you."

"Yes. You selfish bitch."

"Sorry, Patty. What did Darth say when he came back to the desk?"

"Nothing! I wouldn't have known anything had happened if you hadn't called me and told me to get your stuff."

"Typical. Once you're gone it's like you were never there."

"That's not true. Poor Drew is freaking out that they're going to sit someone painful next to him, and Reese ordered swine burgers for lunch in your honor. You need to call them. They're pretty bummed you didn't say good-bye."

"Anyone else?" I wasn't sure why I cared. But I wanted to know.

"He didn't say anything, but I think he's upset. I glanced at him as I was on my way out and he looked like someone sucker-punched him. I think he's afraid he's never going to see you again."

"He's not."

Asshole.

"What are you going to do now?" Patty asked.

"No idea. I don't really have any idea what I'm going to do next. And that's a first for me. Although I'm pretty sure I'm going to freak out in a few minutes." The reality was starting to hit me: I QUIT MY FREAKIN' JOB.

"I'm so proud of you," Liv said, tilting her head to the side as if she was talking to a three-year-old. "You gave up a lot for that job, and the only thing you got back was money and a few good friends. It wasn't worth it."

"I know. But we're in a recession. It's not going to be easy trying to get another job right now."

Annie reached over and grabbed my hand. "I think this is the greatest thing you've ever done for yourself. You did the right thing. The glass is half full. Not half empty."

"Speaking of half empty, can someone top off my pinot, please?" I pushed my glass toward the bottle of wine and drummed my fingers on the table.

"Got it!" Liv answered.

Annie continued her pep talk. "I'm serious. I'm surprised you lasted as long as you did there. Now you can try some new things. The recession is forcing a lot of people to look at their lives and make changes. It's a great opportunity actually."

I flipped my cell phone open to see if I had any text messages. Drew and Reese. I had just left Cromwell, and I already missed them terribly. My friends on the desk were the one thing I was sad to leave behind. Well, them and the stock.

"Well, I need to get going. I'm looking forward to waking up tomorrow without a hangover," I said as I stood.

"Can't we get another bottle?" Liv asked as Patty sullenly stared at the box on the floor.

"Nope! I have to go."

"Where? You have plans?"

"Sort of. You know that bartender I ran into at Tortilla Flats?"

"Yes?" Liv asked hopefully.

"He started working at an Italian place down on Carmine. I called him earlier, and he asked me if I wanted to swing by tonight and check it out. I told him I would."

"Look at you; you're like a whole new woman, trading in preppy Will for a tattooed bartender."

"Oh stop. The only thing I traded in is my Cromwell ID for an unemployment card. Swell."

"I can't believe I'm not going to see you tomorrow!" Patty said as she hugged me good-bye. I found myself fighting back tears. I was really turning into a sap.

"You'll do great, Patty. Don't let anyone tell you differently. Tell everyone I miss them already."

"The feeling's mutual," she said as she sadly waved good-bye.

I HAD THE CABDRIVER TAKE me through the windy streets of the West Village. The air was crisp for August and I decided to get out a few blocks away and walk, soaking up my newfound freedom.

My phone rang and my caller ID displayed the number that used to make me quake with fear. Tonight, it made me smile.

"Well, hello there, boss."

"Is it true?"

"How'd you find out already?" I asked.

"Alex, I may not be your boss anymore, but I still know everything that goes on at that firm."

"Of course you do." I laughed, enjoying the luxury of talking to Chick without being restricted by employer-employee boundaries.

"So did you really tell Darth Vader to go fuck himself?"

"No! Is that what everyone thinks? I just left. It wasn't very dramatic, all things considered."

"That took balls, Alex. I'm proud of you."

"For quitting?"

"No, not for quitting. I talked to Will. He told me everything that's been going on with Rick and what he's been trying to do. I'm pissed as hell that you never said anything to me about that."

"You really had no idea he was bothering me?"

I heard him sigh. "I knew he was messing with you a little, but that's just his way. He does it to everyone, and I thought I was keeping an eye on it. I guess with everything going on in the markets, I stopped paying attention. I'm sorry about that. I had no idea it had gotten so out of hand. You should have told me when he crossed the line."

"I wanted to, but I was worried you were the one who gave him my number in the first place."

"You should know better than that, Alex. I thought I took good care of you."

"You did. You were a good boss, for what it's worth."

"Good to hear. That brings me to the second reason I'm calling. I got an offer to run another group. I can't tell you where because my contract isn't completely negotiated yet, but how would you feel about coming to work for me again? I'll even make sure I have a desk ready for you this time."

"You're offering me a job? I don't even have to interview?"

"I've known all I need to know about you for a long time, Girlie."

"I'm flattered, Chick, really. I'd love to work with you again, but I'm actually thinking about doing something else with my life."

"What else is there? Are you skilled in anything else? Do you have any secret talents I don't know about? Yodeling?"

"No."

"Baton twirling?"

"No."

"Fire breathing?"

"No!"

"Then what are you thinking about doing? Are you going to go back to school? That's not a bad idea. You could go get an MBA. I'll write your recommendation for Harvard."

"Actually, no. I wasn't thinking about going back to school. I have a few ideas. I'll fill you in when I figure it all out."

"Fuck that. You'll tell me now."

I stayed silent.

"Please don't tell me you're going to turn into one of those bitter bitches who leaves the Street and then write a book or something. I hate those women."

I laughed. "I'm not writing a book, Chick."

"Good. I don't deserve to be slammed. I treated you well. I gave you extra cash at Christmas and my U2 tickets, if I remember correctly."

"You also made me spend a thousand dollars on a wheel of cheese."

"That's called tough love, Alex. It made you a more punctual salesperson."

"I know, and I don't think I ever thanked you for that. If I did write a book, I'd probably talk about how you put your feet up on your desk and made me look at your socks though. Which never matched, by the way."

"I can live with that. I'm a busy man, Alex. I don't have time to style myself. Besides, you're the only person who ever noticed the difference between navy blue and black."

"It's more likely that I'm the only one who ever told you."

"Fine. Whatever. Alex, listen. The last thing I want to be is a fucking dating game host, but for what it's worth, Will feels like a schmuck about everything."

"He should."

"No doubt. But when I talked to him, he asked if he should call you. I think he felt bad that you didn't say good-bye when you left. I told him I'd talk to you first and feel it out. What should I tell him?"

"Tell him to fuck off."

That felt good.

"Okay, then."

"Yup. Well, I'm about to meet a friend for a quick dinner. Thanks for the call though. It means a lot."

"Don't go getting all sappy on me. Listen, if you need anything, you know where to find me. When you decide what you want to do with your life, let me know. If I can help you in any way, I will. Capiche?"

"Capiche."

"Go get 'em, Girlie. I'm rooting for you."

Click.

He hung up.

I walked the last half block to the small Italian restaurant on Carmine Street to meet Matt and sample his culinary talents. I was a free woman. And for the first time in a long time, I could breathe easily.

The small sign hanging next to the door said BUONA FORTUNA. Italian for "good luck."

It was fitting. I was going to need it.

acknowledgments

THANK YOU TO everyone who helped and supported me as I wrote this, and through just about everything else. Your encouragement meant more to me than you will ever know. (And, side note, thank you for buying many copies of this book without the threat of my revoking our friendships or family ties, at least out loud.) Really, you guys are the best.

Thank you to Joanna Adler, Kristen Baer, Eileen Berkery, Kurt Brown, Patricia Byrnes, Megan Collins, Whitney Cox, Avery Duffy, Barbara Duffy, Calleigh Duffy, Cathy Duffy, Karen Duffy, Merri Duffy, Ronan Duffy, Quinn Duffy, Rob Farrer, Lauren Fischetti, Marianne Filipski, Maura Fitzgerald, Harvey Gould, Jordan Keating, Mary Kay Kemper, Christina Kingham, Pat Langdon, Karen Macdonald, Stacey Mon, Greg Mone, Colleen McNellis, Casey Nicholas, Erica Noble, Catherine O'Connor, Kevin Penwell, Susan Puglisi, Jennie Quinn, Katie Regan, Jennie Robin, Kelly Sanderson, Kevin Sexton, Derek Solon, Susan Stewart, Sarah Tilley, Mark Tortora, Lee Ann Truss, Todd Vender, Michaela Wenk, Jeannine Wiley, Kirstine Wilson, and Kelly Zaremba.

Thank you especially to the rest of the Duffys and the Sextons, both the in-laws and out-laws. I am so lucky to have such a large extended family that it is impossible to mention everyone; thank you all. I have no doubt that I will hear about who wasn't mentioned specifically at Christmas. Truth be told, I'm a little scared.

For all of my friends on the Street, who made this life more fun than anyone deserved to have had at work, and whose nicknames are used to protect the innocent: They know who they are . . . and that's all that matters. Thank you:

Agency Ian, B, Bernie, Boss, Brendan, Bury, Charlie, Chanimal, Cleve, Disco-Dot, Doug, FX Ray, Gargi, Guy, Hammer, Harry, Hegs, Hey Tiger, HI RAY!, Jedster, JB, Joe, Joey D, JZ, Keith, Laips, LP, Lynchie, Magantor, Mangia, MB, Microsoft, Milweed, Moose, Muchacho, Murray, Okay terrific, Pado, PT, Ranz, Robo, Rocket, Santee, T, Tank, Team Central Bank, Ted, Tokyo Rose, Silver Fox, Sharptooth, Sobes, Smitty, Sweet Lou, Wayno. Thank you all. I miss you.

A few people deserve special mention. Without them, this book would still be nothing more than the world's heaviest paperweight. I still can't believe it's not. Neither can more than a few people reading this. Most of them are family.

Thank you to my lawyer, Eric Rayman: for spending his time and massively strong brainpower on an unknown author, and for making sure I didn't make any colossally bad decisions. From day one, you believed, and I thank you. You didn't have to. I know.

Thank you to my manager, Will Rowbotham: for convincing me that this project was something worth pursuing, for fighting all the battles I'm too afraid to fight on my own, and for always calling me back. Let's get dark and stormies. Tomorrow. Hell, today, I'm not busy.

Thank you to my agent at William Morris, Erin Malone: for believing in me, and for cutting a seven-hundred-page book down to size. It wasn't easy. You are amazing, and I hit the jackpot when you took on this project. You held my hand through everything, and then sold this book from a coffee shop on your vacation. That, I won't soon forget. Trust me.

Thank you to everyone at William Morrow: especially Jennifer

Brehl, the world's best editor, who has the patience of a saint, the mind of a scholar, and the spirit of a teenager, which I love. And to her second-in-command, Emily Krump. Thank you for dealing with me, my stupid questions, and my countless neuroses. Thank you for believing in this book, thank you for your hours of work, and thank you for teaching me that the word *toward* does not have an *s* on the end. Who knew? I didn't. One of many things you taught me. The list is endless.

Last but in no way least, thank you to Kelly Meehan, and the amazingly generous, fantastically talented, and unbelievably kind Adriana Trigiani: This Cinderella does not deserve to have you as her fairy godmother. Without you, I'd never have had the courage to write it all down. You told me to. Thank you, Adri, for everything.

Words cannot express my gratitude. To any of you.

Insights,
Interviews
& More . . .

About the author

About the book

Read on

Meet Erin Duffy

Elena Seibert

ERIN DUFFY graduated from
Georgetown University in 2000
with a B.A. in English and went on
to spend more than a decade working
in fixed-income sales on Wall Street.
Bond Girl is her first novel. ∾

Almost Everything You Ever Wanted to Know about Wall Street*
*But Didn't Know Who to Ask

Q: *Do women on the Street really wear high heels?*

A: You bet they do. Men on the Street have the power suit, women have the power shoe. Most women don't wear them outside on the pavement unless absolutely necessary, though (these shoes ain't made for walkin'). So, at any given time, look under any Wall Street woman's desk, and you are likely to find thousands of dollars' worth of footwear.

Q: *Do you know a real-life Alex Garrett?*

A: I know more of them than you could imagine. The Street is full of young, fun girls with drive, humor, and more than a few flaws. The ones who seem normal are just better at faking it.

Q: *What's a "Bond Girl"?*

A: A Bond Girl is a new breed of heroine. Instead of a bathing suit she wears a pantsuit and carries a HP12C calculator instead of a gun. However, she can be just as deadly as the original. ▶

Almost Everything You Ever Wanted to Know about Wall Street* *(continued)*

Q: *What is a "bonus"?*

A: A "bonus" is a mythical payment that Management dangles in front of you like a carrot to make you work like crazy for the entire year. You rarely get the carrot. You usually get the stick.

Q: *What's an interesting fact about trading floors?*

A: That they're acceptable places to conduct personal hygiene. Although not noted in any company handbook, this must be true because nail-clipping (finger *and* toe), tooth-flossing, and gargling followed by spitting into a garbage can while sitting at your desk are fairly widespread practices.

Q: *How common is dating on trading floors?*

A: More common than you'd think. There are so few women on trading floors that odds are one or more guys will try to date them. These relationships almost never end well. They almost always end with wallets, cell phones, BlackBerrys, calculators, or even entire purses being thrown against the wall in the ladies' room with enough force to crack tile.

Q: *What is the strangest thing you ever saw or heard of happening on a trading floor?*

A: There was a guy who had been working at the same firm for his entire career. The day he retired he rode a Harley around the trading floor three times. To this day, no one can figure out how he got that bike on the floor.

Q: *Perception is that everyone on Wall Street makes a ton of money. How close is this to reality?*

A: Only a select group of people get paid a ton of money. Unfortunately, those seem to be the only people anyone outside of the business hears about. While people employed in the financial sector are paid well by any standard, there is a huge disparity between the big bucks made by a few top guns and the paychecks of most Wall Street employees, the overwhelming majority of whom will never earn anywhere near the kind of money it is popularly presumed they will.

Q: *Why are there so few women in the industry? Why is there such a disproportionate male-female ratio?*

A: It takes a very specific personality type (male or female) to handle working in a stressful, male-dominated industry like finance. It's not easy. Business is also an industry more suited to "male" character traits. I think the natural competitive, ▶

risk-seeking personality required for success on Wall Street is more commonly found in men. Nothing is ever good enough, and that's hard for a lot of women to embrace.

Q: *Do you think the industry has been unfairly portrayed in the media?*

A: Sometimes, especially in the current environment. In most cases, greed is not the reason people are drawn to the financial sector; the majority of people working in this business really love the markets, love math, and love the way they can apply their skills in a lively environment. Again, those are rarely the people anyone hears about.

Q: *Do you think that women are treated fairly in the industry, that they are given the same opportunities as men?*

A: I think if a woman is smart, hardworking, and ambitious, she can find success on Wall Street. There are a lot of very strong female role models out there, and most of them are more than happy to help mentor younger women as they come up the ranks. The opportunities are there if you work hard enough. Ꮧ

The Story Behind *Bond Girl*

BACK IN 1999, when I accepted a job offer to work on Wall Street, I thought it would be an easy adjustment. Finance is basically the Duffy family business. My brothers, aunts, uncles, cousins, and, yes, father all work on "the Street," and I somehow presumed that years of listening to their lingo, hearing about their commutes, and seeing their office buildings (from the outside) meant that I knew all that was needed to join the financial district rank and file. Piece of cake; it's in the blood.

I didn't have the first damn clue what I was in for.

I thought I would do a little math, sell a few bonds, and clock out at five P.M. every day to go home to my normal life. Hah! No one told me that there would be no more "normal" life. No one told me I would have to start mainlining caffeine and alcohol in an attempt to keep up with the men I worked with. No one told me that in addition to learning office practices and protocol, I'd also have to educate myself about wine, golf, sports, even poker, because that's what's required if you want to be on a Wall Street team. No one told me that a job on the Street isn't just a job—it's a *lifestyle*.

Working on the Street demands 100 percent of your time, your energy, and, if necessary, your sanity, and it ▶

> 66 No one told me that a job on the Street isn't just a job—it's a *lifestyle*. 99

doesn't leave much room for a lot of relaxation. And contrary to popular opinion, you can't say no to anything. Especially if you're a woman; if you are a woman, you do not ever, ever say no.

No one told me to expect any of that. I'm still waiting. Any day now.

So while I'm pretty sure my career choice has shortened my life span by a good ten to fifteen years, it has also taught me a lot about people and about life. I realized that if I couldn't have imagined the life I was living—and I grew up surrounded by it—how could anyone else even begin to understand what it was like? More important, would anyone even *want* to? And *why*?

Then one day a few years ago, right around the time that Wall Street became responsible for the destruction of the American dream, I realized that Gordon Gekko, the fictional character who entered the pop culture pantheon with the line "Greed is good," was who came to mind when most people thought of Wall Street. And that made me feel bad. It's not that there weren't—and aren't—greedy people working on the Street, it's just that that is not all there is. I know that there's a lot more to the people who work on the trading floors than shiny cuff links and ice in their veins.

At the same time, it seemed that suddenly the entire world wanted to know what actually went on at the top financial firms. And I knew that whatever it was they were imagining, it wasn't even close to reality. I thought it would be instructive—and fun and funny—to give people an idea of what our days are really like, of what really can, and does, happen. I wanted to set the record straight, and present an honest portrayal of what life on the Street is really like. And so I began writing. And the result is *Bond Girl*.

The culture, the business, the relationships, the *life* of Wall Street is oft-maligned and almost always misunderstood. It's easy to see why. I hope to change the popular perception, if only a little bit, if only for the few hours that someone spends reading my book. At the very least, I want readers to understand that real-life Gordon Gekkos know how to crack a smile, and frequently do. I was inspired by ten years spent in a business that provides more laughs and enjoys itself more than any other that I can think of. And that's something that I think will surprise a lot of people. I hope it does. It sure as hell surprised me. ᖷ

66 I wanted to set the record straight, and present an honest portrayal of what life on the Street is really like. 99

The Top Ten Things You Probably Don't Know About Working on "the Street"

10. The number of U.S.-owned banks and/or brokerage houses actually located on Wall Street: zero.
9. Office windows that open are overrated.
8. Moran's Bar & Grill, located in the heart of Manhattan's Financial District, caters primarily to Wall Street employees and people who want to marry them, and serves more beer between Memorial Day and Labor Day than any other bar in the city.
7. Free pizza cures all. Especially before 10 A.M.
6. A $65.00 limo ride with road sodas is a completely acceptable way to travel ten blocks.
5. Five blocks if it's raining.
4. Knowing math is important— but nowhere near as important as knowing wine, golf, and watches.
3. Gucci loafers go with every outfit, in all weather, all year round.
2. Socks are optional (and rarely necessary).

And the #1 thing you probably don't know about working on "the Street" is . . .

1. A bet is a bet is a bet. If you lose at Credit Card Roulette, you will pay the bill. No one cares that you're only twenty-two and the bill is $1,000. ᨦ

Questions for Discussion

1. Alex is a relatable character for many women despite the fact (and maybe because) she is ambitious and determined to make it in a male-dominated world. What does Alex represent that makes her likable to both men and women? Why do you think she's relatable even though many people don't know much about day-to-day life on Wall Street?

2. When we meet Will, he seems to be charming and interested in Alex. Do you think it's possible to pursue a girl while being unavailable? Do you think it's something Alex should have foreseen? What do you think Will's expectations were if he knew he was never going to be with her?

3. Sexual harassment is a prevalent theme in the book. Do you think Wall Street encourages this kind of environment more than other industries? How should Alex have handled the problems with her client? Should she have done anything differently?

4. Chick is a complicated character, but he seems to genuinely care about his employees. Do you think Chick did enough to look after Alex and the other team members, or did he inadvertently encourage the environment by being too nonchalant about some of the attitudes on trading floors? Would

you want to work for someone like Chick? Why or why not?

5. Alex and her coworkers are a pretty tight-knit group. How important is camaraderie in the workplace? Do you think it's necessary in order to be successful? Or is this kind of close environment toxic?

6. At the end of the novel, Alex has to make some decisions about what she wants to do with the rest of her life. Should she take the job with Chick and return to Wall Street? Or do you think she should pursue another career? If so, what should she do?

7. Do you think Alex and Will's relationship is an accurate depiction of young love? Do you think she should have heard him out when he tried to apologize to her? What do you think will happen between them in the future?

8. Alex seemed to have been driven to work on Wall Street through a desire to be like her father. How important is family history in determining who you become, and should it play a role at all? Do you think Alex's father would be happy with her decision to quit the firm? Why or why not?

9. Gender roles are explored in the novel. Do you think there's still a glass ceiling for women in certain industries, or do you think in this day and age females are given equal opportunities? Are there some careers that women, by and large, are not cut out for? If so, what?

10. Alex faces multiple challenges in *Bond Girl* that she did not foresee ▸

when she took her dream job at Cromwell Pierce—brutally long hours, creepy clients, etc. How has she changed by the end of the novel? What challenges impacted her the most?

11. What movie(s) would you compare your life to? If *Bond Girl* was to become a movie, who would you want to see cast as Alex, Will, or Chick? ᨞

Erin Duffy Recommends

THERE ARE A FEW BOOKS that
I absolutely love, and love to
recommend to friends. In my
free time, when I can find it,
I could snuggle up with one of
these again and again. Well, one
of these, and my bear.

I LOVED, I LOST, I MADE SPAGHETTI by Giulia Melucci

Good Lord, Giulia Melucci knows
about dating in New York City. Her
book is spot-on funny, and truthful
in a hysterically painful way. Plus, as
an Irish girl with no cooking heritage
whatsoever, I love a book with good
Italian recipes. *I Loved, I Lost, I Made
Spaghetti* is like the jackpot for a single
person who wants to learn how to cook
and find love in untraditional places. I
highly recommend her Fuck-you Cakes
with Chocolate Bourbon Frosting . . .
perfectly delicious every time.

VERY VALENTINE by Adriana Trigiani

Set in Manhattan's historic Greenwich
Village, *Very Valentine* made me fall in
love with New York City all over again.
Valentine Roncalli and Alex Garrett
have a lot in common. They are both
hardworking, ambitious ladies trying
to juggle work, dating, and the not-
always-forgiving day-to-day of life in
New York City. While Valentine ▶

struggles to keep her family's
floundering shoe company afloat
(and takes a dreamy trip to Italy to
accomplish just that), she gives us
a look at a strong working woman
who can seemingly handle it all. If
that isn't enough, this book is also
the first in a trilogy. Once I fell in love
with Valentine, I had two more stories
to look forward to. And, besides, who
doesn't want to learn a little something
about shoes?

CHASING HARRY WINSTON
by Lauren Weisberger

Single ladies unite! This book
examines being single and looking
for love (and maybe diamonds) in
Manhattan. Emmy, Leigh, and Adriana
are all very funny, endearing, and
relatable in their own ways, and are
also motivated to get themselves off the
singles market. Who can blame them?
Being single and living in New York
City, I felt like I was reading about my
own life in a lot of ways, and it made
me feel like maybe there actually is
safety in numbers. Reading this book
was like sitting down with good friends
and rehashing the latest dating drama.
I laughed, I cringed, and then I reached
for my secret stash of ice cream.
Another New York City single gal
classic.

BONFIRE OF THE VANITIES
by Tom Wolfe

My favorite book of all time is one I first read in high school: Tom Wolfe's *Bonfire of the Vanities*. Is there anything better than the Social X-rays and the Lemon Tarts? I don't think so. This book takes politics, Wall Street, and social unrest and molds it into one amazing story. This was the first thing I ever read about Wall Street, and I thought it was fantastic because it so vividly captured the ego and the machismo that the industry promotes. Tom Wolfe describes the psychology of his characters better than any other author I have ever read. My high school years are gone longer than I wish to admit, and most of the time I can't remember where I left my wallet, but I still remember this book. It changed my life. But. (There's always a but . . . isn't there?) It's not small. Beware; you must be ready to tackle its more than 700 pages.

AMERICAN PSYCHO
by Brett Easton Ellis

I thought about including a classic, *American Psycho* by Brett Easton Ellis, here—a quintessential book about Wall Street style and finance. The problem is that book traumatized me within an inch of my life. I read it because I wanted to sound smart, and didn't want to have to admit that the last thing I read was my horoscope in *Cosmo*. I thought it would give me ▶

street cred, and I would sound worldly at cocktail parties. What it *actually* gave me was nightmares. It scared the hell out of me, and forced me to sleep with a nightlight for longer than I am willing to admit. Nightlights don't help your dating cause, ladies, trust me. For that reason, I choose not to mention it here. Forget I said anything.